Lafitte and You moved forward slowly, and looked through the wired glass of the skylight. Mejia was propped up on the bed, nude, with his back to the skylight. The three women were also nude, dancing wildly to a portable record player. But it was not the light from the skylight that made the scene unreal. In a corner was a flashing red strobe light that made the women seem like manikins, dancing in a jerky silent movie. From time to time they would come together, fondle each other, and then two would throw the other one to the floor and crawl all over her. Then Mejia would lash one with a knotted rope and the one struck would leap up and impale herself on top of him. He would allow her to stay a few moments, then fling her to the floor where she was engulfed by the other two.

LAFITTE LOWERED HIMSELF OUT OF SIGHT. THE MAN WITH THE ROPE WAS RESPONSIBLE FOR THE TERROR AND TORMENT OF THE PAST HOURS. HE WOULD PAY FOR EVERY MINUTE, BUT BEFORE HE DID, HE WOULD TALK...

D1457564

Lafitte's Legacy
is an original POCKET BOOK edition.

Books by John Whitlatch

Cory's Losers
Frank T's Plan
Gannon's Vendetta
The Iron Shirt
The Judas Goat
Lafitte's Legacy
Morgan's Rebellion
Stunt Man's Holiday
Tanner's Lemming

Published by POCKET BOOKS

 *Are there paperbound books you want
but cannot find in your retail stores?*

You can get any title in print in **POCKET BOOK** editions. Simply send retail price, local sales tax, if any, plus 25¢ to cover mailing and handling costs to:

MAIL SERVICE DEPARTMENT
    POCKET BOOKS ● A Division of Simon & Schuster, Inc.
    1 West 39th Street ● New York, New York 10018

Please send check or money order. We cannot be responsible for cash.   *Catalogue sent free on request.*

Titles in this series are also available at discounts in quantity lots for industrial or sales-promotional use. For details write our Special Projects Agency: The Benjamin Company, Inc., 485 Madison Avenue, New York, N.Y. 10022.

Lafitte's Legacy

by
John Whitlatch

PUBLISHED BY POCKET BOOKS NEW YORK

LAFITTE'S LEGACY

POCKET BOOK edition published September, 1971

3rd printing..........March, 1973

 ▬▬▬▬▬▬▬▬▬▬▬▬▬▬

This original POCKET BOOK edition is printed from
brand-new plates made from newly set, clear, easy-to-read type.
POCKET BOOK editions are published by POCKET BOOKS, a division of
Simon & Schuster, Inc., 630 Fifth Avenue, New York, N.Y. 10020.
Trademarks registered in the United States and other countries.

L

Standard Book Number: 671-75670-2.
Copyright, ©, 1971 by John Whitlatch. All rights reserved.
Printed in the U.S.A.

Lafitte's Legacy

Part One

THEY HAD BEEN DRIVING FOR SOME TIME THROUGH THE LUSH Louisiana farmland in almost complete silence. From time to time he would pat her on the knee and she would look from the scenery to him and smile. He would smile in return and then look back to the road. Now she was staring off to her right at a grove of ancient oaks, dripping with Spanish moss, content to take in the countryside. As his eyes followed the gently curving road he wondered again about his grandfather. Perhaps he had waited far too long. Though he'd corresponded with the old man from time to time through the years, after the fashion of busy men who seldom write personal letters, he'd never been back. . . . Her hand on his arm returned him to the present and he looked at her with an inquiring smile.

"Is that a swamp?" she said, pointing to the right of the bridge ahead, at the tangled line of dark green that marked the edge of the water.

"Not quite," he replied.

He pulled the rented Chevy convertible to the shoulder, just short of the concrete bridge, and got out to let her see her first bayou. He went around the back, opened her door, and then had to wait a moment while she fixed her wind-blown hair.

"Come on," he grinned, "the bullfrogs won't mind."

She ignored him, pushed at her hair once more, then took

his extended hand and stepped out of the car to be led to the edge of the bank, some twenty feet above the water.

"To answer your question," he said, "it's not a swamp, it's a bayou. . . . See there, down past those big trees? Well, on the other side, maybe five miles or so, the bayou flattens out and disappears into the swamp and you can't really tell where one stops and the other begins."

She nodded and her eyes came back to the dark, placid water and the overgrown banks. "It's so peaceful."

"Uh huh," he said dryly, pointing to the middle of the stream. "You see that?"

"You mean that floating stick?"

He grinned and stooped down and picked up a rock and pitched it with a sidearm motion within a foot of the object. The "stick" wiggled quickly a couple of times and then disappeared from the surface.

"Some stick," he said. "It was a water snake."

"Ooh!" She shuddered and got back into the car.

He pulled onto the deserted highway, crossed the bridge, and continued at a leisurely forty miles an hour. After they'd gone a mile or so, she broke the silence.

"Why haven't you been back before this?"

"Nothing to return to, really," he replied. "The old man and I like each other, but we have little in common."

"I presume your grandfather married late? I mean the second time."

"Yes," he nodded. "But twice. That's one too many for me."

"Any regrets?" she asked, then immediately wished she hadn't.

"No, not really." He grinned at her, sensing her discomfort at having asked such a question. "I'd probably have screwed myself to death by now."

"Men!" she said, though she wasn't angry.

"In fact," he said, "I've never even met the madam."

"Shouldn't that be madame, with an 'E'?"

"No, not at all. Madam, like in whorehouse."

"Jean!" she exclaimed, properly pronouncing her husband's name "Jhoan," though she was an Arizona girl who spoke no French.

"Well, that's what he's always called her, maybe she was. She's almost seventy now, but I hear she's still a beautiful

woman. . . . The old man always said if he married again it
would be to a broad who knew about men."

He stopped talking as he pulled out to pass an ancient
wagon being drawn by a plodding mule. He waved at the old
black man and the old man smiled and waved back. When
he'd returned to his side of the road he picked up the conversation again.

"I guess the real reason I never returned was that I didn't
want to be the old man's flunky. . . . Oh, I could've gone to
work in the business in New Orleans, like Jeremy did, but I
couldn't see that. Besides, Jeremy and I never did hit it off.
We've disliked each other from high school."

"He's your cousin's husband?"

"Yes," he nodded. "Jeremy Duroc. From one of the oldest
Creole families, and the son of a bitch always liked to flaunt
his ancestry. I think that's why my cousin married him. She
thought a lot of dough went with the old name."

"Did it?" Sandy asked.

"Not a pot or a window," Lafitte grinned.

She grinned with him a moment and then said, "But your
name, and her maiden name, is also one of the oldest, isn't
it?"

"Yeah, maybe," he allowed. "But it has a certain spice to
it . . . there may be a bar sinister across the escutcheon, depending on which Lafitte you think sired the American
branch of the family."

"Pardon?" she said with a frown. Then, when she saw his
face she knew he was putting her on a bit and she smiled
good-naturedly and added, "Oh, you're so smart! Well, I
won't even ask you. I'll just look it up when we get there."

He chuckled and said, "Good girl!"

"Well, I still think it's a bit strange . . ."

"What is?"

"You've been gone all these years and you suddenly get
the urge to see the old homestead once more."

"Plantation, dear," he said, correcting her gently.

"Well, anyway . . . whatever."

"No, not really." He shook his head. "It's just sort of a
matter of timing. With the company picking up my half of
the tab, and then the old man writing and saying he'd like to
see me once before he died . . . well, I thought it'd be a good
idea."

"It has so far, it's been a wonderful vacation." She squeezed his arm again. Then, "Is he really?"

"Is he really what?"

"I mean is your grandfather dying?"

"Apparently. He already had that one massive stroke. But he thinks he's dying, otherwise he wouldn't have written. . . . Besides, I'd like to see what's left of the old place. It's probably run-down as hell now."

"But he was once wealthy. Didn't he save anything?"

"Not that I know of. And yes, he was once a millionaire several times over. But fast women and slow horses took care of that."

"You don't seem to mind."

"Mind what? That he spent his money? No, of course not. It was his and he lived a good, full life. If you're wondering if he might've left anything . . ."

"Jean! I didn't mean that . . . I'm not the mercenary type."

"I know," he said. "You couldn't be and live with me all these years. But there's nothing left and that's fine. He earned it the hard way, and he blew it all by himself. Besides, I don't need much but the four things I've got."

"Four?"

"You, the kids, and a strong back."

She laughed and leaned over to kiss him on the cheek. He smiled and slowed the car as they approached the outskirts of the town where he'd gone to high school. The sign read:

WELCOME TO BAYARD, POP. 7,382.

"Bi-yard?" she said, trying to pronounce it correctly.

"Bi-yar," he said. Then his eyes widened as they entered the town. "My! The town's really grown."

"It has?" she said, one eyebrow raised.

He nodded good-naturedly and pulled to the right lane so he could observe the changes. Bayard had started as a general store sometime before the Civil War and had barely grown to be a sleepy, rural town. The older buildings showed the regional architectural style, a mixture of antebellum and Creole influence, and were mainly two-storied with lots of iron grillwork. These venerable structures were now in the minority and when one was condemned, it was replaced by a building of almost no style at all; a rectangle with a plastered front and a sloping, flat roof.

The streets were still narrow, but the cobblestones Lafitte

remembered had been replaced with blacktop and the board sidewalks were now concrete. The telephone poles were newer and some held overhanging streetlights. The hitching poles with their big iron rungs were gone; in their places were parking meters. There were, however, a few civic improvements of which Lafitte approved. There was a new, one-storied city hall and police station, and he grinned when he thought this one probably didn't have a single gaboon and a barefoot boy could go in without having to watch where he stepped. The old post-Depression high school had been replaced with a concrete building large enough to house fifteen hundred students and Lafitte knew its solid construction was hurricane-proof.

He turned onto the main shopping street which, with the exception of a J. C. Penney's and a Sears catalogue store, was one long block of small shops. The drugstore was still there, though the front was a bit fancier and with more neon. Lafitte found a parking place three doors down. As he pulled to the curb he said:

"I want to get some cigarettes."

"Goody," she said. "Do I have time to browse?"

"Yeah," he replied cautiously, "a little bit."

He got out, went to the sidewalk, and held the door for her, then put a dime in the meter and took her arm as they strolled toward the drugstore. Two neatly dressed women shoppers were chatting at the curb as they approached. One of the women stared at him, then nudged her friend. Lafitte nodded politely and as they passed, one of the women said in a stage whisper:

"That's him! It has to be, he's the spitting image! He's back!"

Lafitte raised an eyebrow and glanced at his wife. If she heard she gave no notice. He steered her into the dry goods store and a lady clerk nudged the manager and whispered something. The man nodded, then looked at Lafitte with a big, toothy grin and said:

"Afternoon. Something special I can show you?"

"Thank you, no," Sandy replied. "Just browsing."

"Fine. Go right ahead."

They went down an aisle with Sandy pausing every few feet to finger the material. After a minute or so she turned to

her husband and said, "Why don't you go on to the drugstore
and then come back for me?"

"Excellent idea," he grinned, squeezing her arm.

As he left the store the man smiled again and bowed
slightly. Lafitte nodded pleasantly and went out to the sidewalk. The two women were still there, only now there was a
third. One glanced quickly at him and nudged the newcomer.
Lafitte ignored them and turned to his left and went the two
doors to the drugstore, wondering how they knew him, or
thought they did, since he certainly didn't know them.

As Lafitte approached the counter by the cash register, the
soda clerk came from behind the old-fashioned soda fountain
and whispered to the druggist who nodded, then hurried forward with a big smile.

"Good afternoon," the man said. "Welcome back."

"Thank you," Lafitte said. His only indication of slight surprise was a raised eyebrow. "May I have a carton of Benson
and Hedges, please."

"Certainly," the man replied and turned to the wall. Lafitte put down a five-dollar bill and the man rang up the purchase with the same big smile.

"Give Mr. John Christian my best," the man said, handing
Lafitte his change and the sack.

"I'll do that, thank you," Lafitte replied.

Sandy was waiting for him in front of the dry goods store.
She took his arm and he walked her toward the car. When
they were a few feet away she spied a small dress shop and
turned and said, "I'll just be a minute. I promise."

"Okay, sixty seconds."

He stepped out into the street and opened the driver's
door. As he threw his sack on the front seat he saw a small,
white cardboard box, a bit bigger than a cigar box. He
frowned slightly and looked up and down the street a moment. There was no one near the car except Sandy, who was
disappearing into the dress shop. Still frowning, he picked up
the box and opened it, and a cold shiver ran up his spine. It
was a small man-doll with blue eyes and dark hair, much like
his. But what had made him shiver was the little plastic
sword impaling the chest. He took a deep breath and whispered:

"Voodoo!"

He shivered again, then quickly replaced the cover and put

the box into the empty glove compartment, got behind the wheel and closed the door, and sat as if waiting patiently for his wife.

"That son of a bitch!" he said to himself. "Him and his friggin' practical jokes!"

He had conquered his anger and was sitting quietly, smoking a cigarette, when Sandy came back to the car.

"My!" she said with a big smile. "The values they have! If we stay a while, I'd like to come back and go shopping."

"We'll see," he replied, turning the key.

Toward the end of town he came to the Shell station. Its glass shack and two old hand pumps had been replaced by a sanitary-looking building and three islands and nine pumps. The revolving sign was a good sixty feet high. He pulled into the station next to a white police car and got out and nodded to the attendant. "Fill it, please. With Ethyl."

"Yes, sir," the man replied.

The police car pulled out slowly and the officer smiled at Sandy and said, "Afternoon, ma'am," and then he nodded politely to Lafitte. The nod was returned and Lafitte followed the car a few feet with his eyes and they came to rest on the adjacent building fifty yards away, across an expanse of blacktop. It was a large, two-story, Colonial building with two wings fanning out into a "V" toward the rear. Everything was painted a spotless white with an occasional dark red trim to complement the brick planters. The large sign hanging over the front portico said: SMUGGLER'S INN.

"Hey! Pretty fancy, huh?" he said to his wife.

She nodded and then pointed to the dark clouds building up in the distance. The attendant saw the gesture and said to Lafitte:

"We gonna have us some good rain pretty quick. Can I help you put the top up?"

"No thanks," Lafitte replied. "We're just going down to Bonne Terre."

The man nodded with a quizzical look on his face. It was obvious that he had a question but he was too polite to mention it. Instead he said, "Well, sir, that oughta do it. Shouldn't rain fer maybe a half hour or so."

The man quickly checked the oil and washed the windshield and Lafitte handed him the credit card. While the man was filling out the ticket the police officer slowly drove back toward town, looked at them and smiled, and continued on his way.

"Does he know you?" Sandy asked.

"No, I don't think so. He just knows we're strangers . . . doing his job, that's all."

Bayard quickly vanished behind them as he picked up his speed down the two-lane highway. The oaks were more numerous now and heavily draped with moss.

"Mattress stuffing," he said.

"Mattress stuffing?" she repeated, as though the remark was slightly daft.

"Yeah. The poor folks use moss for mattress stuffing. It's a little stiff, but the price is right."

"Umm," she nodded at this informative bit of trivia and then pointed to the bushes lining both sides of the road. "What are those?"

"Blackberries."

"Really?"

"Sure. Wild blackberry bushes. They use 'em as hedges. Most effective, they're brambles, keeps the cows in. I remember when I was a kid they used to send us out in our oldest clothes with baskets to pick the berries."

"Why? Your clothes get torn?"

"No, silly. I can see you're a city girl. It's 'cause kids eat as much as they pick. And the stain just doesn't come off."

"Oh," she grinned, then lapsed into silence and watched the stately trees again. After a short interval she said, "Did you notice how many people were staring at us in town?"

"Oh sure," he grinned. "They were just saying look at that lucky guy with that gorgeous woman. . . . Bayard's just like any small town. Everybody knows everybody else. And here's a strange car, a convertible at that, with two strangers in it . . . an obvious object of interest, and something to wonder at."

"I suppose," she replied with a small shrug. Then she pointed to the clouds and added, "That looks pretty black. You think we'll make it?"

"Hope so. At the first drop the top goes up."

She nodded and settled back to enjoy the ride.

It was now as dark as twilight and there were no more

shadows under the trees. The air was muggy and there was no breeze. He had about decided that they might not make it before the rain came and he pushed the accelerator a bit, but almost at once he had to slow for a sharp curve. Then he was jamming his foot onto the brake pedal and fighting the wheel as he skidded to a stop. At the outside of the curve was a large oak, cutting into the shoulder and overhanging the highway. A huge branch was down, blocking both lanes. He came to a lurching halt, well under the big tree with the hood in the fallen branches.

"Wow!" he said, grinning at his wife, who had both hands on the dash.

Something dropped onto the back seat and he turned his head to see two cottonmouth moccasins wiggling on the upholstery. He froze, his throat constricted, and he almost panicked, but then he thought of her and he conquered his fear and tried to think what he could do to get her out of the car. He took a deep breath, clenched his teeth, and looked quickly up into the tree. There was a faint rustling sound, but he could see nothing and he didn't dare take a leisurely look. Another quick glance told him they were still on the seat and he leaned carefully toward his wife and said in a calm voice:

"Easy now. Do as I say. Put your feet on the seat."

She turned to stare at him, but the fierce look on his face and the quiet insistence in his voice stopped her from asking. He slid his right hand under her knees and pulled and she leaned back as she pulled her feet to her right and up on the seat.

"There's a snake on the back seat," he said, almost conversationally. "It dropped out of the tree. Don't move."

Her eyes widened in instant fear and she started shaking.

"Easy, it looks harmless," he lied. "Just sit still and don't look back. I'll come around and get you."

She nodded, swallowed hard and, to her credit, stared straight ahead. He turned his head a bit and one of the snakes was gone. He fought down a shiver and wished he were wearing boots, and for a moment he was again afraid he was going to panic. He forced himself to take a deep breath and glance again at the back seat and the other snake wiggled to the floor. He clenched his teeth, faced forward, and made sure he didn't move his legs and then slowly raised up on the door handle and pushed. When the door was all the way open he pulled his left hand to the back of the seat, put his right hand on the door post, and paused for another slow breath, then quickly swung his feet to the left and propped them on the door. He shivered, Sandy gasped, but his legs weren't touched. Feeling a bit safer, he let out his breath and leaned back a moment, then vaulted out onto the pavement and took two quick running steps, stopped and turned back to grin weakly at his wife. She didn't see him, she was still staring through the windshield.

As he turned to run behind the car he saw a white Jaguar roadster skid to a stop behind him. He continued to her side, pulled the door open and stepped back and looked at the floor; there were no snakes in sight.

"All right, honey," he said quietly, "turn and take my hands."

She did as she was told, white-faced and silent.

When both her feet were straight out and he had a firm grip on her hands, he said, "Now, when I pull you out, put your feet on the ground and run for that car."

She glanced to her right and saw a man getting out of the Jag, and she nodded. Lafitte gripped hard and pulled her out of the car. At the moment her feet hit the ground one of the snakes took that instant to escape and its body scraped across her nylon-covered ankle; she screamed and ran as the snake quickly slithered off the road.

The Jag driver was coming toward them and intercepted her a few feet behind the Chevy. He grabbed one arm and she spun around to face him with a hysterical gasp. He grabbed her other arm and held her fast for a moment and then she took a deep breath and nodded that she was all right. The man released her and stepped back. He was expensively dressed in a camel's hair sport coat and tan slacks. Though shorter than Lafitte by a few inches he had very wide shoulders and a barrel chest. As Lafitte joined them, the man turned his darkly handsome face and said in a bass voice:

"What happened?"

"Some snakes dropped out of the tree on us."

The man frowned and his dark eyes looked at the oak and then to the center of the road next to the Chevy. A snake was wiggling diagonally across the opposite lane. The man trotted to the snake, coming up behind it, and quickly put out a foot and pinned the reptile just behind the head. The man bent over, studied his captive for a moment, then raised up and said to Lafitte in a slightly French accent:

"Sir? In my glove box is a knife. Would you bring it, please."

Lafitte nodded and led the still pale Sandy to the right side of the Jag. He opened the door and put her in the seat, took out his cigarettes and matches and handed them to her. She swallowed hard, nodded once, and managed a slight smile. He ran his hand lightly over her cheek for a moment, then opened the glove compartment and reached in and took out a long knife and grinned tightly; he hadn't seen one like it in years. It had a dark wooden handle and an eight-inch, tapered blade, somewhat thinner than a Bowie knife. Locally called a "Cajun toothpick," it was deadly in hand-fighting because of its weight, but it was also an excellent throwing weapon. Lafitte raised an eyebrow for a moment, squeezed his wife's shoulder, then hurried to his Samaritan.

The man nodded as Lafitte handed him the knife, butt first. Then Lafitte got another look at the dirty, olive-colored, three-foot snake, and he shivered.

"It is a water moc!" Lafitte said in a low voice.

"It is indeed, sir," the man replied.

He bent over and forced the blade into the mouth, turned it sideways and showed a long set of evil-looking fangs. Lafitte shivered again and the man started cutting the head off at the base of the neck and blood spurted onto his expensive boot. He stopped when the knife was just past the spinal cord and was still attached by the underskin. Then he changed hands with the knife and grabbed the wildly gyrating tail and said, "If you'd stand back, please."

Lafitte nodded and backed up a good ten feet and the man moved his foot and swung the snake by the tail in a low, wide arc into the bushes. He took a handkerchief from his breast pocket, put the knife on the ground, and wiped his boot. Then he rubbed the blade clean, checked his hands, dropped the handkerchief at the edge of the road, and retrieved his knife.

"I have a thing about snakes," the man said, almost apologetically.

"You hide it well," Lafitte said dryly. Then, "Christ! Maybe one's still in the car. Maybe I didn't see a third one."

"I can help there," the man said, looking at the clouds.

"But we'd better hurry." They went to his car and he said to Sandy, "Are you all right, ma'am?"

She swallowed and managed a weak smile. "Yes, thank you. I'll be fine as soon as I stop shaking."

"Good girl!" Lafitte said, proud of his wife.

The man grinned and took the keys from the ignition; he went to the rear of the car, opened the trunk and carefully took out a shotgun and broke it open to make sure both barrels were loaded. As he handed the weapon to Lafitte he said, "You know about these things?"

"I certainly do," Lafitte replied, taking the gun.

The man nodded, took out a long flashlight, and they went to the tree where he cut off a three-foot branch and trimmed it with quick, sharp strokes. He nodded Lafiitte to the open Chevy door and stooped down to flash the light under the seat. Then he looked up with a friendly grin and said:

"I suggest you don't shoot unless you have to. It won't help your car."

"I'll make sure you're not in the way," Lafitte answered.

The man's dark eyes stared openly at Lafitte for a moment and then, apparently deciding he could turn his back, he flashed the light under the seat again and poked with the stick while Lafitte kept the shotgun pointed at the ground. In a moment the man grunted and got to his feet and they went to the other side of the car and repeated the process. When he was satisfied, he turned slightly and guided the barrel of the shotgun over the open quarter window. He reached in gingerly and pulled out the small rear seat. There were no snakes.

The man nodded, Lafitte raised the barrel of the gun, and the man replaced the seat and got to his feet.

"Well," he said, smiling slowly, "that should do it. But you'll never make it to your destination tonight. It'll take a road crew to get this out of the way."

"Uh huh," Lafitte agreed, his eyes going to the broken branch.

Then he frowned and trotted to the tree, followed by his new friend. They stood a moment in silence and saw where the giant limb had been cut with a chain saw.

"It, uh, didn't just fall," Lafitte observed.

"No, sir, it surely did not," the man agreed, staring from the tree to Lafitte with a slightly quizzical expression on his face. "Well, you'd best spend the night in town. Uh, may I suggest the inn? Excellent facilities."

"Yes, I saw it on the way out, sounds fine."

"Hey!" Sandy called. "I felt a raindrop!"

The two men grinned and Lafitte hurried to his car, started the engine, and put the top up while the man escorted Sandy from one car to the other, put her in and closed the door. When the top was clamped down, Lafitte got out and met the man at the back of the Chevy.

"Yours is manual, isn't it? Let me help you."

As they went to the Jag a few big drops began to fall and they pulled the top up in a hurry. When it was secure, Lafitte went to the driver's side and extended his hand and said:

"I certainly appreciate your help, Mister . . . er?"

"You," the man said. "My name is Dominique You."

"You're kidding!" Lafitte said, then burst into laughter. "Dominique You!"

"Yes," the man replied, the smile disappearing into an irritated frown.

"Then we've got to be friends!" Lafitte said, keeping his grip on the man's hand and clapping him on the shoulder. "Ho! That's great!"

"I don't understand," You replied, still frowning.

"My name is Jean Lafitte. Dominique You has to be my best friend!"

You's eyes widened, the frown disappeared, and he joined Lafitte in laughter for a moment.

"*Mon Dieu!* But, of course! We must be! I thought you looked familiar!"

The big drops increased a bit and Sandy stuck her head out of the driver's door and shouted, "It must be funny, but you'll get soaked!"

"She's right," You said. "Follow me to the inn. We must have a drink on it."

"Absolutely!" Lafitte said, clapping You on the shoulder again.

He ran to his car and Sandy pushed the door open for him. The windows were quickly rolled up and he started the windshield wipers. As both cars made a tight U-turn and headed toward town the full force of the rain squall hit.

"What was that all about?" Sandy asked.

"Wait 'till we get to town. I'll buy you a drink and explain it."

"I can use one." She shuddered, then added, "I've never been so frightened in my life."

"I know," he said, patting her knee. "Couple of drinks and you'll be all right. Then we'll talk about it."

She nodded, took a deep breath, and Lafitte noticed that her hands were still shaking and his eyes narrowed to slits for a moment.

"All right, by God," Lafitte thought, "if he wants to play jokes, maybe we should see how he likes to play 'em with a broken nose!" Lafitte's sense of humor did not extend to water moccasins, especially when dropped on his wife. With a great effort he forced down his anger, there was no use in upsetting his wife further. He would wait.

When they pulled under the portico of the Smuggler's Inn it was still raining hard. The white Jag was there, You standing next to it. Lafitte pulled alongside and You opened the door and helped Sandy alight. She smiled her thanks and the three quickly climbed the steps.

"Your keys?" You said with a grin. "Are the bags in the trunk?"

"Yes," Lafitte replied, handing him the keys.

You, in turn, tossed the keys to the young parking attendant who was holding the door for Sandy. "Ron, bring the bags out of the Chevy, please. Then park both cars?"

"Yes, sir."

As they entered the foyer Lafitte turned to You and said, "I don't think I've introduced you to my wife, Sandra. Honey, this is Mr. You."

"Mrs. Lafitte?" You said with a brief, polite bow. "My pleasure."

"Mr. You?" Sandy smiled.

You indicated the desk against the far wall and escorted them across the big, low-ceilinged, Colonial decorated foyer. The elderly, bald desk clerk smiled, nodded, and said:

"Good afternoon, Mr. You."

"Give them Number Twenty-One," You said, returning the nod.

"Yes, sir."

Lafitte registered, then turned to You with a slightly raised eyebrow.

"Oh, I forgot to tell you," You said. "I own the inn. After you're settled, I would like to buy you a drink."

"Do it now," Sandy said with a wide grin. "I've already seen the snakes."

"Fine," You replied.

Lafitte nodded to the clerk, and You escorted them into the large, almost empty bar. As they were about to take seats at the booth nearest the fireplace, Sandy said to her husband:

"Order me a double."

Both men smiled politely as she quickly headed for the powder room.

The bar was richly paneled in dark wood and the booths were dark red leather. The large brick fireplace took up one corner and a bandstand the other. The opposite wall was all bar. Behind it a bartender was busily fixing snacks for the expected cocktail crowd. He nodded to You, picked up a tall glass, and turned to speak to the waitress.

In a moment the large-breasted young lady was there, smiling at You, and bending over close to Lafitte to wipe the already clean table. She was dressed in the modern version of a Colonial gown, but with several noticeable differences. While it was lacy and had a small bustle, it was very short and cut as low as the law, the law of gravity, would allow. Lafitte grinned lasciviously into her cleavage and You said:

"I would hate to disturb an art lover, but what will you drink?"

Lafitte grinningly took his eyes from the two huge mounds and said, "A tall, double bourbon and water and a Scotch and water, please."

You nodded and added, "And my cognac and soda."

"Yes, sir," the girl replied and headed toward the bar.

Lafitte took out his cigarettes and offered one to his host. It was declined with a raised hand and You reached into a coat pocket and took out an almost black cheroot. Lafitte held a match for him and then held the match to his cigarette while he studied his new friend. After a few moments he confirmed his first impression, he liked this darkly virile man. While You was ruggedly handsome, and his manners would shame a French courtier, Lafitte was a good judge of men and felt that the fine manners would disappear should Dominique You be offended. . . .

"Well," You said, breaking the polite silence, "may I, without intending to be nosy, ask what a man with such a famous name is doing in Bayard? And no doubt you're the grandson of the old . . . pardon, the elder Monsieur Lafitte?"

"The old man?" Lafitte grinned. "Yes. And we were headed for Bonne Terre when the tree . . . uh, managed to get in the way."

"I see. . . . Ah, the drinks." You stopped talking as the buxom waitress approached from the bar.

"My," Lafitte said, watching the girl jiggle across the room, "that was quick."

"The bartender started fixing mine when we walked in," You explained, as the girl put the glasses on the table. "And, of course, we pride ourselves on our service. Archie's hands are faster than a magician's."

"I can believe that."

Then they saw Sandy approach and both men started to rise. She shook her head and held out her hand to stay them and her eyes turned to stare at the retreating waitress. She shrugged slightly, then grinned at the men and slid into the booth next to her husband and picked up the glass.

"That was quick," he whispered.

"It certainly was," she nodded and extended the glass toward Dominique You. "To you, Mr. You, with our thanks."

"Amen," Lafitte said, raising his glass.

"You're very kind," You replied, raising his glass. "And let us also toast a hundred-and-sixty-year-old friendship."

"Well said," Lafitte chuckled. "I'll drink to that."

The two men sipped their drinks while Sandy drank over half of hers without putting down the glass. When she did, she stared at each man, her brows knitted, and said:

"Now, you two seem to have a big secret. Like just now, a hundred and sixty years. And what was so funny out on the highway? You were standing in the rain laughing like crazy."

Lafitte smiled and You chuckled and puffed on his cheroot.

"You're not up on your history, dear," Lafitte said. "It's our names, his and mine."

"I don't understand."

"Honey," Lafitte said, "Dominique You was Lafitte's . . .

the first one, the pirate . . . You was Lafitte's best friend. He was the artillery expert who helped Andrew Jackson save New Orleans from the British in 1812."

"Oh," she grinned. "I didn't get the connection. And are you any kin to the first one, Mr. You?"

"Supposedly," You replied with a slight shrug.

"A coincidence," Sandy said, her orderly mind made up.

"Perhaps," You allowed, sipping his drink. "If you believe in such things."

"Don't you?" Sandy said.

"More like fate, Mrs. Lafitte," You said. "The coincidence is almost too much. The names, my arrival at the propitious moment. . . . Ah, some shrimp."

You moved the ashtray as the waitress appeared with a big platter with large, shelled shrimp, sauce, and thin slices of French bread. Sandy's eyes widened and she finished her drink; You motioned for another round.

"I don't usually guzzle my drinks," Sandy explained, "but every time I think of those snakes it makes me shudder."

And, as if to demonstrate the point, she shuddered and her husband squeezed her arm.

"You carry it off very well," You said. "Most women would have been in complete hysterics."

"I'm still thinking about being hysterical," Sandy said with a forced smile and another shiver, "but a couple more drinks and I won't worry about it."

"Watch it, honey," Lafitte said. "Those are doubles."

"Yes, I know," she answered primly. "We are going to spend the night here?"

"Yes, dear, we are."

"Good, then I'll have several more. And in the morning I won't worry about it."

Lafitte shrugged at You as if to say that he couldn't argue with his wife's logic. You grinned slightly over the rim of his glass, then put it down and said:

"Excellent. . . . Shrimp, Mrs. Lafitte?"

"Yes, thank you," Sandy said, spearing one with a toothpick. "My, these are the biggest shrimp I've ever seen."

"Yes, ma'am. The best of the catch. Brought in daily."

"Umm, delicious!" she said, reaching for a cocktail napkin.

They watched her finish three shrimp as they finished their drinks and then the waitress was there with another round.

"Would you bring me another one, please?" Sandy asked.

"Yes, ma'am," the waitress replied, managing to keep a straight face.

"Although he'd mentioned a grandson," You said to Lafitte, "and I'd read about it in the paper, still I'm happy you have the proper name."

"Of course!" Sandy giggled. "He has to be Jean Pierre . . . Jean Pierre Lafitte! It wouldn't sound right if his name was Max Lafitte. Or Fred."

She giggled again and took another big drink, determined to make herself sleepy. Lafitte smiled indulgently and decided to let her have her way. To You he said:

"You know the old man well?"

"Oh, yes. Though I haven't seen him in some months, not since his last attack. I called once and he sent a message that as soon as his hand got better he would take my money at another poker game. . . . Is this your first visit to Louisiana, Mrs. Lafitte?"

"Yes, it is," she said with a wide smile. She finished her drink in two gulps and Lafitte shuddered while You grinned politely. "And in spite of this afternoon, I think the country is beautiful. It's just as green as Jean said it was."

The waitress replaced her glass with a fresh drink and Sandy stared at it a moment in some wonder, then said, "My, that was fast."

"The waitress signals the bartender as she turns from the table," You explained. "A highball is usually ready by the time she gets to the bar."

"My, isn't that interesting?" she said to her husband as though You's remark was a great revelation. She took another large drink, then put the glass down and looked at You with a frown. "Were those snakes dangerous?"

"No, I don't think so," You said, lying easily.

"Then why did you kill that one?" she asked pointedly.

"I, uh, don't like snakes. They kill chickens and get the eggs."

She nodded, then smiled and said brightly, "Look at that. I didn't even shudder."

"Good girl!" Lafitte said.

He offered her a cigarette and then held a match. She took a drag, then a long sip. Another puff, another drink. Lafitte made a face and You grinned into his glass. In a few mo-

ments her third big double was gone and she put the glass
down with a firm gesture.

"There," she said. "That ought to do it. Now I think I'll go
upstairs and take a little nap."

"I'll take you up," Lafitte said, starting to slide out of the
booth after her.

"Nonsense," she said, "I'm just slightly . . . and I can certainly walk upstairs."

"And I want to wish you the very best of luck, dear," Lafitte said dryly.

You got to his feet and said, "Your bags will be in the
room. There are two keys at the desk."

"Thank you," Sandy said, extending her hand. "You're a
charming host and thank you again for your help this afternoon. And please ignore my drinking. I usually sip one or
two light ones. It's just that I want to be sure I'll go to sleep."

"It was my pleasure," You said, bowing slightly over her
hand. "I hope to see you again while you're here."

"I'm sure we will. We'll have to think of some way to
repay your help."

"Don't mention it."

"You sure you don't want me to see you up?" Lafitte
asked.

"No, of course not. Stay here and enjoy your talk. But be
quiet when you come in."

She leaned over and kissed her husband on the forehead,
picked up her bag and walked steadily, if somewhat carefully, across the room. You sat down again, smiled, and said:

"Will she be all right?"

"Oh sure. She's not bombed. But she'll sleep the night
through, and that's good."

"A most charming woman. My compliments. Not many
women would carry it off as well as she did."

"Thank you. And yes, I consider myself most fortunate.
You wouldn't know that she's the mother of two teen-aged
kids."

"No! Really? You are to be complimented. I envy you. I
never married . . . except for a night at a time, of course."

"And there's much to be said for that form of marriage,
too," Lafitte replied with a smile as he raised his glass.

Dominique You raised his, drained it, and waved to the

bartender. As the man nodded, You said, "And bring yesterday's paper."

You picked up the matches from the table and held one to
his cold cheroot. Lafitte took a cigarette out of his package
and You held the match for him. As he shook it out and
dropped it into the ashtray he said:

"Are you really descended from the original Lafitte?"

"Maybe. I don't really know. If one listens to the stories,
half the boys in Louisiana are descendants of Jean Lafitte."

"But you have the name."

"Sure. And the old man swears it's true . . . but he could
never really prove it. If you'll recall, the original Lafitte never
married so, if I am descended from him, I come from a long
line of bastards. But brother Pierre, though he had many bastards, did have one legitimate son. Occasionally, the old man
said we came from him. The story varied, depending on his
mood. But it's a fairly common French name."

"Yes, and I've even heard of several other men named
Jean Lafitte. But still, *mon ami*, I am taken by the coincidence. May I ask, what business are you in?"

"I have a piece of a trucking line."

"Ah, how interesting. We're both in the transportation business, sort of. . . . The inn is only a side thing with me." You
studied his cheroot for a moment, then added, "I own a
number of small boats. We rush the finest shrimp and frog
legs, and I mean the finest, and several other delicacies, to
New Orleans to be flown in ice to the greatest restaurants in
the country."

"Sounds lucrative," Lafitte nodded, then changed the subject. "And Dominique You, are you a descendant of the first
one?"

"It is possible," You allowed with a smile. "And I like the
idea."

"It does make one wonder," Lafitte agreed. Then, "Hey!
I'd better call Bonne Terre and tell 'em we won't be there,
they're expecting us."

You nodded and called to the waitress who was about to
leave the bar, "The phone." The woman nodded, turned back
and was handed a phone by the bartender. She pulsated her
way to their table, put down the tray and plugged the phone
into the jack in the wall, put down two fresh drinks and the
paper, smiled and left. Lafitte dialed the number, smiling as

he remembered that it was not the same one he'd dialed as a boy, even the phone numbers had changed. It rang three times and then a woman's voice, thick with a Southern accent, said:

"Lafitte's residence?"

"Sedonia?" Lafitte said.

"Jean Pierre!" she shouted, then regained her decorum a bit and added, "Mistah Lafitte, where are you?"

"Sedonia, it's good to hear your voice. How are you?"

"Ah'm fine, jes' fine, suh."

"Sedonia, a big tree's blocking the road and it's raining like hell. Tell the old man we won't be out until the morning, okay?"

"Yes, suh, but we wuz expectin' you."

"Can't help it, old girl. Tell the old man we won't be there until about ten in the morning. We're staying in town, at the inn."

"Yes, suh, I'll do it."

"Good girl, see you in the morning. 'Bye."

"Good-bye, Mistah Jean."

Lafitte replaced the phone and pushed it to one side. You was reading the local paper, folded into quarters. He looked up, smiled slightly, and took a sip from the fresh glass.

"My friend," he said seriously, "I think it is time we talked of snakes."

"I thought you might ask," Lafitte replied.

"And I may be presumptuous, two grown men, barely met, and acting like old friends because of the linking of the names, but I do believe in fate."

Lafitte nodded and sipped his drink.

"When Dominique You makes a friend it is a damn rare thing, so I do speak with some concern. That was deliberate."

"I know," Lafitte answered.

"Do you have any idea who did it, or why?"

"Yes," Lafitte said calmly, "I think so."

"But you do not seem concerned," You said with a frown.

"Oh, I'm concerned, all right," Lafitte said with a thin smile. "I'm goddam mad about the son of a bitch dropping snakes on my wife, or having it done, more likely. But I'll take care of that in due time."

You raised an eyebrow and studied his new friend, amazed at Lafitte's calm words. "Well, I will not pry further, except to add that those were indeed cottonmouths, at least the one I killed was, and they are not tree snakes."

"I know," Lafitte said in the same placid tone, "and the branch didn't just fall down, it was cut, and then dropped just as my car started into the turn. But, really, I think it was a prank. Admittedly a bad one, but that's what I think it was."

You chose his words carefully. "To . . . uh, scare you away?"

"Obviously, though I'm not sure why. But I think I know who did it and, of course, he knew I was coming, and about what time. I figure I was spotted in town."

"Ha!" You exclaimed, handing Lafitte the paper. "I knew you were coming. The whole town did! And with a picture of your grandfather forty years ago for comparison."

The article was captioned, "LAFITTE RETURNS." The subcaption said, "To Claim the Legendary Treasure?" The article said that John Lafitte, the last adult heir of the family, was returning for a visit and the question was raised about the legendary treasure of Lafitte, the pirate, buried perhaps at the plantation, before the pirate's hold on the Delta was broken before the War of 1812. The concluding line was a beauty, "Does this last in the line of Lafittes return to claim the fabulous treasure of his famous ancestor?"

"Where the hell did this come from?" Lafitte demanded, putting down the paper.

"I know the people at the paper," You replied. "And the old man's wife is friends with our genteel society editor. She probably gave it to her. And on the phone, no doubt."

"How do you know it was on the phone?" Lafitte asked.

"Note the spelling of your name," You grinned. "Mrs. Lafitte used the French pronunciation and our esteemed society editor, being a foreigner, spelled it John."

"A foreigner?"

"Yes, she's from Ohio."

Lafitte grinned, sipped his drink and said, "She certainly is."

"But it's news," You said. "Lafitte is a legendary name in Louisiana."

"Big deal!" Lafitte snorted. "That's a lot of bull!"

"Maybe," You shrugged. "But you look somewhat like him."

"Like who?"

"The pirate." You grinned and flicked his cheroot toward the big ashtray. He made it. "The old man has a portrait of Lafitte in his study. At least it's supposed to be the one. Now, you don't look exactly like him, just sort of. Your hair is dark brown, instead of pure black, but you have the high cheekbones and those blue eyes. You're only middle-sized, but I understand the first Lafitte was under six feet. And you've got the broad shoulders, and the Creole shows in the brown skin."

"Ha!" Lafitte grinned. "That's the desert sun. We live in Tucson."

"Even so, you're the heir. And everyone thinks he gave you the secret, or is going to."

"Bullshit!" Lafitte exclaimed a bit loudly, but the waitress was at the far end of the room and there was no one to notice but the bartender and he merely grinned and went on cleaning his glasses. "The secret to what? The old man blew whatever he had on women and horses. There's nothing left."

"I see," You said, making rings with his glass on the table top. "Now, certainly without doubting your word, and not wanting to pry, the question comes, as it will to the whole parish . . . why did you return after all these years, when he's had several strokes before and he probably has but little time?"

"Mainly because he asked me. And because I respect him, and he's never asked a thing of me. Not a single damn thing in all the years I've known him! There's nothing left. He made it the hard way and he blew it gloriously on the good life. . . . The pirate thing is just what the paper says, a legend. The mere fact that I'm the last in line and all that bull about pirate gold is pure fantasy. . . . Don't you think that if there had been a map and gold that some member of the family would've gotten it long ago . . . and spent it?"

"All right," You nodded. "I'll accept that. But then why the tree and the snakes?"

"Because," Lafitte grinned, "somebody in my family is not real sure. But I don't really have any enemies, and once he finds out that the legend is just that, he'll know too. . . . But, back to what I said a few moments ago, it was just a prank . . . on the off chance that the old man might really have something left to leave me."

"Mon ami," You said with a shake of his dark head, "if you don't mind my saying so, it was one helluva prank! Did you ever see what a bite from a cottonmouth does?"

"Yes," Lafitte replied, with a small shiver as he flexed his bad ankle, "I have. And that's what makes me believe that it really wasn't an assassination plot, if that's what you think. Besides, it would have been easier to shoot me. Consider this; had they wanted me dead, all they would've had to do would be cut down the tree, or obstruct the road in some way, then when I stopped they could've shot me several times with a good rifle. . . . This way was clumsy. The snakes were as afraid as we were. They wouldn't've bitten me unless I'd tried to reach for one. Forget it."

You shook his head and nudged the newspaper and started to speak, but before he did, the bartender was at the table.

"Pardon," the man said. "But Marcel called. He is ready."

"Thank you," You said, getting to his feet. The bartender returned to his trade and You put out his hand and said, "Pardon me, but I must go."

"That's all right," Lafitte smiled, rising and taking the strong hand. "I've certainly enjoyed your hospitality. Thank you again."

"Not at all," You replied, smiling. "Whatever you desire, except the waitress, of course, is on the house. Call me as soon as you're settled and we'll get together for a drink. I'd like to see the old man again, if you can arrange it."

"I can do that. Tomorrow, maybe the next day. But, thank you, I'll join my wife."

"Fine, my new, old friend," You said, picking up the paper. "And if you don't mind one parting bit of uncalled-for advice?"

"No, of course not."

"As to your thought about not having an enemy," You said, waving the paper. "I think you do now."

Part Two

LAFITTE OPENED HIS EYES, STARED AT THE CEILING UNTIL IT came into focus and wondered if he had a hangover. Despite what he'd told Dominique You he'd stayed in the bar for three more drinks, eating those big shrimp. He swallowed a couple of times, grinned, and concluded that he didn't. He stretched slowly, took a deep breath, and decided that it was nice to be on a vacation, despite the day before. He propped himself on his elbows and gave some thought to getting up as his eyes scanned the room. It was comfortably dim, thanks to the heavy drapes over the windows. He looked to his left and she was there, on her back with the covers at her waist. She was nude and the curve of her breasts was softened because she had her hands above her head. He smiled as he studied the nipple closest to him and then he put his finger on it, as though ringing a doorbell. She sighed and took a deep breath. He removed his finger and the nipple was larger.

"Isn't that nice," he said to himself, "and the kids won't be pounding on the door demanding breakfast."

He grinned at the pleasant thought and was faced with a choice, that of making love to his wife, or falling back on the pillow for some more sleep. As he thought about it he was pleased that he actually had the time and the opportunity to make such a choice. Before he could make what was obviously an important decision the fancy telephone on the night stand on her side of the bed jangled politely.

25

"Damn!" he whispered and reached over her for the phone. He put it to his ear and said, "Yes?"

"Jean Pierre?" the loud, deep voice said.

"Hello, you old bastard," Lafitte replied with a smile, recognizing his grandfather's voice.

"Well, for Christ's sake! Is that any way to talk to the head of the family?"

"In this family, yes. How are you?"

"Never mind! Are you coming down today?"

"Yes, we'll be there in a few hours."

He grinned down at his wife who had opened her eyes and was smiling at him as he balanced over her, the phone just above her head.

"Good. I got lotsa things to talk to you about."

"Hey! What time is it?"

"It's after nine o'clock . . . time a full-grown man was out of bed. Now, don't y'all be late, ya hear?"

The phone abruptly went dead and Lafitte grinned, shook his head and leaned over his wife again to set the instrument on the night stand. She grinned sleepily at him and murmured:

"Good morning."

"Hi," he said, and then lightly kissed a nipple.

She cleared her throat, pushed him away, and pulled the sheet to her neck.

He tugged the sheet to her waist and stared at her breasts with a big grin. "And what a glorious inspiration I have. A sight like that could inspire even me to poetry. . . . Ode to a Boob. . . . Let's see, hmm, yeah. . . . There you are, O glorious boob, so round and firm and fully packed, and, uh . . ."

"Oh, for heaven's sake," she giggled as she pulled the sheet up again. "It's a good thing you're a better husband than you are a poet."

"Come on, you can't have everything."

He leaned over her again and picked up his watch from the nightstand, but without his reading glasses he couldn't see the dial. His glasses were across the room on top of the chest and instead of getting up he put the watch down and picked up the phone.

"Desk?" a pleasant young feminine voice said.

"Would you please have room service bring up a couple of

double Bloody Marys? And with a shot of Tabasco in 'em, please? This is, uh, room . . ."

"Twenty-One. Yes, sir. Just a few minutes."

"Thank you."

He replaced the phone and slowly got out of bed and limped to the bathroom. Just as he finished brushing his teeth the bell rang. He came out of the bathroom, headed for the door, then stopped suddenly in the middle of the living room as his wife giggled. He was naked. He grinned through the door at her and reached into the bedroom and grabbed his slacks from the chair.

"Just a moment," he called, and hurried to pull on his pants.

He opened the door and the bellboy nodded, stepped inside and put the tray on the table by the door. With the two tall drinks was a neatly wrapped package the size of half a cigarette carton.

"What's this?" Lafitte asked, taking a dollar from his pocket and giving it to the little man.

"Left at the desk about an hour ago, sir."

"Uh huh," Lafitte frowned. "Okay, thank you."

"Thank you, sir," the bellboy nodded, closing the door behind.

Lafitte looked over his shoulder to make sure his wife couldn't see him from the bed and then he picked up the package and read the card. It was typed:

MR. J. P. LAFITTE, PERSONAL

With an eyebrow raised anticipating the contents, he pulled the ribbon and lifted the lid. He was right. It was another voodoo doll, the twin of the first one.

"Damn you!" he whispered, more in irritation than anger.

"Honey?" Sandy called from the bedroom. "What's taking you so long?"

"Just a minute," he said, trying to sound relaxed. "I want to get some cigarettes."

He put the lid back on the box and hurried to put it in the bottom of his suitcase. He grabbed a package of cigarettes, picked up the tray, and went into the bedroom, forcing himself to smile. As he entered, she looked at him a moment, then quickly raised up and said:

"What took you so long?"

He grinned again and put the tray on the night stand. As he handed her a glass he held his up in a toast.

"I'm just moving a bit slowly after last night, that's all. This'll fix me up. . . . Here's to our vacation."

"Yes indeed," she said pertly, "and on vacations I require a big breakfast."

She got it; scrambled eggs, bacon, toast, and, though she wanted potatoes, she was served grits with melted butter. The first sip of the hot, black coffee made her blink.

"Chicory," he grinned. "All the restaurants down here serve it that way."

"Wow!" Then she added, pointing at his bowl of Wheaties, "There you go again, making me the pig. I have a big breakfast and you have a bowl of cereal. . . . And did you notice the way the waitress grinned when you gave her the order?"

"Tough," he said, reaching for the milk. "I've got to watch my weight. Besides, that's an indirect compliment to your cooking."

"Well," she said, somewhat mollified, "all right. . . . Say, grits aren't half bad."

The sun was shining brightly, the land was drying and it was a sparkling day. Lafitte looked at the sky and was grateful; had the day been wet he doubted that Sandy's fears would have been dispelled. But she was as naturally cheerful as he, and if the smiling woman next to him held any bad memories she hid them admirably. The tree branch had been removed and they passed the spot without comment. Within a few miles the farmland disappeared and was replaced with subtropical vegetation. Lafitte pulled off the shoulder at a small rise and pointed to his right.

"Look, the beginning of the swamp."

She nodded and studied the almost impenetrable greenery where it started on the other side of the bayou, and shuddered. After a bit she turned to him and said:

"You're not going to try it again, are you?"

"Try what?"

"The swamp. The last time it almost cost you your leg. Honey, you said you'd never go back to the swamp."

"The old man doesn't live in a swamp! Really, you'll like the house. It's old and graceful and the rooms have a musty smell. . . . As to the swamp, no; you couldn't get me in there. Hey! What the hell got you on the subject, anyway?"

"I don't know. You always said you'd never go back."

"I know. But I'm not going back to the swamp, honey! We're going to visit a mean, foul-mouthed, miserable old bastard who happens to be dying."

She stared at him a moment, then nodded and said, "Drive on, sir."

He drove a few miles farther and picked up the conversation again.

"You know, the old bastard really is something. . . . He got into the East Texas oil fields after everyone said they'd reached their peak and he made a fortune. He once lost two hundred thousand dollars in an all-night poker game. . . . He went into stocks when they were way down, and he came back home to wait. He bought General Motors when it was a few bucks a share, Coca-Cola stock for a pittance when some guy was about to go under. When it went up again he had another fortune to blow on women and gambling. And when it was all gone he came back to the old place to wait out his days."

"And it doesn't bother you that he spent it all?"

"No, not at all. He made it the hard way. . . ."

"And you could've been rich," she said in admiration. "Good for you, hon!"

"Big deal!" He grinned, patting her on the leg. "I've got it knocked . . . I've got everything but money."

"And that's another right answer," she said, squeezing his arm.

They left the jutting arm of the swamp and the land grew firm again and the bayou had two discernible banks. Another mile and he slowed at a rickety old bridge which had a badly weathered sign on it which said LAFITTE. He crossed the bridge at a cautious five miles an hour while Sandy made a face at the creaking noises.

"Don't worry," he said with a straight face, "this bridge was built over a hundred years ago."

"Oh, I don't doubt that," she agreed.

"Now you're on the island," he said, as the car cleared the boards and eased onto a dirt road. "Though it isn't really an island. It's a chunk of high ground. You know, like twenty feet higher than the water. On the north and south it borders the swamp. On the east is the bay. The road we've been on has paralleled the bay, but at a distance of a few miles."

"My, it's really isolated, isn't it?"

"Sort of. But the dry part is superb farmland. It's almost pure delta silt."

"How nice," she replied.

He grinned at her and picked up his speed a bit as the road made its way through an oak grove for a half mile, then turned sharply north and the oaks were replaced by big magnolia trees and the dirt became a white, hedge-bordered driveway. As the tires crunched into the surface she said:

"What is it, white gravel?"

"No. Shells."

"Shells?"

"Sure. You know, like the gasoline. They're dredged up from the bays, make excellent driveways. Besides, there's not much gravel down here."

She leaned over the door and studied the driveway for a few moments, then nodded to herself, confirming her husband's statement.

"Look," he said, pointing through the trees, "there it is."

"Oh, how beautiful!"

The two-story white house with the tall, Grecian columns was indeed beautiful, with a grace that gave it an enduring quality as its age attested.

"Hey!" he said. "They've got TV. . . . You know, when I first came here as a little kid with my mother the Lafitte from the Civil War was still living here. Of course, he was well into his nineties . . . but I told you that."

"I know," she smiled, "but now's the time to tell it again."

"Oh, come on," he said, exchanging smiles with her. Then he decided to tell her again to make sure she would remember if the occasion arose. "Well, you know, the old boy was a twenty-year-old lieutenant in the Civil War and he made the mistake of marrying a Yankee girl. He brought her and her sister here and they lived in ostracized solitude, except for the field hands, and they worked the land clear up into the twentieth century, until their grandson returned, that's the nasty old bastard you're about to meet. Anyway, grandfather stayed, and he took over. From here he went out to make his fortune, and each time he had trouble he came back here to start again. And when the old folks died, within three months of each other, they left the place to the old man."

"Well," she said mischievously, trying to keep a straight face, "it must be true. The story hasn't changed in all the years I've known you."

"Smart!" he said. "That's what you are, an oversexed smart-ass!"

"Well, if you object . . ."

"No, no, no! Don't change."

As he pulled the car to a stop in the middle of the circle driveway and got out, the big front door opened and an old colored woman, middle height and fat, stormed out onto the front porch and down the wide steps, wiping her hands on her ample apron. Lafitte grinned and met her at the bottom of the steps to be engulfed in a big hug.

"Mistah Jean," she said, tears in her eyes. "It's good. It's good!"

"Sedonia," he said, "you're losing weight."

"You're joshin' me, like always," she said, releasing him. She turned to the car and pulled back on the door as Sandy got out. "Is this the missus? How'd do, ma'am?"

"Sedonia?" Sandy grinned, putting out her hand. "I've heard so much about you."

"Thank you, ma'am, there's lots of me to hear about."

Then a stately old black man with almost white hair came out of the house to shake hands with Lafitte.

"Sam!" Lafitte said. "It's good to see you."

"And it's good to see you, Mistah Jean," Sam replied.

"Hey! Congratulations!" Lafitte grinned. "I hear you and Sedonia finally got married."

"Yes, suh," the old man grinned. "The kids kept insistin' and I got too old to run so, fat as she is, she finally caught me. . . . Where's the bags?"

"On the back seat," Lafitte said, glad that they weren't too heavy.

"Well, goddam!" a voice like a foghorn bellowed from the second floor. "You finally got here, late as usual!"

Lafitte looked up to see a wheelchair in the doorway of one of the upstairs bedrooms. He couldn't see the face, but there was no mistaking that voice.

"Hello, you old bastard!" Lafitte called cheerily and Sandy grimaced.

"Don't pay them no mind, Missy . . . is it Sandra?" Sedonia said.

"Call me Sandy."

"They been cussin' each other since Mistah Jean wuz a boy. But they don't mean it."

"I hope not," Sandy grinned.

"Come up here!" the old man called. "I want to talk to you. . . . Is that your wife? Well, she's goddam pretty . . . probably much too good for you!"

"Yes, sir," Lafitte replied.

"Young lady!" the old man continued his shouting, though there was no need. "Welcome! Sedonia will make you comfortable, and I'll come down in a bit and welcome you properly, but first I want to talk to this . . . this . . . well, I'll greet you in a bit."

Sandy smiled and waved and turned to help with the bags. Lafitte grinned at his wife and she motioned for him to go on up. He nodded and began to mount the steps when his cousin Suzanne, followed by her husband and three young girls, came out onto the porch.

"Hi!" Lafitte said, taking both his cousin's hands.

"Jean!" she replied. "It's good to see you."

He stared at his beautiful cousin a moment and decided that she had grown more voluptuous through the years. She was almost as tall as he was and she was still large-breasted with well-rounded, but not too wide, hips. Her face was as attractive as he'd remembered and showed little sign of aging. Her dark, shoulder-length hair framed a wide, sensuous mouth and she had the vivid blue eyes of most of the family. For a fleeting moment Lafitte almost wished he hadn't passed up the offer she'd made so many years ago. He turned from her, forcing himself to be civil as he faced the large, curly-haired man at her side.

"Hello, Jeremy," Lafitte said pleasantly, resisting the urge to smash the tall man in his slightly puffy face.

Jeremy Duroc, always the French aristocrat, always conscious of savoir faire, stepped forward with his dazzling smile and took Lafitte's hand in a firm grip.

"Welcome, Jean," he said, "It's good to see you after all these years."

"Thank you," Lafitte forced himself to say, and turned to see his wife on the steps behind him. As he took the bag from her and put it on the porch Jeremy said:

"And you're Sandy. Welcome to the old dump. And, my God, if I may say so, on the same porch we have two of the most beautiful women in the parish."

"Jean!" Suzanne said, "she's a beauty."

"Thank you," Sandy said, smiling. "Nice to meet you."

"And this," Jeremy said, "is Suzanne."

"Hello," Suzanne said warmly, taking Sandy's hand. "And though my husband is usually full of French hot air, this time he is correct."

"Thank you," Sandy said.

"Jean," Jeremy said, glancing upward, "I heard you called. You'd best go up before he has another one."

"I guess," Lafitte grinned. Then he turned to the children and said, "Hello, girls."

"Hi," the oldest one said, and the other two, several years younger than their fourteen-year-old sister, nodded and grinned.

"Jean," Suzanne said, "these are our girls, Claudette, Marie, and Lucille."

"Ladies?" Lafitte inclined his head and the girls giggled as he passed.

"We'll take care of her," Jeremy said, taking Sandy's arm. "We may even fix her a drink."

"Do," Lafitte said. "And have one waiting for me."

"Don't worry," Jeremy replied. "I'm sure the old man will have one for you, despite the doctor."

Lafitte nodded and entered the large foyer he'd remembered as a young man. He paused and took a deep breath of the cool, faintly musty air and nodded as he went up the wide, curving staircase. He knocked at the master bedroom door and the old man said:

"Come, for Christ's sake, it's open!"

Lafitte clenched his teeth to make sure he betrayed no emotion at what he might see, and opened the door. He was glad he did. Gone was the big man-among-men, the giant wherever he went, the man with the firm jaw and the dark brows who had a way of intimidating lesser men. In his place was an old, old man in a wheelchair. The face was drawn and wrinkled and his hair was pure white. The hands were

gnarled with arthritis and the veins stood out of the skin that
had the parchment-like quality of very old age. But the voice
was strong and the eye penetrating, the handshake firm, as
the old man said:

"Well, goddam, it's time you got here. You think I'd live
forever just to wait on your lazy ass gettin' here?"

"Hello, you old bastard," Lafitte grinned, releasing the
hand. "And yes, old goats like you never die, they just sit
around and bitch! How are you anyway?"

"How the hell do you think I am?" the old man said, then
chuckled. "Look at me. The last of the big-time studs . . .
old, worn-out, having strokes. . . . I'm so goddam old that
now when I look at a woman I forget what for!"

Lafitte chuckled and sat on the edge of the bed. "Well,
you're still your cheerful self."

The old man fixed him with one bloodshot eye, the other
closed in a squint. "Oh, you! You're still the smart-ass. . . .
Hey! Is that pretty little broad I saw down there really
yours?"

"That's no broad, you filthy old man, that's my wife."

"Hmph! I told you not to bring her. Things like that
around just make me feel bad 'cause I can't do anything
about it. . . . Incidentally, you meet the madam?"

"No, not yet."

"Well, she's around somewheres." He reached under the
blanket that was wrapped around his legs and pulled out an
almost full quart of bourbon and handed it to his grandson.
"Couple glasses in the bathroom. Straight for me, no water.
Goddam doctor won't allow me to drink."

"So why do you?" Lafitte grinned, getting to his feet and
taking the bottle.

"Ain't none of his goddam business!"

Lafitte shrugged and went to fix the drinks. As he came
out of the bath with the bottle and two glasses on a tray he
saw the old man locking the door.

"So we won't be disturbed," he explained, wheeling around
and taking his glass. He took a sip and then said, "Now, why
the hell did you come down here?"

"Why, you old son of a bitch, because you asked me!"

"Yeah, but I asked you things before and you never did."

"Well, I just came to see you once before you died, you
old bastard," Lafitte said cheerfully, raising his glass of bour-

bon and water. "I didn't come to see you so you'd will me anything. Besides, look at you. . . . You had to spend it all on yourself, otherwise you wouldn't look like that!"

The old man raised up a bit in his chair and stared at his image in the mirror, then broke into a loud laugh, took another sip, and nodded cheerfully.

"Goddam!" he said. "You're the only one of 'em who'd tell me the truth. And you knew I blew it all and you still came. By God, that's good! I almost wish I had something to leave you. Well, no matter. Here, to the last two Lafittes who understand. You and me, boy!"

Lafitte raised his glass in the toast and finished half his drink. The old man finished his and motioned for another one. Lafitte shrugged, and poured his grandfather another double and the old man said:

"Well, it's good you finally got your butt down here. I really am about to die. I'm like an old swamp bear . . . and there ain't many of them left around here, either . . . and they say the old bear knows when his time's about up, and I got that feeling."

"Balls!" Lafitte snorted. "You're just being dramatic."

"No, really. Pretty soon, now. There's not much of me left and one more stroke oughta do it."

"Then lay off the booze."

"No! Goddam, I gave up women and gambling. Take the booze and they can shoot me now!"

"All right," Lafitte said with a straight face. "Two out of three is pretty good."

"Ha!" the old man laughed, then grew quickly serious. "You got a good woman?"

"The best. And two fine kids."

"Good, good," the old man replied. "How's your leg? You do a day's work on it?"

"Oh, sure. I can't run, but it doesn't bother me much."

"Good for you! I remember that other goddam doctor saying you'd never live out the year. Well, that's good. You got it made, then. Hey! You know, the madam's been damn good to me these last . . . Christ, it's been almost twenty years. . . . Anyway, I'll leave the place to her. And, if you're goddam lucky, I'll leave what booze I don't drink to you."

"Good!" Lafitte said, adding to his grandfather's glass. "Then don't drink so damn much."

The old man grinned, tossed off his drink, and said, "It's a good thing I had enough left to see me to the grave, you wouldn't have supported me!"

"Me? Hell, no! It was your money and you shot it . . . that's fine . . . but I wouldn't 've lifted a finger to take an old goat like you into my house. I've got kids to raise!"

"Ha!" The old man grinned again and nodded, studying his grandson. "Well, you look in fine shape."

"Yes," Lafitte nodded slowly. "I have to . . . to make up for my leg."

"Uh huh. Hear tell you work for a trucking line. Pay good?"

"It's all right."

"Uh huh. Ever keep up with your fencing?"

"No. With the leg I can't move fast enough."

"Damn! I spend *beaucoup* money on fencing lessons and you give it up. . . . say, you were supposed to be here yesterday. What happened?"

"Oh, a tree fell. . . . say, you're bouncing from subject to subject like a Ping-Pong ball. Relax!"

"Relax, my ass! Goddam, I told you, I'm dyin'. I gotta get it all in. What tree?"

Lafitte started to banter with the old man, then decided to be serious. "Just out of town. Somebody cut it just as I got there and it blocked the road. I didn't mind that so much, but the son of a bitch dropped a couple of water mocs on us. One crawled across my wife's leg just as I was pulling her out of the car . . ."

"No!" the old man exclaimed, his brows furrowed.

"Yeah," Lafitte answered, the anger rising.

"Now who the hell would do a thing like that?"

"You know goddam well who! That smart-assed practical joker, that's who!"

"Yeah," the old man nodded, "he would. . . . Whatcha gonna do about it?"

"We're going to have a little discussion at the proper time," Lafitte said with a thin smile. "Now, tell me this; who knew when I'd be coming down here?"

The old man considered this a moment, then said, "Me . . . and everybody in the house, and probably half the town. So, best be careful, it might not be him."

"It almost has to be him. Why would anybody else do such a thing?"

"Didn't you read the paper? They think I'm gonna give you the supersecret treasure map and the pirate decoder ring!"

Lafitte laughed and nodded. "Yes, I read it. Are you?"

"Sure. You'll find two big swamp frogs and maybe a muskrat. . . . By God, I'll bet those snakes made you mad."

"Yeah, and they did something else. It made me respect my wife more. She's as afraid of snakes as most women, but she carried it off well. She's a damn sight braver than I am. I was scared, I tell you. On top of that I got two voodoo dolls!"

"No! Somebody really playin' games, huh?"

"Seems so. Somebody left one on the car seat before we left town yesterday and I got another one at the inn this morning. Both had a little sword through the chest."

"Son of a bitch!" the old man said, his eyes flashing. Then the brows contracted again as he looked at his grandson. "But . . . uh, you seem awful easygoin' about it. You weren't that good-natured a feller before, seems to me."

"Maybe you're right," Lafitte allowed. "I've forced myself to be. I used to be a hell-raiser, but now I've got a wife and family, and I work at it. Besides that, I'm just no longer the wild young buck. I smoke too much and I drink too much, and I'm beginning to slow down. I even have to use reading glasses."

"Oh bull crap!" the old man said. "You've got no problems. Look at me. I can't even get the goddam thing hard anymore!"

Lafitte laughed and sipped his drink. "Well, that's one problem I don't have. In fact, the reason I'm so easygoing is my wife . . . I've got the woman I want."

"Well," the old man nodded, "that certainly makes a man complacent."

"Yes indeed," Lafitte answered with a big grin.

"Well, give 'em hell, kid. Hey! A short one. Then I'll have a good nap before dinner."

Lafitte shrugged and poured his grandfather another drink which was quickly consumed. The old man handed Lafitte the glass and said:

"Here. Rinse 'em, please."

When he came out of the bathroom the bottle had disappeared and the old man was dozing in his wheelchair. Lafitte shook his head and left quietly.

Jeremy and Sam were each carrying a bag to the guest room next door. Sam grinned and Jeremy said:

"We stopped for a drink on the way up."

"Can I bring you a drink, Mistah Jean?" Sam asked.

"Yes, Scotch if you have it, Sam."

"I imagine you'll want to freshen up a bit," Jeremy said. "Join us around five. We can have a few drinks before the cocktail hour. That's at six. The old man likes to eat at seven."

"Fine," Lafitte replied, still forcing the cordiality.

"I've got to have a shower," Sandy said from the bedroom. "I'm soaked already."

"It's the humidity," Jeremy grinned. "It takes a bit to get used to it. . . . Well, see you in a while."

Lafitte nodded as Jeremy put down the bag and followed Sam out the door. Lafitte closed it and while Sandy hung his suit and dinner jacket and her dresses in the closet he went to the big French windows and opened them to stand in the doorway, looking past the veranda out to the cotton fields. His eyes wandered past the fields and to the northeast and the swamps. He shivered slightly and turned to the east and the wide expanse of the mud-colored bay. In a few seconds she came and stood behind him, looking over his shoulder and said:

"It's just beautiful . . . good to be home?"

"No, not really," he said quietly. "This isn't our home. It's just another place I used to live a long time ago."

She put her arms around him and said, "And that's another right answer." Then, "I'm going to get into the shower. Fix me a drink when it comes?"

"Okay." He continued to stare at the familiar sight and in a few moments she said:

"Hey, honey! This is a beautiful bathroom."

"See? I told you they had inside plumbing."

He heard her turn on the shower and in a few moments there was a discreet knock at the door. He opened it and Sam stepped inside with a new bottle of Scotch, two tall glasses, and an insulated bucket of ice. Sam nodded and put the tray on the night stand.

"Well, Sam," Lafitte said, "how are things?"

Old Sam shook his grizzled head and said, "Things ain't the same, Mistah Jean. Mistah John's dying and the house is fulla bad spirits."

"Come on, Sam. You don't believe in spirits, now, do you?"

"Well, I try to be a good Christian, Mistah Jean, especially as Sedonia gets mad iffin I don't take her to church on Sundays, but . . . well, I been hearin' the drums agin."

"What drums, Sam?" Lafitte said carefully.

"Mistah Jean, it ain't everybody I can tell, but I can tell you. It's them drums agin, the same ones."

"Aw, come on, Sam!"

"Now . . . now I ain't sayin' it's voodoo, though I did hear in town that some of the young ones is at it agin. . . . But, whatever it is, they's out there of a night and I hear 'em. . . . And the young ones, they's changed. They's uppity. And they demand their rights, whatever that means."

Lafitte grinned as he pulled the foil off the bottle. "You're getting old, Sam. But you've still got your health . . . and Sedonia."

"Yes, suh." Sam brightened a bit and managed a smile. "If you want anything, just lean outa the door and yell."

"Thank you," Lafitte said, following him to the door and closing it behind him. He turned the latch and kicked off his shoes and fixed two drinks and took them into the bathroom to add the water. He took a sip, decided it was very good Scotch, and sat on the dressing stool with both drinks. In a moment the water was turned off and Sandy stepped out and reached for a towel. She grinned at her husband, pulled off her shower cap, and he grinned in appreciation at his wife's figure. She still had the shape of a schoolgirl, almost, though her hips were a bit wider and she had an extra inch or two around the waist. When she saw him staring at her she held the towel above her head with both hands and wiggled so that her breasts quivered. He leaned forward and she took a step toward him and put a breast in his mouth. She let him suck her but a moment and then stepped back and dropped the towel.

"Shower first," she said and leaned forward and he held a glass while she took a sip.

Then she turned away and began to dry herself and when she turned back he had put the glasses on the sink and was reaching for her.

"Shower!" she said with mock seriousness, wrapping the towel around her.

"Nag! Nag! Nag!" he said and began to pull off his shirt as she took her glass and went into the bedroom.

When he came out of the bathroom she was propped up on the bed, nude, and the drapes were drawn. He came toward her, still drying himself with his towel, and she grinned and slid down on the bed, put her hands behind her head, and began to undulate slowly while she stared at him with half-closed eyes. He stood close to the bed and finished drying his close-cropped hair while he watched her. She put out a hand and began to feel him very gently and he felt himself begin to grow hard and he threw the towel onto the bed and got on top of her and she guided him into her, wrapped her legs around him, and began to move slowly as she cupped her breasts for him.

Suddenly she threw her arms around him as she began to move quickly and she whispered, "Faster! Faster . . . now!"

She was on her side, still asleep, when he awoke at four thirty. He gently patted her bare white bottom and got up and dressed in a fresh shirt and slacks. She had taken out their travel alarm clock and he set it for five and wrote her a note on the back of one of his business cards telling her to join him downstairs.

The big living room that had been, a hundred years ago, a formal drawing room was empty when he entered and he went behind the well-stocked bar and fixed himself a drink. Then he wandered next door to the study, darkly paneled in pecan, and as big as the living room. Glass in hand, he began to make the rounds of the ancient walls. Over the fireplace was another portrait of the old man, as big as the one in the living room, except that this one was a virile, strong man with a firm jaw and penetrating eyes, a leader of men.

Lafitte shook his head at what the passage of time had done and turned to look at a smaller picture next to the bookcase that he had not seen before. It was a three-quarter size painting of a man in a dark red waistcoat with a white stock at his neck and a lace-fronted shirt. In his waistband was a long knife with a fancy handle. The man's hair was pure black and he had dark skin and vivid blue eyes that were slightly squinted. He was a man of action, a gentleman fighter . . . he was Jean Lafitte, the pirate.

Lafitte studied it for some moments and then shrugged; he saw little resemblance, and he turned to the opposite wall. There were some pictures of his ancestors, and then his eyes stopped at the two-by-three, walnut-framed map and he smiled. Under the glass was the original surveyor's map with the metes and bounds described in archaic English, in a flowing script. He grinned as he put on his glasses to read the first lines below the hand-drawn map of the "island." The surveyor had written in 1823:

"Pursuant to an order from the Surveyor of the Public Lands south of the State of Tennessee, and in conformity with the request of the present claimant . . ."

He put away his glasses and turned to look at the hundred-year-old crossed foils with which he had tried to learn the gentlemanly art of fencing, with but moderate success. From the dust and the faint amount of rust on the long shafts and the steel guards it appeared that they had not been touched since. He raised his glass to what might have been, though, to his credit, without rancor, and was still staring at them when the door opened and Suzanne said:

"Jean!"

He turned to see his cousin, in a short skirt and a deep-cut blouse, enter the room.

"Hello, Suzanne. Where's the rest of your tribe?"

"Oh, Jeremy's helping the girls get dressed. They'll all be down in a few minutes."

"Uh huh. Want a drink?"

"Yes, please. Bourbon on the rocks."

He nodded and prevented himself from shrugging at her masculine choice of drinks and went behind the small bar and grinned slightly when he remembered that the old man had put in both bars during a time when he had lots of money. He found an Old-Fashioned glass and stooped to put in a couple of ice cubes from the tiny refrigerator. When he stood up she was leaning over the bar smiling at him, as though she were nude. Her blouse was open and she wore a half bra that showed her ample breasts to the top of her nipples. He stared at them a moment, as he knew she wanted him to, then he looked up with a bland smile and said:

"Boy! You still got big knockers!"

"And they're still available," she said in a low, husky voice.

"Well goddam, you don't make any bones about it."

"With you, Jean, no. Cousins or not, I'd still like you to try me."

"Well, I appreciate the offer but, no thanks. Even if I wanted to, I can't seem to keep up with my homework."

He poured a double shot over the ice and slid the glass to her.

"Maybe later," she said, hooking a thumb in the bra and tugging so that one large breast popped out.

"No," he said, staring, "no, I don't think so. But, thanks anyway."

"Hi there!" Jeremy called from the door and Lafitte looked up to see Duroc enter with his three girls and Sandy. Suzanne shrugged and slipped the breast out of sight and turned her head to smile cheerfully.

Lafitte began to fix Sandy a drink and said, "Duroc?"

"Scotch and water, please," he replied, coming to sit by his wife.

"Ladies?" Lafitte smiled at the girls. "What may I fix you?"

The girls giggled in unison and Suzanne said, "They may have one glass of cola before dinner."

Duroc came behind the bar and said, "Here, I'll fix them."

Lafitte nodded, finished making the two highballs and left the bar to kiss Sandy on the cheek and hand her a glass.

The conversation was easy and friendly. Suzanne and Jeremy took turns telling Sandy of earlier years of the family and small stories of the plantation while the girls sat quietly on the couch and sipped their cola. Six o'clock came and went, but the old man didn't appear until ten of seven. Then the doors were opened and Sam wheeled him in. Standing beside him in an out-of-date organdy dress was the madam. She was an elderly, dainty woman who had obviously been a beauty in her day. She smiled and came forward and said to Lafitte as she extended her petite hand:

"Jean Pierre! You look like John Christian must have looked."

"Bull!" the old man roared. "I was much better looking!"

"Horse——!" Lafitte said, then stopped as he remembered the children.

The madam went to Sandy and they shook hands and the old lady said, "Welcome, welcome. It's my pleasure to have you visit us."

"Thank you," Sandy replied. "It's nice to meet you. You have a wonderful home."

"Hmph!" the old man grunted and wheeled himself forward. "I guess you've heard of me. I'm the old bastard."

"Grandfather!" Suzanne said, and the children stifled a giggle.

Sandy raised an eyebrow, then said, "Yes, sir. I heard that my husband had a grandfather, if that's what you mean. But I heard he was an old man. I hardly expected such a virile man as you."

"Ha! What a goddam lie!" the old man said in a loud voice.

Then Sedonia put her head in the door and said, "Girls? Time for dinner."

The girls got to their feet in unison, smiled at their parents, and hurried out the door. The little one came back in a moment, grinned at Lafitte, and closed the door.

"Thank God!" Suzanne said in a stage whisper.

The old man heard her, raised a scornful eyebrow, decided to ignore her, and turned to Sandy. "Hey! How'd you like to fly to Vegas with me this weekend?"

Suzanne shuddered, the madam smiled and shook her head, the two men grinned, and Sandy said:

"That sounds like a lot of fun, but what would we do after we got tired of gambling?"

"Goddam!" the old man said, then burst into laughter. "Son of a bitch, Jean Pierre, she put me in my place!"

He waved his hand toward the bar and Sam went to fix him a drink.

"No . . . no, sir," Sandy said with a demure smile, "I think it would be wonderful. But you wouldn't want me to throw rocks at my husband now, would you?"

Everyone chuckled except the old man; he was howling with laughter which quickly went into a cough. Sam hurried to bring him a glass of water and his double shot. The old man waved away the water and tossed off the bourbon and said:

"Hell no! I've no time for water! Another one!"

"And then dinner's ready," the madam said gently.

The old man nodded, and waited for his second drink and Lafitte went to his wife's side and whispered, "Did you rehearse that?"

"No," she replied with a grin, "but I thought I'd better be ready."

"You were that," Lafitte said and squeezed her arm.

While the old man sipped his second drink Lafitte took his wife around the room to look at the old portraits. Sam was watching his employer and as soon as the old man had finished his second drink Sam announced:

"Dinner is ready."

Sedonia and Sam served them a wilted lettuce salad and roast lamb and rice with a rich, brown gravy, and black-eyed peas and several kinds of wine. Out of deference to the old man, who ate his small meal rapidly and without conversation, the table was generally silent until he'd finished.

"Enjoy your food," he said. "I don't seem to eat as much anymore." He waved to Sam who came forward with the brandy bottle and filled the old man's glass.

"Ha!" Lafitte said. "No wonder. You don't have room."

"What a wise-ass," the old man said in a conversational tone.

"Maybe so," Lafitte answered, "but it's too bad you don't eat more. The food is excellent."

"Yeah," the old man agreed. "Pretty good meal for a broke old man to be serving to the last male descendant of the pirate."

"Aw, come on," Lafitte said. "There you go again. There's no proof that we're related to him."

The old man began to cough and Sam was there to gently pat him on the back. The madam nodded to Sam and the old man stopped coughing and said:

"Yeah. It must be the thrill of it all. . . . Seeing my beloved grandson again has been too much for me. To bed, Sam."

As Sam turned the wheelchair the old man grabbed the brandy bottle and winked at Sandy. To Jeremy he said,

"There's another bottle in the sideboard, Jeremy. . . . 'Night, all. See you in the morning, probably."

As the diners mumbled "Good night," Sam wheeled him out of the dining room and to the foot of the stairs and hooked the chair to the electric lift. The madam got up and nodded, the men half rose, and the dainty little lady went to join her husband. As the old man was halfway up, he called:

"Enjoy your brandy. Tomorrow night's the big dinner and I promise to make the evening."

As Jeremy got up to get the bottle of brandy, his three girls trooped in from the kitchen, and the oldest one, who slightly resembled Sandy, said to her mother:

"Mother, may we watch TV?"

"Yes, Claudette, but see that Lucille goes to bed in one hour."

"Yes, ma'am," the girl said and began to herd her sisters out of the room.

Duroc returned to his seat and took out two cheroots and offered one to Lafitte. It was accepted with a nod and Lafitte held a candle for a light.

"Thank you," Duroc said. He tried his cheroot and then said, "I think the old goat did."

"Did what?" Lafitte asked.

"I think he really did find some gold."

"Come on," Lafitte said with a slightly acid note in his voice. "That's pure legend."

"Oh, it may not have been Lafitte's gold," Jeremy agreed, "but the old goat went broke a couple of times and each time he mysteriously came up with another stake and made another pile of money."

"Maybe," Sandy suggested, "he never really went broke."

"A good thought," Duroc said with a nod. "He was always devious with his money. Even now. He says he's broke and I have no doubt that he's no longer wealthy, but I wonder how much he does have left. I don't think he's broke, not by a long ways."

"Excuse me," Suzanne said, getting to her feet. "I think I'd better check on the girls and make sure they don't have the TV so loud it disturbs Grandad."

"Certainly," Lafitte said, as both men got partially to their feet.

Sandy finished her brandy and held the glass out for a re-fill.

"Careful, cousin," Jeremy grinned. "That's good French brandy. It'll sneak up on you."

"That's all right," she smiled, "it's delicious. Besides, I'm not driving tonight."

Sedonia came in from the kitchen and started clearing the dishes. "We have cherry pie or ice cream, or both."

"No, thank you," Sandy said, and the two men shook their heads.

Sedonia quickly scooped up the dishes and put them on a large tray and said, "There's coffee, just yell."

"Thank you," Duroc said. He waited until she'd gone through the swinging doors to the kitchen and then said, "Another thing that makes me think there might be some truth to all the rumors is the fact that although he was alleg-edly broke several times, he never sold this place, or even put it up as collateral . . . at least, as far as I know."

"Maybe he's really sentimental under that tough old hide," Sandy said.

"Ha!" Duroc snorted as Lafitte grinned. "Not on your life!"

Suzanne rejoined them and Duroc asked, "Is everything all right?"

"Yes," Suzanne nodded, "they're watching a movie."

"Good," her husband replied. "We were discussing the possibility of the old man really having some treasure buried around here."

"Don't concern yourself, dear," she said, a nasty tone creeping into her voice. "If he does, considering the way he feels about you, you won't get any of it."

"No doubt." Duroc grinned ruefully. "If there's any left, he'll figure a way to take it with him."

Lafitte raised an eyebrow at the exchange as the thought came to him that the old man's dislike for Duroc hadn't changed over the years. Changing the subject, Suzanne turned to Sandy and said:

"So what do you think of Bayard? Quaint, isn't it? Or did you get a chance to see much of it?"

"What I saw was charming," Sandy replied.

This started a polite round of conversation that lasted until almost eleven and ended on the front porch with several more brandies. When they'd said good night and were on their way up the stairs Sandy was giggling and yawning at the same time. Lafitte grinned indulgently; he too was feeling the brandy.

As they went into the bedroom Sandy kicked off her shoes and began to pull her dress over her head. There was a light on in the bathroom and one beside the bed. As he went around the bed to turn off the light on the night stand, he saw it. There was another doll on the pillow. He said "Damn!" under his breath and grabbed it quickly; he dropped it behind the chair and turned to see if she had noticed. She had not, she was still trying to pull her dress over her head without unzipping it. He turned back to the bed and pulled the covers down and went to the French windows, closed and locked them, and pulled the drapes. Then he crossed the room again to make sure he had locked the bedroom door and turned to help Sandy with her dress. She grinned at him when her head appeared again, struggled out of her slip, and sat on the bed to fight her way out of her pantyhose.

"Night, night," she said, as she slipped under the covers and pulled the sheet up, squirmed a moment, and then flung her bra toward the foot of the bed. Despite his anger he couldn't help grinning at her as he picked up her dress, turned it right-side out, and put it on a hanger in the closet. Then he turned back to the bed and leaned over her; she was already breathing deeply. He kissed her on the cheek and then his jaw clenched as he stooped and picked up the doll.

He took it into the bathroom and closed the door. He put it on the sink and shivered as he got his first good look at it. It was a female doll, obviously Sandy, even to the white dress she'd worn on their arrival in Bayard. It had short, blond hair, even green eyes like hers. But what had made him shiver was that, in addition to the sword through the chest, there was a small, plastic snake coiled around the neck. He took a deep breath and began to examine it closely, his insides churning. He had seen voodoo dolls before, but none as well-made as this. It was made out of flour sacking, instead of the usual burlap, and seemed stuffed with moss. It was properly formed and neatly stitched, the hair was spun glass and the eyes were little green beads, both probably from a child's doll; the features were painted on by a careful hand.

"Damn!" he said in a low voice. "What kind of a sick mind would do a thing like this?" He thought about it some more, trying to rationalize a decent solution, but one thing he was sure of, he didn't want her to know. He raised his leg to massage his suddenly aching ankle and then quickly put his foot back on the floor, immediately aware of his physical manifestation.

"By God!" he mumbled. "I'm not gonna let the son of a bitch run me off!"

"Hell!" he thought, a bit of his naturally cheerful disposition coming to the surface. "Next thing, Lon Chaney will be coming out of the swamp like a zombie!"

But he checked again to make sure the doors and windows were locked and the air-conditioning turned up before he undressed to begin a fitful night's sleep.

His confrontation didn't go exactly as he'd planned. He'd thought he'd get up early the next morning, have a big breakfast, and get a paper sack for the dolls from Sedonia and go looking for Jeremy. He did do those things, including a long chat with Sedonia over a plate of grits and eggs and slab bacon. They talked of his youth and the many times she'd pulled him into the house by the ear for his bath. But while she was smiling and friendly, he noticed a certain reticence when he asked her about current affairs. Her reply to a question about how the old man and the madam got along was a brief:

"All right, I guess."

To the question if Jeremy and Suzanne came down often she said:

"Every weekend. They's sittin' around like vultures, just a waitin'."

To a question about Sam's health she replied:

"It ain't his health so much, he's in good shape fer his age."

"All right," Lafitte finally said, putting down his coffee cup. "What's with Sam?"

"Nothin'. He's all right."

She began to clear the dishes rapidly and he stopped her with a hand on her arm and said, "Come on, now. You've known me most of my life, what's with Sam?"

"Ask him."

"I intend to. But if I did, would I hurt his feelings?"

"Mistah Jean," she said, "I'm sorry I spoke so sharp . . . but it's them damn drums!"

"What drums?"

"Ask Sam."

"Sedonia," he said, getting up and following her to the sink, "you tell me about the drums."

She looked around as if they might not be alone and said, "Ain't another white man I'd say this to, including Mistah John. . . . But Sam thinks it's voodoo."

"All right, don't stop now." He spoke loudly as she turned on the faucet.

"Come on," Lafitte said, trying to ignore the dolls, "we're in the nineteen seventies, not the last century."

"I know it, and you know it, but Sam, he ain't as good a Christian as I am, and he thinks it's directed toward the house."

"The house?"

"Yeah. All of us. But I don't believe it. . . . Mistah Jean, they's a new crop of black kids nowadays, they's got an education, sort of, and they talks all the time about civil rights . . . and lots of 'em been to college and now some of 'em, white kids, too, they go out in the swamp and they practice voodoo."

"Big deal!" Lafitte grinned. "In the East they practice witchcraft. Just dumb kids, playing dress-up."

"Uh huh. I think so. And you think so. But Sam, he's a nigger frum the old school, and he's afraid. . . . Mistah Jean, you talk to him. You tell 'im."

"I certainly will. Where is he?"

"Out doin' his gardenin' somewheres."

"Okay. Say, have you seen Mr. Duroc?"

"He ate early, with his girls. They're up washin' their hair. Mistah Jeremy said he wuz goin' for a walk."

"All right," he grinned. "Thanks for the sack. And the breakfast."

He went to his room and eased the door open and slipped in quietly. She was still sleeping soundly. Her breasts looked inviting, but he reluctantly decided that now wasn't the time. He put the dolls in the sack and left silently.

It was a beautifully bright morning and he took a turn around the old house and noticed how well Sam kept the grounds. The lawn was good enough for a putting green and the big oleanders were neatly trimmed and there were no dead flowers or leaves under the giant magnolia trees. It was when he had mounted the steps to the large, whitewashed summer house and was going into the dim interior that his plan went awry.

Two big hands grabbed him, one on his right arm and one by the back of his shirt, and crashed him into the top of the wicker table. As it leaned forward, Lafitte pulled his head down and twisted his left arm under him so that he landed on his shoulder in the corner. He saw a dim form fly forward and try to land on top of him and the thought flashed through his mind that his assailant wasn't particularly adept at ambush; otherwise, the man would have stepped forward and kicked him in the head. With a faint smile he waited a split second, then rolled quickly out of the way, and Jeremy landed on the floor where Lafitte had been.

Jeremy grunted and Lafitte rolled back and smashed the flat of his right hand across the back of Jeremy's neck, not enough to do any real damage, only enough to stun. Jeremy grunted again and then Lafitte was on him. He put his right foot on the outstretched right hand and twisted the left arm behind Jeremy's back, forcing the hand back toward the wrist.

Jeremy cried out and Lafitte relaxed his grip a bit, but not much. Then he took the little finger in his left hand and started to twist it out of the socket, but slowly. As Jeremy groaned in pain and began to realize that his wife's cousin had changed since he'd last seen him, Lafitte grinned coldly and said:

"You haven't changed a bit, Jeremy. You never could do anything right, even when we were kids. Now . . . give me your word that you won't attack me again and I won't break your fingers . . . like one at a time."

Jeremy grunted again and tried to break the hold, using his greater weight to roll out of the way.

"All right," Lafitte said with a shrug, and held Jeremy in place and began to twist the finger out of its socket.

"No!" Jeremy yelled. "I promise!"

Lafitte eased the grip and said, "Promise what?"

"I give you my word I won't attack you again!"

Lafitte grinned at the little-boy exchange, released the grip, and stood up.

Jeremy got to his feet and began to massage his little finger. "All right," he said almost petulantly, "what do you want?"

"Me?" Lafitte said angrily. "Why you son of a bitch, you jumped me! What the hell do you want?"

Jeremy stared at him a moment, then went to a chair in a corner and picked up a part of the morning paper which was wrapped in a bundle. He righted the table, put the bundle on it and opened the paper to reveal two dolls, similar to the ones Lafitte had.

"This!" Jeremy said in a low voice. "That was a dirty goddam trick! Trying to scare me was childish, but to try it on Suzanne was disgusting! It's a good thing she never saw it, otherwise I think I'd 've shot you!"

"What are you talking about?" Lafitte said, knowing the answer, but not really believing Jeremy.

"You know damn well! You planted those things in our bedroom hoping you'd scare us off. You know that either you or Suzanne will inherit everything! Well, go on . . . do your damnedest, but I won't leave! You'll have to kill me first."

Lafitte shook his head, then looked around the room for the sack. He found it and dumped the contents on the table next to the paper. As Jeremy's eyes widened, Lafitte said:

"Wrong again, Jeremy. It wasn't me. And I, too, was fortunate; Sandy knows nothing about 'em."

Jeremy looked at the dolls with an uncomprehending stare and Lafitte said in an irritable voice, "Look, you dumb butt! If it wasn't me, and it wasn't you, and at this point we should at least partially accept that fact, then someone else is trying to set us both up. . . . Now, two things. Who the hell is it, and why would they do it?"

Jeremy shook his head again, then whispered, "For the treasure."

"Bullshit!" Lafitte said derisively. "You too? Now look, Jeremy, old boy. There is no pirate treasure! And, assuming, and it's goddam remote, that there might be, you won't get it and neither will I. The old man told me he's leaving the place to the madam. So that ought to cut out the competition."

"Then who?" Jeremy said, still staring at the dolls.

"How the hell do I know? This is the first time I've been

here in years! You're the local citizen, you figure it out. . . .
But I'll tell you one thing. You try me again and I'll break
off that finger and shove it in your eyeball, or any other
handy orifice. You understand me?"

Jeremy took a deep breath, looked at Lafitte and said,
"Yes. . . . I don't particularly like you, Jean, you know that.
In fact, to be real honest, I guess I shouldn't blame you for
that. You've always had such an easy way about things, and
you've never shown any interest in this place, while I always
wanted it. . . . And, well, I guess I thought you were the only
one who would do such a thing."

Jeremy, still rubbing his hand, drew his cloak of aristocra-
cy about him and forced himself to say, "I'm sorry, I should
never have accused you. I . . . I'm sorry."

Then he turned quickly and left the summer house. Lafitte
shook his head at Jeremy's retreat and said in a low voice:

"Jeremy, either you're a born loser, or you're one of the
best liars I've come across."

As he turned to compare the dolls again there was a tap-
ping at one of the laths and he turned to hear Sam say:

"Mistah Jean, it's me."

Lafitte relaxed, grinned, and said, "Come on in, Sam."

As Sam entered the summer house Lafitte said, "You
heard?"

"Yes, suh. I wuz here all along. I saw you come in."

"Then why the hell didn't you come to my rescue?"

"I didn't think he would jump you," Sam said, a reproachful tone in his voice. "Besides, 'tain't fittin' fer me to get in a
fight between two of the family."

Lafitte grinned and said, "I'm sorry, Sam. I shouldn't have
said that." Then, pointing at the dolls. "So, what do you
think of those?"

Sam's eyes went to the dolls and he shivered and looked
quickly at Lafitte. "I don't like to think about such things."

"Well, do. They're a fact."

"Yes, suh, they are," Sam replied, turning so he wouldn't
have to look at them.

"Sam," Lafitte said, firmly, but kindly, "now's the time to
get it out in the open. And I don't want any bush-beating,
you understand?"

"Yes, suh," Sam said, shuffling his feet.

"All right. I need your help. You know more about these things than I do. Look at them."

Sam shuffled his feet again, stared at Lafitte, and seeing the determined look on his face, finally forced himself to stare at the dolls. He shivered, took a deep breath, and nodded once.

"Yes, suh. They's voodoo. . . . And they mean business . . . those little swords, and the snake on that one."

"Any idea who?"

"No, suh. 'Cept someone don't want you around. Nor the Durocs, either."

"All right. What about the drums? When did they start?"

"Maybe a week ago . . . only at night."

"Uh huh. Where from?"

"From the swamp, north somewhere."

"Now, you're sure they're voodoo drums?"

"Yes, suh, I'm sure!"

Lafitte nodded and studied the old man. There was no doubt that he was telling the truth, as Sam knew it.

"Mistah Jean," Sam said, almost in a whisper, "I heard rumors in town about the old . . . the old . . . what's called an old story?"

"A legend?"

"That's it. About the old legend that if the treasure is taken away, the drums will start up again . . . and bring big trouble."

"Oh, bull!" Lafitte said. "That's a lot of rumor, all right. Look here, Sam. I lived here a good long time as a young man, all through high school and the summers of college and I never heard any such tales."

"No, suh, but that's no sign there ain't any such legend."

"Sam! Don't believe it! Somebody's just working on your superstitions."

"Maybe. And maybe some ain't real smart, and that's surely me. . . . But, Mistah Jean, don't give no count to voodoo. I seen it kill a man by his wastin' away. And I seen several men who had a spell put on 'em . . . smarter men than me . . . and when they started to get sick they moved away. . . ."

"Balls! Sam, there's no gold, no Lafitte treasure. At least, none that the old man knows about. If there was, he would've used it long ago. Look at him. He made millions and now he's broke. Don't you think that if he knew there was a treasure he would've used it by now?"

"No, suh!" Sam said emphatically. "It's 'cause he's old. He don't need it anymore. He's dyin', Mistah Jean, and he knows it. He don't need the money. He's a wise enough man to know it ain't gonna help him now."

"Maybe, Sam, maybe. But I tell you there's no treasure."

Sam shrugged, then nodded. "You're a lot smarter than I ever wuz and might be you're right. But I do know for a fact there's a group goin' strong in the swamp, and the kids, both black and white, they's practicin' voodoo."

Lafitte grinned. "You don't really believe in voodoo, do you, Sam?"

Sam shook his head quickly and frowned, though Lafitte thought he was putting it on a bit. "No, suh. . . . But I don't disbelieve."

"Then what about the treasure?"

"I guess not. What you said sounds right, or old Mistah John would've used it up by now. . . . But that ain't the point. Most folks around here do believe that there's a treasure, they've always wanted to think that."

"Well now," Lafitte said with an appreciative raising of an eyebrow, "you've got a point there. It's not what's the truth, it's what people want to believe. . . . Can you find out some more about the kids and this voodoo thing for me?"

"Yes, suh, I've got a friend who knows things. He can find out. I'll let you know."

"Good. Now, can you dispose of these for me?"

Sam stared again at the dolls, but he could not hold back the shiver. "If you'd put 'em in the sack, I'd burn 'em. That's the best way. I got to burn some leaves and I'll git a good, hot fire goin'. That'll do it, I hope."

Lafitte grinned and put all the dolls in the bag, twisted the top, and Sam took it like it was a bag of scorpions and left hurriedly.

Lafitte thought a bit about the power of voodoo as he watched the old man scurry across the grass and then he said, "Fuck 'em!"

As he headed for the house he decided that Jeremy was weak, greedy, and not the most convincing of liars.

*   *   *

Sandy and Suzanne were having breakfast with the madam in the kitchen. He said good morning to everyone, kissed his wife on the cheek, and accepted another cup of coffee from Sedonia; reluctantly, but he hid it well. He pulled a chair close to his wife and said in a low voice:

"You want to take a tour of the place?"

"Maybe later, honey. Or tomorrow. I've promised Claudette to help her with her jigsaw puzzle."

"My!" he said, "that sounds like fun. . . . Well, okay. I'm going to find Sam and take a look around. . . . Madame, where's your shy husband?"

The dainty little woman smiled and said, "Mistah John Christian is on the upstairs veranda."

"Well," he nodded, taking another sip of the horrible coffee and getting to his feet, "enjoy your puzzle."

"Jean," Suzanne said, "I already invited her for a swim, to which she said no. But she did agree to go into town with me this afternoon for some shopping."

"Huh!" he said. "Take the swim, hon, it's cheaper."

"Not on your life," Sandy said, smiling broadly. "Suzanne told me of several real old shops in town that sound absolutely exciting. Besides, we're going to have lunch in town."

"All right, I give up. See you for cocktails."

He kissed his wife on the cheek again, nodded to the others, and wandered outside.

He dropped down the front steps and crossed the driveway and turned to look up to the second-floor balcony, but he couldn't see his grandfather. He turned again and crossed the big lawn and went down the grassy slope to the edge of the bay, then made his way toward the old wharf. He smiled nostalgically and studied the weathered old planks over which thousands of tons of cotton had once been shipped north. Though the wharf was badly in need of repair and had a slight list to port, it still appeared serviceable. Sam stood up from the other side where he had been clearing weeds and grinned, took off his hat and wiped his brow.

"Is it still safe?" Lafitte asked.

"Certainly, suh," Sam answered. "It's only about a hundred years old."

"Ever used anymore?"

"By me, mainly. I've got a couple of pirogues tied up over on this side and I use 'em once in a while. Then there's Mistah John's outboard . . . you probably seen it in the garage. . . . We used to go huntin' in the swamp, but no more. But you kin still go to town offen this old wharf."

"Oh? How so?"

"Mistah You's paddlewheeler comes by every mornin' and every night, takin' the men to and frum town. They got a thing called a 'lectronics factory now and lots of the Cajun men figure it's better'n froggin' or shrimpin'."

"Is that right?"

"Yes, suh. All we have to do is hang out the lantern and the boat stops."

"You say Mr. You? Is that Dominique You?"

"Yes, suh, you know 'im?"

"Yeah, I met him in town. We stayed at the inn last night and had a couple of drinks with him. Very pleasant man."

"Yes, suh. One of the few gentlemen we got left, present company not included, of course."

"Thank you. Hmm, I wouldn't think running a backwater paddlewheeler would pay."

"It pays real well, frum what I heard," Sam grinned.

"And just what the hell does that mean?"

"Well suh, I wouldn't tell any but you . . . but seems he makes somethin' outa it. There's talk that Mistah You's a sorta high-class smuggler."

"Ha!" Lafitte laughed. "And he owns the Smuggler's Inn. He's got guts."

"Yes, suh. And he's got more'n that. He's got smarts. Hear tell he's the biggest gambler in the parish . . . with that paddleboat goin' out on the Gulf on weekends."

"My! And what does he smuggle?"

"That I don't know, but he lives mighty high offen the hog, and I mean mighty, with those fancy race boats, and that Jaguar, and the fancy house up on the nice end of town. Cain't make that kinda money frum a motel, fancy as it is, and a run-down riverboat."

"Well now," Lafitte raised an eyebrow, "and what can the ubiquitous Mr. You do for money?"

"I ain't never had the bad sense to ask."

"Good boy!" Lafitte grinned. "Say, did you burn the dolls?"

"Right away."

"Uh huh. . . . Sam, I'd like to see the place, if the roads are still in shape?"

"They are, fur the jeep. I don't think your car would make it, we got some big potholes these days. In fact, I'd like to drive you, iffn you don't mind. That way I can let these weeds git a bit higher so they's easier to pull and Sedonia won't git on my black ass 'cause I'd be drivin' you."

"A great deduction," Lafitte said with a straight face. "Let's go."

Sam got the jeep out of the garage and they set out at a leisurely pace under the hot Louisiana sun. They drove past the now fallow fields and Lafitte saw where the weeds were returning as advance scouts for the swamp.

"How long has it been like this?"

"Oh, jest this year. Before that, Mistah John let it out to sharecroppers, and it at least kept the land clean and useful."

"Why not this year?"

"Well, suh, when he had that first stroke he tells me, 'Sam, old boy, ah'm gonna die before you after all,' and he plumb lost interest in the land. And I guess it's a good thing, he couldn't handle the sharecroppers now, and I cain't 'cause I'm black. And it's sure the madam couldn't."

Lafitte nodded once and Sam drove quickly past the last hundred acres and slowed at the point where the road turned sharply left and the land began to disappear into the edge of the swamp. The shallow water covering the quicksand and the ooze of centuries was only a few feet deep but under the overhanging protection of the trees and vines it was almost unnaturally smooth, as though covered by a heavy film. Sam shot a quick sidelong glance at his passenger and started to make the turn, but Lafitte held up his hand and Sam stopped and shifted into neutral, glancing again at Lafitte, and then looking quickly away and stared at the other side.

Lafitte grinned slightly at Sam's discomfort, knowing the old man was thinking of Lafitte's trouble. As he looked at the deadly tangle of growth and backwater his ankle ached again and he propped it on the dash and rubbed it and was glad that he wasn't terrified at the sight.

As he was about to tell Sam to drive on, a pirogue suddenly appeared from behind two big cypress trees. It was poled by a grizzled man in his fifties wearing torn overalls and a tattered hat. The man grinned at Sam, tipped his hat politely to Lafitte, and let the boat ground itself.

"Hi!" Lafitte said, waving at the man.

"How'd do?" the man replied. "Sam?"

"Mistah Daudet?" Sam replied. "Any luck?"

"Some," was the reply. "You must be Mr. Lafitte."

"I am."

"I heard you wuz back. Welcome home."

"Thank you."

"The old place changed much?" the man asked.

"Some," Lafitte nodded. "The land's fallow."

"Um. Too bad. But mebbe you'll change that."

"Not likely," Lafitte replied with a shake of his head. "I'm only here for a short visit."

"I see. . . . Well, I've got some hours yet to go. Nice to have seen you."

"Thank you, Mr. Daudet," Lafitte replied.

With another nod at Sam, the man turned around and with two quick strokes of his pole the pirogue disappeared and in a few moments the water was again calm. Lafitte waved his hand and Sam shifted into low gear.

"Now," Lafitte said, "how do you suppose he knew I was here?"

"You're news. Ain't much to talk about fer these folks and you're a Lafitte. Probably every Cajun in the bayous fer miles around knows you're back."

Lafitte shrugged and said, "What does he do?"

"Well, he's one that don't work in town so he lives like his grandaddy did, he catches muskrats and frogs, mebbe collects moss. Mebbe he gits snakes, sometimes a 'gator, though there ain't many of 'em left. It ain't much of a livin'."

Lafitte nodded and remained silent.

The dirt road led them past the back of the house, at some distance, and to the other end of the peninsula. There the road made a sweeping turn as it crossed the main road from the bridge and continued on down to where the land again disappeared into the swamp. The road ran along the last edge of dry ground for about a half mile where on one side the land was overgrown farmland and on the other was a large stand of cypress, their convoluted trunks rising out of three feet of brackish water. As Sam rocked along at a bumpy fifteen miles an hour, Lafitte observed:

"Seems to me, Sam, the swamp is moving in quite a bit."

"Yes, suh, we's losin' an acre a year."

Lafitte shook his head at the waste of more than a hundred years of back-breaking labor and couldn't think of anything to say that wouldn't sound trite, so he remained silent.

Sam stopped the jeep at the oleander hedge by the dressing rooms at the back of the pool and they exchanged grins and Lafitte made his way through the breezeway to the pool. Suzanne's three girls were throwing a beach ball to each other in the shallow end as though they were six girls. He waved and they waved back and he went around the side of the house to the front veranda. His grandfather was dozing in his wheelchair next to the front door. Lafitte tried to walk silently on the shells, but the old head snapped up and the old man saw him and said by way of greeting:

"Well, where the hell have you been?"

"Good morning!" Lafitte said with a cynical joviality. "Sam took me for a ride."

"Not much to see anymore."

"I found that out," Lafitte said, sitting on the steps. "How do you feel this morning?"

"Dry. Join me for a drink?" The old man pulled a fresh bottle from under the robe and began to take the top off.

"No thanks, it's a bit early for me. Besides, you're having a big dinner tonight. I'll do my drinking then."

"Hmph! Then go get me a glass and some ice."

"All right."

Lafitte got up and went into the house and made his way to the kitchen. He was leaving with a tall tumbler full of ice cubes when Sedonia came in from the back porch. She grinned and shook her head rather sadly and said:

"That for Mistah John?"

Lafitte just grinned and she put her hand on his arm and added:

"Sedonia ain't that dumb, and I know he's drinkin' himself to death. And I know the doctor says he's dyin' anyway. And if it makes it any easier, fine. I jest wanted you to know that I know that Sam's smugglin' it in to him."

"Well now," Lafitte said, "seems we've got lots of smugglers around here."

He returned to the front porch and handed the glass to the

old man who took it and promptly filled it half full of bourbon. He sloshed it around a moment, then took a long drink.

"Ahh," he sighed. "Now I can make the day."

"Goddam," Lafitte said conversationally, "if you did have
another stroke, nobody could tell it."

"Good boy!" the old man grinned, thumping his thigh.
"You're the first one wise enough to know it . . . and the first
one wise enough not to tell me I shouldn't."

"Not me," Lafitte said. "You were a full-grown man before I was born."

They sat in the silence of the morning sun a while as the
old man sipped his whiskey. When his glass was half empty,
he said:

"Sure you won't have a drink?"

"No thanks. I'll wait a bit."

The old man shrugged and added to his glass.

"Besides," Lafitte added, "this is sort of a working vacation. I've got some paper work to do. And I've got to see a
man in New Orleans before we leave about some shipping
agreements."

"Like the job?"

"Yes, suits me fine. I've got a piece of the company and it
looks like I might make something yet."

"Hmph! Well, doesn't look like you'll make a lot. Otherwise, you'd be living higher on the hog by now."

"Maybe," Lafitte allowed. "But I had enough hell-raising
in the army to last me. . . . I like the easygoing life."

"Yeah," the old man nodded. "Maybe that's your trouble,
you're too easygoin'."

"Maybe."

"Yeah. You know, when you came home that last time on
leave you were as nervous as a whore in church. I thought
then you mighta had enough fighting to hold you. . . . Damn,
that's good whiskey. Say, ever have any more work done on
that leg?"

"No," Lafitte lied easily. "The army did a good job. They
even kept me over a while to make sure I was okay before
they released me."

"Uh huh. I see you limp a bit."

"Yeah, but it's no big bother."

The old man nodded again, finished his glass of whiskey

and put the glass on the porch beside him. After another short silence Lafitte said:

"Say, I've been meaning to ask you how come the land isn't planted, and . . ."

He stopped talking as he looked at the old man and saw that he was asleep. Lafitte grinned and stood up and left quietly.

He spent the next several hours in his room working on his shipping schedules so that he'd be ready for his conference. He was almost through when there was a discreet knock at the door and Sedonia entered at his call with a large can of beer and a tuna sandwich. When she saw the papers scattered on the desk she smiled, put the tray on the bed, and left quietly. He finished up quickly as he sipped the beer, then ate the sandwich and stretched out on the bed for a nap.

When he awoke it was late afternoon. He heard the rather pleasant sound of the girls playing in front of the house. He yawned, stretched, and got up and went to the windows and looked out. Sandy and the three girls were on the lawn, pitching quoits and laughing at every toss. He smiled at Sandy's strong maternal instinct as he headed for the bathroom to brush his teeth and wash his face. Rather than disturb the game, he went downstairs and fixed himself a tall Scotch, a thin one with lots of water, and went out to sit by the pool. He'd expected to be alone, but he found Suzanne there, swimming with long, leisurely strokes. When she got to the other end she turned, saw him, and waved.

"Join me?"

"No, thanks," he said, taking a chair under one of the metal umbrellas.

"No matter," she grinned. "I was through anyway."

She climbed out of the pool and came toward him at a fast, feminine walk that almost made her big breasts jiggle out of the black bikini. She grinned again, picked up the towel and ran it over her hair, then quickly rubbed it over her body, a bit seductively he thought, but then added the additional thought that with a body like that she could move no other way. She picked up his glass, took a long drink, and said:

"Ah, Scotch. But you always did have good taste. And in women, too, I might add."

"Thank you," he replied with a nod. "Can I get you a drink?"

"Not now, thanks. I'll change first. Be only a minute, don't go away."

He nodded and she picked up the terry-cloth robe on the other chair and went to the dressing room at the far end of the pool. He sipped his drink and wondered what his ancestors would think if they knew the old man had replaced their genteel croquet court with a swimming pool where the women of the family would cavort in open view almost naked. He had another sip and decided the men would like it.

"Jean?" Suzanne called from the dimness of the breezeway. "Would you come here a moment, I seem to have a small problem."

He put down the glass, circled the big pool, and went into the opening between the two dressing rooms. Suzanne was standing in the doorway of one, wearing the robe.

"What's your problem?" he asked, anticipating a zipper.

He was wrong.

With a swift shrug of her shoulders the robe dropped to her elbows and she stood facing him, nude, holding her breasts in her hands.

"Me!" she whispered, grabbing him by the waist and kissing him hard, with her mouth open and her hot tongue darting out.

For a brief moment he was almost aroused and then he thought that, despite the Puritan ethics involved, he preferred his wife. He took her by the shoulders and pushed her away gently, not wanting to hurt her feelings, and stared down at her now undulating pelvis. His ethics didn't go that far, he thought, and enjoyed the peep show. That she was ready to lie down on the hard concrete he had no doubt, but he was now in control of himself and he merely stared, shifting his gaze to the big, inviting breasts. He was trying to decide how to say no gently when he saw a flash of red at the far end of the breezeway and his eyes darted to the right and he saw Claudette standing there, biting her lip, a hurt look on her gentle face.

Suzanne turned to see what he was suddenly staring at and saw her child. She caught her breath, but the child turned and was gone. Lafitte shook his head, his heart going out to the child, and he looked at Suzanne and his feelings quickly turned cold. Instead of a mother's feeling of terrible guilt at being caught in such a scene, her face showed nothing but irritation and Lafitte had to quickly control his expression to hide his anger.

"Oh!" Suzanne said petulantly. "That child! She's always spying on me!"

Lafitte kept a blank face and stepped back, and Suzanne, knowing her opportunity was gone, pulled the robe up and tied the belt.

"I guess you think I'm terrible," she said, feeling that she had to explain her position.

"No," he answered evenly, "that's between you and your family."

She nodded and reached into the robe pocket for a cigarette. He held a match for her and she blew a stream of smoke into the warm air, then said:

"And I guess that's right. I made my bed. . . . Jean, you can't imagine what my marriage has brought me. . . ."

He turned and they walked toward the tables.

"At first I thought I had the man I wanted," she said in a low voice. "Family, bearing, manliness. . . . Ha! That lasted until the children were born. Perhaps he thought by marrying me that Grandfather would make him a full partner. But he was wrong. Grandfather never really approved of him, though he did take him into the business. I guess the only thing that's kept us together was Jeremy's thought that Grandfather would leave him a bundle, even through me."

"That's not an unusual story," Lafitte said, pulling out a chair for her.

She sat down and tugged at the robe. "And then the women started." She paused to take a long drag on the cigarette and added, as she flipped the ash toward the big tray, "Then Grandfather caught him padding the books so that Jeremy got most of a year's profits. . . . I didn't think, despite my knowing that he was weak . . . I didn't really think he was a thief. And if there's some friction between you and Jeremy . . . and Jeremy hasn't said a thing . . . it's because he thinks you'll get whatever the old boy leaves."

"You know that's zero, Suzanne. The old man hasn't got a pot or a window, except this place. And he told me he'll leave it to the madam. You must know that."

"Yes, I know," she said almost sadly. "And that's just what

we deserve; me for picking a louse and then sticking with him, and him for being a common thief. . . ."

Lafitte didn't reply and she stared at him for a moment, smiled sadly, and said:

"And you must know that you're not the first man I've ever made a pass at." Then she laughed, but without humor. "But I must admit that you're the first one who ever said no."

Lafitte looked at her a moment and then got to his feet and said quietly, "See you at dinner."

He went through the house and out on the fronch porch. Sandy looked up from the girls who were gathering up their game and came toward him, a big smile on her face. Lafitte looked at the girls; the other two grinned happily, Claudette just stared at him, her face composed.

"Look, honey," Sandy said, holding out a huge blue pencil and the tissue that had been wrapped around it. "Look at my nice gift that Claudette just gave me for being her nicest new friend."

"Oh, how nice," Lafitte said with a smile. Then he looked again at Claudette and, wise beyond her years, she shook her head slightly, meaning that she had kept a secret. Lafitte nodded and winked at her and Claudette managed a thin smile. Sandy marched up the steps and said:

"Your timing's perfect. I've already told the girls that we have to go in and get ready for dinner. I have to shower and fix my hair. They start cocktails promptly at six . . . according to Sedonia."

"Well," Lafitte replied, "she's the sergeant-at-arms."

"Honey," she said, squeezing his arm, "we had a fine time. Did you have a good day?"

"Most interesting," he replied without inflection.

They made a handsome couple as they came down the big stairs for the party. Lafitte was dressed to suit his normal inclinations, conservatively. He wore his white dinner jacket and a black cummerbund. His only deviation from conservative dress was the fact that he tucked his bow tie under his collar. He was the perfect complement to his wife. Sandy was dressed in an iridescent green taffeta cocktail dress. Around her neck was a jade choker he'd picked up in Mexico. She carried no purse or kerchief and the effect as she came down the steps was one of casual sophistication. As many times in the past, he was quietly proud of his wife.

The big living room doors were open and they entered to find the adult members of the family already there. The old man was properly dressed in a white dinner jacket and held a sizable glass of bourbon in his hand. The only indication that he might ever have been sick was the chrome wheelchair. The madam was wearing a full-length ivory-colored lace gown that made Lafitte think of the Civil War. Jeremy, too, wore a white jacket, but Suzanne was radiant in a skin-tight blue dress that left little to the imagination. As they nodded all around, Sedonia and Sam stepped forward, dressed as a butler and a maid. Sedonia seemed quite at ease serving shrimp from a large platter, but it was obvious that Sam was uncomfortable. At Lafitte's nod Sam went behind the bar to fix two drinks. The amenities of the evening were exchanged and the two younger women complimented each other on their dresses. Jeremy stepped close to Lafitte and whispered as though nothing had happened:

"You have a ravishing wife, cousin."

"That's a no-no, Jeremy," Lafitte whispered.

"Not me!" Jeremy protested. "My hand still hurts." He grinned and raised his glass and Lafitte took it as a sort of a truce gesture.

Lafitte nodded good-naturedly and, as Sam brought him a drink, the doorbell rang. In a few moments Sam ushered in two well-dressed couples in their late fifties who obviously knew the old man and his wife, and had a nodding acquaintance with the Durocs. After the general meeting the madam brought them forward and introduced Dr. George Glover and his wife. They were pleasant, very Southern. Dr. Glover had a firm hand and a sharp eye as he said:

"John Christian was right. You are a Lafitte."

"How should I take that?" Lafitte grinned.

"Oh, my dear sir, that was a compliment."

Then the madam said, "And this is Mistah John Christian's attorney, Mistah Calvin Davis and his charmin' wife."

As Lafitte shook hands with the tall, portly man and nodded to his birdlike wife, he thought that the attorney reminded him of someone and it came to him almost at once, Daddy Warbucks. Lafitte grinned and the attorney nodded pleasantly and the madam steered them toward the bar. Suzanne was standing by Lafitte's side and she whispered:

"He ran for everything. He was a state senator for a term or two, but when he tried to go farther he found that he couldn't buck the Long dynasty or the Italians, for that matter, so he returned to private practice."

Lafitte nodded and was about to say he thought that made the attorney a very wise man when Sedonia ushered in Dominique You, resplendent in a powder-blue dinner jacket and a frilly foulard jabot, looking like a riverboat gambler. On his arm was a tall, striking woman, very tan and obviously Creole, with raven black hair and light blue eyes. She was wearing a champagne-colored dress that showed a figure that moved with a hydraulic motion that made every man in the room stare. You grinned at Lafitte and his wife and came forward to kiss the madam's hand. He exchanged a quick handshake with the old man and introduced his companion as Miss Eugenia Mornay, "of the New Orleans Mornays."

The old man handled the general introductions from his wheelchair in such a courtly manner that it made Lafitte's left eyebrow rise. He had forgotten what a charmer the old bastard could be. Dominique and his lady made the rounds of the other couples and got to the Lafittes last. Then the old man said in a dry voice:

"I seem to recall that you've met Mr. You before."

"Yes indeed, we have," Lafitte grinned, realizing that Sam must have told him.

"And how are you, my friend?" You asked with a broad smile as they shook hands.

"Things are fine," Lafitte said with a nod that You correctly interpreted as meaning that nothing more had happened.

You then bowed low as he took Sandy's hand and kissed it lightly. "Madame, you look devastating tonight. I trust you've recovered from the other day?"

"Yes, thank you," Sandy smiled.

As You turned around to bring his lady forward for the introductions, Sandy whispered to her husband:

"My! They don't do that in Arizona."

"Sure," Lafitte replied in a low voice, and with an almost straight face, "but what comes after, they do."

Then You was approaching again with his date and Sandy said, "You're drooling."

Lafitte grinned and the other couple thought it was because he was polite and then Miss Mornay was presented. She was properly formal and a bit more warm to Sandy than her husband, which pleased Sandy and relieved her husband, though he hid his feelings behind the same smile.

When he saw that everyone had a drink in their hands, You raised his glass and said, "I propose a toast. To the return of Jean Lafitte."

Lafitte shrugged, but he smiled politely and said, "Thank you."

"And to his lovely lady," Duroc said, and the glasses were lifted again.

When You's hydraulic machine learned that they were from Arizona all the ladies gathered to ask her about the desert and You took the opportunity to pull Lafitte aside and say:

"Everything all right?"

"Yes, sort of. But Duroc showed me two dolls that he got."

"Then someone is very devious," You observed and Lafitte raised his glass to his friend's perspicacity.

"Time for one more," the old man said, rolling forward.

"Not me," Sandy grinned, showing a half-filled glass. "I want to enjoy your wine."

"Ha!" the old man said loudly, banging his glass on the arm of the chair. "Jean! You got one of some considerable intelligence."

"I could've told you that," Lafitte said with a smile.

"My!" Duroc said to the men. "I didn't know they drank wine in Arizona. I thought they only drank red-eye."

"Oh yes," Lafitte replied easily, picking up the verbal challenge and winking slightly at his grandfather in his wheelchair. "Why, just last week I managed to buy a case of Meursault, 1966 yet. Imagine that! It has such a bouquet, yet is so dry and mellow at the same time that it defies description. I'm sure, dear cousin, that you also enjoy the finer white burgundies as a rare treat, don't you?"

"Uh, certainly, " Duroc said lamely, afraid to go further.

The old man grinned at Jeremy, wickedly.

The dinner was magnificent and the old man was the most charming of hosts, holding court from the head of the table

and making sure that he had a pleasant remark for each of
the ladies. The meal was a gastronome's delight of Louisiana
food, properly augmented by the right kind of wine. With the
bouillabaisse Sam poured a dry Madeira; with the stuffed
crab a white burgundy; the entree, rare roast beef accompa-
nied by mounds of fluffy white rice and fresh cow peas cooked
with bacon and small onions, was served with a deep red
burgundy. Lafitte held his glass to the candlelight and said:

"Excellent! And properly decanted, Sam."

Sam beamed and the old man grinned, almost viciously,
Lafitte thought, and then he knew when his grandfather
stared at Duroc a moment and then said:

"Thank you. This is a Côtes de Nuits, from the commune
Vosne Romanée. . . ."

Dominique raised his glass in appreciation, but Duroc remained silent, afraid to test the old man's expertise, and the
old man added:

". . . as a matter of fact, I've been saving it for years for a
special occasion and the way I've been going I decided we'd
better drink it before I missed out."

"Ha!" Lafitte said and grinned while the rest of the diners
were silent. The old man took no offense and grinned at his
grandson in the silence. Then Sandy said to the madam:

"The food is wonderful! I've never tasted such things."

"Thank you, my dear," the madam smiled. "But I was only
the planner. Sedonia was the real builder."

Sedonia smiled with an embarrassed shrug and mumbled,
"Thank ya, ma'am."

The table was cleared and Sam served anisette to the ladies
and brandy to the men, and he and Sedonia quietly retired to
stand by the sideboard.

"To a fine dinner," You said, raising his glass. There was a
toast and the old man nodded and said:

"Thank you. And now to business. . . . I've got my only
two heirs here, excluding of course, my dear wife, several
close friends, and my lawyer and my doctor, not necessarily
the same people. . . ."

There was a round of chuckles and then the old man became serious.

"I've decided to announce my will while I'm still here, and

to save Davis from the onerous chore of reading what might seem to several a vituperative document."

The old man paused to sip his brandy and the guests were now completely serious.

"Anyway," the old man continued, "without further explanation I leave the house and grounds to the madam. . . ." He raised his glass to her and they exchanged loving smiles past the candles. "I have left Sam and Sedonia a sum that should do them for life. To you, my dear grandson, I leave you what you already have; my best wishes and that glorious wife of yours. Besides that, there doesn't seem to be anything you need. To you, dear Suzanne, and husband Duroc, I leave you the business you already have. Duroc, I know you've been milking it for years, so that's the best thing I could leave you. That way, there'll be no inspection of the books and your mathematics won't be the subject of public scrutiny."

The old man said it so casually that many of the ladies took it as a partial joke, but the men, who knew him better than the women, knew that he meant exactly what he'd said. Duroc remained silent, but red-faced. Not so his wife.

"Grandfather! You're always making jokes."

"I am like hell!" he said loudly, pointing a crippled finger at Jeremy. "With his gift of chicanery, if he had my brains he would've been a millionaire. What do you think of that?"

Everyone was silent for a moment, somewhat embarrassed for Duroc who managed a wry smile and shake of the head.

"Great!" Lafitte said, breaking the impasse. "It's better than I expected. At least I didn't have to take care of you in your dotage!"

"Oh!" the old man said in mock disgust. "You always were such a smart-ass Yankee kid."

"Yankee!" Lafitte said loudly. "Why you old Rebel bastard! We lived in Texas when I was a kid."

"Yes, suh, you did," the old man replied seriously. "But in northern Texas."

Dominique You laughed and the others smiled politely.

"But," the old man said, pointing his glass at Lafitte, "my lawyer says that if I leave you something it stops the breakin' of the will once I've gone to my noble reward."

"Bull!" Lafitte said loudly and grinned. "You'd better save something to get that goddam place air-conditioned because that old Devil, he's gonna fry your fanny!"

"Yeah?" the old man replied, obviously enjoying the exchange. "Well, Mistah Smart-ass, I've got something for you so you can't start no ruckus. Sam! Bring me that map from the study."

"Yes, suh." Sam grinned and left the room.

The old man grinned again. Jeremy's eyes widened a moment, but Lafitte saw it and reached for one of You's proffered cheroots and lit it casually from the candelabra while they waited. In a moment Sam returned with the map and put it in front of his employer. The old man held it out a moment, then laid it flat on the table again and said:

"Now, this ain't worth nothin' much, except as a genuine antique, but, you use it wisely, if you've got the brains, and it's worth a fortune."

Lafitte clamped down on his cheroot to make sure he didn't change expression, though the message was not lost on him, and several others, and reached out and took the map as the old man handed it to him and laid it flat on the table. It was still in its frame, covered with glass, but something caught his eye. There were now seven "X's" on it, in the swamp at the south, with a larger "X" at the top of the chain. Lafitte dared not pick it up for fear of drawing Jeremy's attention, though it was probable that his cousin's husband had already noticed the markings. Instead he casually dropped his napkin on it and got to his feet and raised his glass and said:

"I drink in sincerity to an old goat who happens to be my grandfather and to a man who lived a good, full life, and who owes a debt to no man."

"Here! Here!" You said and the others joined in, in various degrees of eagerness.

"Thank you. Thank you," the old man said, obviously honored. He waved his glass at his guests, smiled and added, "On that, I'll give it up for the evening. It's time I went to bed, but please, enjoy the brandy . . . and the company. Sam!"

Sam came forward and wheeled his employer toward the lift as the diners chorused a good night and the madam got up to kiss her husband on the cheek. When the wheelchair was out of sight, the madam picked up her glass and the liqueur bottle and said, "Ladies?"

The women got to their feet and followed their hostess to

the living room while the men gathered closer and Duroc refilled their brandy glasses.

"Well," he observed, trying to be a good sport, "at least we broke even tonight."

"Good for you!" Lafitte said, feeling momentarily sorry for the weaker man.

Dr. Glover asked Lafitte about the trucking business in order to change the subject and this led to a discussion of business in general. In a few minutes Sam came to Lafitte's side and said:

"Mistah John would like a word?"

Lafitte stood up and said, "Excuse me," and picked up the map and his glass and followed Sam up the stairs. Sam held the door for him, the old man waved Sam away, and Sam nodded and closed the door quietly. Lafitte sat in the chair next to the old man's bed and his grandfather said caustically:

"Now we can talk, Sam's already taken me to the pot."

Lafitte chuckled and said, "That's a helluva way to go for the biggest whoremonger on the river."

"Fuck you," the old man replied casually and reached for the glass of bourbon that Sam had left on the night stand.

"Okay, you old bastard," Lafitte replied, "what shall we talk about?"

"Well, you got any questions? Better ask 'em now."

"Okay," Lafitte replied. He thought a moment, then said, "What about Dominique You? Sam tells me he's the biggest gambler and the biggest smuggler in the parish."

"Yeah," the old man nodded. "He's the biggest gambler, all right. He controls the bookmakin' and that's a big thing down here and it's usually run by those dago bastards. And he runs that old paddlewheeler out into the bay, maybe the Gulf . . . though I don't believe that . . . one or two weekends a month for those who want to gamble for high stakes. He's got roulette, baccarat, blackjack, and poker going, but only for gentlemen. He runs it right. Only high-class customers and he's got enough muscle to keep the grifters out."

"Huh!" Lafitte said with an appreciative nod. "What about the smuggling?"

"Heard tales. Heard that he smuggles booze, but it's only a rumor. Whiskey is about a buck and a half a quart without the federal tax, and it'd sure be easy for a man with the boats he's got . . . half a dozen fast speedboats that I know of . . .

and it'd be easy to smuggle it in from Mexico and rum from Cuba. And that son of a bitch knows the swamps like no one I ever heard of. . . ."

The old man paused to take a drink of whiskey, wiped his hand across his mouth, and continued, "But I don't think he'd do that."

"Oh? Why not?"

"Cause he's one of the most honest men, and I think patriotic, and I don't think he'd cheat on the government. I even found out, and I won't tell ya how, that he reports all his gamblings on his income tax."

Lafitte nodded. "That's not unusual. There's no federal law against gambling and the smart operator reports all his winnings to Uncle."

"Well, he's smart all right," the old man nodded. "And that's why I think he's been doin' his damnedest to run out that gang of voodoo nuts."

"Oh?" Lafitte said with considerable interest. "I heard about the voodoo from Sam when I tried to find out who might've sent those dolls, but he's a mite scared."

The old man grinned and nodded paternally. "Yeah, he would be. Sam's a good man, a great man, but he's an old-time Louisiana nigger."

"Oh? And what does that mean?"

"That means that he believes all that bull crap!"

"Yeah," Lafitte nodded, "I guess he does."

"You bet your fanny he does! I've tried and tried to tell him that it's nothing but blind African superstition, but old Sam won't believe me."

"Uh huh. What about Dominique You and the voodoo?"

"Well," the old man said, taking another sip of whiskey. This one seemed to have a more salubrious effect on him than the first sip because he began to talk a bit more rapidly, and with gestures from his free hand. "Mainly the group is a bunch of college kids, some drop-outs, some hippie types, and some just plain nutty kids out for kicks. Everyone in town knows of it . . . you know, sorta like an open secret . . . but the police don't do anything about it anymore, mainly because they can't. It's known that they hold their . . . meetings, I guess you'd call 'em . . . on an island in the swamp that's, you know, one in three feet of water?"

"Yes," Lafitte nodded, keeping a straight face, "I know the swamp."

The old man stared at him a moment with one bleary eye, then decided to ignore Lafitte's reference to his injury and stick to the subject. "Anyway, they set up lookouts and it's been impossible for the police to get in without being seen. They tried it a few times and always when they got close, the kids got the word and were gone. . . . There's been a number of cases of parental bitching about daughters getting knocked up and sons getting high on something or other, but the law's answer has always been lack of parental supervision. . . .

"So, there's an impasse, the cops don't want to waste their time anymore and the parents can't do much about it."

"Okay. So what about Dominique? You said he tried it."

"Yeah, he told me one night after a poker game that he'd taken several runs at it, but they'd always heard his boats comin' in. Says next time he tries it he'll pole in and bring some muscle to . . . uh . . . convince Mejia of the error of his ways."

"Mejia?"

"Yeah." The old man let his accent thicken as he said, "He de big high muckey-muck of de voodoos." Then his speech returned to normal. "Tomas Mejia."

"Why would Dominique spend time and money on that? He doesn't strike me as the most civic-minded type."

"Oh," the old man grinned widely, "he's not. It's purely business. . . . Now this Tomas Mejia is a wild ass. He's a Puerto Rican. Incidentally, he was once an Olympic fencer, got a good go in life but somehow got disillusioned, dropped out of official sight . . . the chief of police is a friend . . . and then showed up here some ten years later. Now, Dominique tells me that Mejia uses this voodoo thing and the swamps to run in narcotics. And Dominique also thinks he's run in an occasional Cuban agent. I guess he also runs jewelry and watches from Cuba, but they say he isn't a Commie, just a goddam pirate, not even a decent privateer!"

"Well," Lafitte nodded and took a sip of brandy, "seems like we've got an honest gambler trying to run out the real bastards to keep the official eye off his gambling."

"Exactly!" the old man exclaimed. "Goddam! Jean, how come you never made a pile of money?"

"I told you," Lafitte grinned. "I've got the woman I want and a full belly. What else?"

"Huh," the old man said reflectively. "Maybe you're smarter'n I thought. . . . Now, we'll see. You know, you can never really tell when I'm lyin'. (Lafitte raised his glass and smiled in agreement.) But, take this for what it's worth. I really was tellin' the truth about the map. It's worthless . . . but you use it right and it's worth a fortune. Value is like Toulouse-Lautrec's eye of the beholder. . . ."

Lafitte raised an eyebrow and nodded.

"And you, you son of a bitch," the old man added, "when you go downstairs, grin like I left you a fortune."

Lafitte grinned, but only to please his grandfather. The old man coughed, almost finished his whiskey, and then became serious.

"I've had some rumblings and, like that swamp bear, I know my time's comin'. The next one is supposed to be it and I've no more time for jokes, no more time for magnificent put-ons . . . so, I want to truly thank you for the pleasure of your company. . . . You know, you were the only son of a bitch I ever knew who wasn't afraid of me, or didn't want something. Had fate done it right, I would've had you for a son, instead of a grandson."

The old man put out his hand and Lafitte rose and took it as the old man gripped it hard and said, now in a whisper:

"Good night. Maybe good-bye."

"Bull!" Lafitte grinned. "Good night, you old bastard. . . . And, if tonight it is, I wish you a pleasant journey."

The old man grinned and raised his glass. "I'll drink to that."

Lafitte joined him, then took the old man's glass and put it on the night stand, put down his brandy glass, and picked up the map. When he looked back at his grandfather, the old man's eyes were already closed.

He went next door to his room and quietly closed the door behind him and leaned against it. He knew the old man was playing a game, the people game, something he'd always played superbly. He studied the map by the light by the bed and saw something he'd missed on his cursory look downstairs. Next to the biggest "X" was a faint notation, "Oak."

After a bit he grinned and nodded, and decided the old

man was partially telling the truth; the map could be very valuable. And then he chuckled once at the old man's presentation of the map at the dinner table. He knew his grandfather would say no more, but that wasn't the immediate problem; right now, the map itself was. Jeremy must have seen the markings and he'd be sure to talk to someone. Without a doubt Sam had seen them, and would probably tell Sedonia, maybe either one of them would mention it at the market in town. That the old man was stirring up the pirate thing again was obvious, and maybe to make the property more valuable for the madam. As it stood now, it wasn't worth what it had once been. Not many people would be interested in buying an old plantation house, and one with fallow land that was rapidly disappearing into the swamp.

Lafitte grinned faintly at the various possibilities, but the grin quickly disappeared as the thought came to him that the map was now highly volatile, particularly if someone believed in old legends. Lafitte had half a notion to follow up on the map, but his common sense told him it would have to wait for a more propitious time; right now he had to hide it. He studied the map in detail and his memory told him that all the "X's" were at the edge of the swamp, but then he nodded to himself; that was the proper place for buried treasure.

His practical mind considered the project for a few moments and then he went to his briefcase and took out a piece of stationery and a pen. Holding the map close to the light he traced the outline of the island, and the markings. Then he wandered around the room, trying to decide where a good spy would hide a piece of paper. He considered, and discarded, the idea of hiding it among his papers in his briefcase, in a book, under the rug, under the bed, under the chair, in his suitcase, and finally anywhere in the bedroom. That sent him to the bathroom where he spent a moment looking at himself in the mirrors and then it came to him. He grinned at his image and slid open one of the cabinet mirrors and opened the tin of Band-Aids. It was full, so he took eight and put six in his pocket. He opened two and peeled off the tear strips and hung them momentarily on the sink while he flushed the wrappers down the toilet. Then he slipped the paper behind the mirror that slid to the rear and fastened it with the two Band-Aids. He moved the mirror from side to side several times to make sure the paper didn't hang up on any of the

articles on the shelf and when he was satisfied that he'd done
a proper job he again grinned at his image and picked up the
framed map and left the room.

He eased open the door and made sure that he was alone.
Then he went to the banister and looked downstairs. There
was no one in sight, though he could hear the guests out on
the front porch. He quickly dropped down the stairs and
checked the foyer and the dining room; still no one. He went
into the study and grinned when he found it empty and the
drapes drawn. He closed the door and, just to be sure, he
checked behind the bar and the drapes. Feeling properly con-
spiratorial he got a straight-backed chair from the wall and
stood it in front of his grandfather's portrait. He climbed up
on the chair with the map and eased it behind the big picture
until it was just above the spot where the bottom of the portrait touched the wall. Then he gently pulled his hands away
and the map stayed in place. To be sure, he opened the
Band-Aids, pulled off the covering of each, putting the refuse
in his pocket, and hung them momentarily on the wall. When
he'd done all six he put each of them from the map to the
ancient wood backing of the painting. When he was satisfied
that the map wouldn't fall, he let the portrait ease back into
place and stood back. Everything was as before. He nodded
and got off the chair.

He looked at the portrait for a moment from the floor and
replaced the chair, making sure to wipe his footprints off the
upholstery. He looked again at the picture, nodded once, and
went to the door to peer into the foyer. It was still empty and
he strolled out calmly to join the group on the front porch.

They were sitting in a loose semicircle, most of the men
with highball glasses in their hands. Jeremy was standing by
the makeshift bar set up by Sam on a card table to one side
of the front door. "Scotch?" Jeremy asked.

Lafitte nodded, winked at his wife who was chatting with
the Glovers, nodded to Dominique You over the heads of the
ladies, and turned back to take the glass.

"Well," Jeremy said wryly, making sure that no one could
hear them, "that was a helluva legacy he left us. You a fifty-
dollar antique and my wife a business I should already right-
fully own."

"Don't feel bad, cousin," Lafitte said cynically. "At least you didn't have to support him."

Jeremy took a sip from his glass and said, "What was all that taking him to bed about?"

"Nothing," Lafitte said casually, though he was instantly on guard. "He wanted to hash over old times and talk about the former glory of the South, and the last summer I was here before I went into the army."

"What did you do in the army?"

"Oh, I was a freeloader," Lafitte lied. Then he added, "I had a good deal. I was a company clerk and got all the three-day passes."

Sandy had joined them in time to hear his version of the army and she frowned a moment as she put her hand on her husband's arm, but let it pass. It was a long time ago, she thought, and he probably wanted to forget it.

Dominique You and his girl were the first to leave. While Sedonia went inside to get her stole they made the rounds, saying good night and shaking hands. You managed to get Lafitte to one side and said in a low voice:

"There's one decent nightspot in town, the Cove. Would you and your wife care to be our guests? I can assure you it's enjoyable, they have a nice band and serve decent liquor. In fact, one has to have a card to get in, so it cuts out the rowdy group."

"Thank you, no," Lafitte smiled, then added a small lie because he didn't particularly feel like going. "My wife's had a most athletic day. But another time we'd love to."

"Fine," You said, shaking hands. "We must get together before you go and celebrate the resurrection."

"Good," Lafitte replied. "Give me a couple of days to do my family duty and we'll be more than ready."

"Excellent. I'll call you."

After a short chat with the madam so that it wouldn't seem that they were all leaving at once, the Glovers and the Davises made the rounds saying good night and then drove off in Glovers' big, white Lincoln Continental.

"My," the madam said, fanning herself with her dainty lace handkerchief, "I do like to entertain, but I'm no longer up to the long evenin' so I'll say good night, myself. But please, enjoy the evenin' breeze. And Jean and Jeremy, the liquor will not run out, so please continue."

Lafitte and Jeremy nodded and smiled, the women said good night, and the men escorted the frail little woman to the screen door. When she had gone inside, Jeremy turned to Lafitte and said: .

"I've got a couple of business calls to make before it's too late."

Lafitte raised an eyebrow but said nothing; it was already ten o'clock. He rejoined his wife and Suzanne on the porch and they sat quietly, enjoying the night sounds of the crickets and an occasional owl calling from the swamp. In the background they faintly heard Jeremy make several calls and then he rejoined them and said, to no one in particular:

"Damn. I've got to go to town and meet Mullins. He was making his calls around here today and I've got to go over an order with him before he goes to Houston." He kissed his wife lightly on the cheek and said, "I'll see you all later."

Lafitte nodded but said nothing as Jeremy dropped down the steps and headed for his car.

"Well," Sandy said, getting to her feet, "I've got to powder my nose. Hon, fix me another, I'll be back in a bit."

Lafitte got up and went to the table where Sam had left the tray with the bottles and the ice and fixed himself and his wife another light highball. Suzanne joined him, poured herself a double, tossed it off, and said:

"Damn!"

"What's the matter?" Lafitte inquired.

"I talked to Mullins' wife a week ago. They left the next day on vacation!"

Lafitte shrugged, not wanting to get involved again in her domestic problems, and before he had to concoct an answer the phone conveniently rang. On the third ring they heard Sam answer, mumble a few moments, and then he called:

"Oh, Mistah Jean? Can I see you a moment?"

"Excuse me," Lafitte said, putting his drink on the table.

He went into the house and met Sam standing by the phone in the entry.

"That waz my friend," Sam explained in a low voice. "For five dollars he stirred hisself and found out somethin'. There's a voodoo thing goin' on in the swamp tonight. Did you wanna see it?"

"No, I don't think so," Lafitte replied with an easy smile. "But I'm interested, mind you. Hey! If they're playing with their dolls, how come no drums?"

"Mistah Jean," Sam said seriously. "This here is the kids. It ain't necessarily voodoo fer real!"

"Well, okay. But I'm not real keen on runnin' around that swamp at night. I may be as brave as the next man, mind you, but I'm no goddam idiot. No thanks!"

"Well, I don't blame ya."

"Here," Lafitte said, taking a five-dollar bill from his pocket. "Thank your friend for me and tell 'im if he hears anything else of interest to let you know. . . . Say, what made you think I'd be interested in going out in that swamp to watch a bunch of nuts?"

"Well, they may be nuts, Mistah Jean, but I thought you might be interested, especially tonight. They's supposed to be holding a ceremony renewing the curse on Lafitte's treasure."

"Balls!" Lafitte said with a grin. "And what exactly does that mean?"

"It means they're puttin' a curse on anybody who puts his hands on that gold."

"Oh, well, that's all right, as long as it's not me," Lafitte replied as he turned back to the front door. But despite himself Lafitte felt vaguely uncomfortable.

He rejoined Suzanne on the porch and in a moment Sandy appeared and the women sipped their drinks and chatted, pausing a bare moment to smile at him, and then continuing their conversation. He picked up his glass and selected one of the large-backed cane chairs and scrunched down with his feet on the railing. After a few minutes he put the glass on the porch and dozed off as the women's voice became a pleasant background drone.

He was awakened by his wife gently shaking his shoulder and saying, "Honey?"

"Huh? What's up?"

"Jeremy's on the phone, honey. His car broke down."

He blinked, swallowed a couple of times, and he was awake. "Where?"

"In town."

He took a deep breath, nodded, and got to his feet and went into the house.

"Jeremy?" he said into the phone.

"Jean, old boy, I hate to bother you, but my car won't run. And at this time of night there're no garages open."

"Okay, where are you?"

"I'm at the Cove. It's the first street past the inn; turn left a half mile or so. It's on the right, you can't miss it."

"Okay, I'll be there in a bit."

He replaced the phone and went out on the porch. The women looked up and he said to Sandy:

"Want to go with me?"

"No," Suzanne protested. "Leave her with me, we're not through talking. Take Sam with you for company."

"You go ahead, honey," Sandy said. "We'll be all right."

"Okay. Be back in an hour or so."

Sam wasn't much of a replacement for Sandy, but he was company, even though he didn't talk much. After a few miles Lafitte figured it out; Sam wasn't used to a sixty-mile-an-hour drive at night in a convertible. He grinned and said, "Nice night for a drive, huh?"

"Oh . . . oh, yes, suh, nice night."

It was after midnight when he pulled into the nearly empty parking lot of the Cove. He saw Jeremy's Cadillac and parked next to it. They got out and crossed the lot toward the bush-lined entryway. As Lafitte got close to the big double doors a big man dressed in a tight tux appeared and blocked the doorway. He had a broken nose and Lafitte wondered at such a place in a small town having a bouncer.

"Good evening," Lafitte said pleasantly.

The man merely nodded.

"I'm here to pick up a friend."

"Do you have a card?"

"You mean a membership card? No, I'm not a member. My friend's car broke down and he phoned me to pick him up."

"Well, you can't get in without a card."

The man wasn't actually rude, but his bluntness slightly irritated Lafitte, though he smiled and tried again.

"Well, can I get a message to him?"

"Look, mister; this here's a private club. That means we don't take messages inside and you can't get in without a card, and him, we wouldn't even let him in with anybody's card."

Lafitte's eyes narrowed at the reference to Sam and the old man backed up a few steps. Lafitte stood his ground and the bouncer advanced to within two feet and glared down from his eight-inch advantage.

"Well," Lafitte replied, now forcing himself to be civil, "you look a little big to debate the race issue. How can I get word to my friend?"

"Call him," the man said, and Lafitte got a whiff of straight bourbon, which partly explained the less-than-friendly attitude.

"All right, what's the number?"

"It's unlisted." The big man grinned for the first time, showing a missing bottom tooth. "And when ya leave, take that nigger with ya."

Lafitte gritted his teeth as his usually easygoing manner began to dissolve, but he tried to hold his temper. He looked up at the big moose and said as conversationally as he could:

"Come on, man; your red neck's beginning to show. What do I have to do to convince you that he asked me to pick him up?"

That was obviously the wrong thing to say, as the man had a much lower boiling point than Lafitte. He demonstrated it by grabbing Lafitte's right shoulder with his left hand, and as he spun the smaller man away from him he said:

"Ya gotta git past me!"

Lafitte, though angry, was ready and he let himself be propelled to his left as he saw the big man raise his right arm to come down with a backhand judo chop. Lafitte hunched his shoulders as the huge hand descended, and he was struck on the top of the left shoulder and knocked ten feet away, finally dropping to his knees.

Lafitte shot a quick glance at a frightened Sam and said in a low voice, "Stay clear," and moved his shoulder. The blow had merely been impeding, not crippling. He got his feet under him and turned on one knee to face his antagonist and saw the bouncer pause to see if his blow would be the only one necessary.

In that instant Lafitte knew it had returned, and he slowly stood up, feeling the cold tenseness of combat again . . . the instinct he'd fought since he'd injured his leg and knew he might not be as tough as he'd once been. He moved in slowly, fighting the urge to maim the bouncer, as the word "war-

rior" flashed through his mind; the profession he'd once prac-
ticed. He knew it would be safer, and easier, to walk away
and continue to be the easygoing man his wife wanted, but
the bouncer was coming at him again and he chuckled and
decided he'd been away from the wars too long. . . .

He put out his hands in a defensive gesture a moment,
opened his mouth and widened his eyes, hoping that the
bouncer would think he was afraid. When the big man
paused a moment, Lafitte's left hand shot out, the fingers stiff,
accurately smashing the bully in the throat. The man gurgled,
put his hands to his windpipe, and turned away, gasping for
breath. Lafitte moved to his right, lightly jabbing at the forehead with his left hand. The bouncer ducked and Lafitte nodded, hoping the man would do that, and raised his right hand
and brought the flat of it whistling down to the base of the
bull-like neck. As the man grunted and fell to his knees, Lafitte said calmly:

"See, you silly bastard, that's the way to do it. You have to
hit the cervical vertebrae."

Lafitte danced clear, waving his bruised hand a moment
and grinning as Sam stared in amazement. But the bouncer
wasn't through yet. He put his hands on the ground and
started to come up and Lafitte moved in quickly, grabbing
the curly head with both hands this time and jerking it toward his rising knee; there was a dull thud as the man's nose
shattered. Almost unconscious, the big body sank to the
ground again, and Lafitte grabbed the coat collar and moved
behind the big hulk and said:

"Come on, on your feet."

He grabbed the man under the arms with his other hand
and the bouncer shook his head uncomprehendingly and
started to struggle erect, but Lafitte quickly spun him around
and shoved him head first into the brick wall. There was another thud, but no sound from the bouncer. He fell away
from the wall and collapsed behind a large oleander bush.
Lafitte looked behind the bush a moment, nodded and turned
to Sam with a calm smile, again his placid self.

"Come on," he said and turned to try the doorknob.

Sam shook his head and whispered, "We'd better git outa
here, Mistah Jean."

"Relax, Sam. It was too dark for him to know who we are.
Come on, the door's open."

Micronite filter.
Mild, smooth taste.
For all the right reasons.
Kent.

America's quality cigarette.
King Size or Deluxe 100's.

Micronite filter.
Mild, smooth taste.
For all the right reasons.
Kent.

© Lorillard 1972

Regular or Menthol.

Kings: 17 mg. "tar,"
1.1 mg. nicotine;
100's: 19 mg. "tar,"
1.3 mg. nicotine;
Menthol: 19 mg. "tar,"
1.3 mg. nicotine
av. per cigarette,
FTC Report Aug. '72.

Warning: The Surgeon General Has Determined
That Cigarette Smoking Is Dangerous to Your Health.

"No, suh. They'd just run me outa there and cause you more trouble."

"All right," Lafitte nodded. "Wait in the car. But if anybody asks you, you don't know anything about a fight, anytime. Got it?"

"Yes, suh," Sam replied and beat a hasty retreat.

Lafitte straightened his dinner jacket and stepped inside to an opulence that he would not have expected in such a small town. The foyer was properly dim but obviously well appointed. So was the hat-check girl. As she came forward he could see that she wore something less than a Bunny costume.

"Good evenin', suh," she said.

"Good evening. I'm meeting a friend at the bar."

They exchanged smiles and he went into the bar which was on one side of the big dining room. The place was less than half filled and the bar was almost empty. He found Jeremy at the far end, watching the floor show. He took the empty chair next to him and said to the bartender:

"A tall Scotch and water, please."

"Hi!" Jeremy said, putting a dollar down on the bar for Lafitte's drink. "Have any trouble getting in?"

"No, not much," Lafitte lied with a grin. "But we'd better drink up. I did have a few words with that bouncer."

"Yes, he's an ugly one. You know, he once beat a man until he got a fractured skull and spent a month in the hospital."

"No!" Lafitte said, picking up his glass and taking a long drink. "Well, let's go. I wouldn't want him to get mad at me."

Jeremy nodded, his eyes lingering on a busty girl who was wearing barely enough to keep from being a bottomless dancer. Then he got off the stool and Lafitte hurriedly finished his drink and followed Jeremy toward the door.

As they stepped outside Jeremy said, "I wonder where the bouncer is?"

"Maybe he went for help," Lafitte grinned, seeing a foot sticking out from under the oleander.

They crossed the nearly deserted parking lot to Jeremy's Cadillac and Lafitte said, "Did you check under the hood?"

"No," Jeremy replied. "A mechanic I'm not."

"Have you got a flashlight?"

"Sure." Jeremy reached in the glove compartment and took out the light and handed it to Lafitte and both men nodded to Sam who had joined them.

Lafitte raised the hood and flashed the light inside and nodded. It didn't take a mechanic to diagnose the trouble; the battery terminals had been neatly snipped with a pair of cutters. Lafitte flashed the light in Jeremy's face, grinned at what he saw, and then flashed the light back to the battery.

"You've got a friend," Lafitte said. Then, to Sam, "Wait for me in the car?"

"I beg your pardon?" Jeremy said, watching Sam go to the Chevy.

"Well, it's damn late. You sure the lady doesn't have a boyfriend?"

"Now just what the hell does that mean?"

"That means, Jeremy, old boy, that you've got lipstick all over the right side of your face."

Jeremy's frown changed to a smile as he took out his handkerchief and wiped his face. "How's that?"

"It's gone."

Jeremy nodded and dropped the handkerchief to the ground and said, almost proudly, "I didn't think she had a boyfriend, though it looks like it, doesn't it?"

"It certainly does," Lafitte agreed dryly. "Besides that, you committed a big faux pas at the house. Suzanne knows the salesman and his wife are on vacation."

"Oh God!" Jeremy said, more disgusted than fearful. Then he added with a small shrug. "Well, yes, you're right. And my, we did have a time between shows but . . . uh . . . that's between you and me?"

"Absolutely," Lafitte said. "That's your problem."

The upstairs lights were on as Lafitte pulled the Chevy to a stop at the steps. As they reached the porch Sandy ran to grab her husband's arm and say:

"Thank God you're back!"

"Honey! What's the matter?" Lafitte said, his good humor disappearing into a frown.

"We had some prowlers. Your grandfather took a shot at them!"

"Is everybody all right?" he asked.

"Yes, yes, I think so," she said, trying to sound calm.

"Come on," he said, taking her by the arm and steering her into the house.

The two men followed him and they climbed the stairs to see Suzanne herding her girls back to their room. The door to the old man's room was open and Sedonia in a flannel robe was standing in the doorway. Lafitte entered to see the old man sitting up in bed, grinning, though his eyes were wide and his face was flushed. The madam was sitting by the bed holding his hand.

Lafitte let out a sigh of relief and then said, "All right, what happened?"

Sedonia started talking at the same time as Sandy, and the old man's voice boomed over them. Lafitte's eyes darted from person to person, trying to make sense out of the babble. He shook his head a moment, then shouted:

"All right! Shut up!"

There was an instant silence and he nodded. "That's better. Now, Grandfather, you were the marksman. What happened?"

"Well," the old man said, pleased that he had the floor, "I was asleep and I awoke and heard someone tearing up the place next door."

"Our bedroom?" Lafitte asked.

"Yeah."

Lafitte turned to his wife and she nodded and said:

"You should see it. It's a mess."

"They take anything?"

"No . . . no, I don't think so. . . ."

"They were lookin' fer that goddam map, that's what!" the old man said.

"Now what the hell makes you say that?" Lafitte demanded, knowing the old man was telling the truth.

"Because I heard 'em, that's why!" the old man replied. "I musta been asleep during most of it 'cause when I awoke they were just coming out on the balcony again and I heard one say, 'A map could be anywhere,' and then they tried my windows. . . ."

"Then what?" Lafitte said, knowing the old man paused so he would ask.

"Well, suh! I reached for my gun and when one of them muthas . . . 'scuse me, ladies . . . started to come in, I cut loose!"

"Hit 'im?" Lafitte asked, going to the French windows to look at the hole in one pane of glass.

"No, dammit!" the old man replied. "I ain't anything I used to be!"

"I checked out there," Sandy said. "No sign of anything."

"You did?" Jeremy was amazed. "That was pretty brave."

"No, not really," Sandy replied with a small smile. "Suzanne and I were in the kitchen having a cup of coffee when we heard the shot. As we came out we heard them run across the drive, so we ran upstairs."

"Them?" Lafitte asked.

"Yes," Sandy nodded. "Sounded like two."

"I said that." The old man sounded angry.

"Uh huh," Lafitte replied. "How come you only shot once?"

"That's all it took," the old man grinned. "I heard 'em run to the other end of the balcony and then in a bit I heard 'em cross the shells; they just didn't think an old man would have a gun, that's what!"

The old boy leaned back on his pillows, a satisfied grin on his face, and the madam held a cup of cocoa for him. Lafitte frowned as he began to think about the event and he went to the windows again and stepped outside on the balcony and stared into the night, pacing slowly to the other end. In a moment his wife joined him and put her arm around his waist and hugged him.

"I'm glad you're back. We were scared for a bit."

"Yes," he said quietly, kissing her on the cheek. "And I'm glad I'm back."

He stared out into the night, considering all the possibilities that came to him, and the only conclusion he could reach was that he had to know more, there were too many possibilities. Realizing that he was neglecting his wife he leaned down and kissed her on the cheek and she said in a small voice:

"Honey? You really think they were after that old map?"

"No, sweetie, I don't really think so. The most logical thing is they were just prowlers and the old man was playing it up. He's got a little game going about the map. He wants everyone to think he really left me something of value so he can save face. After all, he's a proud old man who was once wealthy. . . . Of course, there's the possibility that they were after the map and that opens up a wild realm of conjecture."

In the dark he could see her eyes widen and he nodded and added:

"Uh huh. If they were after the map how the hell did they know I had it?"

"Oh!" she said. "Then . . . then, who?"

"Yeah," he nodded. "There were . . . let's see . . . the old bastard and wife, you and me, and, uh . . . Sam, Jeremy, Dominique, and the other two, and their wives. . . . There were fourteen adults here tonight. Now, it's a damn cinch that you and I didn't rat on ourselves, so that leaves twelve. Now, any of them could've hired it done, or, more likely, they probably mentioned it on the way home, maybe like at a bar or something . . . they all left early and . . ."

He stopped talking as a loud echoing voice came out of the darkness.

"La-fitte . . . La-fitte . . . La-Fitte . . ."

"Aw, come on!" He said it irritably, like they were putting him on.

The sound came from the direction of the swamp to the north. It had an eerie sound that he recognized as coming from a loudspeaker system.

"For Christ's sake!" he said to his wife. "They're making like an old movie!"

"La-fitte! The map. La-fitte! The map . . ."

"Well," he said, grinning down at Sandy, "so much for the prowler theory."

"Jean Lafitte!" she exclaimed, though she wasn't really angry. "You don't seem to be particularly disturbed."

"No, dear heart," he replied with a grin, "I'm not. I just think it's a couple of losers trying to steal a buck."

"What in the world do you mean?"

"Well, consider this. If it really was a group trying to get the legendary map of the Lafittes they certainly wouldn't wait until I'd left the island, I might've taken it with me. They would've moved in while I was here, cut the phone lines, and taken me before I had a chance to dispose of it. Bullshit! Besides, none of us pirates are afraid!"

He laughed and she couldn't help but grin as he took her arm and they went back into the old man's bedroom.

"You heard?" Jeremy said.

"As a matter of fact," Lafitte grinned, "I barely did."

"La-fitte! La-fitte!" the call came again. "Follow! Follow!"

Lafitte stepped to the windows, cupped his hands to his mouth, and shouted, "What do you want?"

"Follow! Follow!"

Lafitte turned to Jeremy with a grin and said, "Hey, you know. That's not a bad idea. Want to go?"

Jeremy frowned a moment, then said, "Yes. I'm game if you are."

"Good. You got a gun?"

"A .38 in the car."

"Good. Get it. And run out the jeep. Sam's got the keys."

Jeremy left the room, taking Sam with him as Suzanne entered.

"Where're they going?" she asked.

"We're going for a little ride," Lafitte said. "You stay here with Sandy."

"Honey?" Sandy said with a worried look. "Should you?"

"Certainly," he said, brushing her cheek with his hand. "This is part of the game. They'll know I won't have the big, old treasure map with me. Sit tight. We'll be back in a few minutes." To the old man he said, "Any other guns?"

"Yeah," the old man grinned, his eyes flashing. "Take the scatter gun. Downstairs, closet behind the stairs, near the pantry. Extra shells on the shelf. Goddam! I wish I wuz going with you."

Lafitte paused to pat the old man's arm and say, "Me too."

Without waiting for his wife to say more he sprinted out of the room and down the big stairs. He found the twelve-gauge shotgun in a back corner, broke it open, and raised an eyebrow when he found it loaded. He searched on the shelf for a moment until he found the box of shells. He grabbed six and decided that if he needed more he wouldn't need a shotgun, he'd need a machine gun. He ran out the front door and the voice called again:

"La-fitte, come! La-fitte, come!"

Despite the eerie sound, Lafitte grinned at the dramatics and said under his breath, "I'm coming, you silly mutha fucka . . . just stand still!"

Sam pulled the jeep to the front and got out and Lafitte got behind the wheel and handed the shotgun to Jeremy.

"Got your pistol?"

"Ready."

"Ready!" Lafitte snorted. "You better by God be ready. Hold tight!"

Lafitte threw the jeep into low gear and spun out of the shells and down the driveway, but to the south, not toward the north where the sound came from. He hit the first cross path and slid through the corner in second gear, going west. Jeremy hung on, his mouth open, and finally decided that Lafitte knew what he was doing. They ran two hundred yards in high gear and when he thought he was getting close to the west road he put his lights on for a moment, then snapped them off and slid through the turn, heading north.

They bumped their way along the ancient road at a fearful sixty miles an hour for the two miles to the turn and then Lafitte slowed a bit and said, "Can you see the turn?"

"Yeah, uh . . . I hope to God that's it a hundred feet ahead."

"Might be," Lafitte allowed, grinning at the frightened Jeremy for a moment. He got to the turn, coming down on it in high, only shifting into second as he began his turn, and pushed the gas to the floor. The little jeep responded as had thousands of its ancestors through several wars, and the back wheels dug in and kicked it out of the turn like the lumpy, ugly sports car it had always been. When he felt it grab, Lafitte laughed in remembrance and Jeremy stared at him like he'd lost his mind. Lafitte ran the half mile to the turn where they'd met the Cajun at full bore, back-shifting to second and slamming on the brakes at the last moment. He cut the ignition and jumped out, grabbing the shotgun, and said in a low voice:

"Come on, we gotta get away from the jeep."

They trotted a hundred feet down the south road and Lafitte waved Jeremy into some bushes. They stopped for breath and listened, and at first they could hear nothing. Then, when he'd regained his breath, Lafitte heard the crackle of the speaker. He grinned into the night. They were in the bay, but below him, and between him and the house.

"You wanted Lafitte?" he shouted. "Well, here I am!"

It was silent for a moment and then the voice called, "The map, Lafitte!"

"Yeah? It's useless! You're welcome to it!"

"Bring it on the paddlewheeler tomorrow morning and

we'll leave the old man alone! All the excitement might be too much for him!"

Lafitte started to shout an answer, then paused; he hadn't thought of that. "Son of a bitch!" he whispered. "They're right!" To Jeremy he said, "They're goddam nuts!"

"What are you going to do?" Jeremy whispered.

Lafitte thought a bit, then grinned. The fight with the bouncer had stirred him to the point where he thought he might try them. He hadn't played that game in a long time. He nodded, it might be fun.

"I'll give it to you!" he shouted.

"And if you don't, the town will know that the last of the Lafittes was a coward! Be there!"

"Fuck you!" Lafitte said in a whisper and grinned, then shouted, "Hey! How will I know who to give it to?"

"Be there!" the speaker blared, then went silent.

They waited a few moments, but they could hear nothing and soon the swamp creatures started their nightly overture again.

"Will you give it to them?" Jeremy whispered, as though he were giving away a million dollars.

"Sure. It's worthless. And even in the remote chance that it isn't, it won't do 'em any good. Come on."

Lafitte trotted back to the jeep and got in quickly. Jeremy seemed about to say something but Lafitte started the engine and roared down the east road as fast as he could, making conversation impossible. As he pulled up in front of the steps Jeremy put his hand on his arm an said:

"What do you mean, it won't do them any good?"

"Think about it a bit," Lafitte grinned and jumped out. On the porch he stopped Jeremy and added, "Say nothing in front of the women, understand?"

Jeremy nodded and followed him up the steps. They were all in the old man's bedroom and Sandy met him at the door and said, "Find anything?"

"Nothing. They were gone. It was just a prank. Now, all of you leave. I want to talk to His Eminence, here."

He escorted his wife to the door, followed by Suzanne and Sedonia, then Sam, and finally the madam.

"Don't worry," Lafitte said to the dainty old woman, "we'll only be a while."

The madam smiled and Lafitte closed the door and quickly

told the old man what had happened. The old boy listened quietly, and when his grandson was through speaking he said:

"You're going, of course?"

"Now what the hell does that mean?" Lafitte demanded.

"It means that you're a Lafitte and you gave your word."

"Bull! My word to a gang of punks?"

"You've got another idea?" the cagey old man said, sensing that his grandson had something in mind.

Lafitte started to answer, but then decided that Jeremy might be a weak link. Instead he turned slightly so that Jeremy couldn't see his face and he winked slightly and said, "Yes, I guess you're right. I gave my word. Besides, the map's not worth anything. I'll give 'em the goddam thing and that'll be the end of it."

"But . . . but," Jeremy said, then added, "when will you go?"

"Oh," Lafitte lied. "I am not about to get up at the crack of dawn and take that boat. I'll go in town and meet it when it arrives . . . I think Sam said about eight."

"Oh," Jeremy said. He started to speak again, then changed his mind and said, "Well, I'll say good night."

The old man nodded and said, "Send in Sam, will ya? I've gotta go to the can."

Jeremy nodded and closed the door and the old man turned to Lafitte and grinned, "You son of a bitch, you've got a plan!"

"I have indeed, O worthy Grandfather. I'm gonna roll it in a small cylinder and shove it right up their asses."

"Good! Goddam good!" the old man almost shouted. "Give 'em hell, boy!"

Lafitte grinned and then Sam entered and Lafitte said, "Anyone in the hall?"

"No, suh. Mister Jeremy's gone downstairs."

"Good. Now listen close, Sam. We're going out in the morning. That motorboat still go good?"

"Yes, suh," Sam grinned. "It goes like a bomb."

"Good. Now, get your ass up early, you got an alarm? . . . Good. Set it early enough to get the lantern out for the packet. Then get that boat out and fire it up and hang out there in the bay 'till it comes by. I'll get on it and then I'm gonna give my briefcase to someone on the boat and then I'm gonna jump. You be close enough to pick me up, all right?"

"Yes, suh!" Sam sounded elated.

"Uh, any snakes out in the bay?"

"No, suh. Nothing to worry about. That is, iffin you kin swim?"

"I can swim. Just be close enough so that I don't have to be in the water too long."

"Yes, suh."

"You gettin' pretty goddam brave, ain't you, boy?" the old man asked. "I mean the way you been so easygoin' and all."

"Yeah," Lafitte grinned. "But I decided that I've been too nice. I don't take to those bastards coming around scaring my wife like that."

"Good for you!" his grandfather said.

"Uh, Mistah Jean?" Sam said. "What for we gonna git you on the boat and then you jump out?"

"Sam, I'm going to give them the briefcase, then we beat the packet to the dock, and we follow whoever has it to wherever he's going and then we're gonna give a little lesson in manners."

"Good boy!" the old man grinned.

"Good," Lafitte said, heading for the door. "Sam, rap on my door when it's time."

Sam nodded and Lafitte slipped outside, hoping the old man hadn't figured that he was doing it for his grandfather's benefit.

Part Three

IT WAS STILL DARK AND A BIT MISTY AS HE STOOD NEAR THE old wharf. He was crouched on one knee in the weeds that Sam was going to pull, the knee resting on the locked, empty briefcase. He was dressed in his light nylon jacket, covering a T-shirt and Levi's. He wore deck shoes but no socks. He had given his wallet and watch and keys to Sam a half hour earlier as he'd helped roll out and launch the outboard. Sam had assured him that it would be no problem to paddle the outboard far enough out into the bay so that the noise of the engine wouldn't be heard. Hopefully, Sam was out in the bay now, waiting to start his engine when the paddlewheeler left the wharf.

Lafitte looked over his shoulder and grinned as he thought how he had double-talked his wife and, fortunately, she hadn't mentioned calling the police and, of course, he hadn't either. Jeremy had, as far as he knew, been true to his word and not mentioned the conversation at the far end of the island. Lafitte told himself he was doing it mainly to keep them from coming back and risking the old man having another stroke, but despite the seriousness of that part of it, Lafitte looked on it as a small foray against some local punks, someone to whom a small lesson should be taught. He'd decided it was good to feel like a warrior again.

He looked at the house, but there were no lights. He nodded and concluded that he and Sam had managed to get up

93

and away without being noticed. He wished he'd had some
coffee, but he didn't have time to dwell on the condition of
his stomach, as he heard the sound of the paddlewheeler approach in the dark. He got to his feet, picked up the briefcase, strolled up the bank, and stepped out on the wharf, the
creaking sounding louder than it had in the daytime.

As the boat drew closer the thought crossed his mind that
if they were professionals they would've already tried to get
rid of him, in case he'd memorized the map. But then he discarded the idea, as his logical mind told him that while many
men were thieves, few set out to be murderers. Besides, if
they had been really smart it would also have come to them
that perhaps several other people would have memorized the
map, or made copies. He shook his head in disbelief; they
had to be just thugs, intent on getting the map for a quick
sale, smart men would realize that outsiders would have but a
small chance. Of course, there was another possibility that
came to him, but he'd have to think that one out a little more
clearly.

The ancient vessel creaked and groaned as it backwatered
to a shuddering halt at the wharf and the mate held out an
arm as he jumped aboard, collected the forty-cent fee, and
turned to replace the gate. As the boat pulled away he made
his way past the closely jammed pickup trucks and cars lining
the outside of the main deck and went into what had once
been the saloon, but was now a dingy waiting room with
wooden benches. There were a good fifty men aboard, some
white, some black, most with lunch pails and almost all wearing work clothes. A few looked at him with mild interest, but
most ignored him. He walked slowly up one aisle to the forward end and then came back down the other aisle. No one
approached him.

He shrugged and went forward again and out the door to
stand on the prow deck. There were a few men taking the
morning air, but in the dark he couldn't tell if anyone was
staring at him or not. He turned and looked down the port
side at the closely packed cars, but they all appeared empty.
There were a few men standing near their cars on the starboard as he made his way along the railing. Again he was
stared at, but casually, and was not approached. As he got
near the stern and its stacked cargo of boxes and barrels he
got a strong smell of seafood and thought it was most proba-

bly oysters in water. He was almost to the railing around the big paddlewheel when he heard the sound of a box being moved. He whirled around to see two dark forms blocking the way back and he started to grin, but it quickly faded as he saw the glint of knives.

"Damn!" he said, mad at himself because he hadn't expected trouble.

He stood his ground a moment, knowing that he couldn't back up. If they really meant to kill him, the obvious thing would be to dump him into the big wheel. While he tried to decide if he could run forward and into the lights, one man said to the other:

"Voodoo man says don't kill."

The other mumbled something that Lafitte couldn't hear but he grinned. They were only out to scare him, maybe a bit more, but he thought he could cope with that.

"This what you want?" he said, holding out the briefcase.

They didn't answer but started to advance, and separate. His first thought was try one and then take on the other, but then he saw the one to his left flip his knife in his hand and he decided that it was discretion time. He whirled the briefcase in a circle and then flung it at the one on the left and ran directly toward him. The man managed to fend off the briefcase but had to take a couple of steps backward. That gave Lafitte the slight leeway he needed. As he saw the one to the right come toward him he cut to his left a bit, took two more running steps, and then dived over the railing into the night, taking a deep breath.

He hit the water and continued downward, diving a good fifteen feet to miss the suction of the wheel, then with six strong strokes swam away from the boat and paused . . . there was nothing but a gentle swirl. He turned his head upward and kicked hard, his breath almost gone. He surfaced and sucked in a great breath and turned to see the lights of the boat over fifty feet away. He grinned and took another breath and kicked in a circle looking for Sam. He could see nothing.

As he treaded water a few moments and tried to decide what to do, it quickly came to him that Sam should be close enough for him to hear the engine. He spun again in a circle, but there was no boat. Then he spun back to get a quick fix on the rapidly disappearing lights of the boat and decided

that land would be at right angles. He stopped his paddling
again to listen . . . still nothing.

"Whew!" he let out his breath and decided that he might
have a long swim. "Goddam! Some plan."

He grinned at his own genius and slipped out of the jacket
and kicked off the shoes. The Levi's suddenly weighed more
than he wanted to carry, and he took a deep breath and doubled over in the water and struggled out of his pants. He
came up for a breath and started to let go of the pants and
then changed his mind; he might need them if Sam didn't
show up. He started to swim toward where he thought the
land should be, and then changed his mind and decided to
put his faith in Sam and began to swim slowly in the boat's
path.

His faith was well placed. He'd decided to swim after the
boat for five minutes, then he'd have to turn toward land, but
he'd gone what he thought was only two minutes when he
heard the sound of the outboard. He spun around once to get
the bearing and then headed that way. When the sound was
close he yelled once, then again, and the sound grew louder.
In a few moments the boat was very close and he yelled as
loud as he could; the throttles were cut and a flashlight
scanned the water. He waved when the light hit him and Sam
yelled:

"I'm comin'!"

When he was alongside, Sam helped him aboard and said,
"Where's your pants?"

"Right here," Lafitte answered, pulling the twenty-pound
Levi's aboard. "Where the hell have you been?"

"I'm sorry, suh," Sam apologized. "But the prop got fouled
in a floatin' tree branch. Took me a bit to get it untan-
gled. . . . How'd it go?"

"Oh, just fine," Lafitte answered in a wry tone.

Sam made good time back to the wharf and pulled in with
a flourish. It was well after daylight, probably after seven,
Lafitte thought, as he jumped into the water to guide the boat
onto the partially sunken trailer. When it was secure, Sam
jumped out and trotted to the house to get the jeep while Lafitte slipped on his damp pants. In a few moments the jeep
appeared and the trailer was hooked on, and Sam towed the
boat slowly to the garage. As they were unhooking the trailer

Sedonia came out of the house and Sam said under his breath:

"Oh! Oh! Now we's in fer it!"

Lafitte grinned as he saw her apron swirl, almost angrily, he thought; to match the look on her face.

"Mistah Jean . . ." she said in a loud voice, then stopped as Lafitte put a finger to his lips.

"Quiet," he said. "Don't wake the whole house."

She entered the big garage and shot a withering look at Sam, who was busily fiddling with the already unhooked jeep, and said: "Now, where you two been?"

"We went for a nice boat ride, Sedonia," Lafitte said, lying easily. "And now we've got to hurry into town."

"Yeah!" she said derisively. "Shore you did . . . and lookit you, you're all wet! Two full-growed men out chasin' hop-head punks. You should be ashamed!"

Lafitte grinned again, the worried look on her face showed that she didn't really mean it. Then his expression grew serious and he put his hand on her arm in an affectionate gesture. "Now look, old girl, this is serious and I can't give you all the details. . . ."

"That's all right," she said firmly, "better I don't know such things."

"Good," Lafitte said, "we agree. Now I don't have much time. I brought out a change of clothes and as soon as I'm dressed we've got to get into town, but in the meantime, you can do your good turn of the day by getting your big fat bottom into the house and bringing us out a cup of coffee and a roll or something. How about it?"

"Hmph!" she snorted, then inclined her head toward her husband. "Him too?"

"Sure, him too! He's hungry."

"Didn't mean that. Mean he's gotta go with ya?"

"Yes, I need him. Now, git."

"Hmph!" she said, heading toward the house at a fast waddle. "And it ain't that big and fat!"

Chuckling to himself Lafitte went to his rented car and opened the door; he sat on the seat and began to change clothes from the skin out. By the time he was decently attired in a sport coat and slacks, Sedonia returned with a tray covered with a cloth. She gave both men a glance that said she still didn't approve and put the tray on the hood of the jeep.

"Anyone up yet?" Lafitte asked.

"Only the girls. And they's busy watching that booby tube."

Lafitte laughed at her adding a Y to the description of the TV and then agreed that the way it was going she wasn't far off. He lifted the cloth and saw two steaming mugs of black coffee and two large sweet rolls. As he and Sam took one of each he decided that he was very hungry. He ate half the roll with sips of coffee and Sedonia turned her back to her husband. She still hadn't spoken to him, as an indication of her displeasure at him for not clearing his activities with her first, and she lifted her apron and gingerly pulled one of the old man's snub-nosed .38's and its spring-clip holster from her dress pocket.

"I don't think they's all kids," she whispered as though they were alone.

He grinned and put his cup on the jeep fender and the roll on top of it and took the gun and slipped the spring clip into his waistband and nodded. After his short experience with the two on the boat, it didn't seem too bad an idea. She winked at him with a common sense wise far beyond her book knowledge and turned to her Sam.

"Now listen, you black mutha," she said as though Lafitte had suddenly disappeared. "You do exactly as Mistah Jean says. Then I know you'll be back in time to pull them weeds down at the wharf . . . you hear me?"

"Yes, ma'am," Sam answered, as though she weren't his wife.

Sedonia nodded again and then left with the parting shot, "I gots to git busy, no time fer play games."

Lafitte chuckled and finished his roll and said to Sam, "Come on, we'll take my car. We can make better time than with the jeep."

"I thought you might say that," Sam said, finishing his roll.

They were waiting at the corner of a warehouse across from the pier as the paddlewheeler pulled in. As the gate came down and the cars came off first, Lafitte said:

"They'll probably be on foot, but check each car to see if there's anyone you know. And I'm sorry, I can't even tell you what they look like."

"They's black," Sam said, pointing to two men who were

moving rapidly past the cars. One was tall and skinny and in his hand he carried a burlap bag tightly wrapped around an object the size and shape of Lafitte's briefcase.

"They certainly are," Lafitte said. "Know 'em?"

"The one with the briefcase, he works for Tomas Mejia."

"Well, that's no surprise. Follow 'em and I'll get the car and follow you. Stay on the sidewalk where I can see you."

"Yes, suh."

Lafitte turned and went to his car, a half block away. By the time he'd picked up Sam and was following slowly, their direction was well indicated, toward the heart of the black section. They went three blocks, turned left a block, and Lafitte saw them enter a run-down, two-story building. Sam turned and looked in his direction once to make sure he was close and then entered the building. Lafitte parked across the street and a few doors past and waited a bit. In a few moments Sam came out and Lafitte got out of the car and crossed the street to meet him.

"Looks like a warehouse, but it's off hours," Sam explained. "Anyway, they went upstairs."

"Uh huh. Follow me at a bit. Stay downstairs while I go up."

"Mistah Jean," Sam frowned, "this looks like bad business. Maybe we ought'n."

"Never mind," Lafitte said, heading toward the grimy door.

He pushed it open and saw a deserted hall and a set of stairs. Glad for Sedonia's concern, he hunched his shoulders and checked to make sure he could reach the gun easily, and mounted the steps. The upper hall was deserted. He stopped at a door, listened a moment and heard the sound of muffled conversation and decided on the direct approach; he tried the knob, found the door open, and pushed.

He was in a cheap brothel and the room contained two dirty beds on which two black men were laying two black whores. One man looked over his shoulder with a curse and Lafitte said, "Oops!" and hurriedly backed away, but not before his eyes scanned the room. There was no other door, or closet, and the only window was too high and too small for a man. He closed the door and turned to face what had to be the madam. She was a fat, tan woman with too much make-up and wearing a frilly dressing gown. As she approached from the end of the hall she stared at him with a big smile and said:

"Something special?"

"No, not exactly," he said with a grin. "I'm looking for two black men."

"Ha!" she chuckled. "Well, we got several on the premises right now, but we don't rent 'em out."

"That wasn't exactly what I had in mind. The two were to meet me here. One was tall and skinny and is probably carrying a burlap bag."

"Huh!" she said noncommittally, studying him for a moment. "You ain't a cop or there'd be two of you, and a white man in here is nothin' but trouble. I got maybe half dozen men here right now, but they're all busy. Now, if I didn't care what happened I'd invite you to check all the rooms. But I don't want no trouble with a white man gettin' beat up in my place, so the best advice I can give is that you'd best git."

"Uh huh," Lafitte said, "but the two I'm looking for just came in——"

"No sir, they didn't," a big Negro said, coming from a door across the hall. "I been in here for almost an hour, with the door open a bit, and no one's come in. Big Mama's right, don't you think?"

The man spoke easily and advanced slowly, scratching his head with one hand. Lafitte saw the muscles ripple under the tight T-shirt and nodded.

"You know," he said, backing to the stairs. "I'm inclined to agree with you."

The big man nodded and Lafitte dropped quickly down the stairs. Outside he let out his breath in a whoosh and again appreciated the value of discretion.

As he crossed the street with a relieved Sam at his side he shook his head and stopped Sam's inquiry and thought about the problem. By now, or soon, Mejia would know that the briefcase was empty. If Lafitte left it at that, he had no doubt that Mejia would send his messengers again. . . . Lafitte shrugged, he didn't like that idea too much. His conclusion was to face Mejia now; at least he might know more and he wasn't particularly afraid. Mejia wanted something, and Lafitte had it.

As they got in the car Sam said, "I can't wait. What happened?"

"Nothing, fortunately," Lafitte grinned. "They must've gotten in and out in a big hurry, probably the back way. There was a big buck there who convinced me that I was in the wrong place."

"He did?" Sam said, his brow wrinkled. "How did he do that?"

"Merely by flexing an arm as big around as your head."

"Oh," Sam said in a low voice.

"Okay, you ready?"

"Ready fer what?"

"We've got to get to Tomas Mejia. Know where he might be?"

Sam clenched his jaw and stared through the windshield.

"Come on, goddammit, do you know?"

Sam nodded, but reluctantly. "Yes, suh. But don't."

"Never mind the don't, Sam. He's got the briefcase by now and he knows it's empty. He'll probably come again."

"Yes, suh, but he's bad medicine."

"Baloney! Sam, all he tried to do was rob the house. And on the boat one of his men could've shot me. They didn't. They just wanted the briefcase. Better I talk to him now. Tell me!"

"All right. He's got an office upstairs on the next street, down a block, but Mistah Jean, it's in the middle of the nigger district; don't go."

"Sam," Lafitte said patiently, "the man wants the map. He sent a couple of punks last night. He set up the bit on the packet, and in that whorehouse just now. Now, he's going to come again. Sam, it's only money he's after. You don't want me to do it the hard way, do you? I can go to the cops and they'll tell me."

"No, suh, don't do that! If he thinks we called the law he might put a curse on us!"

"Aw, come on! Let's go see him in the broad light of day and you'll find that he puts his pants on one leg at a time, just like the rest of us. If you don't, I'll find him anyway."

Sam took a deep breath, then nodded. "All right. But I'd never do this at night."

Lafitte grinned and silently agreed that he wouldn't either.

He drove two blocks down the street, watching the rear-

view mirror, but there were no cars behind him. He went another block and made four right turns, just to be sure, then
turned left on the proper street and pulled up across the
street from the run-down building that looked like its neigh-
bors; the next high wind would raze the block. As he turned
off the key, Sam pointed to the building, but made no effort
to get out of the car.

"Come on," Lafitte commanded, "you'll be better off with
me."

They crossed the street and Lafitte pushed open the door
to a dingy hallway. A black woman was just coming out. She
shot him a furtive glance and tried to pass quickly. Lafitte
blocked the door and said:

"I'm looking for Tòmas Mejia."

"Upstairs," she said in a low voice and brushed past him
and hurried down the almost deserted street.

With his coat open, and Sam behind him, Lafitte mounted
the steps to the second floor. There were three doors. The
middle one had a dingy card on it which read: TOMAS
MEJIA. The other two doors were closed, this one was ajar.
Lafitte pushed with his foot and the door swung all the way
back on rusty hinges to reveal a tall, well-built brown man
with a nasty scar running from the center of his hairline
down to the bridge of his nose, which gave him a rather Sa-
tanic look. He was seated behind an old desk. The top was
clear except for a four-foot length of broom handle. He was
wearing a tight, white, knit sport shirt and both hands were
flat on the desk top.

"Come in, Señor Lafitte," the man said in good English,
slightly tinged with a Spanish accent. "I am Tomas Mejia. As
you can see, I'm alone. And you want to talk. Come in, and
bring your nigger with you."

Sam started to back away, but Lafitte reached behind him
and grabbed the old man's sleeve. Lafitte stood in the doorway a moment and recognized the broom handle for what it
was, a jabbing stick, then inched forward a bit until his periph-
eral vision told him that there was no one on either side
of the door. Then he pulled a quaking Sam inside and kicked
the door closed behind them. Another quick glance told him
that the room was empty and that there were no other doors.
Mejia held up his hands to show that he was unarmed, and
said with a cold smile:

"And you want to know why I want your map?"

Lafitte nodded, his eyes narrowed, and said, "Something like that."

"Well, let me put it this way. I want it. I will get it. By the way, that was clever of you on the boat. But, of course, you had no way of knowing that they had orders not to harm you in any way. However, you could've saved yourself a dunking by just letting them have it."

"And why should I?" Lafitte asked. "It's mine."

"True," Mejia allowed. "But you're just a visitor. You'll not be here long enough to pursue the thing. Better you let me have it before you find out it'll do you no good."

Lafitte shook his head and matched Mejia's grin as Sam started to pull away, and he grabbed Sam again.

"Perhaps you don't understand the power I have over these people. And with the two of you, I might feel at somewhat of a disadvantage. . . . Let me show you." Mejia got to his feet, leaving both palms flat on the desk and stared at Sam. "Sam, you believe in voodoo."

"No, suh, I do not," Sam said, but without conviction.

"Oh, but you do," Mejia replied, his voice deepening. "I have looked at the insides of a frog while saying your name. I've got some of your hair from the last time you came to town and got a haircut. I beat the voodoo drums and I burned your hair with the words . . . I said the words, Sam. . . . I've called up the curse for the time I would see you. . . . And the curse is you cannot raise your right arm, Sam. It is numb. . . . And, when I choose, the rest of you will be numb until you are a clod in your grave. . . ."

"Knock it off!" Lafitte said. "That went out a hundred years ago! Sam doesn't believe in that crap!"

"Yes he does!" Mejia shouted. "Yes! Try to move your arm, Sam!"

Lafitte turned to see a terrified Sam back away a step, move his shoulder, and wiggle his fingers, but his right arm wouldn't move.

"Mistah Jean!" he said in a frightened whisper. "I cain't! I cain't!"

"Bullshit!" Lafitte shouted. "It's just superstition. Move your arm, Sam!"

Sam shook his head, beads of perspiration on his forehead.

His fingers moved, but his arm would not. Lafitte shook his head and turned back to Mejia and said in a low voice:

"Well, there's one way to end this crap!"

He moved a step forward and instantly realized his mistake. He should have gone for the gun first. Mejia had the stick in his hand and it whipped out and rapped Lafitte on the wrist with a stinging blow. He tried to flex his fingers, but they were numb. He backed out of the way of the following jab and tried to reach for the gun with his left hand, but the stick was there to knock his hand away. Lafitte backed up and Mejia rounded the desk, holding the stick like a foil.

As Lafitte backed farther away, the stick was still there, keeping his hands spread. An almost forgotten reaction made Lafitte glance at his opponent's eyes and his other hand. Mejia lunged again and Lafitte grabbed for the stick, but it whirled away in a flawless parry and he was again rapped on the forearm. Lafitte darted to his left and back again and then he was hit on the side of the head by something heavier than a broom handle, the room turned red, and as he was about to lose consciousness he heard Mejia's voice:

"I will have it. In fact, Mr. Lafitte, you will give it to me. . . ."

Then he was hit again and everything went black.

A bright light was shining in his eyes and he groaned and put his hand to his head as he became aware of his surroundings. He was sitting behind the wheel of his car, still parked across the street from Mejia's office. The light was the hot morning sun. He felt the lump on the side of his head and his hand came away sticky with drying blood. He groaned again and sat erect and saw Sam sitting next to him, staring straight ahead.

"You all right, Sam?"

"Yes, suh," Sam said in a flat tone, " 'cept I cain't use my arm."

Lafitte swallowed hard and as his head cleared he turned to look up and down the street. On the sidewalk were two black men who glanced once at the strange white man with the bloody head and then hurried on; it was not business for them. There were several people at the end of the block, but other than that the street was deserted. He turned the rearview mirror until he could see his face and said, "Ick!" and grinned at Sam. His shirt and the side of his head were bloody. He felt the lump again and decided the cut was fairly small, but the lump was a good one. He looked at his watch and raised an eyebrow; it was after nine; he'd been out over a half hour. Then he felt under his coat; the gun was still there.

"We been sitting here all this time?"

"Yes, suh."

"Well, why the hell didn't you go for help?" Lafitte said in an irritated voice.

"Cause Mejia and them two brought us outa that building and when they put us here he says fer me to stay put until you comes to, less'en he does my other arm."

"Bull! Goddam, Sam, that's pure superstitition, and you know it! Snap out of it!"

"You kin say that," old Sam replied patiently, " 'cause he didn't put no spell on you . . . but I cain't move my arm."

Lafitte shrugged and his eyes wandered two doors down the street to a run-down saloon that was open early, presumably for the all-day drinkers. He pointed to it and said, "You want a drink?"

"No, suh. And better you not, too. That place is fer blacks."

"Goddam!" Lafitte said, managing a smile as he got out of the car, "You segregationists are all alike!"

He entered the swinging doors to a dirty, sour-smelling, dingy bar with three shaky patrons at the far end who stared at him a moment, then turned to their breakfast. The fat bartender stared at him a moment, nodded politely, but said nothing.

Lafitte dropped a dollar bill on the bar and said, "A shot of good Scotch, please, and a water chaser."

The bartender poured him an ounce and a half of Lang's and backed it with a glass of water. Lafitte waved that the man should keep the change; he dipped his fingers in the whiskey and turned his head so he could see in the bar mirror and gingerly dabbed at the cut. He whistled silently while the bartender grinned, and then Lafitte dabbed some more, picked up the glass, and tossed off the remaining shot of Scotch. As he made a wry face he took out his handkerchief, sipped the water, and then dipped the handkerchief in the glass and began to wipe the blood from the side of his head and neck. The bartender came up with a paper towel and Lafitte nodded his thanks and dried the side of his neck, looked at the image and snorted:

"Some pirate!" he said in a low voice.

He nodded again to the barkeep and returned to the clean air. Another glance at his shirt told him that he shouldn't go home like that. He considered buying a new one, but a better idea came to him. He nodded and got into the car and took the keys out of his pocket.

He pulled into the parking lot at the inn, shut off the engine, set the brake, and went around the other side to help Sam out of the car. He started to remonstrate again with the old man but changed his mind and silently walked him into the foyer and up to the desk clerk.

"Mr. You?" Lafitte said.

"Through the bar . . . if he's in," the man said.

Lafitte nodded and walked Sam into the darkened bar where a man in a sweatshirt was cleaning the mirror. When he heard them he turned and smiled.

"My name's Lafitte. Dominique You here?"

"I'll see," was the cautious reply.

The man went to a door at the end of the bar, knocked, and then stuck his head inside. In a moment he backed out and was followed by the stocky Frenchman. As he came forward to shake hands, You saw the bloodstains and gripped Lafitte's hand but a moment and then stepped aside and said:

"Come in, come in."

Lafitte nodded and walked Sam into the expensively appointed office, put him in a leather chair in a corner, and turned as You indicated a chair in front of his desk. Lafitte grinned and sat down. When he was seated behind the big desk, Dominique said:

"You've . . . uh . . . had a bit of a workout?"

"Yes, you might say that," Lafitte allowed, smiling at the Frenchman's dry question. "I met a man named Tomas Mejia. I gather you've heard of him?"

"Yes," You smiled. "I certainly have." The grin disappeared and You added, "I think, my friend, that perhaps you should tell me what happened."

"I will . . . and I need your help."

"But you have that without asking. What can I do for you?"

"First, I need to borrow a shirt. If I went home looking like this it might raise too many questions."

"Of course," You replied. He got to his feet and opened the closet behind the desk and selected a tan sport shirt from ten or twelve hanging neatly in a row. "It's not the same, but it's close enough that it might not cause too much comment."

"It'll do nicely," Lafitte replied.

He stood up and shucked his coat, laid the .38 on the desk (which Dominique considered with a raised brow but no comment), and stripped off his bloodied shirt. You, noticing the big chest and the well-muscled arms, observed:

"My, you're in good shape for a man who works in an office."

"Trying to make up for my leg, I guess," Lafitte admitted, taking the shirt from the hanger and slipping it on. The sleeves were a bit long, but his coat would cover that.

"Oh," You said, as though he should've mentioned it earlier, "would you like a drink?"

"Thank you, no. But I think Sam could use a cup of coffee."

"I surely could," Sam nodded. "Thank you."

You nodded and left the room for a few moments. When he returned with a tray with a pot and two cups, Lafitte had the shirt buttoned, tucked in, and was replacing the gun. He grinned at You and the Frenchman shook his head, meaning that no explanation about the gun was necessary. He poured two cups and handed one to Sam. The old man took it with his left hand and nodded.

"What happened to him?" You said to Lafitte.

"Do you believe in voodoo?" Lafitte asked, replacing his coat so the gun wouldn't show.

"No. No, of course not. But I've seen some things you wouldn't believe."

"Uh huh," Lafitte nodded. "Well, Sam does."

You nodded slowly without speaking as he stared at Sam's limp arm. Then he looked at his friend and said, "Uh, perhaps it goes with the bang on the head?"

"It certainly does."

While he sipped his coffee, Lafitte told Dominique what had happened since he and that gorgeous creature had left the plantation the night before; of Jeremy's call from town and his going in and picking him up (though he omitted the part about the bouncer), of the scene at home when they'd returned and his chasing them to the edge of the swamp and agreeing to go on the packet, and finally his somewhat less than spectacular doings of the morning. When he was through, Dominique poured him another cup of coffee and Lafitte added:

"And, you know, that son of a bitch is a fencer! He could've killed me with that goddam stick . . . almost; except when he lunges he barely flicks his fingers on his other hand. Just a bit, but he does . . . he has to be out of practice."

"I see," You replied, leaning back in his chair and playing with a knifelike letter opener. "And how is it that you noticed such a helpful thing?"

"I used to fence some, but that was a while back."

"Well," You said, "I heard he was a good one, too."

"I don't doubt it," Lafitte grinned ruefully, rubbing his sore forearm.

"So why didn't he kill you with that stick?"

"He doesn't want to kill me. He can't and get that map. Useless as it is, he thinks it's worth a lot of money. But . . . uh, we didn't debate the issue too long."

"Of course not," You replied with a smile. "But, other than being knocked out, you weren't harmed further, and you still have your gun?"

"Oh yes," Lafitte grinned. "It's a little game we're playing. Like I said, he has to have me alive to get that map. He'll risk a brawl, but I doubt that he'll risk breaking any sizable law; the old man still carries a lot of weight in this parish."

"My friend," You said, dropping the letter opener with a frown, "I do not recommend playing games with Tomas Mejia. He is a bad one."

Lafitte nodded. "I thank you for the advice. But, at this point, anyway, I have to play games. Remember, in a few days I'll be leaving here and Mejia can whistle for the map."

"So? Why don't you leave now?"

"I can't," Lafitte replied, smiling. "My dear wife doesn't know of any of this and I don't want her to, for another reason."

You shrugged and said, "Well, I will certainly not attempt to advise you about your own wife. But a dead enemy . . . well, he is no longer one."

Sam almost dropped his cup, but Lafitte ignored him and replied:

"I've played this game before, in Germany. And, until things change—that is, until Mejia doesn't need me anymore, and as long as I've got the map that won't happen—I don't think I'm in any particular danger. Besides, I have in mind to dispose of the map so that Mejia will know and not be able to get it. For instance, I have to go to New Orleans on business; I can leave it with a bank with instructions that should anything happen to me that it will be left to the State Historical Society."

You leaned back again in his big chair and studied his friend a bit, then smiled and said, "Incidentally, I heard that the bouncer at the Cove finally got his last night."

"Oh?" Lafitte smiled, rubbing his still sore hand.

"Yes," You replied seriously, and with a straight face. "The story I got was that the bouncer, rather a big bully for a number of years, tried to keep some citizen out. The citizen was unknown to the bouncer, though admittedly it was dark, but it seems the bouncer was found behind some bushes, well worked over."

"And, uh, what does 'well worked over' mean?"

"It means, my friend, that he was found with possible fractured vertebrae, a fractured nose that was plastered all over his face, and unconscious, all two hundred and forty-five pounds of him."

"My!" Lafitte said mildly. "He must have been worked over by a professional. (Sam's cup rattled loudly.) But the door was open when I got there."

"I see," You said, smiling broadly and accepting it for what it was, a partial truth, but too polite to inquire further. "But you must admit it was an obvious setup to get you out of the house?"

"Yes," Lafitte nodded, "it was pretty obvious. Someone spotted Jeremy in town, disabled his car, and he called home. I was the likely one to go after him, and I did, and that left no one at home but the old man and the women."

"My friend," You said, "do you know of Mejia's background?"

"Yes, some. My grandfather told me."

"And let me add what I know. Tomas Mejia had more opportunities than most young men, black or white or Puerto

Rican, and he has chosen unwisely. I have heard that he is a Communist, but I do not know this for a fact, but the things he does . . . a good man does not do such things to his country. He is a smuggler of two things that an honest man would not touch"—Lafitte kept a straight face and sipped his coffee —"heroin and hashish. And as his cover he plays high priest of voodoo. Many times when the young and misguided come out in their boats to the swamps, other boats, fresh from the Gulf, join them."

"Has the government tried to stop him?" Lafitte asked.

"I am informed so," You smiled, "though I do not enjoy the confidence of the Coast Guard. I have heard that Uncle has chased his boats several times, but always lost them in the other small boats or in the swamp . . . the swamp is not on the side of the searcher."

"Well," Lafitte said, choosing his words carefully, "I would think that the local smugglers would have put him out of business by now for fear that he might expose . . . uh, all of them."

You chuckled, leaned back, and said, "I will partially answer that question by saying that I've heard that the locals do not engage in murder. And we've been fortunate. The Mafia has no interest in us." He paused a moment to offer a cheroot to both men from a box on the desk. The offer was declined by a shake of heads and You took one and held the big lighter to it. When it was going he said, "Sam, I'm surprised at you, believing in this voodoo trash. You know it is nothing but lies."

"Yes, suh," Sam said, though he obviously didn't agree. "But Sedonia will be the first one to tell ya that I wuz always weak . . . well, I'm still weak."

"Superstition, Sam!" You said.

"Yes, suh," Sam replied, trying to phrase a proper answer. "But I seen it work before . . . and, and it still does."

You gave it up and turned to Lafitte. "Before I forget, should you need me in a hurry, check with the front desk. Even should I be away they can either get a message to me or else guess how long I'll be, and I always check in."

"Thank you," Lafitte said sincerely. "I appreciate that. However, as I told you, I'll play the game a while. I don't think Mejia will do anything for a few days, it should take him a bit to figure something out. Besides, I've got two reasons; one, I don't want my wife to know about this if I can help it, and then there's the fact that more excitement wouldn't be good for the old man."

You nodded and decided to leave it at that. "All right. But remember, should you need my help, and that of several strong men, just call."

Lafitte grinned, nodded, and stood up, and they shook hands warmly. Lafitte turned to Sam and said:

"Come on, old boy, you've got to face Sedonia sooner or later."

Sam swallowed hard and stood up.

Lafitte drove home in silence. Talking to Sam would be a waste of time, he was engulfed in the fear that showed on his set features. Lafitte thought about the map and decided again that he would soon have to rid himself of it. There was always the possibility that one of Mejia's men might not be as smart as his boss, and the controlled violence might get out of hand. Yet he hated to think of actually giving it to the Historical Society. Of course, he could take his wife and leave quickly, but that went against the grain, he just didn't like the idea of running. Besides, now he owed Sam; he got the old man into it, and now he'd get him out. That thought brought up several possibilities, but he didn't have time to mentally explore them all before he reached home. . . .

He pulled the car into the big garage and they went into the house through the kitchen. Sedonia was the only one there to greet them. Her eyes widened as she saw her husband's limp arm and she glanced back to Lafitte and said:

"What happened?"

"Sedonia . . . you may not believe this, but Tomas Mejia put a curse on 'im."

"Oh Lordy!" she said, wringing her hands. "Sam! I told ya about that!"

Sam looked at the floor and mumbled, "I know. But I just cain't help it. I cain't!"

She nodded, her firm jaw set. "All right. Go on to the room. I'll be there directly."

Sam nodded in his shame without looking at either of them and shuffled out of the kitchen. When the door was closed, Lafitte told her briefly of their encounter with Mejia and concluded:

"Now, goddammit, Sedonia, don't you say a word to anybody!"

"Mistah Jean," she replied evenly, "you know me better'n that. Whatcha gonna do?"

"I've, uh . . . got a couple of thoughts in mind, but one thing I'll promise you, Mejia will lift that curse, one way or another. . . . Trust me, old girl. It'll take a few days, week maybe, but I'll get it done."

She stared at him a moment, then said, "I'll not say a word. Besides, I know ma baby kin do it."

He grinned, squeezed her arm, and said, "Good girl. Say, who's home?"

"Only Mistah Jeremy. 'Course Mistah John and his missus, they's upstairs. But the two ladies and the girls, they's in town, shoppin' and lunch."

"Good. That'll help. When you see this shirt in the laundry, do it up nice and put it in a plastic bag, please?"

"I'll do it," she smiled.

"Thank ya, ma'am," he grinned, whacking her on her ample backside.

He went upstairs to his bathroom and stripped off his clothes and examined the side of his head with the aid of the two swinging mirrors on either side of the medicine chest. It was a sizable lump, though it was smaller than it had been, and it was sore, but the cut was small and wouldn't be noticed under his hair. His right hand and forearm were bruised, but serviceable. He shrugged and stepped into the shower.

When he came downstairs the house was quiet in the midday heat. He went into the kitchen to find Sedonia beginning to fix dinner. She grinned and put four big shrimp on a plate for him and handed him a bottle of catsup.

"You want a sanwich?" she asked. "Long time 'till dinner."

"No thanks. Couple more shrimp and a piece of bread'll do me."

She nodded and opened the bread box and took out a heel of French bread, buttered it, and put it on his plate with three more shrimp. He grinned and began eating, suddenly realizing that he was hungry. He finished them quickly and left the table to reach up in the liquor cabinet; he took down a bottle of Scotch and fixed himself a tall, thin drink.

"Hey, by the way," he said, "where's Jeremy?"

"He's been out in the summer house since just before you came home, workin' on a bottle of that there Scotch."

"Yeah? I thought all Southern gentlemen drank bourbon."

"Yes, suh, most do, but he's sorta strange."

Lafitte grinned, said, "Thanks for the shrimp," and wandered outside with his drink.

Jeremy watched him climb the steps of the summer house without moving from his position in the big wicker chair. His feet were on the table, next to the tray. On the tray was a bucket of ice and a three-quarters-full bottle of Scotch. Lafitte grinned easily, pulled up another chair, and put his feet on the table. Jeremy lifted his glass in greeting, took a sip and said wryly:

"Cousin?"

"Jeremy?"

Lafitte sipped his drink and studied his cousin's husband and reprised the previous night in his mind. He started to speak, but he saw a trickle of sweat run down Jeremy's brow and decided to wait. He smiled slightly and took another sip. Jeremy swallowed hard, shot a glance at Lafitte, and then looked away quickly. Finally he could stand it no more and he said:

"Well! Now what?"

"Jeremy, old boy," Lafitte said quietly, "if I had a suspicious nature, I might think you set that up last night."

"Set up what?" Jeremy demanded, taking his feet from the table and sitting erect.

"Well, I've considered the fact that when your car was conveniently disabled, you called me to come pick you up."

"Convenient for whom?" Jeremy said.

"For whoever tried to break in and find that map, that's who . . . or is it whom?"

"Damn you!" Jeremy said, putting his glass on the table with a bang. "I don't have to take that from you!"

"No?" Lafitte inquired calmly, his feet still on the table. "You want to try me again? Maybe this time I'll break your finger right off."

Jeremy took a deep breath, picked up his glass, and leaned back in the chair.

"That's better," Lafitte nodded. "I always think it's better to talk first. Now, listen. . . . It does seem more than a passing coincidence that someone broke into the house last night, obviously looking for the map, and they tried my room . . . and on a night when there were six men present most of the evening. Compound that with the fact that you arranged to get yourself out of the house to see the broad and then 'somebody' cuts your wiring. You have to admit it looks like you set it up."

Jeremy inhaled deeply, the corners of his mouth turned down, started to speak, thought better of it, and poured himself some more Scotch. Lafitte waited silently while Jeremy added a couple of ice cubes, swished them around a couple of times, then took another sip. Finally he nodded and said:

"Cousin, I must admit I look guilty as sin but, so help me God, it wasn't me. You've got to believe that."

"Now why the hell should I do that?" Lafitte inquired calmly.

"Because despite what you may think of me, and my relationship with my wife, I think you'll admit that I love my children and I'm a good father."

Lafitte considered that a moment, then nodded. "All right, I'll concede that."

"Then you must also concede that I wouldn't set a couple of thugs on this place and risk my children getting involved."

"Uh huh. And that's possible," Lafitte agreed.

"Besides," Jeremy added, "I don't think you look on me as a stupid man. And therefore, I wouldn't have to set it up like that."

"So?"

"I mean that the thing was too obvious to have been a frame by me because it would look exactly as it did, that I rigged it for an alibi. I know you never thought I was particularly brilliant, but please give me more credit than that!"

Lafitte stared at Jeremy for some moments and then nodded, much to Jeremy's relief, and said, "All right, Jeremy, I agree." He leaned forward to add a little Scotch to his glass and grinned. "And I'm glad it wasn't you, Jeremy. I wouldn't want to have to kill a cousin."

"You and your jokes," Jeremy said with a grin, glad that he was off the hook.

"Sure," Lafitte said dryly. "By the way, any idea who tore up your car?"

"No . . . except maybe the lady's boyfriend."

"Maybe you're lucky he didn't try you first. Any idea who he is?"

"Oh, no . . . I never inquired, though she may have several."

"And who is she?"

"Come now, Jean. Gentlemen never reveal such things."

"Come on, you phony Creole bastard!" Lafitte's voice was suddenly hard. "I'm on the well-known spot. Somebody tried it last night. Next time they may try me. Now, did it occur to you that she might have been the bait? That if you hadn't called her she might have called you and got you into town? Then she would've had your car disabled and you would've done just what you did, call me and get me out of the house the same time that you were gone."

Jeremy's mouth opened and closed. He had not considered that possibility. Lafitte almost decided to tell him of the incident on the boat and Mejia, but Jeremy decided it for him.

"By the way," Jeremy tried to sound casual. "You didn't give them the map, did you?"

Lafitte's eyes narrowed for a fraction of a second, but he smiled easily and lied, "No, of course not. I went into town this morning and stood by the dock and a black came up to me and asked if I had a map for him and I told him hell no, that it was already on its way to a bank vault in New Orleans. . . . Now, what about the girl who got us both into town at the right time?"

"All right," Jeremy said, his shoulders dropping as though he had just lost all his money. "Her name's Marie Tour. She's the featured dancer at the Cove. . . . My God, if this ever gets out, I'm ruined!"

"How so?"

"Well," Jeremy said, leaning forward and reducing his voice to a confidential whisper, "she's a quadroon."

"Huh!" Lafitte chuckled and shook his head. "You Southerners! Son of a bitch! It's okay to cheat on your wife, shack up, have a mistress, but just think of the scandal if anyone found out she was a quarter colored. . . . Jeremy, your logic escapes me! But your secret's safe. . . . One of the strongest guilds in the world is the husbands' union. I've never known a man to tell another man's wife that her husband was cheating on her. And I won't tell Suzanne."

"I thank you for that," Duroc said sincerely, his head nodding.

"Besides," Lafitte grinned, "like I told you last night, she already knows."

"Yes," Duroc said in a low voice, "that explains the cold reception."

"No doubt," was the dry answer. "Now, two things. When will you ask the girl?"

"Not tonight, you can be sure," Jeremy grinned. "I'd better stay home and be the good husband. . . . What's the other thing?"

"How touching!" Lafitte said sarcastically. "The other thing is your car. Anything other than the cables?"

"No. Just that they were cut. Say, that reminds me. It'll be ready by six. Will you drive me in? The man said five thirty and he closes at six, so . . ."

Lafitte nodded. "We'll be there by six." It was excellent timing, he could look for the girl.

They heard a car crunch along the shells and stop in the garage and the sound of the children laughing as they went toward the house.

"I'd better be a good boy," Duroc grinned, getting to his feet. He put his hand on the tray and said, "Shall I take this?"

"Yes. I'll stay here and finish my drink. Tell Sandy I'll be there in a bit."

Duroc nodded and forced his charming smile, happy to be able to leave. Lafitte watched as the tall man descended the steps and crossed the lawn. He grinned and raised his glass and made the final decision he'd partially made earlier in the day.

"Jeremy, old boy," he said quietly, "I'm going to sell you the Brooklyn Bridge. If you sent the dolls, you'll think your plan worked. If you didn't . . . well, you're still a coward and you're greedy. . . . You'll fit perfectly!"

He drank a grinning toast to cousin Jeremy, finished his drink, and went to find his wife.

As Jeremy got into Lafitte's car at five thirty he grinned and said:

"My! Suzanne's still mad. She even thought I was going to see the girl again. But when I told her you were driving me to the garage to pick up my car she seemed to think that it was all right, as long as I was with you."

"Sure," Lafitte grinned. "See how nice it is to be a good boy?"

"Oh!" Jeremy laughed. "You saints!"

Lafitte drove fast and got Jeremy to the garage just before six. He hadn't wanted to leave his wife alone, though he thought his errand was important. Just to be sure, he got Sedonia alone in the kitchen and asked if she had another gun. She opened the spice cabinet, moved a few cans aside, and showed him a large .45 caliber Colt, ancient, but serviceable, and loaded. He'd smiled, whacked her once on the fanny, and gone outside to meet Jeremy. As Jeremy got out of the car Lafitte said:

"Tell Sandy that I might be a bit later than you. I'm going to stop by and see Dominique You. What time's dinner?"

"Eight. The old man won't be joining us, I hear. It'll just be the four of us."

"All right," Lafitte nodded. "I'll be there."

He drove a bit more leisurely this time and parked his car in the almost empty parking lot of the Cove and went to the big door. It was open. He went into the dimness and made his way to the bar. The place was empty except for a smiling bartender.

"Good evening," the man said cheerily. "What can I get you?"

"Evening," Lafitte said, leaning on the bar. "I thought this was a private club."

"It was," the man replied, "until last night."

"Oh?"

"Yeah. Somebody nearly killed our bouncer, so the manager wisely decided to open the place to the public."

"Doesn't look like it did much good."

"Oh, it'll show later. By ten we should have a good crowd."

"Uh huh." Lafitte took a five-dollar bill from his pocket, folded it once, and stood it on edge in front of the bartender. "I don't really want a drink. I want to talk to Marie Tour. Know where I can find her?"

The bartender grinned and pushed the bill toward Lafitte. "I can't really take your money for that, mister. She's in the back. Dressing room two, right through there."

"Well now," Lafitte grinned. "Thank you. An honest bartender. But keep it. If we're about to be disturbed, let me know. And when I leave, forget it. My wife would understand lots of things, but not this."

The bartender grinned, nodded his thanks, and the bill disappeared. Lafitte went past the bar, behind a large drape and down the hall. He rapped lightly and a woman's voice said, "Come in."

He opened the door wide, scanned the small room quickly, and stepped inside and closed the door. The attractive girl at the dressing table turned and smiled at him with a wondering look and Lafitte nodded politely and looked over the dressing screen, then turned and locked the door.

"Hey!" the girl demanded. "Who are you?"

"Don't get excited. My name is Jean Lafitte. I think you've heard of me."

"Oh!" the girl said in a small voice. Then, quickly recovering her composure, she nodded and indicated the couch. "Yes, I should have known. Monsieur Duroc was so weak. . . . Please, have a seat."

"Thank you."

Lafitte stared for a moment at the couch, which had to be a Salvation Army reject, and sat down carefully, opened his coat, and leaned back and studied the girl as she came to stand in front of him. She was wearing a short dressing gown, and probably nothing more. She was of medium height and moved with the sensual suppleness of a busty woman with a small waist who was perhaps five pounds too heavy.

"Well, Mr. Lafitte, did you come to see for yourself?"

"Something like that. I wanted to see what it would take to make Jeremy Duroc forget his alleged social position."

"Oh, but it was only a passing thing, a . . . what do you call it? An infatuation?"

"On his part," Lafitte agreed. "What about yours?"

"Just fun and games. And maybe a few nice things from time to time. . . . Will you have a drink?"

"No, thank you."

"All right," she shrugged, then added. "Pardon me."

She reached past him and leaned over to get the cigarettes from the table to his right. As she did so the gown came open a bit and he could see one well-rounded breast. She smiled and stood erect and said:

"Do you have a light?"

He nodded and took a book of matches from his pocket, struck one, and held it up to her. She bent over again and this time he could see both breasts. She smiled and stood erect and they disappeared.

"Well." She blew a stream of smoke into the air, smiled and added, "Just how much did you want to see?"

"My!" he grinned again. "That's an interesting offer. But that's not why I'm here."

"Oh?"

"Uh huh. I want to know who put you up to it." His voice now had a flat sound.

"Up to what?" She said it quickly.

"Keeping Jeremy here last night so that his car could be disabled."

"I don't know what you're talking about." Her voice rose an octave.

"Sure."

"Really! He called me! Wanted to come over. He'd been good to me in the past so I said okay . . . that's all."

"Yeah. Then who did you call?"

"Call?"

"Yeah. Who did you call and tell that Duroc was on his way to see you? Someone had to know he was here in order to fix his car like that. I saw the cables. They'd been cut with heavy wire-cutters. Now damn few people go around carrying diagonal cutters like that. Somebody knew!"

"I don't know anything about it," she said quickly. "I called him and he said he'd be right over. When it was time for me to go on I made him leave!"

She started to get mad and then thought better of it, grinned, and went to a small record player on the dressing table and turned it on, then faced him.

"Mr. Lafitte, you don't understand me. I'm only built for pleasure. I don't know anything that goes on outside here . . . or my apartment. I'm a dancer. . . ."

The recording was a slow, sensual drumbeat with a flute accompaniment. The girl began to undulate slowly, and as the beat picked up she began to twirl and then her breasts were free of the gown. She smiled at him and licked her lips and he sat back to enjoy the show. Now she was gyrating wildly and suddenly the gown was on the floor and she was nude. The dance was pure African mixed with the oldest of mating dances, the belly dance. She dropped to her knees and wiggled toward him. As the music stopped, she forced his legs apart and held her breasts up to him.

"Any way you want it," she whispered.

"How 'bout this way," he said coldly, the .38 suddenly pressing on her cheek while his other hand held her by the back of the head.

She froze, her eyes wide with fear.

"You don't seem to understand, young lady," he said mildly. "I want to know who made you do it. Now, who was it?"

He pushed the cold muzzle of the gun a bit for emphasis and she gasped, swallowed a couple of times, her eyes trying to focus on the gun, and then said:

"I . . . I can't. He'll kill me."

Lafitte nodded calmly and said, his voice still quiet, "And I'll kill you if I have to. No one saw me come in and I can get out the same way. One of these pillows will do nicely. . . . Now you're in over your head. I'll give you one chance to get out. As you said, as soon as he finds out he'll kill you. Now tell me."

The girl was on the verge of panic, and as she began to shake Lafitte thought for a moment she was going to faint. But she didn't.

"Tomas Mejia," she whispered. "He told me a few weeks ago to play up to Duroc, that he usually came down on the weekends and always managed to stop in the Cove at least once. He . . . he told me to lay him if I had to. . . . If I didn't, he said my mother wouldn't know me. . . ."

"And he meant it," Lafitte said, pulling the gun back a bit. "Now you know he put you onto Duroc, and in the wrong hands that could get Mejia into big trouble. You know what'll happen . . . he'll kill you anyway when it's over."

Her mouth opened, but she could form no words. Satisfied that she was properly scared, Lafitte added, "No, no, he won't. Tell me what you know and I'll let you get out of town."

"But . . . but I don't know nothin'!" she wailed. "I'd been livin' with Mejia for a few months and he forces me to lay Duroc . . . some big deal he had. But he never told me what. He never! Honest to God he ne——"

As her voice rose, Lafitte put his hand across her mouth and said:

"All right. It'll be all right. Put your robe on."

The frightened girl nodded and got to her feet, picked up the robe and wrapped it around her, suddenly cold. Lafitte put his gun away and stood up and said:

"Pack. Do your first show, maybe the second, but pack and get the hell out of town tonight. If he finds I've been here your life won't be worth a Confederate dollar."

She nodded, swallowing the lump in her throat, and managed to say, "There's a ten o'clock bus."

"Be on it. Otherwise you're going to the law in the morning . . . if you're still alive."

She nodded again and Lafitte left quickly, pausing a moment at the door to check the hall. The bartender was still alone, getting ready for the night's work.

"I've been alone for an hour," he said with a brief smile.

Lafitte was home soon enough not to raise questions and in plenty of time for dinner. The four of them had a pleasant, leisurely meal with Duroc's three girls coming in from the other room from time to time to tell of the scary horror movie they were watching on TV. All except Claudette. She came in once to tell her new "aunt" Sandy that "It's a fake. And a poor one."

As soon as they'd finished dinner Suzanne suggested to Sandy that they go into the other room with their coffee and watch the movie a bit. Sandy nodded and looked at her husband who shook his head and pointed to the brandy bottle, then toward the front porch. Jeremy grinned and went to get the bottle and the women picked up their cups and went to see how Vincent Price collected his residuals.

When they were seated on the porch, feet on the railing and brandy glasses in hand, Lafitte said:

"Jeremy, I have to go to New Orleans tomorrow on business. You have nothing on?"

"No. Why?"

"Will you stay close to the women?"

"Certainly. You think they'll try it again so soon?"

"No, not really, or I wouldn't go at all. But I'd feel better."

"Don't worry, cousin, I've got four females to your one."

"Good. You got that gun?"

"Yes. And the old man's got some locked in the closet in the study. I told him he should have 'em hanging on the wall, but he's old-fashioned, he said guns were for killing and he wanted 'em hidden."

"Good for him," Lafitte nodded. "Keep one handy."

"Will do," Jeremy replied. "Don't worry, I won't let them out of the house. They said they're going shopping maybe the next day again, and they went today, so I don't think they'll want to leave tomorrow. If they do I'll think of something to keep 'em home."

"Fine," Lafitte said, finishing his brandy. "Let's go in."

He'd had the foresight to tell Sandy that afternoon that he had to go to New Orleans the next day, and when he and Jeremy came into the study she was the one to suggest that they go to bed early. He agreed and good nights were said all around; he grinned easily at his cousin and her weak husband and hoped the rest of his plan went as well.

He left early the next morning, before Sandy was awake, after having again cautioned Sedonia to be alert and run for her gun at the slightest suspicion that anyone was around who didn't belong there.

His business went about as he had expected, though it took far longer; he had to make some concessions, but he had planned to make them, and he got a couple of small bonus agreements for his firm so, all in all, he was pleased.

In California or Arizona the transaction would've taken no more than a half hour, forty-five minutes at most. But he was dealing with a Southern gentleman of the leisurely school whose father had done business in that manner, and very successfully. There was a necessary chat about the trip back home, the weather, the cotton, and politics, all over a freshly brewed cup of strong coffee served by the man's secretary. Though he was in a hurry, Lafitte followed the local protocol and waited for his host to get around to business. When they finally did, the man discussed the issues as fast as Lafitte could've hoped for and he was glad that the opening amenities hadn't signaled an all-day session. As they were parting, Lafitte asked if he could use a phone. He was shown to an empty office wtih a phone and a book, and the man shook hands and left.

Lafitte looked up the numbers of several war surplus stores and called three until he found one that carried Geiger counters. He called four coin stores before he found what he wanted. The man proudly said that he had the best collection of coins from 1800 in the state. Lafitte thanked him and looked up the address of a hardware store that was on his way out of town.

The war surplus store had a number of Geiger counters, several used. Lafitte selected an inexpensive one and the man said:

"May I ask what you want it for, suh? We don't get much call for 'em."

Lafitte grinned and said, "Well, I just had my tennis court and my driveway paved and now it seems we've got some leaks in the old water main. Will this find iron?"

"Yes, suh," the man grinned, not believing Lafitte's lie. "If it's within ten feet of the surface."

"Fine," Lafitte nodded. "I'll take it."

At the coin store Lafitte spent ninety-five dollars on some old coins dated from 1797 to 1808; a half dozen pennies, three silver dollars, several Spanish reals, and a few French centimes. All were in poor condition and the dealer said that if the coins had been graded "fine" they would've been worth much more. Lafitte replied that he knew that but the coins were a gift for his young nephew and by the time the boy was grown they would be worth many times their present value. The man hastily agreed and while Lafitte vacillated on the ninety-five dollars the man hurried to add that if any of the coins weren't satisfactory he would redeem them within thirty days for the purchase price. Lafitte agreed and the purchase was made.

At the hardware store he bought two burlap bags, a gallon of muriatic acid, "for his pool," a four-foot square of plastic sheeting, and a shovel.

Once he got off the main highway and was making his way south he drove slowly through several small towns until he found a combination "antique" and junk shop. The first one didn't have what he wanted and he had to drive another ten miles before he found one that did, an ancient iron pot with a lid. He examined it closely, though casually, so as not to run up the price. It had no manufacturer's stamp and was badly rusted, one of its three legs was only a stump.

He shrugged under the watchful eye of the proprietor who had sized him up as a city feller and he went on to pay con-

siderable attention to several old iron grates, a chipped porce-
lain chamber pot (with lid), and a number of iron trivets. Finally they got down to bargaining. Lafitte explained that he
was looking for a gift for his wife, something old to put in
the garden, next to the big windows where it could be seen
from inside. He worked the man down fifty percent on the
chamber pot, decided it was too much, and said that he
might go for the iron pot, if it wasn't too expensive. They
started at twenty-five dollars and Lafitte walked out at seven-
teen fifty, stopped, turned and said:

"Fifteen dollars, no more."

The man nodded and another great American deal was
consummated. The buyer had what he wanted at a price he
was willing to pay and the seller was overjoyed, he'd paid
fifty cents for it as junk.

At the next quiet bayou Lafitte pulled off the road and
rolled up his sleeves and took the two sacks and the gallon of
acid down to the water. He found a stick and thrashed the
water and then, satisfied that he was alone, he immersed the
bags, pulled them out onto the bank, and poured some acid
on them. As the yellow liquid smoked its way out of the bottle and onto the burlap he was careful to avoid the fumes. He
let the acid work a few moments and then soaked his bags
again and nodded. Where the acid had eaten into the rough
fabric it looked like the burlap had rotted. He did a few more
spots, soaked his bags again, and when he was satisfied that
they looked properly old, he pulled them through the water
for a minute or so to make sure the acid was all gone and
then squeezed the bags damp dry. He dumped the acid on the
ground and tossed the container behind a bush. The bags
were dragged through the mud of the riverbank to make sure
they looked old and properly dirty. Then he tested one by
pulling at the fabric and was able to easily tear a hole in the
now ancient bag.

At the car he wiped the bags on the pot to add some rust
and then he took some of the coins and rubbed them on the
bags to make them dirty and put them in the bottom corners
of each bag. He studied his work a moment, then tore a large
hole in each one as though the original cache had spilled. As
he laid them in the plastic and covered them he allowed himself a wide grin.

*   *   *

When he got to the family bridge he slowed to make sure that there were no cars in either direction and then he crossed the ancient structure and turned right, taking the dirt road that ran in a loop to the south, toward the swamp. It was late afternoon and the last rays of the sun were on the treetops; beneath them it was rapidly getting dark. He drove very slowly, looking for the spot. The road was close to the edge of the swamp and now he could see the giant oak. He stopped the car and took the contents of his trunk and slowly and carefully made his way to the tree, being careful to watch for snakes. On one side of the tree was dry land, on the other side it was dry for no more than three feet and then the water began. He stopped and said to the oak:

"Perfect! This must be the big X on the map. Any kid knows that pirates buried their treasure at the base of a giant tree that could be seen from the ship!"

He grinned at his big plan and set about adding the last of the bait. He took off his coat and shoes and socks, rolled up his pants, and reached for the shovel. With but a few minutes of light left he worked quickly as he stood in the soft sand and scooped out a hole a good four feet deep. A few of the remaining coins were put in the pot, and it was half filled with sand, and the pot was put in the bottom of the hole, not quite upside down. The hole was filled and the excess sand was pitched out into the small backwater of the swamp. Then he brought the counter to the water for a test. There was no sound as he waved it around the other side of the tree, but when it was over the pot it pinged most satisfactorily and the needle jumped. He grinned and held up the counter and used the shovel to smooth his tracks as he backed away from the tree.

His timing was good. Sedonia met him at the back door and said:

"They's all in for their first drink."

"They?"

"Yeah. Mistah John and the madam are down for dinner tonight, and Dr. Glover and his wife."

"Sandy?"

"She's in there with 'em, and the Durocs."

"Good. I'll shower and change and be right down. Tell Sandy I'm here, will you please?"

"Yes, suh. And wear your dinner jacket."

Lafitte nodded. "How's Sam?"

"Jest the same," she said with a shake of her head. "And he ain't much use."

"Okay. Fifteen minutes."

When he joined them they were on their third drink, so Jeremy fixed him a double. Lafitte kissed his wife on the cheek, nodded to everyone, and Sandy said:

"How'd it go, love?"

"Fine. The deal's all set. I'm well pleased."

"Didn't give the store away, did ya?" the old man said from across the room.

"No, sir." Lafitte grinned. "I remembered what my grandfather told me about business."

"Horse puckey!" the old man roared and his wife blushed. "If you had, you'd be a millionaire by now!"

Lafitte nodded pleasantly and Sedonia announced dinner.

The old man was quiet during the meal and Sandy whispered that the doctor was there to examine Mr. Lafitte because he'd had a minor setback earlier in the day. The diners were relatively quiet and the meal went quickly. As soon as they'd finished, the doctor got to his feet and said to Sedonia, who was already clearing the table:

"We'll have our coffee upstairs. And thank you. Your dinner was excellent, as usual."

"Thank you, suh," she replied with an almost shy smile, flattered that the doctor would compliment her.

"And to show you that I mean it," the doctor said with a wink at the old man, "as soon as I poke at my patient a bit to substantiate my exorbitant fee we're going home, but I've been invited back tomorrow, ostensibly to talk business, but it's really so I can enjoy your excellent cooking again."

"Ha!" the old man said. "The business we got is so small the profit won't hardly pay for the gas to run that big Lincoln out here again, so maybe he's right, Sedonia, it has to be your cooking."

Sedonia grinned again; they were joshing her, but she liked it.

The old man winked at her, took out a cigar, and allowed the doctor to wheel him to the lift. The ladies got to their feet, following the lead of their hostess to have more coffee

in the living room. Lafitte winked at his wife and he and
Duroc stood up, smiled, nodded, and Jeremy took two
cheroots from his pocket and gave one to Lafitte. When
they'd gone, the doctor and his patient were out of sight, and
Sedonia had returned to the kitchen, Lafitte said:

"Good. I've got to talk to you."

"And I to you." Duroc would've said more, but Sedonia
quickly appeared with a tray.

She put the tray on the table, poured coffee for the two
men from the carafe, and picked up the tray with its four
tiny cups and headed for the ladies. When she closed the
door behind her, Lafitte said:

"You go first."

"She's gone!" Jeremy said, as though he didn't believe his
own statement.

"Who's gone?" Lafitte sipped his coffee, knowing the answer.

"Marie! I called her and she's gone. Her landlady said she
left with her rent paid up for almost a month. She offered to
show me her apartment. I called the Cove and they said
she'd quit, drew her pay and left . . . before the second show!
It looks like you were right."

"Jeremy, you're a genius!" Lafitte grinned derisively over
the rim of his cup. "Well, that's the end of that. But you
probably couldn't 've gone much farther with her without Suzanne being on your back."

Duroc grinned philosophically, shrugged, then grew
serious. "True. Oh, uh, what was it you wanted to tell me?"

"Well," Lafitte said in a tone that he hoped sounded properly serious, "when I was in New Orleans today I bought
some things to prove that the map was a fake . . . a Geiger
counter and a shovel. I wanted to prove that the whole damn
thing was a figment of the old man's diabolical imagination,
so that whoever wanted the map would leave me alone. . . ."

Lafitte let his voice trail off and it had the desired effect.
Duroc's dark eyes flashed a moment, then the lids drooped
and he leaned forward and said in a low voice:

"Well?"

"Well, I have to tell someone." Lafitte also leaned forward
so that he could whisper. "I just can't keep it a secret. . . . I
found some old coins, not worth much, mind you, but they're
all dated before 1810."

"No!" Duroc could hardly keep his voice down. He glanced at the closed door to the living room and then said, obviously forcing himself to be casual, "Where did you find them? Did you check all the X's on the map?"

"Jeremy!" Lafitte's voice was properly reproachful.

"Well," Duroc admitted, "that night when the old man gave you the map I couldn't help but see those marks. And I knew they weren't there before . . . did you?"

"No," Lafitte said, taking a slow sip of coffee. "I checked only one. And I didn't have time to check that one properly. The counter gave off a bleep and I began digging at the water's edge. Pretty soon I came to two old sacks and I pulled them out of the sand. They were almost rotted through and I guess most of the contents have long since sunk into the sand . . . but I got a few coins."

"Yes? Then what?"

"Well, it was getting dark, and I didn't want to be too late, so I covered the hole again and my tracks . . . I didn't want anybody to accidentally stumble on it after all these years. . . . But the counter was still making noises, must be a box or something down deeper."

Duroc's eyes were sparkling now and he made an effort to control his breathing. Lafitte decided it was time to slacken the line a bit.

"But it may not be much," he said, trying to make the remark sound casual. "They're just a few old coins. A couple of dollars from the period and a few pennies and a couple look like Spanish dollars. I don't know old coins . . . but they can't be worth much. There was no gold. . . . I just thought you might be interested."

Lafitte leaned back and sipped his coffee and waited to see if he had properly set the hook. He had.

"But, cousin!" Duroc could barely contain himself now. "The fact that there was no gold indicates that it probably is a Lafitte cache!"

Lafitte silently agreed that Jeremy was absolutely right. Aloud, he said, "How so?"

"Most of the old pirate stories about buried gold might apply to Henry Morgan and some of the older pirates, but not the brothers Lafitte. Most of their . . . uh, conquests were on local shipping out of New Orleans. Most historians agree that the money taken from the brothers when the United

States government raided Barataria was local U.S. money. Dollars, pennies, and surely reals, because that was a common coin of the time. But gold? Maybe. Some, yes. But, being heavier, it would've most likely sunken deeper. But, on the other hand, some historians say that Jean Lafitte got away with millions. And there's no evidence that he ever spent that much."

"No!" Lafitte hoped his reaction showed a mild shock. "What d'ya know? Maybe I've really got something." Lafitte stared at the ceiling in a mild wonder, then shook his head. "No, Jeremy . . . certainly not millions. Something less, perhaps. But no, I'm just not the type to believe in pirate treasure."

"But you don't understand," Duroc said, leaning forward. Then he forced himself to close his mouth, finish his coffee, and say calmly, "May I see them?"

"Sure," Lafitte agreed. "They're in the trunk of the car."

Duroc got to his feet, grabbed a bottle of brandy and two glasses from the sideboard, and said, "Come on. The ladies won't miss us for a while. If they do they'll just think we went outside for some air."

Lafitte nodded and stood up. "We'll need a flashlight."

"In my car."

They went outside quietly and Duroc got his flashlight while Lafitte put the bottle and glasses on the porch table. They met at Lafitte's car and he unlocked the trunk, lifted the plastic, and stood back. Duroc flashed his light on the tattered, damp bags and lifted one and the coins fell out. Breathing quickly and shallowly he examined each coin carefully, feeling the worn edges and checking the dates on each. Then he reached for the other bag and repeated the process.

"May I take a couple inside?" He said it in a whisper.

"Sure," Lafitte said nonchalantly, and silently wondered at the greed that had closed Duroc's eye.

Lafitte closed the trunk and they returned to the dining room and Duroc examined each coin again. Sedonia came through the room carrying a pot of coffee and headed for the living room. Duroc quickly put his arm over the coins and grinned lamely. Sedonia smiled at the two men and continued on her way, closing the living room door behind her. Lafitte held out his hand and Duroc reluctantly returned them. Lafitte casually put them in his pocket, inclined his head toward the front of the house, and they went outside to the veranda. When they were comfortably seated with their brandies Lafitte said:

"Maybe you're right. There must be more. No one would've put just a few in such big sacks. Most of the coins must've sunk deeper into the sand. . . . Well, I guess it's obvious, now that I mention it. Otherwise, the counter wouldn't have kept on bleeping. . . ."

Lafitte stopped talking and sipped his brandy and tried to see Jeremy's face, but it was too dark, even though there was a light coming from the living room where they could hear the ladies chatting. Now he decided to reel in the line.

"Of course, now I've got a problem."

"Oh?" Jeremy said casually. "How so?"

"Well," Lafitte replied, settling back to try his salesmanship, "I wanted to prove that the map was worthless so that they wouldn't try again. Now, it's more trouble. The old man said it was valuable, but I didn't believe him. And, on top of that, I don't really want it. . . . Oh, not that I don't want money, mind you, I just don't want the hassle. I don't live here, and to get it out properly and avoid the taxes would take a bit of doing. Besides, I wouldn't want to take time off from my job for it . . . which I can't afford . . . or try to explain why I'm spending so much time down here. No, I'm just not that much of a gambler."

Lafitte sipped his brandy again and the fish jumped into the boat.

"I'll take it off your hands," Jeremy's voice sounded strained.

"Yeah, sure," Lafitte put a bit of derision into his voice. "I know you. You're just trying to sucker me into it. Well, no thanks. I can sit on it for a while. Maybe I can form a syndicate when I get back . . . lots of guys would put a few bucks into a thing like this . . . and it seems I've got the old man's blessing, otherwise he wouldn't've given it to me. But whatever, we're leaving in a few days and I think I'll leave it at that."

Ten feet away the drapes in the living room were pulled by the madam and they saw her open the French windows for the air and step back. The women's voices were louder, but no one looked out. By the increased light Lafitte saw Jeremy twirl his glass thoughtfully and say:

"I'll give you ten thousand dollars, tax free."

"Up your ass!" Lafitte replied without rancor. "If there's anything there it's worth a half a million bucks!"

Lafitte mentioned the figure half jokingly, just to get Jeremy's reaction, but the one he got, tacit agreement, was absolutely amazing.

"Possibly," Jeremy said seriously. "But by the time you get it out after exploring all those marks on the map, and the old man and the madam get a hunk of it . . . and if the map's not stolen first, and if you manage to fence it, or sell it some way, you'll be damn lucky to come out with a twentieth and I'll give you just that, twenty-five thousand cash."

Lafitte took a quick sip of his drink to hide his face and said, "Cash?"

"In traveler's checks. Small denominations you can dump over the years. Or in hundred-dollar bills. Tax-free."

"Can you?"

"Certainly," Jeremy said confidently. "The business is easily good for that. If she finds out it'll just be something more for her to gripe about."

"No, no it's not enough," Lafitte replied, negotiating again. "Besides, there could be nothing there, and I'd feel bad. It could be a fake. The old man could've salted it, for that matter, just another of his big jokes."

"Come on!" Jeremy had a chiding note in his voice. "I don't think the old boy would've done that. Not now, not in the shape he's in, and when he knows he's about to meet his maker."

"No, Jeremy. I think I'll wait till I get back to the city."

"Oh? And to whom would you sell it?"

"Maybe I'd form a syndicate."

"I don't think you can!" Jeremy tried to sound somewhat indignant.

"Why not?" Lafitte was enjoying himself now, baiting Jeremy and trying to see how big a fool Jeremy would make of himself. "I've got the map. I'm the last of the Lafittes. Even the local paper supports me."

"But it might take you years to get enough backing, or even meet my offer."

"Maybe." Lafitte shrugged. "But the more I think of it the more I think the old bastard was telling the truth. Remember his stake? He always said he'd pirated the money."

"No." Jeremy shook his head. "I don't think he ever used any of it. I think he saved it until it was too late."

"Okay." Lafitte nodded. He'd hoped that Jeremy would reach that conclusion. "Then he left it to me . . . 'cause he doesn't like you or Suzanne."

Lafitte reached for the bottle and refilled each brandy glass and leaned back to let Jeremy sweat a bit. Jeremy, a poor businessman, less of a negotiator, didn't wait long.

"All right. I'll make you one more offer. Fifty thousand dollars, in cash, in small bills. The banker may wonder, but he won't be able to talk. I'll get the money and we can do it in the bank's conference room. What say?"

Lafitte gritted his teeth to keep his face impassive and stared into the night for a moment. He was dumbfounded at Jeremy's offer. He would've taken the ten thousand and was just trying to run the offer to twenty. My God, he thought, what a greedy, gullible ass Jeremy is! Lafitte wasn't at all sure that Jeremy could produce but he wasn't about to let the opportunity slip by, as wild as it seemed. Besides, now he had to see if Jeremy would actually pay.

"No," he said, speaking the word carefully, "it'll cost you seventy-five grand. That way I can pay the income tax on it . . . no matter how you charge it off I'll chalk it up to gambling winnings . . . and still have fifty grand tax-free."

"Done!" Jeremy said, getting up to shake Lafitte's hand. Then Lafitte learned why Jeremy would pay such a sum. "And she won't have anything to say about it."

So that was it. Jeremy would risk all the money he could steal from the family business to be rid of Suzanne's nagging influence. Lafitte shrugged in the dim light and was glad that he'd never had such problems but merely said:

"Okay. But . . . uh, we'd better not do it until later. I don't think we should march into that little bank and transact such a deal while the place is full of people. Can you set it up for, say . . . five o'clock?"

"Yes," Jeremy replied. "But why?"

"Well, you can't go digging until after dark, anyway. If your kids, or your wife, or any of the family found out, it wouldn't be long until everybody in town knew you were digging for treasure. That would bring two groups, neither of which you'd want . . . Uncle Sam and maybe the same guys who tried to steal the map."

Jeremy considered this bit of advice for a moment, then nodded. "You're absolutely right. Patience. But I've had years of that."

Lafitte nodded and picked up the bottle to go in the house. Then he decided that he was angry, somehow he'd been too kind.

The next day was hot, windless, and leisurely . . . for Lafitte. For Duroc it was probably one of the longest days of his life. They spent most of the day around the pool, sunning, swimming, playing with the children in the water and drinking with their wives. They had a late lunch served by Sedonia at poolside and afterward they pulled the chaises longues to the shade and had siestas while the children continued at the same frantic pace.

About three Lafitte awoke to the sound of tires on the shells and went to the side of the house to see Dr. Glover get out of his car and carry his black bag to the front porch. Lafitte smiled and waved as the doctor nodded to him. He'd determined to stall Jeremy on going into town if the doctor hadn't arrived by the time he and Jeremy were ready to leave for the bank, and he was happy to see that Glover was early. The doctor stood on the top step and watched Lafitte very carefully cross the shells in his bare feet. When Lafitte joined him in the shade to shake hands, the doctor smiled and stared down at Lafitte's lumpy ankle and slightly atrophied calf.

"From the looks of the scars," the doctor said in a professionally flat tone, "you seem to have recovered well. It ever bother you?"

"Only when I laugh," Lafitte replied with an easy grin. "You inquiring as a doctor, or for a client?"

"Yes," Glover nodded, then smiled. "John Christian asked me to inquire."

Sedonia appeared at the screen door, bobbed her head, and said, "Mistah John's still nappin'. Go by the pool and ah'll bring you a drink."

Dr. Glover nodded. "A bourbon, with lots of water, please."

"Yes, suh."

They descended the steps and Glover smiled as Lafitte

minced his way quickly across the shells again until he was on the grass. Lafitte grinned and said:

"You will stay for supper, won't you, Doctor?"

"Oh yes. I meant what I said about Sedonia's cooking."

"Good. I'd like to talk to you about the old man later."

"We can do it now, if you like."

"No. The group's awake." He pointed to his wife and the Durocs, who were waving at them. The doctor waved back. "I'd rather do it after dinner. . . . I have to go into town first. You'll wait for me?"

"All right. I'll be here until nine or so," the doctor replied.

"Thank you." Lafitte smiled and indicated with a wave of his arm that they should join the group.

Sedonia appeared with the doctor's drink and the amenities of the afternoon were exchanged. Lafitte decided that maybe it would be a good idea if he and Jeremy had an excuse to suddenly go into town, so he quietly backed out of the conversation and went into the house and called Dominique You. When the burly Frenchman answered, Lafitte said in a joking tone:

"This is the pirate."

"Mon ami! How are you? Any more visitors?"

"Only friendly ones."

"Bon. What can I do for you?"

"I thought you'd call me about four to come into town, and bring Jeremy with me, so we could have a drink and explore the possibilities of shipping some seafood from Grand Isle by truck rather than the slower way of keeping them on the boats and beating their way up the passage."

Dominique You was not a slow man. *"Certainement, mon ami!* You want an excuse to come into town."

"I certainly do," Lafitte replied. "And we'd really like to stop by for a drink."

"Better yet. Meet me at the Cove at five, if that's a good time?"

"How about five thirty?"

"Fine. They have a new policy at the Cove for the cocktail hour. I'm sure you'll enjoy the service."

"The service?"

"Yes. They have some new girls. I'm sure you'll enjoy it."

"Good." Lafitte grinned. "Call me at four or so, will you?"

"It will be my pleasure."

"Thank you."

When he returned to the pool the children were grouped around Sandy. She looked up at her husband and he smiled and said:

"What's the big attraction?"

"Honey, I hope you don't mind. We've agreed to take the girls to the show in town, there's a new Disney film. It starts at four."

"No, of course not." Lafitte grinned at the three girls, much to their relief. "Jeremy and I will lie around and listen to the magnolias drop."

"Good." Sandy got up and kissed her husband on the cheek. "We'll be back by seven thirty or eight. In time for the girls to have a snack and go to bed and then we big kids can have a leisurely dinner."

Lafitte grinned good-naturedly at this small stroke of fortune and didn't particularly begrudge his efforts in setting up a meeting with Dominique. Besides, after their business it would be nice to have a drink or two. He turned to wink at Jeremy, and the big man grinned and relaxed.

The meeting at the bank went properly, efficiently smooth. By prior arrangement, the map was left hidden. Jeremy trusted Lafitte to give his word "as a gentleman."

"As a gentleman?" Lafitte had asked with a wry smile. "I'm flattered. And yes, I'll give you the map when we get home."

While the local banker might have wondered at such an enormous transaction on such short notice, he was not going to insult the grandson of one of his most important clients and question the transfer of cash, even seventy-five thousand dollars, from the well-known and respected Mr. Jeremy Duroc to the old man's obvious heir. He merely told himself that it was some family matter and besides, the business of which Mr. Duroc was the president had more than enough cash to cover such a transaction and it was certainly not a good banker who would be so indiscreet as to inquire.

Lafitte carefully counted the traveler's checks—there were twenty-five—signed them once, and Duroc signed his papers and the transaction was done. The manager saw them to the door of the already closed bank, making sure he vigorously shook hands with both men. They slipped out the door and

Lafitte paused to look up and down the street, but none of the few people even gave them a glance.

"Well," Lafitte said, feeling like some sort of an embezzler, even though he had decided to declare it as income, "we shouldn't keep Dominique waiting."

"No, of course not," Jeremy agreed.

The parking lot was packed, though it was not yet dark. There was a polite attendant to take their car and there was a tall, husky doorman in a dark suit to hold the door for them. Lafitte and Duroc exchanged wondering glances and Duroc said:

"Dr. Glover told me last night he'd heard the place changed hands suddenly. Looks like they're after the carriage trade."

Lafitte glanced at the many big cars in the parking lot and nodded. "How come so suddenly?"

"The story I got was that the former owner had been on the verge of selling for some time. Then, the other night, his bouncer was almost killed in some sort of a fight out here on the lot with a bunch of rowdies and then Marie left . . . well, Dominique was there with the money."

"Oh?" Lafitte said wonderingly, keeping a smile back about the story of the "bunch" who'd beaten the bouncer, "I didn't know Dominique was the new owner."

"Oh yes, he's a man of many talents. I understand he's a wealthy importer, retired."

Lafitte smiled and they entered the foyer. There was no guard in evidence, though Lafitte knew the suave man outside the door could well be one. Things were handled much more smoothly this time. There was a newly installed reservation desk and a new velvet rope barring the way to the main dining room. Behind the desk, dressed in a tux, was the former clerk at the inn. Next to him, also wearing a tux, and holding some huge menus, was a burly man Lafitte had not seen before. His brows were heavy with scar tissue and his nose had a slight list to port, indicating that he had not always been a "host." Lafitte smiled; this was a much more genteel way to display a bouncer. The clerk looked up and smiled.

"Ah, Mr. Lafitte," he said. "Mr. You is expecting you."

"Thank you." Lafitte returned the smile, then nodded to the "host," as they followed the monster to a ringside table. It

was quite dim and they were almost to the table before Lafitte could recognize the Frenchman. You got to his feet, a
wide grin on his swarthy face, and shook hands with his two
guests and indicated chairs.

"My!" Lafitte observed, "you, uh . . . move rather fast."

"Yes," You replied, holding up his hand for service, "we
had been negotiating for some time. Then the unfortunate af-
fair of the bouncer tipped the former owner in my favor. I
certainly wish I knew who had challenged the man. His tab
would be on the house for as long as I own this place."

He winked slightly at Lafitte and Lafitte grinned.

"Gentlemen, what'll you have?" You said as the waitress
appeared at the table.

Lafitte couldn't help but stare a moment. The beautiful girl
was wearing what looked like a hip-length, diaphanous night-
ie, a mini G-string, which partly disappeared from time to
time, and nothing more, discounting, of course, the high
heels. She smiled and leaned over to put a fresh ashtray on
the table and Jeremy almost knocked it to the floor, staring at
her large, wiggling breasts. Lafitte chuckled and said:

"A tall Scotch and water."

Jeremy nodded and managed to croak, "The same."

"Well now," Lafitte said as the girl disappeared. "Where
did you get that innocent little child?"

"She's hardly that," You observed dryly, "but I imported
her, and six more, from New Orleans yesterday."

"I bet that cost a pretty penny," Jeremy said.

"Yes," You replied, "and even more for our two featured
dancers. But it appears that I've struck gold. . . . (Jeremy
coughed.) We're booked solid for two weeks already."

"How did that happen so quickly?" Lafitte asked.

"Hoping that I would finally be able to buy the place, I
had some brochures made up several weeks ago. Then I sent
a batch out by special delivery, as soon as I knew I'd made
the buy, to every businessman I knew who I thought would
be interested . . . from Houma to Grand Isle, and a bunch in
New Orleans . . . extolling the advantages of a charter membership in the finest club in the bayous and explaining how
almost everything could be written off as a business expense."

"I didn't get one," Jeremy complained.

"Ah, but I wouldn't send such a document to a man's

home, or even to where I knew he was visiting. There's one waiting at your office."

"My compliments, sir," Jeremy grinned. "I should have known."

Then the waitress appeared again and Jeremy's smile changed to a leer as he stared at her. She smiled, the false smile of women who make their living without their clothes, and served the drinks, nodded at You, and disappeared in the dark. The men raised their glasses and You said:

"To the bouncer's downfall. And to the unknown winner. Should he ever need a favor . . ."

Lafitte nodded once over the rim of his glass and the stage lights went up and there was the sound of two Arabian drums. Then the lights went out except for a blue spot. A supple, well-built girl in a transparent harem costume appeared and began to slowly undulate to one of the world's oldest introductions to procreation. Lafitte had seen exotic dancers before but none as sensuously adept as this one. As the drumbeat quickened, she twirled faster and faster and the costume dropped to the floor until she was wearing nothing but a provocative smile and the jewel in her navel.

It was an enjoyable evening and the three gentlemen chatted on current affairs and drank and enjoyed the dancers, particularly Jeremy. Lafitte was still amazed and he smiled into his glass when he realized that the money had actually been paid to him, and the more he thought about it the more he became convinced that the old man had found a way to . . .

"Another drink, *mon ami?*" You asked.

Lafitte grinned and held up his almost empty glass.

It was such an enjoyable time that the hours went quickly and Lafitte did something he almost never did, he stayed longer and drank more than he'd planned. It was eight thirty before they thanked their host and reluctantly left. Jeremy, though not obviously drunk, hadn't held his liquor as well as Lafitte, so Lafitte drove Duroc's big status symbol home.

Part Four

As Lafitte turned the Cadillac onto the driveway he pointed to the big house. A light was on in every room.

"Hey!" Duroc said, "we having another party?"

Lafitte shook his head and frowned; something was wrong. He pulled the car to a sliding stop on the shells and the two men jumped out and ran up the steps. They could hear Sedonia wailing from upstairs and then Suzanne shouted:

"Oh, for heaven's sake, Sedonia, shut up!"

"Suzanne?" Duroc shouted as he fumbled for his key. He got the big door open and they started for the stairs. With his good legs Duroc made the steps two at a time as his wife called to him:

"Up here."

When Lafitte reached the second floor he saw Suzanne facing her husband, flanked by her two younger children. Suzanne's face was pale and the children were wide-eyed with a fear they didn't quite understand. Sedonia was standing in the doorway of the old man's room, her fat body quivering with each sob.

"What happened?" Jeremy asked.

Suzanne was barely in control of herself and kept biting her lip. She blinked at the loudness of her husband's voice and then replied, "Claudette . . . Claudette and Sandy. They've . . . they've been kidnapped."

Lafitte was suddenly cold, and his mouth was dry. His first

thought was of anger and disgust toward himself. He'd been playing pirates for big kids and the money had made him careless. He clenched his teeth and took a couple of deep, controlling breaths while Jeremy said to his wife:

"Now, dear, you must be mistaken. I'm sure it'll be all right if we . . ."

"Shut up, Jeremy!" Lafitte commanded in a cold voice as his common sense returned. To Suzanne he said gently, "How long?"

Jeremy's mouth opened and closed, he blinked, then went to his wife, but she turned aside to look at Lafitte. Jeremy, embarrassed at the rebuke, went past Sedonia to the bedroom.

"They're gone!" Suzanne's voice had a wondering note in it. She was on the verge of hysteria. "My Claudette's been taken and . . . and Sandy . . ."

"Quit it!" Lafitte said sharply, gripping her shoulder hard.

She stared at her cousin for a moment, then her eyes cleared. She hugged her frightened girls closer to her and she nodded. "Ten minutes maybe."

He nodded, his mind racing. If it'd been that long, and they'd met no one on the road, that meant that they'd left by the swamp, or the bay. Either way they were long gone, the chances of catching them now were remote. But then, he thought, maybe they'd left by the road and had pulled off when they saw the lights of another car. But no, that wasn't too probable. He shook his head once and decided he'd have to hear it all. A small wave of nausea started in his stomach when he thought how big that bay was, but he shook it off, took another big breath, and said to his cousin, "Go on."

"We were . . . we were about to put the girls to bed and we heard a shot and we ran upstairs and they were gone . . . and Grandfather's had a stroke. He's just lying there, staring at the wall. . . . Oh Jean, I'm afraid he's dying. . . ."

Lafitte nodded and stooped down to put a hand on the shoulder of each child. "Girls, it's time for you to be very brave and take care of your mother. Take her down to the living room and put her on the couch and one of you get her a glass of water . . . all right? I'll be down in a minute."

The two little girls nodded seriously and the older one took her mother's hand and said, "Come, Mommy."

As they took her down the stairs Lafitte went to his grandfather's bedroom and looked over Sedonia's shoulder. The old man was in bed, his wife and Dr. Glover at each side, Sam in one corner and Jeremy at the foot of the bed. The room was torn up, the drapes half off their rods. He quickly decided that they would wait a moment and he whispered to Sedonia, "Run down and get me a big glass of milk. Quick!"

She nodded and turned from the door without protest, happy to have someone tell her what to do. Lafitte went next door to his own room and, though he'd expected it, he drew his breath in sharply. The room was a shambles. The bed had been torn apart, the chairs were overturned, the rug had been kicked to one side and the contents of their suitcases were scattered. The closet doors were open, but their clothes were only partly disarrayed, as from a quick search of pockets. He went into the bathroom, slid open the mirror, and checked for the tracing. It was still there. Then he shucked his coat, pulled off his tie, and leaned over the toilet and stuck his finger down his throat. When he was through he rinsed his mouth with water, brushed his teeth quickly, and doused his head and face with cold water. He was drying his head with a towel when Sedonia rushed in with the glass of milk. He drank it quickly, returned the glass, and sighed.

"Thank you," he said. "This is no time to be even half drunk."

"Yes, suh," she replied with an approving bob of her head. "You heaved, didn't ya? Most men would take another drink."

"Well, listen, fat girl," he said, allowing his Southern accent to return for a moment, "you may have seen me do lots of laughin' and scratchin' the last few days, but that's only show . . . ah ain't most men."

"No, suh," she agreed. "You surely ain't."

She followed him to his grandfather's room and he stood in the doorway again while his eyes took in the room. The old man was propped on his pillows, very pale, hardly breathing, his eyes staring blankly. His wife was sitting on the floor by the bed, holding his limp hand. Dr. Glover, at the other side of the bed, looked up as Lafitte entered and shook his head. Lafitte nodded once and his narrowed eyes moved on. Jeremy was by the windows, Sam still standing in the corner, his eyes wide with fear. The madam turned her head toward him and said in her dainty voice, as though it made things all right:

"Dr. Glover is here."

"Yes," Lafitte nodded and turned to Sedonia, who was sobbing again, and said in a low, firm voice, "Sedonia, goddammit, this is no time for my mammy to go to pieces. Now get hold of yourself and tell me what happened."

She dried her eyes on her apron and whispered, "Miz Suzanne, she knows it better, we wuz in the kitchen."

"All right," he replied, patting her shoulder. "I'll talk to her."

"Did you see this?" Jeremy said.

Lafitte turned to see him pointing at the windows. The drapes were badly torn and there were several strips missing, obviously cut with a knife.

Lafitte shivered involuntarily and his anguish started to rise again, but he gritted his teeth and forced himself to be calm and handle it rationally. He took out a cigarette and lit it, took a long drag, and looked around the room again. It had been thoroughly ransacked; the pictures had been pulled from the walls, the rugs were in heaps; Lafitte frowned and turned toward the bed as the madam said:

"The bed had been overturned and the mattress was slashed. We found him on the floor. . . . When we heard the shot we ran up but the door was locked. . . . Oh, for one terrible moment I thought Mistah John Christian had done away with himself. By the time I could fly to my room and get a key and come back . . . well, he was on the floor, the gun in the corner and they . . . they were gone."

Lafitte nodded, stared at his barely breathing grandfather for a moment, then wandered around the room again, looking for something, but he didn't know what. Duroc stretched out a portion of the drapes and Lafitte nodded that he knew that a part had been used for bonds. He turned to go down stairs and Sam stepped forward, holding his dangling arm, and spoke for the first time:

"Mistah Jean, I did find something . . . in your room."

Lafitte nodded and followed the old man out the door. As they entered his bedroom Sam said:

"It ain't here, Mistah Jean, it's out on the veranda."

Lafitte shrugged and followed the old man through the open doors where Sam pointed to the heavy wooden railing.

There were two sets of double gouge marks on the inside of the railing, clearly visible by the light from the bedroom. Sam pointed down the porch, toward the old man's bedroom and held up two fingers. Lafitte went to examine them, looked over the railing at the heavy, two-by-four trellis, and nodded.

"Grappling hooks," Lafitte said, dropping his cigarette into a big iron tray.

"Yes, suh. That's what I figgered."

Lafitte turned and went into his grandfather's room through the open French windows and nodded to Duroc. Jeremy followed him out of the room and down the steps.

"Jeremy," Lafitte said in a low voice, "if they want that map, the deal's off. They can have it."

To his credit Jeremy quickly replied, "Of course. I had already considered that. There's no question."

"Good." Lafitte nodded and went to the living room to talk to Suzanne. She was sitting on the couch, flanked by her girls. Duroc stopped Lafitte at the door with a hand on his arm.

"I'll take the girls into the kitchen for a snack or something," Duroc said. "That way you can get a better story out of her."

Lafitte raised an eyebrow at Duroc's idea and said, "Fine."

"Come with me, girls," Duroc said to his children.

They got dutifully to their feet and went to their father, and he took each girl's hand and headed for the kitchen. When they were gone Lafitte sat by his cousin and offered her a cigarette. She took it with a shaking hand and he held a match for her and said quietly:

"Tell me all of it."

She nodded, leaned back on the couch for a moment before she spoke. "Grandfather was in bed and the madam had been back downstairs a few minutes when Claudette asked Sandy if she could go up and say good night to him. The madam said she thought that would be fine and Sandy took her up. Marie and Jeanette were being very good because they knew it was well past their bedtime and we thought it was rather charming and we thought no more about it . . . until the shot. Then we ran up the stairs. . . ."

"We?"

"Madam, Dr. Glover, and the girls. . . . Anyway, the door

was locked and the madam ran and got a key and we came in and found . . . well, you saw it."

"Uh huh," Lafitte replied, forcing himself to keep his face blank. "What did the rest of you do while you waited for her to get the key?"

"We . . . uh, we waited . . . and Sedonia came up and kept pounding on the door. I guess they all told you the rest."

"Yes. . . . Why, do you suppose?"

"Why, what?"

"Why did they take them?"

"They came in and they saw them, that's why . . . and then they panicked. That had to be it, Jean. Otherwise they wouldn't have taken my child . . ."

Her voice trailed off and Lafitte continued to stare at her. Suzanne's hands were still shaking and she had trouble snuffing out her cigarette. Lafitte decided that he'd get no more. He stood up, patted her on the shoulder, and wandered out into the hall, trying to decide what to do. He knew he might have to call the law eventually, but Dominique You would know. He went to the hall phone and dialed the operator and asked for the new number of the Cove. While he waited he saw Jeremy and his girls come from the kitchen and meet Suzanne at the door of the living room and then the family went upstairs.

"Yes, thank you," Lafitte said, jotting the number down on the pad. He dialed quickly and asked for his friend, telling the man his name and adding that it was an emergency. Jeremy came down the steps with Sam in tow and Lafitte put his hand over the phone and looked at Duroc.

"Sedonia finally got her senses together," Jeremy said, "and remembered that she saw some lights, flashlights probably, just as she entered the old man's room."

"Which way?" Lafitte asked.

"Mistah Jean," Sam said apologetically, "I'm sorry. I shoulda got it outa her sooner. . . ."

"Never mind! Where were the lights?"

"Toward the landin'."

"Uh huh." Lafitte nodded. "Well, we'd better take a look. Rifles? Pistols aren't much good at a distance."

"Yes, suh. He's got a coupla rifles. And two shotguns."

"Good." Then he heard You's voice say:

"Jean? What's the matter?"

"Dominique? Hang on a minute." He put his hand over the phone and said, "Go with him, Jeremy. Load 'em all. I'll be right there."

Duroc nodded and he and Sam headed for the study. Lafitte removed his hand from the mouthpiece and said:

"I'd hoped it wouldn't be necessary, but that guy who worked over the bouncer needs a friend; like right now."

"Certainly!" You replied. "What can I do?"

"My wife's been taken, and one of Duroc's girls. While we were enjoying your free booze someone broke in here looking for the map and tore the place apart. On top of that, the old man had another stroke."

"No!" You said, the concern evident in his deep voice. "I'll be there as fast as I can. Do you need men?"

"I . . . I don't know. Maybe later. Right now I need your advice more than anything. They could've gone in any direction. . . . And, Dominique? Don't mention this, I haven't even called the police."

"Of course not. My friend, I'll be right there. Are you armed, should they return?"

"Yes."

"Good! I'll be there as quickly as possible!"

"Thank you. I'm sorry to have to tear you away on opening night."

"Don't concern yourself, *mon ami*. The place is so packed no one will know if I'm here or not. A few minutes, I'll be there."

"Thank you."

There was a click and Lafitte replaced the phone and went into the study. The door to the closet was unlocked and Jeremy was inside loading a double-barreled shotgun. Sam backed out of the way and Lafitte looked in and saw a familiar weapon; the Winchester deer rifle he'd always used when he was home. He pulled it from the rack with a faint smile as he noticed the scratches on the stock. He'd put them there the day he hurt his leg. He eased open the lever and looked into the chamber. As he turned it sideways Jeremy said:

"Wouldn't you rather have a shotgun?"

Lafitte shook his head. "No. This is accurate a helluva lot farther."

He didn't bother to explain that if he had to use a weapon he might want a lot smaller pattern than that of a shotgun.

He turned toward the light, the chamber open, and looked through the barrel and nodded. The weapon had been properly cleaned. He checked the action again and then, satisfied that it was serviceable, he reached into the closet and opened the box of shells. Five were forced into the magazine, one was put into the chamber, the lever was closed and the safety put on. He put six shells in his hip pocket, six in his right pants pocket, and he was ready. To Jeremy he said:

"Give the shotgun to Sam. Load another one and keep it handy. I'll take Sam with me. I don't expect to find anything, but it's worth a try. You stay here, even if you hear some shots, stay! I don't want to fill your ass full of holes in the dark."

Jeremy nodded, a strained look on his face.

"And tell Glover nothing, except what you have to, understand?"

"But he's the family doctor!" Jeremy protested.

"Big deal! Now I know a doctor's prone to keep his mouth shut, but he already knows too much. The less people know, the better off we are. If Dominique You gets here before I get back, tell him everything. I've got an idea we'll need his help."

Jeremy nodded again and was wise enough to remain silent this time. He handed the shotgun to Sam and it was taken by the grip, the barrel pointed at the floor.

"Can you use this?" Lafitte said to Sam.

"Yes, suh! I ain't in the best of shape but I kin surely pull the trigger."

"Good boy!" Lafitte said, clapping the old man on the back. "Get a flashlight and let's go."

Sam nodded, handed the shotgun to Lafitte and hurried toward the kitchen. Jeremy walked Lafitte to the porch where they waited a moment in the dark until Sam trotted through the foyer and out onto the porch. Lafitte took the light and handed Sam the scattergun.

"Sit tight," Lafitte said to Jeremy, "we'll be a while."

Duroc nodded and they dropped off the porch, crossed the shells as quietly as they could, and made their way down the grassy slope to the landing. When they got close, Lafitte pulled Sam to the shadow of a tree and whispered:

"If they've got someone watching they saw us, so be damn

careful. Don't shoot at anything unless I give you the word. It might be one of the girls."

Sam nodded and they moved forward until they were a few feet from the bank, and then Lafitte paused to check the shoreline in either direction. It was fairly light and he could see nothing. The only thing near the dock were Sam's old pirogues. When he was satisfied that they were alone he flashed the light to the ground around the dock. The earth was soft and there were footprints, but no drag marks or any indication of a boat having been nosed into the dirt. Sam stood at his shoulder and whispered:

"I kin still track as good as eny. Lemme look."

Lafitte nodded, and Sam exchanged the shotgun for the flashlight and moved forward slowly, stooping low to look at the soft ground. He checked both sides to the water's edge and then returned with a shake of his head.

"No fresh tracks. Most of those prints is frum you and me 'tother day."

"Then it's north," Lafitte said. "Sedonia saw a light from the old man's window, which would be north of here, so we work up."

"Yes, suh. Seems so."

"You think they would've gone up the road, or across the fields?"

"No, suh. Don't seem likely. They'd stick to the bushes at water's edge."

"How far, you think?"

"Well, probably almost to the swamp. Anywhere 'tween here and there ain't much fer landin' a boat, have to go through the bushes and probably get yer feet wet. Weren't no wet foot marks on the porch or in Mistah John's room."

Lafitte raised an eyebrow and inclined his head at Sam's observation, he was still a tracker. Then he nodded and pointed the rifle north. They followed as close as they could to the water's edge for three hundred yards without seeing so much as a bent grass blade. When they got to the spot it was so obvious that he could've found it without the light. At a point a few yards south of where the bay met the swamp they saw two directions of footprints in the soft earth ending at a long gouge mark leading into the water.

"Pirogue," Sam said. "They went into the swamp."

"What's our chances of tailin' 'em tonight?"

Sam shook his head. "Iffin they got guts enough to come outa there at night, they's local boys and know the swamp. Ain't a nigger's chance in hell."

With a quick shiver Lafitte nodded his head in forced agreement. But at least he knew where to look. "Okay, come on."

They turned and headed back toward the house.

Jeremy met them at the front door. "Find anything?"

"Yeah," Lafitte answered, "they went north, into the swamp."

Jeremy raised an eyebrow and quickly and correctly said, "That means they . . . uh, know their way around."

Lafitte nodded and they went into the house. He and Sam leaned their guns against the wall near the phone. As he turned to go upstairs he met the doctor. Glover nodded, a serious look on his face, moved a few feet away from Jeremy and Sam, and said in a low voice:

"I haven't told his wife, but I gather you've guessed. I don't think he'll recover from this one. I should call the hospital and get a room ready."

Lafitte's eyes narrowed and he put his hand on the doctor's arm. "If that's so, what good would a hospital room do? Is he dying now?"

"No," Glover replied carefully, "I didn't say that. But he's almost dead. He can't talk, or move. The mere fact that he can still breathe is some sort of a minor miracle."

"Is there anything you can do for him?"

"No . . . not really."

"Well then, leave him here. If he needs oxygen, or something like that, you can bring it in, can't you?"

"Yes, I suppose I can."

"My point is, if he's still got a mind, and he's close to dying, I'm sure he'd rather do it here than in a hospital."

Glover smiled a little, then nodded. "All right. I'll have some things sent over."

"Doctor," Lafitte's voice had hardened a bit, a fact not missed by the perceptive physician, "I don't want to sound particularly dictatorial, but to put it nicely, I'd appreciate it if you'd not mention to anyone what happened here tonight, except the fact that a probably dying man had what seems a terminal stroke."

The doctor studied the broad-shouldered, determined man in front of him a moment, then nodded again, added a faint smile, and said:

"All right. As a doctor, I'm confined to my patient's welfare. As a long-time friend of John and the family, I'm constrained to ask . . . are you now head of the family?"

Lafitte grinned. The smile was wide but without warmth, and his eyes were narrowed. "You don't see anyone in the house forceful enough to take that exalted title away from me, do you?"

"No . . . I guess not," the doctor nodded.

Lafitte nodded, then turned at the sound of a car sliding to a halt on the shells. He crossed the foyer in wide strides and met Dominique You as Sam opened the front door. Lafitte took him by the arm and steered him into the study, closed the door, and quickly told his friend what he knew. You listened without interruption, only nodding from time to time, and when Lafitte was through the Frenchman said:

"You sure you don't want the police?"

"No, not yet, anyway. I thought about it some while we were out looking for tracks. I can't see a kidnapping for the map, no matter what they think it's worth. And it certainly wasn't planned."

"Agreed." You nodded.

"Sandy and the child must've popped in on 'em just as the old man was pulling the trigger. Then . . . maybe they thought they killed 'im when the old boy had his stroke."

"Yes," You nodded. "And, I don't want to add to your troubles, *mon ami*, but I would be remiss if I didn't add the obvious, that the kidnappers think your wife and the child are witnesses to a murder, at least a death during a felony, and it's the same thing almost . . . but surely that occurred to you."

"Yes." Lafitte replied, his face set. "And that's what makes 'em dangerous. We call the law and they're likely to do something rash."

"I agree," You said with a nod. "Do you . . . uh, want to wait until you hear from them?"

"You know better." Lafitte shook his head. "That's why I need your help. I mean to go in there. I don't think they'll expect anybody to try 'em."

"But you will?" Dominique said.

"You bet your ass I will! I can't take Sam with me. And Jeremy is a city boy, he wouldn't be much good."

"*Mon Dieu!* If you go, Dominique You will go too! I'll get my boats out."

"You, uh, got any idea where to look?"

"*Oui,* I think so. Seems they would go to Mejia, especially as they went north. . . . I, uh, know where they hold their little games."

"Uh huh." Lafitte nodded. "You used the word 'boats.' More than one?"

"Yes." You grinned. "I've got some good ones. I'll call, they'll be here in less than an hour." You started for the phone, then stopped and turned to stare at his friend. "You'll need some dark clothes . . . I have some that'll fit. You have a weapon?"

"Yes, a good rifle. And plenty of ammunition."

"*Très bien.* I shall be on the phone for a time."

"Okay. I'll check on the old man again."

Lafitte entered the bedroom and closed the door quietly. The doctor was sitting in a chair by the bed. As the doctor turned his head to look at Lafitte, the old man, though his head didn't move, winked his right eye. Lafitte was momentarily startled but recovered quickly and said in a low voice:

"Any change?"

"Just as I told you downstairs."

"Uh huh." Lafitte stared at his grandfather. "Did you make the call?"

"Oxygen's on the way. And Sedonia took madam down for a cup of tea."

Lafitte nodded and went to stand at the foot of the bed so that the doctor would have to turn away from his patient.

"Have you called the police?" the doctor said.

"No, not yet," Lafitte replied and the old man's right eye winked rapidly three times. "I hope to hear from . . . from them before the night's over. I'm afraid if I call the law it might scare 'em off."

The doctor considered this for a moment, then said, "It's your prerogative, of course. My only duty is to my patient."

"Thank you. By the way, do me a favor while you're here. Go down and take a look at Sam's arm."

"Certainly. I noticed last night he wasn't using it, but I

thought it was none of my business so I didn't ask. What happened?"

"Voodoo."

The doctor looked startled and Lafitte added:

"That's right. A man put a spell on him. Sounds stupid, I know, but that's what it is. I thought maybe you might be able to talk him out of it. . . . Go ahead, I'll sit with the old boy."

The doctor got to his feet and walked toward the door. "All right. But if Sam believes it, there's not much I can do. But I'll see."

"Thank you."

Lafitte opened the door and waited until Dr. Glover had gone down the steps before closing and locking it. He went to the open windows and locked them and pulled the drapes as best he could. As he turned to the bed he nodded, the old man's face couldn't be seen from the windows. He stood at the foot of the bed and stared at the old man for a moment and then said quietly:

"All right, we're alone. Can you hear me?"

The old man winked his right eye, then the left, then blinked frantically.

Lafitte grinned widely. "Yeah, you old son of a bitch, you're not out of it yet."

The eyes blinked rapidly.

"Can you talk?" Lafitte said.

There was no answer. Lafitte thought a moment, then said, "All right, let's do this. Can you blink one eye, then the other?"

Both eyes blinked rapidly, the chest heaved.

"No!" Lafitte said firmly. "Now if your mind's still all right, calm down. Right eye for yes. Left eye for no. Now, do you understand me?"

The right eye winked.

"Is your mind clear?"

Right eye.

"Can you talk?"

Left eye.

"Did you see what happened?"

Yes.

"Was my wife kidnapped, and the girl?"

Yes.

"Do they . . . whoever took them . . . do they know that you saw it?"

No.

The old man's mouth was hanging open, drooling. Lafitte took a Kleenex from the table and wiped his mouth, then gently closed the jaw. It stayed in place. "Okay. You had a stroke and they were taken. From this room?"

Yes.

"You had the stroke before my wife came in?"

No.

"The women were here when you had the stroke?"

Yes.

"And Sandy was taken from this room?"

Yes.

"And you saw it?"

Yes.

"Do the kidnappers know you saw it?"

No.

"No? Oh, they think you're dead?"

Yes. Yes.

"All right. . . . Uh, let's see. The kidnappers came in, or were in the room, and then Sandy and the girl came in?"

Yes.

"Uh huh. Then you had the stroke?"

Yes.

"Yet the kidnappers don't know you saw it?"

Yes.

"All right, we're on the right track. You were in bed?"

Yes.

"You saw the kidnappers as they came in from the windows?"

Yes. . . . No.

"Yes and no? Oh. . . . Hey! Did you hear them in my room first?"

Yes, yes, yes.

"Good! All right, relax. You were in bed, heard them tear up my room, then they came in here?"

Yes.

"Then Sandy and the girls came in afterward? How long?"

No, no.

"They didn't? The girls were already in the room with you?"

No, no, no.

"Huh?" Lafitte scratched his chin, then it came to him. "You mean the kidnappers came in from the French windows and Sandy and the girl came in at the same time?"

Yes, yes.

"Okay." Lafitte thought a bit. "Then you hauled out your gun and shot at the same time as everyone entered?"

Yes, yes, yes!

"Okay, okay! Now, there was no blood on the floor or the porch, so I guess you missed."

Yes and no.

"You did and you didn't?"

Yes and no. Yes and no!

"Oh, you don't know if you hit them or not?"

Yes.

"Is that when you had the stroke?"

Yes.

Lafitte scratched the back of his head, thinking of what his grandfather had said. Then he asked, "All right, you said a while ago that the kidnappers don't know that you saw them take Sandy and the girl, is that right?"

Yes, yes, yes!

"Ah! Okay, let's try this. Everybody entered at the same time, you took a shot, had the stroke . . . then the kidnappers probably tried to jump you at the same time as you shot and then they thought you were dead. Am I right?"

Yes, yes!

"Good. Then you'd had the stroke, they thought you were dead, but you weren't, and you saw them kidnap my wife and the girl?"

Yes.

"Okay. Let's get to 'they.' I saw two hook marks on the railing outside. Was it two men?"

Yes.

"Did you know them?"

Yes and no.

"You knew one of them?"

Yes.

"Do I know him?"

No.

"Would Sam know him?"

The old man stared a moment, the breathing seemed to increase for a moment, then each eye blinked in turn.

"All right. I know you're getting tired, but for God's sake hang on a bit. I'll try and hurry. You said yes and no, does that mean that Sam might know him?"

Yes.

"Is he a local resident?"

Yes.

"Were they white?"

Yes and no.

"One of each?"

No.

"Humm. Was one white?"

Yes.

"I see. . . .Then the other one was a mulatto of some sort?"

Yes.

"Do you know the white man?"

No.

"Then it's the other one. Do you know him very well?"

No.

"Do you know his name?"

No.

"But you know him . . . like you've seen him around town?"

Yes, yes.

"Okay," Lafitte grinned, "let me take a wild guess; is the man a friend of, or does he work for, Tomas Mejia?"

Yes, yes.

For a moment Lafitte almost thought he saw the brows widen in surprise, but as he stared closely at his grandfather the eyes didn't move, only a reflexive blink. Lafitte passed his hand in front of his grandfather's eyes, but they didn't track.

"Goddam!" Lafitte whispered. His grandfather was even unable to see, he could only breathe and hear and wink. In a louder voice he said, "I'll say this for you, you old bastard, you got guts."

Yes.

Lafitte shook his head and then the thought came to him that no one else should know of his grandfather's power to communicate. Helpless as he was, the old boy was still a witness to a felony.

"Okay. We'd better hurry. Is the mulatto light-skinned?"

No.

"Dark?"

No.

"Medium?"

Yes.

"Any distinguishing marks, like scars?"

No. The winks were coming rapidly now, as if the old man felt he was tiring.

"Okay. I'll hurry. Is he my height?"

No.

"Taller?"

Yes.

"Skinny?"

No.

"Fat?"

No.

"Over six feet?"

Yes, yes.

"Six two, six three?"

Yes . . . yes.

"Like six three?"

Yes.

"My, he's a big mutha. You know his name?"

A pause, then, No.

"Okay. I won't try and ask how they were dressed, take too long. Let's get back to the women. Uh . . . were they harmed?"

No.

"Gagged?"

Yes.

"Huh! That took a bit of doing. You said they all came in at once, you took a shot, they jumped you . . . they had to, you were on the floor . . . and the bed was slashed like they were looking for the map, and the room was searched. . . ." Lafitte stopped talking and paced the room a moment, turned and stared at the slashed drapes, finally turned back to his grandfather, talking aloud, but more to himself than his grandather. "Huh. Then that explains the timing. It seemed strange that Sandy and the girl would've been in the room, then a shot with no blood, and they were taken with those outside not hearing anything. Try this; you shot, one jumped

you and you were knocked to the floor. The other one
must've threatened them, with a knife or a gun, and the first
one tore up the drapes, gagged them . . . by this time the others were pounding on the door, and while the madam ran for
the key my wife and the child were tied and hustled out of the
room. . . . Or maybe they heard the madam say about the
key and that gave them a quick chance to tear up the rest of
the room. . . . It was a mess, obviously done quickly, but not
thoroughly. . . . How's that? Am I close?"

Yes, yes, yes!

"How 'bout that?" Lafitte said, somewhat amazed at his
own deductive powers. "That was damn clever of me, wasn't
it?"

The old man didn't move for a moment, then the right eye,
almost reluctantly, winked slowly.

"Huh!" Lafitte said. "Then tell me this; if I'm so goddam
clever, how come I was so stupid as to go off and leave my
wife alone? Damn!"

The right eye winked slowly, then the left.

"Okay. Spilt milk. Did the kidnappers say anything . . .
anything at all?"

No.

"Damn! Can I forget this line?"

Yes.

Lafitte nodded and thought some more, finally said, "Now,
my wife and the child were taken because they were witnesses to what those guys thought was your killing, right?"

Yes.

"And it's all your fault too, isn't it, you old son of a
bitch?"

There was a pause, then, Yes.

"Uh huh. Somebody wanted that phony map, right?"

Yes.

"You bastard," Lafitte said without rancor. "No? Oh, I see,
you just wanted to play a little game, you didn't think anyone
would get hurt by it, did you?"

No.

"And you're sorry?"

Yes.

"Fuck you," Lafitte said in a conversational tone. "Now,
you old son of a bitch, you're the witness and if anybody

knows you saw it. . . . Hey, you sure the kidnappers think
you were out of it?"

Yes.

"So you just stared. You didn't wink or anything?"

No, no.

"Good. All right, I'll keep quiet, so don't wink for anyone
else . . . not the doctor, or even the madam. I know that's a
hard thing to say, but you're a tough old goat, you can understand. You agree?"

Yes. The wink was immediate.

"Good boy! You got any idea which way they went?"

No.

"Okay. Couple more things. Important. Can I trust Sam
with my life?"

Yes.

"Can I trust Dominique You with my life?"

Yes.

"Absolutely?"

Yes, yes.

"Okay, you old bastard. You set it up about the return of
Lafitte the pirate—"

There was a quick knock at the door and Lafitte turned
and said, "Just a moment." He leaned close to his grandfather, his eyes narrowed and his face set as he said in a low
voice. "Okay. You set it up as a joke. Well, the fun time's
over and, by God, they're gonna get just that. Lafitte the
pirate has returned!"

He forced down his anger and went to the French windows and opened them and rapped several panes and said,
"I'm at the windows, Doc, be right there."

He crossed the room quickly but paused at the bed and
leaned close to his grandfather again and whispered, "If you
think of anything else, write it down, will you?"

One eye winked, then the other, then both rapidly.

Lafitte grinned and whispered, "I do believe you invited
me to go make love to myself."

Yes, yes, yes!

Lafitte stifled a chuckle and whispered one last time,
"Okay, sit tight. Don't go 'way, you hear?"

He went to the door, unlocked it, and stepped back to
allow the doctor to enter. The doctor stared at Lafitte a moment, then went to look at his patient.

"Never moved," Lafitte lied. "What about Sam?"

"Nothing!" the doctor said disgustedly. "He's so superstitious that you'd have to kill him to change his mind. Yes, he knows it's a curse. Yes, he knows it's mere superstitition. No, he can't move his arm. And, you know what? He can't."

"I know," Lafitte replied. "He believes."

"He certainly does!" the doctor said. "I doubt if a psychiatrist could do it."

"Well, thank you, Doctor. That's what I expected. . . . You'll stay with the old man?"

"Yes. I'll certainly spend the night."

"Thank you."

Lafitte went down to the living room and found the Duroc family downstairs again, with Dominique, sitting quietly. Suzanne was drinking what looked like straight whiskey. When she saw him she said in a shaky voice which bordered on hysteria:

"Why did they take my girl. Why?"

"Because she was with my wife," Lafitte answered quietly. "And because of that map."

"It's his fault," she said, looking at the ceiling. "That old son of a bitch! They didn't have to take my child! Give them the map!"

"All right," Lafitte said quietly. "All they have to do is return your child and my wife. . . . Now, if I knew who they were, it would be easier."

Lafitte stared at his cousin with narrowed eyes, but his cousin wouldn't look at him.

"We can block the island until they come to us," Jeremy said, but it sounded so ineffectual that he blushed.

"Sure," Lafitte said. Then he shivered at the thought that they must not get the map before he got his wife back. If that happened, she and the child were dead. Staring at the weak Jeremy, he was glad that he hadn't told him where the map was hidden. For the few hours he'd be gone he doubted that Jeremy would have an opportunity to search, should he gather the courage to try.

"Do something!" Suzanne demanded of her husband.

Duroc, still looking embarrassed, stood up, motioned his girls to come to his side, and very firmly took the glass from his wife and put it on the bar. Then he and his anxious daughters managed to steer Suzanne to the door. Lafitte touched his arm and the girls led their mother from the room.

"See the doctor," Lafitte whispered. "He'll knock her out."

Duroc nodded and followed his children. Lafitte turned to Dominique.

"Where are the others?"

"The doctor gave madame a sedative . . . she's in bed. Sedonia and Sam are in the kitchen."

Lafitte nodded, closed the door, and quickly told his friend about his winking conversation with his grandfather.

"Good," You said, "that's two things. It confirms your idea that the kidnapping was incidental and that the mulatto is Mejia's man. . . . You know, I've seen that man around town a number of times."

"You sure?"

"Mon ami, I am sure. And I am sure that Mejia is a dirty bastard. A man like that should be killed at the earliest opportunity. Besides, he may bring the spotlight of federal intervention down on our well-run little parish and cause some great discomfort to the more honest and moral entrepreneurs of the district."

"Ha!" Lafitte grinned. "Would you include yourself?"

"But of course, *mon ami,* and you know it."

Lafitte shook his head. "I know nothing but good of my friend, Dominique You, the man who runs the Smuggler's Inn."

They exchanged the warm smiles of two friends and Lafitte was about to suggest a drink when they heard the sound of throttled-down motors outside.

"The boats," You said, getting to his feet. "I'll check my men and be back in a few minutes."

Lafitte went behind the bar, feeling his still somewhat queasy stomach, and decided that he might need the hair of the dog, but lightly, so he poured himself a small Scotch over lots of ice and water. He wandered out of the living room and into the den and closed the door. The drapes were drawn and he looked around the room, making sure he was alone, before he stood in front of the big picture of his grandfather and sipped his Scotch.

"You son of a bitch, you really did it this time," he whispered to the portrait. "You knew it was worthless, but you knew greedy Jeremy would buy it. Only you didn't think it

would come to this, did you? I'll give you that. You were
only trying to do me a favor. . . ."

He wandered around the room, staring at the foils and the
pictures of his ancestors, and then he stopped at the two
crossed knives below the picture of the original Lafitte. He
put the glass on an end table and reached up and pulled one
of the knives and cut the cords holding the still serviceable
leather scabbards to the wall, replaced the knife and held the
two scabbards in his left hand as he retrieved his drink and
sat in a big chair and stared at the picture of the pirate. After
a few moments he whispered:

"By the time I get through with that son of a bitch he's
gonna think the first Lafitte was a soprano in the eunuchs'
chorus!"

He waved the knives at the portrait of the first Lafitte and
took a long drink, his eyes narrowed, and his mind full of
cold, killing anger. He was still staring at the picture when he
heard Dominique call, "Jean?"

"In here," Lafitte answered and got up to meet his friend
at the door.

You entered with a pile of clothes and said, "Here, we'd
better dress properly. Basic black is de rigueur for such affairs."

He handed Lafitte a pair of black denims, a black sweatshirt, and a pair of dark blue, worn, but serviceable deck
shoes.

Lafitte waved the knives and said, "I'm ready."

As they changed clothes Lafitte found the denims and
sweatshirt tight, but the shoes a proper fit.

"The shoes all right?" You asked.

"Just my size."

"Good. Otherwise you'd have to wear your own. . . . Your
weapon?"

"By the phone."

"I'll send a man with a rifle and a radio to the bridge by
the bayou and leave a radio here. That way no one will be
allowed in without permission."

Lafitte nodded and went to the open closet; he grabbed the
box of shells for his rifle and they went into the hall. Jeremy
was coming down the stairs.

"Jeremy," Lafitte said, "we're going out. You stay here and
watch the women and keep one of those shotguns close. And

one for Sam, he can use it with one hand. Dominique will leave you a radio and a man will be at the bridge with one, so keep it handy. The man will let the nurse in. No one else. If he has any problems he'll call you. Now, don't make any mistakes."

Duroc's eyes widened in amazement at Lafitte's flat delivery. "You're not going out there in the dark?"

"Jeremy," Lafitte said patiently, "we surely are. Now stay here and watch things. No goddam drinking until I get back and, for Christ's sake, pay attention. And, whatever you do, don't call the law! You understand?"

Duroc nodded, opened his mouth, then closed it.

Lafitte nodded, picked up his rifle, and followed Dominique out the door.

Near the wharf were four black, twenty-five-foot catamarans. As he stepped on the boardwalk Lafitte showed his amazement with an appreciative nod. Each boat had two big outboard engines with the numbers "110" in white scroll. You grinned and proudly pointed to his fleet.

"They're the very best in the parish. Of course, I use them for bringing in fresh shrimp."

"Sure, you do," Lafitte said dryly. He stepped over the railing of the closest boat and was greeted with a friendly nod from the "host" of the Cove.

"Good evening, monsieur . . . again."

"Hi," Lafitte replied, trying to sound pleasant.

He looked past the man into the dimly lit, half-enclosed cabin and was again impressed by Dominique's boats. There was a two-way radio with a gyro-compass.

"We'd best have a parley first," Dominique said. Then, raising his voice so that he could be heard on the farthest boat, *"Venez!"*

The men manning the other three boats jumped onto the dock to join them, and as Lafitte stepped over the railing onto the creaking planks he hoped the old wharf would last one more night. All four men, including the one behind him, were dressed as Lafitte and You, black denims and sweatshirts. As the men came forward, Dominique introduced each one in turn.

"This is Abe," he said, indicating a tall, rangy black with a broken nose.

"Abe?" Lafitte said, shaking the big hand.

"Suh?" Abe replied with a bob of his head.

"And this handsome creature is called Blondy, obviously," You said.

Blondy was medium-sized and had, as his nickname implied, very blond hair. Though he appeared in his thirties and had even features, he wasn't exactly handsome; there were too many lines at the corners of his narrow eyes and his mouth turned down as though he were constantly mad. But he smiled in a friendly fashion as he stepped forward to shake hands and exchange nods with Lafitte.

"Obviously," Lafitte replied, turning to meet the third man.

He was smaller than the average man, perhaps five and a half feet tall, but he had extremely broad shoulders and a big chest that made Lafitte think the man must have been a weight lifter. In his belt were four knives.

"This is Marcel," You said, "originally from Martinique, but now a good U.S. citizen."

"Monsieur?" Marcel extended a big, burly hand.

"And this, of course, is Albert," You indicated the "host."

"We've met," Lafitte said, concluding the round of handshakes.

"I have told them of your problem," You said. "They are eager to help. *Mon ami,* they are my most trusted men . . . the best in the state."

There were four silent nods and Lafitte felt better than he'd felt since he came home that night. He stared from one face to the next and got four reassuring smiles. He took a deep breath, nodded, and said:

"Dominique says you're good men and that's word enough. I cannot tell you how grateful I am. Thank you."

The men shuffled their feet and big Abe cleared his throat. Dominique smiled and said:

"Mon ami, what if Dominique You had not been able to bring his good men, or what if Dominique You had not been here at all?"

"Huh," Lafitte said, considering the question. Then he answered quietly, and truthfully, "I would've taken Sam's outboard and the rifle and gone alone."

"You see?" Dominique said to his men and they nodded again. Lafitte was accepted. "Now, Marcel will tow the four pirogues we brought, so he'll lay back. When we get close we'll tie together and take the pirogues in. Remember, no shooting, or even fighting, unless by signal from me or Jean Lafitte. We drew straws and Albert, here, will guard the road."

Albert grinned ruefully and reached into the boat and picked up two walkie-talkies and a rifle and nodded to his friends.

"You know where it is?"

"Yes, I was here once before on an errand. Dominique says to give one radio to Mr. Duroc and then go to the bridge and let no one in without Mr. Duroc's approval."

Lafitte nodded and the man started toward the house. You waved the other three back to their boats and he motioned to Lafitte to get aboard. Lafitte stood on the portside behind Dominique as the burly Frenchman started his engine and waited for the others to move away from the dock. When they were in open water You took the lead. He kept easing the throttle open until the agile boat had its prow out of the water and Lafitte had to grab the stanchion to keep his balance. The noise was so great that conversation was hopeless, unless they wanted to shout, so Lafitte kept his thoughts to himself. You consulted the compass, his watch, and a map from time to time, and Lafitte was glad his friend gave the appearance of knowing what he was doing because there was nothing to see but the open bay.

After a quick ten minutes You abruptly cut his engine and spoke quietly into his microphone: *"Venez! Venez à mon bateau!"*

Lafitte creased his brows as he remembered the bit of Cajun French he used to know and then he nodded; Dominique was calling his men to his boat. You went to the stern and threw an old auto tire over the side where it hung by its rope just above the waterline. Abe eased his boat alongside and Lafitte stood out of the way while Dominique took Abe's rope and tied the boats together so that Abe's prow was a few feet in front of Dominique's stern. In a few moments Blondy's boat was tied to Abe's and Marcel's to Blondy's, with the pirogues bobbing off the stern.

You whispered to Lafitte, "Voices carry over the water," and held up a finger for silence. Lafitte nodded.

Without further words Dominique slipped a .38 from under the instrument panel, tucked it into his belt, and nodded Lafitte to Abe's boat. With motions You indicated that the big black would stay with the boats and Abe shrugged and his teeth showed in the moonlight, but he made no protest and held Blondy's prow while they jumped aboard. They edged their way down the side and into the last boat while Marcel and Blondy were already climbing into a pirogue. Dominique pulled another one to him and held it while Lafitte got in, then Lafitte held the log boat fast while Dominique got into the stern and picked up a short, wide paddle. The other pirogue was already making its way toward the now barely visible outline of the island.

When they were still a good fifty yards out, the little man with the big shoulders stood up and pointed to his left and Dominique waved his paddle; they could see the dim glow from a fire. Then Dominique put down the paddle and held up the pole and waved it, and Marcel waved one in reply. They would now pole their way in, it would make less noise than a paddle.

The boats veered to the right a bit and they were guided toward the shore as silently as what they were, floating logs. The boats were steered under some overhanging limbs and to solid sand. As they got out, You directed them a few feet away where they gathered on the small beach.

You nudged Lafitte and pulled two lengths of nylon fishing cord from his pocket, each about three feet long. He gave one to Lafitte and held the other in both hands, threw a loop, and pulled his hands together. Lafitte nodded that he knew it was a strangling cord. You smiled and kneeled down and drew a long, thin oval in the sand. Then he made an X near one end and said in a whisper:

"We are here. Here is the fire. On the other side of the fire is a sort of river leading into the swamp to the north. On this side of the fire is where they land. The boats should be there. From what I've heard they have two guards in the trees on either side of the landing. I think we should take the two guards before we proceed, as they're probably armed. *Mon ami,* have you ever been in this sort of thing before?"

Lafitte grinned and looked at the circle of men and nodded, then whispered: "Yes. I did ten months in Korea before Uncle sent me to Germany. . . . I'll take one of the guards."

"C'est bon," You said. "Blondy will go with you. I'll take Marcel and we'll go down the water a way and come in from the other end of the beach."

Lafitte nodded. "All right. Then what?"

"Then we work our way in toward the fire. Most of these affairs are an opportunity for the kids to get high on something, purchased from Mejia at an exorbitant price, of course. If your wife is here, she will be off to one side somewhere. After we take the guards we will join and decide from there. How's that?"

The other men nodded and looked at Lafitte. He could not think of a better plan, so he nodded.

"*Bon*," Dominique said. "Give us fifteen minutes to get in place."

Lafitte held his wrist up so he could see the watch and then said with a wry smile, "Aren't you supposed to say something about synchronizing our watches?"

"No!" You said with a chuckle. "That's for war films. Fifteen minutes on your watch is fifteen minutes, assuming it's running. No matter what the time says."

"Huh!" Lafitte replied. "You know, you're right. One thing. Shouldn't we maybe just get the guards aside and talk to 'em? They might know something."

"I considered that," Dominique replied, "but I think not. From what I've heard they are nothing but barflies, hired from nearby towns for the night. It is a rather vulnerable position and it seems Mejia does not want to risk his own men. Anyway, we can always come back and, uh, discuss it with them."

Lafitte agreed by clapping his friend on the shoulder and You grinned once; then he and Marcel turned toward the boats. Lafitte turned to Blondy and whispered:

"We have more time, but I suggest we get into place."

Blondy lifted his sweatshirt on the left to show the butt of a pistol and then took a length of nylon cord from his pocket and nodded that he was ready. Lafitte nodded in reply, checked again to make sure the safety was on, and they moved forward. Blondy led the way into the lush growth a few feet and stopped. There was no sound. After a few moments Blondy moved again and they went a long ninety yards, slowly and quietly. Lafitte suddenly realized that he was sweating. He took a deep breath and kept moving. When they were close they heard a man moving restlessly and Blondy turned and held out a hand. Lafitte nodded and then Blondy pointed to a tree. Lafitte could make out the dim outline

of the guard and then the man turned and they could see the
glow of a cigarette.

The guard on their side was near a wide path, some ten
feet from the small beach. There were a good ten boats
pulled up on the sand, pirogues, several rowboats, and five or
six small outboards. The slight wind changed and from the
direction of the fire they could hear a wild acid-rock record
played on someone's portable recorder. Then there was a distant shout followed by a feminine squeal. Lafitte could not
see the other guard, but his man had not moved from the
tree. Blondy looked at Lafitte again and Lafitte backed away
a few feet until he could see his watch by the dim moonlight.

Six minutes. He moved up again and held up five fingers to
Blondy. Blondy nodded and his teeth showed faintly as he
waved his left hand in a gentlemanly manner, indicating that
the guard was Lafitte's.

Lafitte nodded at the dubious honor and changed places
with Blondy and handed him the rifle. After what seemed
many times the five minutes he'd expected, Lafitte heard a
slight scuffling sound. His quarry moved from the tree and
was about to cross the path when Lafitte took a deep breath
and went after him, the cord in both hands.

His man was taller by a good four inches and Lafitte had
to reach high to slip the cord over the man's head and pull it
tight. The man grunted once and grabbed at the cord that
was already biting into his neck and dropped to one knee and
pulled forward, flipping Lafitte over his head.

When he realized that he couldn't halt his impetus in mid-
air, Lafitte wisely tucked his head to his chest and did a
creditable roll, landing on his shoulders. As he hit, he let go
of the cord and finished his roll, coming up on his knees, and
twisted quickly to face the man who was struggling to get
both feet under him. Before he could get erect, Lafitte, staying on his knees in the sand, launched a roadhouse right low
into the man's gut and grinned at the satisfying retching
sound but didn't wait for the result. He was already counter-
ing with a short left to the man's exposed jaw. The blow
lacked the power that Lafitte knew he used to have, but it
was right on the mark. The man fell to his left, leaning on his
elbows, gasping for breath, and Lafitte remembered the lessons he'd learned at Uncle's expense, and he raised his tightly
pressed hands and brought the heels down on the back of the

exposed neck. There was a slight grunt and the fight was over.

Just to be sure, Lafitte pulled a knife and held it under the man's jawbone, but there was no need, the man was unconscious. Then Blondy was there, the rifle between the fallen man's shoulders. Lafitte backed away, exchanged quick grins with Blondy, retrieved his cord, and got to his feet. There was another quick exchange of grins as Dominique and Marcel came forward dragging an inert body, and both victims were hidden under a bush.

As they moved forward, the sounds of laughter and the shrieks of young feminine voices grew louder, even over the cacophony of the music. They moved cautiously, watching the trail ahead and behind. As they drew closer to the firelight and peered between the trees they saw such an orgy that even the broad-minded Lafitte blinked in surprise.

The group of some thirty odd young people, mostly in their teens, mostly white with a few blacks, were in various stages of undress; over half the girls were stripped to the waist. But what had made Lafitte blink was the gathering at the edge of the firelight. A group of spectators were watching a young girl, nude and flat on her back on a blanket. Two nude boys were kneeling at her shoulders and she was masturbating them while another nude boy was in her. Two other girls, also nude, were flitting around the group, laughing wildly. Lafitte shook his head and saw that everyone in the group of watchers was smiling inanely and weaving his body and mumbling to the music. They were all high on something, as were the rest of the group scattered across the clearing, but they weren't all on heroin. Lafitte knew a vicarious bit about drugs and realized that the mainliners were on the other side of the fire; some alone, some in lethargic groups, relaxing in their deadly euphoria. Lafitte nudged Dominique and the four backed some thirty feet away for a quick conference.

"Goddam!" Lafitte whispered. "I'm in favor of group therapy, mind you . . . but this is terrible! They're nothing but children!"

"*Oui, mon ami,*" You replied. "I told you what Mejia was doing. I know my opinion does not coincide with the law of the land, but I think he should be eliminated."

"Yeah!" Lafitte replied, his eyes narrowed, not only at the

thought of the children but what such a man would do to his wife. He took a couple of deep breaths to get himself under control and then added, "Okay, you take Marcel and circle that way, we'll go the other, and meet over there."

"*Bien.*"

Lafitte nodded to Blondy and they began to circle to the left, slowly and carefully, making sure they stayed out of view of the participants. They met at the far side behind some bushes, their backs to the swamps. Dominique shook his head.

"There's no other place on the island where they can be," he whispered. "It's too small and the rest is but marshland."

"Okay. Let's talk to the guards."

Before Lafitte could stop him, You entered the firelight and put a bullet into the record player. The sound of the explosion, followed by the silence of the music, made the participants react in several ways. Some, heavily sedated, stared dully at him and some began to yell and started to run.

"Stand still!" You shouted. "We're federal officers!"

His two men quickly circled the inner edge of the clearing and began to herd the young people toward the center. A couple of boys tried to dart away but were quickly grabbed and flung toward the fire.

"Get dressed!" You commanded.

The young people were so cowed by the sight of the guns that those who had the reflexes began to scramble for their clothes. Some moved slowly and placidly in aimless circles. Lafitte stepped forward and Dominique nodded that he thought he had the children under control. Lafitte called to Marcel, who was closest to him:

"Come on."

They went into the darkness toward the beach and suddenly Marcel held out a hand and Lafitte cursed himself for not insisting that they tie the two guards; there was only one man at the bushes where they'd left them, the one with whom Lafitte had fought. Marcel moved cautiously forward, his pistol ready and pointed to himself, then toward the beach. Lafitte nodded and crossed the path to check the other side. He felt suddenly exposed and then he caught a movement out of the corner of his eye and spun back toward the bush to see the man up on his elbows, shaking his head.

The move saved Lafitte a fractured skull. He felt a slight

burning sensation on the left side of his head and there was a
tugging at the back of his sweatshirt. He instinctively ducked
out of the way and backed across the sand, the rifle ready, to
face the other man who was advancing with a stout club in
his hand. Now Lafitte was between the two men and he
danced quickly backward toward the fire and shot a glance at
the prone body; that one was still out of it. Another two steps
and he was clear. He stopped, the rifle shifted to port in case
he had to fend off another blow, and called:

"Marcel!"

Lafitte watched the man, and then Marcel was on the path
and aiming his .38 at the man's back.

"No!" Lafitte said. "No shooting!" He lowered the rifle a
bit and advanced a step, motioning to the man and, to his ad-
versary's surprise, grinned and nodded once.

The man was well over six feet with a big beer-belly and
he didn't look too bright, but he was smart enough to realize
that for some reason these men didn't want to use their guns.
Then he showed his lack of intelligence by suddenly charging
Lafitte with the club held high, instead of darting into the
darkness at the side of the trail.

Lafitte, still grinning, wider now that he knew he had the
man, timed the charge, and as Marcel watched in amazement
Lafitte wiggled the barrel twice, then stepped forward and to
his right at the last moment, and the butt of his rifle caught
the taller man flush on the side of the head. Lafitte stepped
clear and the body continued its forward motion to land
heavily in the sand. Lafitte looked at Marcel with a pleased
nod and said:

"Not bad, huh? It's been a while."

"It would not seem so," Marcel observed in his French accent.

The little man moved forward lightly, his gun on the first
man who was now on his knees, staring at his fallen friend,
and took a Zippo lighter from his pocket and held it to Lafitte's head. Then he tucked his gun away and while Lafitte
held his rifle on the captives Marcel probed at Lafitte's head
with gentle fingers.

"You bleed good," Marcel commented. He pulled a blue
bandana from his hip pocket and shook it out and explained,
"Brand clean. . . . Are you faint?"

"No," Lafitte said. "It just laid open the skin."

Marcel nodded and wrapped the bandana around Lafitte's head and tied it in a firm knot. "Tight?"

"No, it's fine. Thank you."

Marcel grinned at Lafitte and turned to the fallen man, grabbed a foot and began dragging the inert body toward the fire as though it weighed less than a hundred pounds instead of a dead weight of two hundred. Lafitte waved his rifle at the other one and the man staggered to his feet, his hands up, and walked toward the fire. The kids were now quiet and huddled to one side of the fire as though they were cold, though it was a warm night. Those who could comprehend were now wide-eyed with fear, and the feeling was intensified as they saw Marcel drag in the body. Marcel let go of the foot and grinned at Dominique and then jerked a finger toward Lafitte.

"You should have seen!" Marcel said in some awe. "This one jumped him from the bushes and Monsieur Lafitte withstood the charge, and he had a club. . . . It was a thing to see!"

Dominique grinned and said to Lafitte, "Are you all right?"

"Yes. He just barely grazed me."

Lafitte handed his rifle to Marcel, pulled a knife, and turned to the prisoner. As the man saw the knife he started to back away, but Lafitte grabbed the sleeve of the man's right arm and stepped forward, letting the man back up until he was against the trunk of a large oak.

"Where are they?" Lafitte said, a measured syllable at a time.

"They?" the man said in a heavy Southern accent. "Who is they?"

The knife was suddenly under the point of the jaw, forcing the man's head back. "Don't play games with me, you son of a bitch!" Lafitte said it in a loud voice and the man swallowed hard. "That woman they took was my wife. If they've harmed her you'll be the first to get your throat cut!"

"I . . . I don't know." The eyes were wide, staring at the glinting blade, but the man said nothing.

"All right." Lafitte shrugged and pulled the tip of the blade down the man's throat, drawing blood. "Let's see how well you talk holding your guts in your hand."

The blade dropped to the man's belt, hooked the dirty

shirt, and Lafitte lifted, tearing the buttons loose and opening the shirt. Then the knife flicked in at the white belly, drawing blood again.

The man shrank back, as though to embed himself in the tree, and said, "No! They . . . they were here. But they're gone."

"Where?" The knife flicked into the skin again.

"I don't know nothin' about it, honest! All I know is two men came in, with a woman and a girl, and . . . and they left."

"How?" The knife gouged a bit, then Lafitte backed off a foot, waving the knife slowly.

"They come in with two pirogues . . . and they took a speedboat and left . . . with the pirogues, headed south. . . ."

"Where?"

"I . . . I heard one say they wuz goin' to Grand——"

The man grunted and dropped to his knees and there was a double-bladed throwing knife in his chest. Lafitte spun around to see Mejia dart from the edge of the firelight and sprint toward the swamp. Marcel raised the rifle and Lafitte shouted, "No!" and began to run.

Lafitte made but ten feet through the sand and knew his bad leg wouldn't let him catch the fleet Mejia; he paused to flip his knife in his hand and throw it. But Mejia didn't stop at the edge of the swamp. He took a running dive into the shallow water, and as Lafitte got to the edge Mejia sank beneath the snake-infested waters and was gone from the dim firelight. As Dominique joined him, his .38 pointed at the water, Lafitte put his hand on the gun and said:

"No. He'll keep." He took a deep breath and shook his head and added, "You know, that son of a bitch has guts."

You stared at his friend a moment, then nodded and said, "Yes, he too."

They turned and hurried back to the fallen guard. He was on his side, holding the knife with both hands as if to extract it. He was dead. You shook his head and stood up as the aware members of the youth group began to scream or groan, according to sex. Dominique silenced them with a mighty shout:

"Shut up!"

They quieted, except for the hysterical sobbing of several girls.

"What did he mean by Grand?" Lafitte asked. "Grand Isle?"

"Maybe that," You nodded. "Maybe Grand Terre. Both are a good twelve miles south."

Lafitte nodded coldly. "Any other Grands you know of?"

"No. . . . No, none. But they're fairly close to one another. One leads back to the mainland and the other . . . leads to the open sea."

Lafitte stared at his friend a moment, his jaw muscles working, then said, "Let's try the other one."

"Blondy?" You said to the pale man who had been examining the man Lafitte had smashed with the rifle.

"No," Blondy said, standing up. "His skull is fractured. I could feel the bones through the side of the head. I think maybe he is dead, too."

Lafitte turned and knelt by the man. The eyes were staring at the night sky, but they were already beginning to glaze. He put his hand on the big chest, but he could feel nothing. He got to his feet and said:

"Damn! Damn me! I didn't have to hit him so hard."

"Would you have said please don't hit me with that big club again?" You said softly to his friend. *"Mon ami,* you had no choice."

"Yeah, but Christ! Maybe he would've been able to talk."

"I doubt that he would've known anything. Had they been anything but the dregs of the wharf they would not have taken such a job. Do not concern yourself."

"It's not me," Lafitte said. "But he might've known something. . . . I guess there'll be hell to pay with the law now."

"No . . . no, I don't really think so," Dominique replied with a confident note in his voice. "I have the ear of one of our . . . shall we say . . . prominent officials. I don't think they'll hold any undue inquiry into a thing that broke up such a bad scene, especially as our respected local police couldn't do it."

"Huh!" Lafitte grinned. "Yeah, you would. But what about the kids?"

"Watch," You said, turning to the frightened young people. "My dear children. What you have seen here tonight will only get you all long sentences as dope users should you repeat such a story, even in your sleep. Consider yourselves fortunate that we have decided to allow you all to go your way.

But, should you return, or speak of this, you will be arrested. Do I make myself clear to you all?"

There were a number of eager nods, several mumbles of assent, and many very wide eyes.

"*Bien!*" Dominique said loudly. "Now, did any of you see two men and a woman and a young girl?"

"Yes, sir," one boy said, frightened but eager to help. "It was like he said. They were here for a bit, talked to a man . . . over there in the shadows . . . and then they went back to where the boats are, and in a bit I heard a big motor take off."

"How the hell could you," Lafitte demanded, "with all that noise?"

"They were changing the record," the boy replied, his voice cracking.

"Huh." Lafitte grunted, not inclined at that moment to feel any pity for the boy's fear. "How long ago?"

"I . . . I don't know, sir. Maybe a half hour, maybe longer."

"All right," Lafitte said to Dominique in a low voice. "Destroy their boats and let's go. Soon as we get a chance we'll call the law."

You shook his head and pointed at the sky. "*Mon ami,* if I may say so, I do not think we should. It is too still and the air is heavy. There's a storm coming. It might only be a rain, but if it hits here without them having boats. . . well, the island is very low. As to the law, no. I suggest we let the children go. What they have seen tonight just might make a few good Christians. . . . And I think my friend will convince them that they should leave well enough alone. . . . What say you?"

"How the hell can you? You can't keep a thing like this quiet. Those kids are bound to talk!"

"Certainly they are!" Dominique grinned and nodded. "And the more they talk the bigger the story will get, and wilder, and no one will believe them."

"Yeah? What about the bodies? That, they'll believe."

"*Mon ami,* now that this thing is broken up, the police will not do much. They'll want to keep it quiet because someone did their job for them. They'll not want the press to point at them for not doing their duty. There'll be wild stories for a while, the law will say nothing, and the thing will become rumor, and legend, and no one will ever really know, not even these kids."

"But they may recognize you. You're a local citizen."

"Didn't I tell you? All the people at the Cove saw me there until closing time."

"Huh!" Lafitte said, staring at his friend. "You should be the president of the PTA. Well, okay. Let's hope that their parents take a board to their butts. But, come to think of it, if they had, most of these kids wouldn't be here. . . . All right, let's get at it."

Lafitte looked at Blondy and Marcel and inclined his head toward the boats. They nodded and started down the path. Then Lafitte turned to the young people and said loudly:

"Be grateful! You got a second chance. The law picks you up for this and you go to jail! And get off the island, there's a storm coming!"

Lafitte nodded to Dominique and they started toward the path. Lafitte went a couple of feet, stopped, turned to the crowd and added:

"And we recognize a number of you! Should any girl be left behind, those we know will get beaten to a pulp, then go to jail!"

As Dominique followed his friend down the path he chuckled and said, "Me and the PTA?"

They quickly paddled to the catamarans and just before they separated, Dominique said, "Marcel, take the pirogues. Check your radios as soon as you're aboard."

The two men nodded, and Lafitte and You climbed into You's boat. Marcel took the pirogue in tow, then Blondy's. While Marcel was tying the pirogues so that they'd tow properly, Dominique took a moment to lean over his railing and talk to Abe. The big man nodded when his boss was through and started his engines. The other boats were fired up and Dominique moved out, his hand on the mike.

"South, at top speed . . . and fan out a few degrees. I'll go due south. Abe to my right, Blondy and Marcel to port, each two, three degrees from each other. And no lights!"

You started to replace the mike, then thought of something else. "Marcel? *Tu comprend mon anglais?*"

"*Oui, mon amiral!*" Marcel shouted almost gleefully.

"Dehors!" Dominique replied with a shake of his head and cut the mike.

Despite the situation Lafitte couldn't help but grin at Marcel's reference to Dominique. The other two boats acknowledged with a simple "Out," and they headed south. After a few moments Lafitte came to stand by You and said:

"What are our chances?"

Dominique turned from the wheel and looked at Lafitte for a long moment, then said, "Only fair. If they're headed for either island, that is. On the good side of the ledger is the fact that there's not a boat around here that can outrun my catamarans . . . that is, if they don't have too big a start."

Lafitte nodded, his face set. He got the answer he thought he would. "What if they're not going there?"

You checked the boat to his right and the two to his left whose wakes were rapidly disappearing in the dark before he spoke. "Then, *mon ami,* we're going for a long boat ride. If that man was telling the truth . . . and *par Dieu,* I think you convinced him . . . then we've got a chance. If not, or if they told him that to deceive us, then there are several hundred miles of bays and bayous that they could have gone into. . . . Whatever this chance, it's our only one."

Lafitte shivered, nodded, and went out of the small cabin to stand on the port side to stare into the night. They pounded down the smooth bay for several miles, You watching ahead and Lafitte scanning either side, occasionally lifting his leg to the railing to rub it; the unexpected activity of the evening had stretched many long unused muscles.

"My friend," Dominique said over the roar of the engine, "more to make conversation than to pry, may I ask a personal question?"

"Certainly," Lafitte answered, going into the cabin so he wouldn't have to shout. "I might not answer, but ask."

"Your grandfather once told me you had a commission in the army before you were hurt. What happened?"

"I was dumb. I thought I knew the swamp so well I could hunt alone."

"I would not be so inclined. You were braver than I."

"No, not really. Dumber, no doubt. She's the constant enemy, and I was giving her another go. . . . Well, that time she got me. You know, Dominique, I always liked the swamp. It had a sort of an ethereal beauty with the cypress and acres of lily pads and the water as smooth as green oil. . . ."

"Yes, it does that," You said. "But if you were expert, what got you?"

"My own stupidity. I let down a bit. I got careless for that split second."

"Yes," You nodded. "That's all it takes. What was it?"

"Well, I wasn't even hunting, I was just out taking pot shots at alligator gar and snakes. I was on my way back, just walking along, taking in all that beauty and quiet. I was going along a log that looked solid, rather than take a chance on some damp sand, and I was almost to the end of it when the last step gave way and my right leg fell through and was pinned. I ended up sitting on the log with my pants leg pushed up and my ankle in the water. And, like a damn fool, I was wearing sneakers. I tried to pull loose, but a split in the log had a grip on my ankle . . . you know, like one of those Chinese hand traps? The harder you pull the tighter the grip? Well, after a couple of tries I decided to be smart, so I turned around and put my rifle on the log and when I turned back there was a water moc. . . ."

Lafitte stopped talking and shivered once. You turned from the wheel, then turned back quickly to stare out the windshield.

"Then," Lafitte continued, "I made a mistake I swore I'd never make again, I panicked. I went out of my mind with fright and I yelled and pulled back on my leg . . . and that did it. My foot wiggled and the snake hit me on the ankle. I twisted it and I only managed to lay open the spot where the bite was and I shoved a batch of dirty slivers into the wound. . . ."

"Ooh! *Mon ami!* Did you get loose then?"

"No, I was still locked in."

"What about the snake?"

"Well, I got a deep breath and tried to get hold of myself and I reached back for my rifle. By then the snake was swimming away and I took a half dozen shots at it."

"Get him?"

"No." Lafitte shook his head and grinned ruefully. "Not even close."

"How long did it take you to get free?"

"I don't really know. Seemed like an hour. It was less than

that, of course, and then I realized that I needed to open the wound and I didn't have a knife. And the more I fought it the quicker the venom ran through me . . . and I knew that, too. So, I finally got hold of my guts and figured out that by leaning forward into the water and using the rifle as a lever that I could force the log far enough apart so I could wiggle my leg, but I couldn't get enough leverage to get free. . . .

"Man, I tell you, I was really scared, and time was running out. I was just about to panic again when I told myself if I did, I was a dead man. . . . Oh, I knew that I'd probably survive one bite. But I also knew that if I didn't get free soon that I'd go out of my head, get delirious, and then I'd either drown or get bitten again. And I was bleeding pretty good, and it was making a big stain in the water."

You nodded. "And that would bring more trouble."

"Uh huh. Anyway, I finally made a decision. I spread the log as much as possible, took a deep breath, yelled like a banshee, and literally ripped my foot free. I tore a lot more skin off the leg and really laid it open. It began to bleed like mad. . . . Christ! What a day."

"I see you made it back," Dominique observed.

"Yeah. Like barely. I wasn't even wearing a belt, so I tore up my shirt as best I could and tied the ankle and the foot, and forced the shoe back on and wrapped the whole thing again, but I couldn't stop the bleeding. I could feel it pump out at every step, but I knew I had to make it out of the swamp so I kept going. . . . Sam found me a couple of hours later, wandering at the edge of the fields. I was out of it by then, of course, but they rushed me to the hospital. The doctors had to take a lot of meat off to save the leg. It wasn't the bite so much, but it seems there was some sort of fungus on the log. . . . Anyway, there went a promising army career."

You shrugged. "It's not much comfort, I know, but such things happen. You were lucky to survive."

"Yeah." Lafitte smiled. "I was, at that. If I'd stayed in the army I'd've never met Sandy."

"Good," You nodded. "That's a proper way to look at it."

"As you say," Lafitte agreed. "Such things happen."

They continued their run down the main channel without seeing a thing. After they'd gone a good eight miles, You pointed to a dark mass to port.

"Mon ami, I made a command decision, as I think I know the waters better than you do."

"I agree. So?"

"So we had a choice. We could've passed on the other side of that island and into the main channel, but I think if I was going to either Grand Isle or Grand Terre I would've passed to this side of the island."

"Okay." Lafitte agreed. "You made a decision."

You nodded and turned back to the business of keeping on course. After a couple more miles the radio crackled and he picked up the mike and said: "Anything?"

"A boat," Abe replied.

"Halte! Halte!" You commanded. "All stop! Blondy! Come west. We should be a mile or so from you and three hundred yards out."

Dominique eased up on the throttle and turned the wheel to starboard and headed toward Abe's boat. When they were alongside, You called to Abe in a low voice:

"Where, Abe?"

The man pointed a few points off his starboard bow and they could make out the dark outline of a speedboat bobbing on the small swells made by the catamarans. They watched for a minute or so, but they could see nothing else. You nodded and waved to Blondy as he came alongside and pointed to the boat. Blondy waved back and approached the small boat at reduced speed. When he was close he set the wheel and stood at the starboard side, his .38 in his hand, and let his boat drift slowly, until he laid his hand on the engine, then opened his throttle and made a tight turn and deftly stopped it at Dominique's port side. Lafitte grabbed the rope and held it fast as Marcel reported to his boss.

"No one. And no pirogues. I think they ran out of gas."

You nodded and turned to Lafitte. "This point juts out into the bay. It is all swamp except for a few small humps of land that stick up a couple of feet above high tide. It is not near Grand Isle or Grand Terre, but it is on the way. They may have a place to hole up, or they may have just run out of gas."

"Uh huh," Lafitte said. "How big is this swamp?"

"Very big."

"Damn!" Lafitte said. Then, "What do you suggest?"

"Run around the other side and check it. I see no point in

going in from this side, too slow. It is possible that they used a pirogue to get through the swamp and then have power boats waiting on the other side. They may have thought they were being followed, they may even have heard our boats in the dark."

Lafitte nodded, considering the possibilities. They were not good.

"And," Dominique continued, "it is pure swamp. Even the catamarans can't get through there."

Lafitte looked at Blondy, still in his boat. "Is it anchored?"

"No," Blondy replied. "And it is about where it stopped. There is very little drift here. . . . One other thing, the engine is still warm, it was not too long ago."

"How do we know it's their boat?" Lafitte asked.

"It is remotely possible that it is not theirs," Dominique said with a Gallic shrug, "but it almost has to be. Who else would leave a good boat like that? And how would they leave without another boat? Only a madman would try to swim to a swamp at night."

Lafitte nodded at this bit of logic and then said, "How long would it take them to get through?"

Blondy shrugged. "Half hour maybe, perhaps an hour. As I recall this place, it is not too wide."

"Uh huh," Lafitte said. "And how long for us to run around?"

"A good fifteen, twenty minutes, even at top speed," Dominique said.

"Son of a bitch!" Lafitte said, his eyes narrowed. "Then they can still make it. . . . Well, it's the only chance, we'd best get at it. Sink the boat, you think? In case it's a trap."

You nodded, looking at the sky with a frown. "Good. Blondy? Then come close."

Blondy again pulled his boat close to the drifting outboard while they waited a moment. Then You returned to the cabin and was busy with the radio. Lafitte heard Abe's radio crackle as Blondy leaned over his railing, and then Lafitte heard the sound of the hatchet. As the outboard started to list, a great gust of warm wind came out of the swamp and the boats bobbed like dry leaves for a moment and Dominique said into his mike:

"Venez! Venez!"

Blondy pulled his boat into a tight circle and tied up next

to Abe who was tossing a line to Dominique. The other boat was approaching fast and it seemed to Lafitte that he cut his engine and pulled on the wheel too late, but Marcel came in smartly and tossed Lafitte a line. The boat was pulled close and all three men jumped onto the deck of You's boat.

Lafitte glanced at the set faces and said: "What am I missing?"

"The barometers are falling madly," Dominique said, "and the Coast Guard is broadcasting storm warnings. A hurricane is crossing the Gulf, we're sure to get a piece of it."

Lafitte looked at the men and they averted their eyes, waiting for their boss to speak.

"So?" Lafitte said.

"If it changes direction a bit," Dominique said in a low voice, "we will get the center of it."

Lafitte clenched his teeth to fight back the shiver that was running up his back. His wife and the girl in a swamp was bad enough, but in a hurricane they couldn't run fast enough. He thought for a moment, searching for the right words, then said:

"And a small boat won't stand a chance. . . . Dominique, I can't ask you to go on. And I want you to know how much I appreciate what you've done for me, but I have to keep at it. Let me have a boat, show me how to run it, and it goes without saying that Jeremy or the old man will replace it if I don't manage to get back in one piece, but please let me borrow a boat."

"No. No, I could not do that," Dominique said with a stern face. Then he grinned and grabbed Lafitte's shoulder. "I will go with you. I have to look after my property."

"Thank you." Lafitte smiled at his friend. "I won't say no." Then he turned to look at the other three, leaning in a row on the rail. "Gentlemen, I thank you for your help, you're free to return. Thank you again."

The three men stared at each other for a moment, then nodded in serious unison to Lafitte, and each man returned to his boat. The lines were freed and the boats pushed apart. You, a small smile at the corners of his mouth, opened the throttles and pulled out, cut hard to port, and ran for the open bay.

He nudged Lafitte as his grin widened and said, "Watch the boats."

Abe revved his engine, pulled into a half circle and fell in behind You's boat and a bit to port. He was quickly followed by Blondy and Marcel until the small armada was in echelon at flank speed. Lafitte grinned and he put his fingers to the bridge of his nose a moment, and then the grin went into a chuckle and he said:

"Damn! Look at that! But of course you knew?"

"Of course," You replied complacently. "I told you they were good men."

"Huh!" Lafitte said, "with a hundred men like that I could take New Orleans."

Dominique raised an eyebrow at the remark and then Lafitte wondered why he'd said it and speculated for a moment on the wild idea that he might, indeed, be a throwback. He grinned widely, shook his head and clapped You on the back, and shouted above the roar of the engines:

"Give her hell, *mon ami!*"

Under different circumstances it would have been the ride of a lifetime for Lafitte. As it was, they couldn't go fast enough, though they never hit less than thirty knots, even when You was negotiating a slipping turn around the edge of the point with the other three flanked out on the port side. Lafitte kept Dominique's big binoculars on the edge of the swamp as they rounded the point at a distance of four hundred yards. Though the moon was still out, he could see nothing but green-black vegetation. The wind and sea increased; not enough to be a problem, but enough so that every man was aware that the storm was coming.

Then they were heading west. They went another three, maybe four, miles and were almost to the point where the swamp joined the mainland when Lafitte saw a slight glow through the glasses. He nudged You and shouted:

"There's a fire!"

You nodded, picked up the mike, and said, "*Venez!* Come alongside and tie up!"

When the four boats were lashed to each other and all the men were in Dominique's boat they had a brief discussion while Lafitte continued to watch the fire. They went over Dominique's map and Abe got another weather report. Then, to Lafitte's surprise, the men quickly returned to their boats and cut loose, heading southwest at a slow, quiet speed. Lafitte watched the fire for a while as they went away from it at an angle, until he could stand it no longer; then he said, almost as a passing comment:

"I've never been this far south. I, uh, presume you know where you're going?"

"Yes. As a matter of fact I do." You smiled and pointed to the map spread out under the dim light on the small plotting table. "And, to ease your mind somewhat, that fire is undoubtedly what we are looking for. Here," You tapped the map with a finger, "the swamp runs due west on the south side. The only thing between us and the Gulf of Mexico are a couple of islands. Now, the water is rising, and so is the wind. The Coast Guard doesn't exactly expect a hurricane through here, otherwise we'd be on our way to our graves, but we will get the end of it and one helluva storm. It may not hit for a few hours, but we must protect the boats."

"Where? They're not submarines."

"True." Dominique pointed to a small dot on the map labeled SM. "That is a salt mound. It is not very big, nor very high, but we can put an oil pot on the south end as a guide and ride out the storm, heading into it. Our greatest danger is in being washed ashore. The wind will rise and the waves will tend to push us toward the swamp. Without something as a marker we could be scattered for miles. Besides, if the storm isn't too great, it can serve us well."

Lafitte nodded in agreement. He'd seen salt mounds before, rising out of the swamp, or close to it, humps of almost pure salt, sticking up like mushrooms. Nothing would grow on them and they usually lasted but a few years, to be washed flat again by the tide. The mounds themselves were of no particular commercial value, except that they usually denoted a sizable deposit of salt. His grandfather had once invested in some of the state's salt mines, but these were great mines under the ground where the salt was taken out by the carload. The thought made him wonder how the old man was doing, but then he shook his head and brought himself back to the terrible present and studied the map and nodded; he agreed with Dominique's plan. They had stopped as soon as they'd seen the light, which put them southeast of the fire. The salt mound, while it was southwest of the fire and could cause them a two or three-mile trip, had one great advantage; it was only about a half mile from the swamp.

You kept the engine throttled down as they beat their way into a rising wind. When they'd gone a good two miles they made a wide sweep to the north and came toward shore, the wind behind them and the mound hiding the dim glow of the fire. When they were close, You directed his boats into a tight turn so they were heading south, one behind the other, and lashed some ten feet apart. Then he waved to his men and held his left fist to his cheek. When they were all on the radio he said:

"Marcel and Abe, take a pirogue and go in for a look. And take a radio with you. If you need help, call at once and we will come for you. If you are seen, try to get to water deep enough for the cats. . . . Go quickly!"

There were two replies, "Okay," and one *"Oui."* Dominique replaced the mike and turned to Lafitte.

"Now, *mon ami,* it may not be them. It may be only some poor Cajun shrimper who took to the beach to ride out the storm. But, if it is not them, still they will have had to stop somewhere for the storm and as soon as it clears we will spread out and run for Grand Isle and Grand Terre."

"I know," Lafitte said quietly, "I thought of that. And also of the fact that we might've already missed them out there somewhere . . . but searching is better than waiting. I want to go with them."

"No!" You said firmly, leaving no room for debate. Then, "Are you good with that rifle?"

"Yes."

"Well, I am the best at running one of these boats and if they get into trouble we stand a better chance of getting them out, not the other way around. Besides, Marcel and Abe are the strongest, therefore the best with paddle and pole in shallow water."

Lafitte shrugged. He didn't like the idea of not going, but he couldn't disagree with the logic.

They had been gone about ten minutes when Dominique said, "They should be getting close."

He picked up the mike and made sure the channel was open and then waited some more. Suddenly You looked to the south and said, "Damn!"

"What is it?" Lafitte asked.

"Look," You said, pointing to the water.

Then Lafitte nodded. He'd been so intent on watching for

the pirogue that he'd failed to notice that the wind had completely died. The water was no longer covered with small, choppy waves. Instead there were long, smooth ground swells. There was no wind and it was completely silent. Lafitte's eyes narrowed, knowing that time was growing short.

"How long?" he asked.

"No way of telling. Ten minutes, an hour maybe. When the rain comes, in those big, hard drops, that is when it will be close."

Lafitte nodded again and leaned against the port rail in stoic silence for a long twenty minutes. He was sweating in the balmy night, but his only outward indication of concern was his clenched jaw, and several times Dominique You shook his head in admiration of his friend's iron patience. Finally the radio crackled and there was a low whistling sound. You grabbed the mike and said, *"Oui?"* in a low voice.

"We're comin' back," Abe whispered. "Nobody saw us. Hang loose."

"Quickly," Dominique replied and replaced the mike.

They watched the east edge of the salt mound for over five minutes before they made out the slim form of the pirogue and the straining bodies of the two powerful paddlers. As they came alongside, Lafitte extended his hand and pulled first Abe, then Marcel over the rail. Marcel tied the hollowed-out log to the stern rail and turned with a wide grin, nodded, and Lafitte let out a large sigh.

When they had their breath after the hard paddling, Marcel said:

"You will not believe it, boss. Let me use your pad, I will draw it."

Lafitte handed Abe a canteen and Dominique got a big pad from the cabin and a pen and Marcel drew a rough map. At the bottom was the salt mound and the four boats. Above that he drew a roughly straight line.

"The edge of the swamp," Marcel said. "From fifty yards out it is very shallow, from two feet down to maybe a foot. But you will not believe what we saw! The fire is on a rise at the south edge of the swamp. But it is dry and solid. The thing of wonder is that there is a house. At first we thought it was but a shack, it looks so. But as we got close we saw that the pilings are great shafts sunk into the water. It has a solid corrugated roof, though it is covered with palm leaves to hide it. Someone built it to stand many storms. But there is no way to get at it."

"Could you see inside?" Lafitte asked. Then added, "What do you mean, there's no way to get at it?"

"Well, suh," Abe said, almost reluctantly, as he handed the canteen to Marcel. "It's like this. The fire is 'bout a hundred feet from the house, and the fire is out in the middle of a big clearin'. There wuz five men around the fire and we moved 'round the side of the house to the little beach; there wuz another man at the door to the house . . . it faces to the land. . . ."

"And why couldn't you get closer or get at it, like Marcel said?"

"Mistah Lafitte," Abe said, "around that house fer a distance of maybe twenty yards is a little bitty fence, wire, sticking up but two or three feet above the water."

"So?" Dominique said.

Abe shivered as he remembered what he'd seen, then continued in a low voice. "We got close, so close the boat bumped the fence . . . and it's a good thing it did. The fence shook and they wiggled all around. . . ."

"They?" Lafitte said, knowing the answer but not really wanting to hear it.

"Yes, suh," Abe replied, his black eyes wide. "Inside that fence is a jillion water mocs. Nobody could git near that house without gettin' hisself eaten alive."

There was a silence for a few moments and Lafitte and You exchanged brief nods, each man realizing that the shack was a sort of barracoon, probably part of Mejia's smuggling, and Lafitte's wife was undoubtedly in there. Lafitte shook his head and turned toward the stern, staring into the blackness, and forced his mind to approach the problem clearly, though there was a cold knot of fear in his stomach. Even though they might be able to take the men by the fire, that had the obvious drawback that the man guarding the shack could dictate his own terms, as long as he held a gun to Sandy's head. They could cut a hole in the fence, perhaps pull out several sections in the dark, but there was no assurance that the snakes would take the hint and leave. They could not try to storm the fence with one or all of the catamarans, even their shallow draft would hang them up in such water. They could not even charge the men on land in the dark, there was too much cover, any attack would have to wait until it was light enough to see. Lafitte was in no mood to wait out the night and the storm; there was but one way. He shivered at his conclusion, then thought again of Sandy and took a deep breath and turned to Dominique.

"Do you have any long rubber boots, or some plastic tarp?"

"Jean!" Dominique said incredulously. "You wouldn't!"

"Dominique," Lafitte said, a flat note of finality in his voice. "My wife is in there. After the storm she may not be. If you've got something I can use, I'm going in. It can be done, if I move slowly. . . . And, Dominique, these snakes won't spook me."

Dominique You stared at his friend for a moment, at the squinted eyes, the jaw muscles showing from the clenched teeth, and then Dominique grinned, slowly at first, then widely until he chuckled. *Par Dieu!* If you will go I will see that you get there! We must have something we can use."

"Yes, suh!" Abe grinned and nodded his head at Lafitte's bravery. "We shorely do. I got a pair of hip waders."

"Bien," Dominique said. "Get them."

Abe nodded and went to the stern of You's boat and with a mighty heave on the line pulled the boats closer together. But even his great strength couldn't make it, and You said, *"Un moment,"* and went into the cabin and eased up on the throttle a bit until the boats drew close enough for Abe to jump. As soon as he was on his own boat You picked up speed again so the boats wouldn't collide and stood by. In a few moments Abe appeared on the prow waving something and the process was repeated. Lafitte and Marcel were there to help Abe aboard and the throttle was pushed forward again and the rope became taut.

"They's big," Abe said with his wide grin. "But ain't a snake alive kin git his fangs through that. They's made for the swamps, got that there fiberglass in between."

"Good boy!" Lafitte said gratefully.

The waders were waist-high and much too big, but they were good and heavy, and Lafitte nodded, they'd do nicely. He struggled into them and pulled the wide waist up to his chest. Dominique grinned and cut a length of light line from a coil in the cabin and rigged a serviceable belt. When it was

secured, Lafitte walked a few steps and turned to the men
and nodded.

"Soigneux," Marcel said. "You must take great care not to
flinch, or go for the snake. One might get your hand."

"Thank you," Lafitte grinned. "In other words I've gotta
let 'em take a bite at my ass without a quiver."

"That is indeed it," You said with a resigned nod, then
added, *"Toque!"*

"I beg your pardon?" Lafitte said, not remembering the
word.

"I said you're crazy," Dominique replied. "You ready?"

"Yes."

You handed Lafitte his rifle and added, "You have extra
bullets . . . and a knife?"

"Yes. And two knives."

You nodded and went to the cabin and pulled a rifle from
a locker under one of the cabin bunks. "A magnum. Cripple
anything it hits."

Lafitte nodded and turned to Marcel and Abe. "You guys
stand by the radio, you hear?"

Both men nodded and Lafitte turned and leaned over the
rail and stared at the last boat and waved at Blondy's dim
outline. Blondy waved back and held his fist to his cheek,
he'd get the news from the radio. Marcel waved and picked
up the mike to relay the news to Blondy as Abe helped Lafitte and You into the pirogue.

They paddled their way around the point of the salt
mound, and for half the distance to the swamp then Dominique stood in the back of the log boat and used the pole
while Lafitte watched the shore. They moved forward silently
over the smooth water, the firelight getting brighter without
either man seeing a sign of life. Then You eased up on the
pole and the boat gently glided into the low wire fence. Lafitte stared down into the water inside the fence and shivered
involuntarily; the water was pulsating with the bodies of the
snakes. Despite himself Lafitte hesitated.

You worked his way forward until he was at Lafitte's
shoulder and whispered, "Jean, I went for the charade in
front of the men, and properly so. But let's cut the wire and
pole in."

"No," Lafitte said, turning his head to reply in a bare whis-

per. "I appreciate the offer. And I know why you're making
it. But don't worry, I won't panic this time. Besides, if we're
both seen inside the wire there's no chance. They have to
have flashlights. If they do, we're both dead, and you know
it. We do it this way."

Without waiting for an answer Lafitte stepped into the
water outside the fence. He was up to his knees and he wisely
took the time to try his footing. He took a few steps, then
moved forward rapidly to test the drag on his heavily weight-
ed legs and almost lost his balance; he quickly realized that
he would have to move very slowly. He glanced over his
shoulder and silently said, "Whew!" to Dominique and then
stepped over the fence, very carefully.

His legs were immediately struck by many snakes and he
flinched and shivered, but paused as the fear washed over
him and his shoulders shook for a moment. Then he thought
again of his wife and he took a deep breath and looked down
stoically as the snakes struck again and again. When he was
in control of himself he looked over his shoulder at You and
nodded once, then turned forward and started a slow, dragging surge toward the pilings of the house, barely visible in
the darkness ahead.

The snakes slithered about him, but he was struck less as
he moved forward and Abe's prediction was right. Still it was
an eerie feeling to have a snake hang onto his leg for a moment before dropping back into the water, and he had to
fight the natural instinct to react. After a shivering fifty feet
he began to think he'd be all right . . . assuming he didn't
lose his footing or wasn't seen. He moved forward steadily,
testing every footstep. The water was only a foot deep now
and he began to gain a bit of confidence; he grinned bleakly
and began to check the shoreline on each side of the shack.
There was no sound except the small swishing noise his boots
made in the water.

Then he was under the shack and his eyes narrowed. There
was no way inside except to go around and come in by the
front boardwalk which slanted out over the water to reach
dry land. The house was a good eight feet over the water,
and as he checked each of the ten shafts his hopes sank. He
slowly worked his way to the front corner of the house and
peered from the shadows and saw the glow of a cigar and the
outline of a man sitting on the ramp. He moved a few feet

toward the ramp, staying in the dark, and stood behind a piling. From there he had a good view of the fire. He watched a
few moments and then his eyes widened in surprise; there
were more than the four men they'd chased, but he couldn't
tell how many. Several were moving about from in front of
the fire and into a small nearby shack. It was low and, from
the fireglow, he could see that it had a tin roof and block
sides, obviously made to withstand the Gulf storms. The
shack was less than five feet high, indicating that it was partially sunk into the ground. After a few moments he was finally able to sort out the men; there were six, and the guard
above his head made seven.

A few minutes more and he was able to discern that two
of the men were darker, either black or Puerto Rican, but
none of the men was Mejia.

The man above him never spoke, and Lafitte was beginning to doubt if he could get into the house when Mother
Nature spawned one of her children and solved his problem
for him. The atmospheric quiet was broken by the sound of
huge raindrops, and the beginning of a squall hit with a beautiful suddenness. The men at the fire began to scurry about
and one shouted toward the house:

"Hey, George!"

The man on the steps grunted and trotted down the ramp
to help his friends move their gear into the shack. Lafitte
grinned and waited a moment or two until he saw the man at
the fire, and then he moved out into the pelting rain and staggered up the ramp in his heavy rubber pants like Franken-
stein's monster. As he crossed the doorway there was a gasp
from the darkness inside and then a woman's voice cried:

"Jean! My God, Jean!"

"Easy, honey," Lafitte said as he lumbered inside. It was
very dark and he couldn't see, but his wife's voice, lower
now, said:

"Over here!"

He followed the sound carefully and then his eyes adjusted
and he could see Sandy and the girl lashed to the center piling which went all the way to the roof and held the ridge-
pole. Sandy was standing but the girl was on her back, her
arms around the post. He pulled in a quick breath and put
his arm around her and kissed her cheek, then knelt quickly
by the child.

"They drugged her," Sandy said. "They forced her to swallow some pills."

"Is she all right?"

"I . . . I think so. Just knocked out."

Lafitte stood again and faced the door, then glanced at his wife as she raised her arm on the piling, and his hopes dropped. Her hands were not tied, they were handcuffed.

"Damn!" he muttered as he felt the cuffs, and then there was more lift from the fire as someone threw some fuel on it in an effort to keep it going and he saw that the cuffs were good ones, stainless-steel police cuffs.

"One of them has the keys," Sandy whispered "but not the one who was just here."

"Do you know who?"

"No," Sandy replied, the strain evident in her voice.

"Okay," Lafitte said, trying to sound positive, "that makes it easy, sweetheart. I'll be back. I've got Dominique You and lots of his men with me. Now don't worry, we'll be back soon. There's a storm coming and we may not be able to get back in until it's over, but we'll be close by. Hang tough, okay?"

Sandy gave him a small grin through the dirt on her face and managed to nod at the same time.

"Now," Lafitte said, adding a big lie, "we've got the island surrounded, so there's no need to worry."

She nodded again, though she was in partial shock and wanted to believe him. He checked the cuffs again and gave it up; even a shot from his rifle would do no good. As he looked around the sparsely furnished room, trying to memorize it for the next time, he heard the sound of heavy footsteps on the ramp and knew he was trapped. He leaned close to Sandy's ear and whispered:

"Get him in here."

Sandy swallowed, then nodded. Lafitte quickly crossed to the right side of the door and held the rifle across his chest, ready to swing the steel-jacketed butt. The man stopped outside, under the tin roof, and turned to stare toward the fire.

"George?" Sandy called, her voice sounding strange. But she didn't speak loud enough, the guard couldn't hear her over the pounding of the rain. She shouted this time. "George!"

Lafitte heard the man's footsteps as he approached and the

rifle was raised a bit as he got a glimpse of a tall form
through the crack in the door. George paused in the doorway
and said:

"Huh?"

"George," Sandy said, "I thought I'd take you up on your
offer. . . ."

"Ha!" George said. "So now you wanna try and fuck your
way outa here!"

Lafitte clenched his jaws and would have killed the man,
but he was still behind the door. Lafitte pulled in a slow
breath and waited, his eyes narrowed to slits.

"Well now," George said, trying to put a friendly tone into
his voice. "Maybe we can work something out."

He took two steps toward Sandy, and Lafitte stepped from
behind the door and said in a flat voice:

"We certainly can."

And he brought the butt of the rifle around in a short arc,
catching the man on the back of the head. There was a dull
thunk and George dropped to the floor. Lafitte glanced
quickly toward the fire, but the rain had stifled the sounds.
There was no one in sight. He turned to the body and rolled
George onto his back with his rifle. George did not move.
Satisfied that he was out, Lafitte knelt and searched the pants
of George's Levi's, then checked the pocket of his soaked
sport shirt. Then he rolled the body on its face and found
the hip pockets empty.

"Damn!" he muttered and got to his feet. To Sandy he
said, "Don't worry, we'll still get you out of here."

"Sure," Sandy replied, her voice quaking. "What about
him?"

"I'll take him with me," Lafitte replied, chancing the fact
that his wife didn't know what was under the pilings. She
didn't. She merely nodded and he was glad he'd lied to her.
He kissed her again on the cheek and turned to nudge
George. The big man groaned but didn't move, and Lafitte
began to worry that he'd struck too hard. He looked around
and saw a pitcher and a basin in the corner. He put the rifle
against the wall and poured some water into the basin and
handed the pitcher to Sandy. She took it with a grateful nod
and while she drank he pitched the water in the basin on the
head of the inert form, replaced the basin quickly, and
picked up the rifle.

"Get up, you bastard!" Lafitte said in a low voice.

George shook his head, groaned and sat up. Then he saw the rifle and his eyes widened. "How the hell did you get in?"

Then he saw the oversize waders and he nodded and rubbed his head as Lafitte said:

"Who's got the key?"

George stared at him a moment, his eyes narrowed, then widened as his thick mind reasoned it out and he stood up, grinning. "And if you come in that way, you come alone . . . so you won't shoot that thing."

"Don't try!" Lafitte said, trying to sound confident, though he knew George was right, he wouldn't shoot.

George paused a moment, then backed slowly toward the door, and Lafitte shifted the gun to his left hand and said, "Hold it! You'll never make it to the end of those planks."

"Huh!" George said, making his final decision. "And if I don't they'll never let me make it outa here. I'll take the chance."

"Yeah, you will," Lafitte agreed, remembering the big man's words to his wife. "You're gonna be playing a game called you bet your ass!"

George didn't reply but backed another step. Now he was in the doorway. Lafitte's right hand moved out and George thought Lafitte was going to swing the rifle; he turned and darted for the ramp and Lafitte's hand whipped to the back of his belt and pulled one of the knives. He took two steps forward to stand in the doorway and tossed the knife in the air so that he could grab it by the blade. His right arm went back and George was halfway down the planks when the knife caught him in the middle of the back, but butt first, and dropped harmlessly into the water. George grunted loudly, spun around and grinned, sure now that Lafitte wouldn't shoot, and started up the ramp.

"And you still won't shoot," George said, a triumphant note in his voice, " 'cause I ain't got the key. And I'm gonna drop you into the water and I'll still git her!"

Lafitte backed up, now holding the rifle with both hands, the left at the upper end of the stock, the right hand lightly on the grip. He knew he was at a disadvantage because of the waders but didn't even consider the man's size, and it was too late for the other knife. He dropped the rifle a bit, backed up another step, and then Lafitte's quick eye showed him a way.

George was advancing with his hands spread at waist height, the fingers stiffly extended, karate fashion. Lafitte suddenly grinned, backed another step, and said:

"Ever hear the story about the karate expert and the jack-handle?"

George blinked and hesitated a fraction of a second and Lafitte rocked on his right foot and suddenly lunged forward, as though his rifle had a bayonet.

"Yaa!" Lafitte yelled in reaction to his charge and his aim was true. The end of the barrel sank into George's chest, just below the sternum.

George grunted and doubled over as the breath was forced from him. Lafitte quickly returned the rifle and lunged again without moving his feet and caught the big man in the throat and the fight was over. George staggered back against the wall, retching and holding his stomach as he fought for a breath of air.

But this time Lafitte decided he'd learned his lesson. As he stepped forward, momentarily lighted by the fireglow from the door, George's surprise turned to fear when he saw Lafitte's face, and then the rifle butt caught George alongside the head, but lightly.

As the big man started to pitch forward, Lafitte let go of the rifle with his right hand and grabbed a handful of greasy hair and impelled his target to the doorjamb. George, incoherent, almost unconscious, instinctively grabbed the rough boards for support. Lafitte stared at the shack, barely visible now as the rain came down in buckets; he smiled as the fire quickly dropped to a dim glow and decided he might not be seen. Then, staring a moment at the unseen water below, he paused, but only for a second, and with a cold rage he pulled George out on the ramp and to the railing and said:

"No, I don't think you will."

With a final lurch he jerked the staggering body to the rail and gasped as the pain came again to his right shoulder; he backed away, gritting his teeth. George hung over the railing, momentarily suspended, and Lafitte put down the rifle and put his arms under George's legs and raised up, dumping the body into the blackness. After the splash there was a shaking in the water over the sound of the rain and Lafitte shivered but quickly controlled it, knowing George never felt a thing.

Rubbing his shoulder, he stooped and picked up his rifle and stared toward the shore, listening. There was no sound but the pounding rain on the roof. Holding the gun in his right hand, the left still on his shoulder, he went into the dark room just as a bolt of lightning lighted the sky.

"Honey?" Sandy said apprehensively.

"Yes," Lafitte said, coming close to put his cheek next to hers. "I'm all right. I'm just getting too old for this sort of thing."

"Sure you are!" Sandy said, and Lafitte could feel her face break into a smile.

"Good girl!" he whispered. "Don't go 'way now, you hear?"

She nodded and he turned away quickly and lumbered to the door. He made his way carefully down the ramp, took a deep breath, and stepped into the shallow water. He purposely forced himself to stand still a moment, though he shivered at each strike. Teeth gritted again, he worked his way under the house and into the open water. When he was halfway to the fence the lightning hit again and he felt horribly exposed, though he saw Dominique waving him on with his rifle. Then the driving rain subsided to a gentle downpour, and Lafitte resisted the urge to move faster and forced himself to make his way to the fence as before, slowly, carefully, testing each footstep before he put his full weight on it. He was only ten feet from the fence when his boot slipped a few inches, but he quickly recovered, knowing how close he came to being a dead man.

At the fence he paused to let out his breath and gave himself a moment, but as careful as he was he almost didn't make it. As he raised one heavy foot to lift it over the wire a snake took one last strike, this time at the inside of his thigh. He yelled out in fear and instinctively leaned back, and almost lost his balance. But the rifle over his head made the difference and he recovered, the heavy boot hitting the water with a splash. He wisely held his position a moment and then the barrel of Dominique's rifle was there to grab for support. Lafitte let out a long breath in a whooshing sound and pulled on it and lifted the other foot over the fence and he was in clear water.

Then the thought came to him that a snake might be still clinging to the heavy rubber. He moved his legs, but he couldn't be sure, so he handed Dominique his rifle and said, "Hold on."

You knelt down and grabbed both sides of the narrow boat and Lafitte pushed it a good ten feet in hopes of shaking off any hooked water mocs. When the water began to rise he whispered to Dominique:

"Get back and watch. Can you see okay?"

"Yes."

Lafitte held the boat steady while Dominique moved back to the prow of the tiny boat, put Lafitte's rifle down, and held his steady. As he held onto the boat, Lafitte lifted his left leg out of the water a moment, then put it into the bottom of the boat. There was nothing clinging to the wader and Dominique extended the barrel of his rifle and Lafitte took it and pulled himself into the boat, being careful to stand erect.

"I think I'm alone," Lafitte whispered, "but I'm not real sure, I can't feel too well through these things."

Then the lightning hit again and You looked into the bottom of the boat and back to Lafitte as he quickly spun around for inspection.

"All clear," Dominique whispered, "but don't sit down. The snakes hit a lot?"

"God yes! Fifty times, a hundred!"

"Hold still," Dominique said.

He pulled a knife and cut the rope belt and reached inside the waist of the waders and sliced the left leg to the toe. He repeated the process with the other leg and the waders dropped. Putting one hand on You's shoulder, Lafitte kicked clear and You hooked them with his knife and dragged them overboard and Lafitte knelt in the stern of the boat. You swished his knife in the water, put it away, and grasped his friend by the shoulders.

"*Mon Dieu!* That was a thing you did! Did you find them?"

"Yeah, but let's get the hell outa here! I'll tell you on the way."

Dominique nodded and they stood up and each grabbed a pole and forced it into the water. When they were well underway, You looked over his shoulder and said:

"Is she all right?"

"Yes," Lafitte replied in a low voice. "They'll both be all right for a time."

"Bon! How many?"

"There were seven. Now there're six."

By the time they'd reached the catamaran Lafitte had told Dominique everything in detail. All three of Dominique's men were now in his boat, leaning over the side to help them aboard. Blondy held the line while Abe and Marcel helped them over the rail. Then Blondy tied the line to the cleat and allowed the pirogue to float to the stern, next to the other one.

When all five were assembled inside the cabin Blondy let the tarp down and Marcel turned the cabin lights up a bit, reached into a locker, and produced a bottle of cognac.

"Against the weather," Marcel grinned and handed the bottle to Lafitte.

Lafitte nodded, took a swig, though he didn't particularly like cognac, and passed the bottle to Dominique. "Good for snakebite, too."

The men grinned and Lafitte began stripping off the thoroughly soaked and now heavy sweatshirt. As he pulled it off his head the bandana came with it. Dominique returned the bottle to Marcel and opened a small locker and tossed Lafitte a heavy towel. Lafitte nodded and threw it over his head and began to dry his head but stopped abruptly. He pulled the towel to his neck and gingerly put his fingers to the left side of his head; he'd forgotten about the cut. His fingers came away bloody.

"Here, let me see," Dominique said. He examined the wound a moment and added, "It's open again. You should have that sutured."

"No, it'll be all right if I can keep it closed for a few hours."

Dominique nodded and reached into the locker again and this time brought out a bandana. This one was green. Lafitte took it in his left hand and shook it open, then folded it until it was a three-inch-wide band and wrapped it around his head, pulled it snug, and tied it at the back. Then he finished drying his arms and body and sat on a bunk and pulled off his soaked sneakers and socks and started drying his feet.

Dominique stripped to his shorts and found himself a towel and sat on the other bunk. As he used the towel he began to speak rapidly in French, with enough English thrown in so that Abe could follow. With a few expletives and a great deal of arm waving he explained the great feat of his friend. When he was through there was a round of grunts of admiration and You looked to Lafitte and said:

"And what do you suggest now?"

"Huh." Lafitte thought about Dominique's wording and held his hand out for the bottle. "Nothing. Goddam nothing! Not until the storm stops and we've got some daylight. Then we go in and get 'em." He took another pull from the bottle and returned it and nodded his head when Abe offered a cigarette and held a match. "Thank you. I'm not real keen on cognac but it sure warms you up." Then, realizing that Dominique had tendered him the invisible cloak of leadership, he added, "Now, if any of you have any qualms about killing that scum, speak up. You heard Dominique tell you about the one who would rape my wife. And I presume the others would have the same idea so, for me, I'll go in as soon as it's light and I'll kill every son of a bitch who tries to stop me. . . . I would be pleased to have you with me."

As he looked from face to face there was a round of dirty words in Cajun, and Dominique, speaking for the rest, said:

"Mon ami, you need not ask."

"Thank you," Lafitte said with a nod and a smile for the other three. "Blondy, you should be the most rested. Will you take the first watch and keep this thing pointed into the wind?"

"Certainement!"

"Then Marcel, me, and Abe," Dominique said. "But first we need some clothes. Your Levi's, are they soaked?"

"No, not really, just the front a bit."

"Bon. Socks and sweatshirts I have, and our shoes will be dry in an hour by the little heater, but I have but one more pair of pants, and mine are soaked. . . . Are you cold?"

"No," Lafitte replied. "The rain's warm, and that cognac's hotter'n hell!"

"True," Dominique grinned. "Are you hungry?"

"Hey!" Lafitte said, suddenly realizing that he was. "I could eat."

"Garçon!" Dominique said to Marcel. *"S'il vous plaît."*

"Oui, monsieur. Un fête. Aimez-vous le fromage rare?"

"Mais oui."

"Et vin rare?"

"Oui," Dominique grinned and Lafitte chuckled at the invitation to a feast of rare cheeses and wines.

"J'ai," Marcel said, holding out his left arm with an imaginary napkin on it, *"fromage ordinaire, vin ordinaire, et pain ordinaire."*

The two Frenchmen grinned and Marcel stooped to open the small refrigerator while Dominique put on dry Levi's and a sweatshirt and threw one to Lafitte. Lafitte caught it, put it on, and observed that the clothing was still black; friend Dominique must indeed transact a lot of business at night. But he kept his thoughts to himself as Marcel pulled down on the small table top and brought out a bottle of Inglenook burgundy, a big slab of jack cheese, a long loaf of French bread, two knives, and two water glasses.

"Have you guys eaten?" Lafitte asked.

"We will eat later," Marcel replied. "There is not enough room."

Lafitte nodded and decided that, as he was now bos, that he would be expected to eat first. He lifted the tarp and tossed his cigarette to the rain and poured himself half a glass of wine, hacked off a piece of cheese and a chunk of bread, and had at it. It was not exactly the feast Marcel had jokingly promised, but he was hungry and it was filling. Dominique joined him and they ate rapidly, finished their wine, and Dominique said:

"Rest, Jean . . . if you can."

"I can," Lafitte replied, then added softly, "I have to."

While the others ate, Lafitte stretched out on the bunk, put one arm over his eyes, and began to count his breaths, one, two, one, two, one. . . .

He felt someone shake him and he quickly opened his eyes and saw Dominique bending over him.

"Jean, it is time."

Lafitte nodded and sat up, rubbing the sleep from his eyes. Dominique handed him a clean pair of sweat socks and indicated his now dry sneakers on the deck. Lafitte swallowed a couple of times and quickly slipped on the socks and the shoes. He got to his feet, stretched, and felt the tightness in his right shoulder. The tarp was gone and he looked toward the stern, but there was nothing to see but a thick, white fog bank.

"How do you feel?" Dominique said, handing him a steaming mug.

"Okay," Lafitte replied, staring from the hot plate on the little table to the mug. He took it, tried a small sip of the hot, black chickory, and gasped. "Wow! That'll wake ya."

He took another sip, put the mug on the table, and went to the stern. The fog was so thick it was solid after thirty feet but he could make out Marcel and Blondy at the next boat, ready to get into a pirogue. Lafitte nodded and grinned at them and they grinned and waved. Lafitte turned to Dominique, rubbing his right shoulder, and said:

"Where they going?"

"Are you all right?" Dominique asked, staring a moment at Lafitte's shoulder.

"Oh sure. It's just bursitis. I get an attack once in a while, just to remind me I'm no longer twenty." Then, at You's frown, he quickly added, "But it won't affect my aim."

"Bon!" You grinned, then extended his hand toward the two men. "We're ready to move into position . . . that is, if you approve? They have pistols and knives and I suggest that they go a ways east of the shack, land, and come in from the other side and await our call. It will take them perhaps a half hour longer, so they should start now. Abe and Marcel are quite proficient at bird calls and I suggested that this be the signal, as soon as the fog lifts."

"All right." Lafitte nodded, not missing You's use of the word "suggest." He looked up, but the fog was as thick that way. "How long you think the fog will last?"

"Not long," Dominique replied. "It is almost dawn. I think the sun will burn it off within the hour."

"Uh huh. Then the three of us will move in from this side."

"Yes. If you approve?"

"I do. Have they had coffee?"

"Yes," Dominique nodded, "we all have. And some chocolate cookies and canned peaches that Blondy fortuitously had on his boat. They saved some for you."

Lafitte nodded again and turned to the two men. He pointed to the pirogue and waved them to Dominique's boat. They jumped in quickly and paddled alongside, and Dominique grabbed the rope from Marcel. Lafitte leaned over the railing and said in a low voice:

"Come in a good ways east so you won't be seen. When you come toward the house, stay a good thirty feet apart. Wait where you can see the clearing and the house on the beach. If you can also see that bunker, so much the better. We'll be on the other side, so be damn careful on the shooting. Shoot only when you cannot miss. . . . They will probably have noticed the missing guard by now, so move damn quietly. In any event I think they'll have a man on the beach; we'll take him. Remember, your prime job is to cover us. Any questions?"

Both men shook their heads and Dominique tossed the rope into the pirogue.

Lafitte was sitting stoically on top of the salt mound, his rifle across his knees. He was staring at the fluffy blanket of fog between him and the shore. From time to time he would rub his shoulder and once he eased the bandana on his head without moving it from the cut. But other than that, he waited. Then there was the whistle of a bird that he knew wasn't a bird, but he didn't move. Now the fog had a slightly orange tint and he took a deep breath, stretched, and rubbed his shoulder again. Below him, at the water's edge, Dominique squatted and stared at Lafitte, a look of slight wonder on his rugged face.

Then the pirogue appeared out of the fog and bumped to a quiet stop on the salt, and Abe climbed out. Dominique tugged on the boat and the two men had a whispered conversation, and then You climbed up to Lafitte and said in a low voice:

"We can talk now, but quietly."

Lafitte nodded, but continued to stare at the fog. As the fog began to turn to a spectacular gold, Lafitte's face was faintly lighted by the glow of the rising sun and You shook his head once, and said:

"You look like your ancestor. . . . How long have we known each other? A hundred and sixty years? Or a few days?"

Lafitte smiled slightly and turned his head to look at Dominique. "It's been longer than a few days, hasn't it? But friend Dominique, don't let the facade fool you. I will be Lafitte the pirate for today, and as long as it takes to get my wife back . . . and Tomas Mejia. . . . Then a guy with a French name will return to Arizona."

"Huh!" You exclaimed quietly. "I do not think so. But then again, I did not believe in ghosts until a few days ago."

"Go on!" Lafitte said. "There are no ghosts. I'm just playing the role. But I'll play it to the hilt . . . you should pardon the pun."

You shook his head and grinned. "I'd better get back to watching. Abe will tell you when they're ready."

Lafitte nodded, and in a few moments Abe came to crouch a few feet below him. After a short silence Lafitte said quietly:

"Abe? What's your full name?"

"Abraham Lincoln Roosevelt Johnson," the big black said with a wide grin. "Ma mammy was patriotic."

"You mean blacks have mammies and whites have mothers?"

"Shore!" Abe said positively. "That's a fact of life."

"No, not necessarily," Lafitte replied. "I had both, my grandpappy was so rich. You know Sedonia?"

"Shorely do. She's a nice woman."

"Well, she gave me more baths in the summertime than my mother ever did. And usually by dragging me in the house by the ear."

Abe grinned. "Yes, suh. She's a fine ol' gal, she is."

"So when we go after these guys and you hear me call one of 'em a nigger bastard you'll know it's just to get 'em rattled."

Abe's brows knitted in thought a moment, then the smile returned, "Well, they is nigger bastards, ain't they?"

Lafitte kept a straight face and said, "They certainly are."

As the fog began to get patchy there was another bird call and Abe nodded and got to his feet and You joined them.

"It's time," he said.

Lafitte nodded and they went to the pirogue. Abe held it while they got in and then the big man began to pole them toward the shore. They landed some two hundred yards west of the house and Abe pulled the boat under some bushes and they got out quietly, their guns ready.

"Ah kin make it around quicker," Abe said, pulling two knives and holding them both by the blade in his left hand.

"But you don't have a gun," Lafitte whispered.

"Don't need one fer a look-see," Abe said. " 'Sides, ah kin run faster'n a nigger at a Ku Klux Klan meetin' and I'm good with these."

Despite himself Lafitte chuckled at the black man's humor. "Well, all right. Go along this way. Dominique and I will work our way in a bit and cut toward the clearing. When you're close to the end of that fence, get to a spot where you can see the door and stay there, unless I yell."

Abe nodded and started along the edge of the small beach. Lafitte and You moved forward quietly, some forty feet apart, keeping to the trees that came almost to the water's edge. They kept each other in sight and checked the over-hanging branches as they went. They went around fallen logs and spun quickly to make sure there was no one behind them; they covered each other as they made their way across small clearings; as they got closer only one man moved while the other fanned the area with his eyes, both realizing that if they were expected the small forest would be the proper place for an ambush.

Then they were at the edge of the underbrush and they could see the house a hundred feet away, to their right. To the left was the sunken shack, some seventy yards across the uneven, grass-covered clearing. They studied both structures and the far edges of the clearing for a few moments, but there was no one in sight. The door to the sunken shack was open, but they could not see into the dark interior. The door to the house on the beach was closed. Lafitte came close to Dominique and whispered:

"Either they're gone or we're expected."

"I, uh . . . doubt that they would've tried the swamp at night."

"Agree," Lafitte replied with a curt nod. "But maybe we caught 'em still asleep."

You shrugged; he didn't think so. Then Abe raised up a bit from behind a sand hummock to their right and pointed to the door of the house. Lafitte studied it carefully and then saw what Abe was pointing at; there was a heavy padlock on the door. Lafitte started to wave Abe to them, then his eyes narrowed; what if the lock was a fake? "Watch the shack," Lafitte whispered to Dominique and then turned and mo-tioned to Abe to run up the ramp. Then he put his rifle down a moment and held both fists in front of him, one on top of the other, and quickly pulled them apart. Abe nodded, he'd check the lock. Lafitte raised the rifle and braced himself against a tree trunk and aimed at the door. In a moment Abe was in his field of vision, sprinting up the ramp. He flattened himself to one side of the door, got a breath, then reached out and tugged at the lock. It was secured. Abe looked toward him and Lafitte waved him back to the brush, then circled his hand behind his head. Abe nodded and sprinted for the trees; he would cut their trail and come in behind them, from the southwest.

Lafitte stepped up behind Dominique and whispered, "Okay, the shack next. We should get on either side of the door."

You nodded. "Should we back out and circle the clearing?"

"No, take too much time. If they did leave I don't think they would've left before it was light, and they couldn't be too far ahead. If we cut straight across from here the only way they can shoot is from an extreme angle . . . assuming they're even in there, of course."

"Well," Dominique replied with a quick shrug of his big shoulders, "it's direct."

Lafitte nodded and they moved diagonally across the clearing, their weapons ready. They were halfway across when two men came out of the sunken doorway with pistols in their hands. Lafitte and You quickly threw themselves flat on the rough ground, but the men seemingly ignored them and cut to the right of the shack and disappeared into the brush in the direction of the swamp.

They exchanged quick glances and two more men suddenly shot out of the doorway, each with a machete, and sprinted directly across the clearing.

"Look at those bastards run!" Lafitte whispered.

Dominique nodded, his eyes watching the brush where they'd disappeared. "They must have seen us. That puts us in a trap unless we back up."

"Uh huh." Lafitte replied, his eyes on the shack as he thought of the alternatives. "How good are Marcel and Blondy?"

"The best."

"Then it's not a trap. They don't know how many we are, and we know they're six. Let's go."

You glanced over his shoulder once, grinned, and got to his feet and began to advance. They'd made maybe sixty careful feet when there was the sound of snapping brush behind them and one of the men, a big black, was running toward them, his machete held high. As Dominique turned to face the charge, Lafitte yelled:

"No! You can run! Get to the side of that door!"

Dominique nodded without a moment's hesitation and started to the sunken shack. Lafitte spun around, slightly crouched, and yelled:

"Hey! Try me!"

The man swerved slightly without breaking stride and headed for Lafitte.

"They'll kill the woman if you shoot!" the man yelled.

Lafitte raised the rifle and his brows contracted as he considered the man's wild charge, but he instantly decided that they'd not shoot Sandy, she was their ticket out . . . and now he knew for sure that she was in there. He sighted on the man's chest, letting him get closer, and then the answer to the wild charge was apparent; the eyes were wide and staring, the big mouth was open; the man was drugged. Lafitte let the man get within twenty feet and then he shot him in the chest . . . and almost made a fatal mistake. The black grunted, broke stride a moment, and raised the blade higher as he closed on his target. Lafitte dived forward as the blade whistled past his head and he landed on his right shoulder, rolled once, and came to his knees, grunting in pain as he felt the impact on his sore shoulder.

He put his left foot under him as he pulled on the bolt, ejecting the spent shell and levering another one into the chamber. He barely got the rifle to his shoulder and the wild man turned and started to throw the machete. The next shot was a shade too fast and caught the man in the side, bringing the long arm to a halt, but the man was still on his feet. Without taking the piece from his shoulder Lafitte levered another shell into place and took just a second to aim as the big man lumbered toward him, now looking ten feet tall. The third slug went directly into the bridge of the man's nose, ranging upward into the brain, and he was knocked on his back, the machete flying free, and the body was still.

Lafitte took a couple of quick breaths, got to his feet, and came forward slowly, the rifle ready again, but there was no need.

"See, ya dumb bastard," Lafitte said to the corpse, "they're right. Speed kills."

Then he spun quickly to cover the west edge of the clearing, but he could see no one. He spun back to see Dominique in the middle of the clearing, between him and the sunken door. He moved forward and then he saw why Dominique had stopped. A man had come out of the bunker, a knife to Claudette's throat. There was a large bandana wrapped around her eyes. Lafitte moved forward cautiously, keeping Dominique in the way, and whispered:

"Careful. This other one was hopped up on something. I had to shoot 'im in the head."

"Yes," Dominique replied in a low voice, not turning around, "that explains the wild charge."

"What about this one?" Lafitte whispered.

"Maybe. If I can see the eyes I can tell."

"There's still one behind us," Lafitte said, turning his head away from the bunker at the slight scuffling sound at the edge of the bush. He saw a bush sway wildly for a moment, there was a loud gasp, and then he saw Abe appear, holding a bloody machete in his hand. He grinned, nodded once, and dropped out of sight. Lafitte turned to stand behind Dominique again, moving backward a few steps until he was ten feet away.

"Abe got the other one," he said.

As You nodded, the man behind Claudette suddenly yelled in a high-pitched voice. "I'll kill her!"

"The same," You whispered. "He might do it."

Lafitte raised the rifle and pointed it past Dominique's shoulder. "Hold still. . . . Does he see me?"

"No," You replied, his lips barely moving. "I'm not even sure he can see me. But, for God's sake, be careful. He may kill the child!"

"Don't move. I'll clear you by a foot."

Down the sights of his rifle he could see Dominique shiver, but the wide shoulders held steady. Lafitte sighted on the man's forehead, well above the child, but he hesitated, though it was an easy shot of less than twenty yards. He shook his head and relaxed his trigger squeeze; the impact of

the bullet could pull the knife across the girl's throat. He
waited. One second, two, then three, and then there was the
sound of two shots from the north edge and a man's voice
shouted: "Lou! Don't! We're cut off!"

Lafitte instinctively turned his head to the left and saw one
of the first men out of the bunker run, waving his gun, then
drop. Lafitte glanced back and saw that Claudette's captor
had also looked toward the sounds, pulling the knife a foot
from the girl's throat.

"Now!" Lafitte called and You quickly replied:

"Oui."

Lafitte sucked in a big breath, let half of it out, and
squeezed the trigger. As the shot began to echo across the
clearing the man's head was snapped back, pierced squarely
in the forehead by Lafitte's perfect shot, and the body
dropped, freeing the blindfolded girl to fall forward. As she
landed on her knees, Dominique was there to break her fall,
and Lafitte turned to face the north edge of the clearing
again, throwing a fresh shell into the chamber.

Marcel stepped forward, waved his gun with a big grin on
his face, and turned as Blondy dragged a body forward to
show that they got both men. Lafitte waved and pointed at
the bunker. The men stopped grinning and ran forward at an
angle to climb to one of the high windows near the small
peak.

"No!" Lafitte shouted and they stopped. He motioned
them to the front and they came forward and took positions
at the far side of the door. He turned back to Dominique as
the Frenchman was picking up the girl, and Lafitte covered
the door with his rifle until they were to the side and out
of any angle of fire from the bunker. The girl was still unconscious and Dominique laid her gently behind a tree, stood
up and came to join Lafitte who was standing behind some
bushes where he could watch the door.

Lafitte waited, his teeth clenched and his eyes narrowed.
He was breathing quickly, but other than that he showed no
emotion. Dominique stared at him a moment, then said:

"Will you call him out?"

"No . . . I don't think so. He may be hopped up, too."

"What about your——" Dominique cut off his words by
biting his lip and wished he'd kept his mouth shut.

"She's in there . . . but I'll wait a bit."

You stared at his friend again, realizing the terrible decision he'd had to make, but it was the right one and he nodded once in admiration.

As Lafitte waited in stoic silence all sorts of horrible thoughts ran through his mind. Perhaps he should have charged at once. Maybe the madman in there was killing her now. He waited a half minute, then a minute, and he could stand it no longer; he began to move forward, intending to storm the door. As he got within twenty feet of the bunker his better judgment made him realize that he might be the instrument of his wife's death, and he stopped. And he waited some more, sweating in the morning sun. When his nerve had about gone and he'd decided to offer himself as hostage in place of his wife, a man's voice called from inside:

"Lafitte?"

Lafitte let out his breath in a long sigh, and said, "Yeah?"

"I've got your wife. And I'm coming out." The voice had a Latin accent but sounded completely rational.

"All right," Lafitte replied, trying to keep his voice flat. "Come ahead."

"And Lafitte? I'm not drugged. I know what I'm doing. Get rid of that rifle!"

Lafitte nodded and tossed it to Dominique who caught it deftly and quickly backed into the brush. In a moment Sandy appeared in the doorway, a big, dark-skinned man standing behind her. He held one knife with the point pressing her chin into the air, another was shoved into her blouse, just below her breastbone. Her hands were behind her back and she had a shocked look on her face that told her husband she must have been on the verge of hysteria for hours. She looked at him through bleary eyes and tried to smile, but she couldn't do it.

"Sandy?" Lafitte said in the same flat voice, suddenly aware that the palms of his hands were sweating. "Are you all right?"

Before she could answer the knife pushed her chin a bit higher and the man said, "Yes, but you'll have a flat-chested wife if you don't do as I say."

"All right, all right!" Lafitte replied, fighting to control himself.

Sandy was marched up the three steps and into the daylight and he saw that her skirt had almost been ripped off, her nylons were shreds, and there were no buttons left on her blouse. Lafitte clenched his teeth and tried to keep the hatred from his face.

The man glanced quickly once in each direction, then back to Lafitte. "Make them drop their weapons. Over here!"

Lafitte looked at Marcel and Blondy and nodded. Impassively the two men tossed their pistols near the man.

"And that rifle."

Lafitte turned to Dominique and nodded. Dominique put the safety on the rifle and tossed it in front of him.

"Make him stand by them!"

Lafitte nodded again and Dominique slowly circled behind Lafitte, keeping his face toward the bunker.

"You'll never make it," Lafitte said.

"If they thought they could kill me without hurting her I would be dead now. . . . And I will point out something else, Señor Lafitte. Both these knives are poisoned. Even if you get me, my reflexes will cut her. . . ."

The man's eyes scanned the clearing once and then he started pushing Sandy in front of him. Lafitte took a step forward and the man spun Sandy around and she almost lost her footing. Lafitte froze, and held his ground. The man grinned crookedly and began backing away. Lafitte let him go a ways, then advanced with him, but never got within twenty feet. Then Abe appeared at the edge of the clearing behind the man and Lafitte blinked but kept a straight face. As Lafitte advanced slowly, Abe put the machete on the grass and ran forward at a silent crouch.

"You can't make it, you know," Lafitte said, trying to keep the man's attention.

The man started to look over his shoulder and Lafitte quickly added, "There'll be a thousand men looking for you before the day's over."

Abe dropped flat, his hands braced at the shoulders.

"No, Señor Lafitte, I think not," the man said.

"Listen, you black bastard!" Lafitte said, getting angry again. "You know what they do to a black who kidnaps a white woman in this state? You'll never make it to the law, but it'll take you a good three days to die!"

"I'm a Puerto Rican!" the man said.

"Yeah? Well, you'd better get your birth certificate ready!"

The man backed another five feet and Abe rose to his full

height. The man backed into range and two huge hands shot
out and grabbed a wrist and a forearm and jerked the arms
apart and Sandy fell to the ground. Abe whirled the struggling man to one side and Lafitte darted in and pulled his unconscious wife a few feet away. He looked up and Abe's
back was to him. Abe was still behind the man and he spread
his arms and the big muscles rippled as he began to squeeze.
Though the Puerto Rican was big, he was no match for Abe
and he quickly knew it. He suddenly flexed his arms against
Abe's, lifted his feet in the air and brought the leather heels
of his boots crashing down on Abe's canvas shoes. Abe
grunted in pain, the grip relaxed, and the man was free. He'd
dropped one of the knives, but he was running for the jungle.

"Stop him!" Lafitte yelled. "He's got the key!"

Abe turned to run, but his foot wouldn't hold him. He
crashed to the ground, looked up at Lafitte apologetically.

"Stay with her!" Lafitte said, pausing to scoop up the
knife. He knew he'd never outrun the man, and when Lafitte
was still forty feet away the man reached the edge of the jungle and was gone. He stopped and yelled:

"Dominique! Bring a rifle! Blondy and Marcel! Stay with
Sandy!"

He started into the bush and ran twenty feet to stop at a
big tree to control his breathing. It was silent. Then he saw
the man's tracks leading north. The toes were dug in and
there was almost no heel mark; the man was still running
when he'd passed here. He followed them another fifty feet
and lost them on some hard ground and quickly took up a
spot behind a giant oak. Now that he'd lost the tracks he was
vulnerable, so he decided to wait for Dominique. He turned
to look back and a bullet nicked the bark of the tree and
there was a sound like a pop gun. Lafitte continued to turn
and dove headfirst past a bush, landing on his left shoulder.
He forced himself to do two full turns and there was the
sound of two more shots. Then he scrambled forward behind
a thick tangle of vines and wiggled his way out of sight, he
hoped.

He pulled in a deep breath and moved his left knee to get
it off a short, thick bit of deadwood. There was no sound and
he moved forward a few feet until he could see through the
vines. The man was standing in a small clearing, holding
what looked like a .25 automatic. He was fanning the brush

where Lafitte had entered. Then he slowly turned Lafitte's
way and Lafitte ducked back and reached for the piece of
wood. He waited a few moments, then wiggled forward on
his belly. The man had turned to Lafitte's right and Lafitte
wondered why the man had shot; he hadn't been seen, he
should've kept going, to lose himself in the swamp. Then Lafitte saw why the man had chosen to fight. At the far side of
the clearing was a small outboard. It was at the bank of a
bayou, the swamp a hundred yards away. If the man made it
to the boat he was gone . . . with the keys.

Lafitte got to his knees, pulled his grandfather's knife from
the back of his belt and, remembering what the man had said
about his knives, shoved the man's knife in the sand and
flipped his own knife to grab it by the blade. He picked up
the limb in his left hand and held it across his body to fling it
backhanded, got his feet under him, and took a deep breath.

He looked at the man; he was still staring to Lafitte's right.
Another breath and Lafitte tossed the limb to his left. When
it hit the brush the man spun around and fired at the spot,
exposing his middle, and Lafitte raised the knife over his
head, grimacing at the fire in his shoulder, and threw it as
hard as he could. His aim was high, and not very good. The
flat of the blade caught the man in the face. He grunted,
dropped the gun as he put both hands to his face and backed
up a step to trip and stumble to his knees.

"Damn!" Lafitte said to himself as he pulled the knife
from the sand and ran through the open spot in the vines. As
the man saw Lafitte he started to lean forward for his gun,
but he didn't make it. Lafitte dived forward and lunged with
the knife. He felt it sink to the hilt and then his impetus carried him forward and onto his sore shoulder again. He yelled
in pain but held onto the knife and scrambled to his knees
with the bloody blade in his hand, ready to lunge again. The
man was on his back, his knees doubled up in pain as he
clutched his abdomen.

Lafitte stood up and circled the man warily, retrieved the
gun, then yelled, "Dominique! Over here!"

When You arrived he found his friend standing by the fall-
en man. Lafitte was clutching his right shoulder with his left
hand.

"Are you all right?" You asked.

"Yeah. But if I keep this up I'd damn well better learn to throw a knife."

"Huh?" You said, staring at the wounded man. "Then what's this?"

"That's from the second knife. It never left my hand. Check him, will you?"

You stared in awe at his friend for the second time that day but knelt by the fallen man without comment and Lafitte searched around in the grass until he found his grandfather's knife. He slipped it into the scabbard at the back of his belt and turned as Dominique said:

"Below the navel; he'll live."

"Don't bet on it. Prop him up and get the keys."

You handed the rifle to Lafitte and dragged the man to a sitting position against a tree. He found the keys in a shirt pocket.

"Good!" Lafitte said. "See to Sandy, please. I want to have a word with him."

You frowned a moment, then nodded and started past Lafitte who thrust the rifle and the automatic in his hands. You nodded again and left. When he was out of sight, Lafitte knelt by the Puerto Rican, the knife in his right hand.

"It's only a gut wound. You'll live," Lafitte said.

The man glared his hate but said nothing.

"Now," Lafitte said cheerfully, "bearing in mind that you threatened to kill my wife, that another of your bunch was gonna rape her, and you promised to, uh, I think the phrase was 'make her flat-chested,' we're going to play a little game. Now you can save yourself some pain if you start talking right now, as fast as you can."

"Fuck you!" the man said, grimacing.

"Well now!" Lafitte said, suddenly smiling. "Let's see."

He hooked the knife sideways inside the man's collar and split the shirt open to the shoulder. Another quick, not so gentle cut on the other side and a quick tug and the man's shirt was in his lap.

"You're not going to leave here," Lafitte said conversationally, "unless you start talking."

He drew the sharp knife across the man's chest. The man cried out, but though it was a thin slice, it drew blood.

"I think I'll handcuff you," Lafitte said, "and leave you for the mosquitoes. They smell that blood and they'll be all over you."

The man's face was now paler, and the fear was beginning to show.

"Come on," Lafitte said, "let's play Tic Tac Toe ... and I bet you lose." Another slice and the man groaned and leaned hard against the tree. "Now, who put you up to it?"

The man shook his head. "I talk and he'll kill me."

Lafitte nodded casually. "All right, so now you've got a choice. . . . Me or him. And I'm here."

Another slice, vertical this time.

"Ai. . . . I . . . I can't!"

Lafitte shrugged and put the point of the knife just below the man's right eye. "Would you like to be able to see how the game comes out?"

"No! It was Tomas Mejia. . . . But you knew."

"Yes," Lafitte said, pulling the knife a few inches away. "But I want proof."

"No chance," the man said, and Lafitte thought he was telling the truth. "He spent the evening in town, at the bar. . . ."

"What bar?"

"Across from his office . . . and he'll have a dozen witnesses, black and white. The society folks slum there."

"But you can testify that you were working for him, that he directed you to do it."

"I didn't do it!" the man yelled, and the knife came close to his eye again. The man shrank back against the tree, his eyes on the blade. Then his voice dropped. "I didn't kidnap them, it was Lou and the big black!"

"Yeah, but you ran it from this end!"

"But they weren't to be kidnapped! They panicked. I just had orders to. . . . It doesn't matter. I'll get killed before I get inside a court. . . ."

Suddenly both the man's hands were on Lafitte's wrist, twisting the arm away. Lafitte was still kneeling and he was being forced over the man's body and to his right. Lafitte grabbed the man's right wrist with his left hand but he could see that he couldn't make it; his wrist was now twisted up and the pressure was getting to his elbow; when it got to his shoulder he knew he would lose the knife, the leverage was too great.

"Damn you!" Lafitte shouted, pulling to his left as hard as he could.

He got the knife close to the man's face but the grip on his wrist was too great and he was unable to twist the knife enough to slash. Slowly the leverage increased again and Lafitte let go with his left hand and raised it in the air and brought the flat of his hand down at the face, but his antagonist turned his head and Lafitte only smashed him on the ear. But now he was about to be tossed on his shoulder. In desperation he reached his free hand behind him, grabbing for the knife at the back of his belt. The man grinned and the pressure increased some more and the man got his right knee into Lafitte's groin and was about to toss him over his head when the knife came free from the scabbard. Lafitte whipped it around in a tight arc and the man's knee slipped, insuring his own execution. The knife sank in just below the rib cage and there was a loud scream, which quickly changed into a gurgle, and the hands dropped away. Lafitte fell on his right shoulder, grunted in pain, and forced his arm to lift him to his elbow.

The man was staring at him, his face contorted with hate and pain. Lafitte shook his head once, his eyes narrowed, and he quickly twisted the knife once each way. The body went limp and Lafitte got to his knees, breathing hard, and withdrew the knife and stared a moment at the bloody blade. He took a couple deep breaths, then cleaned the knife in the earth, wiped it on the dead man's pants, and replaced it in the scabbard.

As he got slowly to his feet he heard the brush crack and Dominique ran into the clearing, the rifle in front of him. He stopped as he saw the body on its back, then came forward slowly.

"Are you all right?" he asked, staring at the huge wound and the slits on the chest.

"Oh yes," Lafitte replied, looking down to see that his hands were shaking. "But I got careless and I landed on my shoulder again."

"What happened?"

"Well, we were having a little talk. . . ."

"No doubt," Dominique said dryly.

". . . and he must not've been hurt as bad as we thought.

Anyway, he grabbed for the knife, and almost had it when I thought to haul out the other one."

You nodded soberly as he studied the corpse, then turned to his friend and said, "Are you sure you don't believe in reincarnation?"

"Yes, I'm sure!" Lafitte said curtly, then grinned a bit. "Only the name is the same. Just like yours."

"You'll never convince me," Dominique said with a big grin.

Lafitte shrugged his shoulders, rubbed the right one, and said, "What about all these bodies? Should we call the law?"

"No . . . I think not," You replied carefully. "It would just cause an unnecessary inquiry."

"Dominique!" Lafitte said in some surprise. "I know it was all self-defense, but it's the law."

"Certainly it is," You agreed. "But consider this. We did nothing wrong, did we?"

"Of course not!"

"Assuredly. And no one knows about it but you and your wife, and me and my men. None of us will talk. And the child is still unconscious. She can be told that we chased the bad men and drove them off."

"Big deal! What about the bodies?"

"Abe just told me that he looked under the house before he tried the lock. The fence is down. The body must have been swept into the bay during the storm. As to the others, Blondy reported that there is a quite adequate area of quicksand at the edge of the swamp, some few yards behind the shack."

"Huh!" Lafitte said in some wonder. "And we can dispose of them without a trace?"

"Well, it's a most fitting end."

"Not quite. . . . Well, let's get at it."

"They're just waiting your word. . . . Marcel!"

"*Oui!*" came the reply from the east.

"Dump them!"

"*Oui!*"

Sandy was kneeling by the still unconscious child when they returned to the bunker. As she saw her husband she jumped to her feet and ran to be enfolded in his arms.

"There, there," he said quietly. "It's all over."

She looked up, her dirty face stained by the tears. She managed a smile and he kissed her cheek.

"How's the child?" he asked.

"She's still out of it. But I think she's sleeping. At least she's breathing easily."

"Did she ever become aware of what was happening?"

Sandy thought a moment, then, with the good sense not to ask why, she said, "Yes, at the beginning, in your grandfather's room. But only for a moment. One of those . . . those men knocked her out. Then . . . I think it was on an island somewhere, she started to come to and they forced her to swallow some pills."

"Nothing since then?"

"No, thank God. . . ."

"Yes," he said gently, then added a well-intentioned lie. "But it's all over. You'll feel better as soon as we get you back to the boat and get some coffee, maybe something to eat."

They stood there a few moments, his arms around her ,and then the men appeared from the north edge of the clearing. They were all grinning and Lafitte waved them forward. They trotted to Lafitte and stood there, waiting for him to speak.

"Honey, here are the men who saved your life; Abe, Marcel, and Blondy."

"Madame?" Blondy and Marcel chorused, pleased at the introduction.

"Ma'am?" Abe said, stepping forward to stoop down and pick up the child as though she were a doll.

"Thank you, thank you all," Sandy said, her voice a bit choked. "I . . . I can't tell you. . . . Thank you."

All three men nodded and Dominique grinned in the background. As big Abe turned to start toward the beach with the child in his arms, Lafitte said:

"Hey, big man! How's the foot?"

"Ain't quite busted," the big man grinned.

Lafitte was standing with one foot on the railing as they chugged toward the landing, the other three boats in a line behind them. Sandy, after a couple of cups of coffee generously laced with cognac, had fallen asleep on the bunk op-

posite the child well before they'd cleared the eastern tip of
the peninsula.

During the trip You had said but two things. "Do you
want some coffee?" and "I know you will go after him. Be
sure and let me help." To both statements Lafitte had replied,
"Yes."

He had sipped many cups of what Dominique passed off as
coffee and he thought about the past night. He weighed the
possibility of packing Sandy in the car and heading home as
soon as possible, assuming he could get past Mejia. That
would be fairly easy; all he'd have to do would be to make
public the knowledge that Jeremy now owned the map. He
owed Jeremy the map. He'd paid for it, and it might serve
him right. But then again, that wasn't part of the deal. He'd
promised Jeremy that he'd keep their transaction quiet . . .
and he would, as long as it served his purpose. But, by doing
that, he'd never find out. . . . Then he glanced at his sleeping
wife and his eyes narrowed . . . he'd stay a while.

As they got within two hundred yards of the landing, each
of the following boats picked up speed and came within fifty
feet in a sweeping arc and Lafitte exchanged waves with each
man. He turned to the small dock and saw Jeremy and Suzanne waiting for them. He shook Sandy gently and she
awoke at once and sat up and pushed her hair back with a
wan smile. Lafitte turned and tossed the line to Jeremy who
made it fast to a pole, and You cut the engine and picked up
the child and carried her to the rail where her father leaned
down and took her in his arms.

"Baby! Baby!" Suzanne said, leaning forward to kiss her
child.

"She's all right," Lafitte said. "She's just knocked out with
exhaustion."

"Thank God!" Suzanne said, and Lafitte turned away and
picked up his rifle and nodded to Dominique, who picked up
his heavy jacket and slipped his pistol in one pocket and a
knife in the other. Sandy held her hand out to Suzanne, but
Suzanne was staring at her child, her eyes wide, as though
she couldn't quite believe that it was actually Claudette. Lafitte climbed to the dock and pulled his wife up, then extended his hand to Dominique and pulled him to the ancient

boards. Jeremy partially turned away from his wife and rather lamely said to Lafitte:

"Uh . . . are you all right. Both of you?"

"Yes."

"Uh . . . uh . . . your grandfather died right after you left."

"Oh no!" Sandy said, turning to put her arm around her husband.

"Damn!" Lafitte said, and Dominique shook his head in sorrow.

Jeremy turned quickly with Claudette and hurried toward the house, Suzanne trailing along, holding the child's limp hand. Lafitte and Sandy, an arm around each other, slowly trudged toward the big house, followed by Dominique, who turned his head from side to side, checking the grounds and the trees. Dr. Glover was waiting on the steps, unshaven, his shirt wrinkled. As Jeremy and Suzanne carried their child into the house, their other two girls appeared and the family trooped toward the stairs. Lafitte kissed his wife on the cheek and said:

"Can you stand up long enough for a shower?"

She nodded and managed a wan smile.

"Get into bed," he said, "and I'll ask the doctor to look in on you."

She nodded and Dominique held the screen door for her. "I'll be at the bar," he said.

Lafitte nodded and saw Sedonia appear and put her arm around Sandy and escort her up the stairs. Then Lafitte turned to the doctor and accepted one of his proffered cigarettes. The doctor held his lighter and Lafitte nodded his thanks and said:

"The child was drugged. She's been out since last night. I don't know what they used. Sandy said they forced her to swallow a couple of pills that made her sleepy at once."

"How's her breathing?" the doctor said, holding his lighter to his own cigarette.

"Seems fine," Lafitte shrugged.

"I'll check. . . . And your wife?"

"Just exhaustion, after the worst night of her life. A good long sleep should do her."

"Uh huh." The doctor nodded, then added the carefully chosen words, "And, uh, she's all right physically?"

"Huh? Oh yes. They didn't get to her, if that's what you mean."

"Good. I'll give her a light sedative."

"Thank you. And I'd appreciate it if you wouldn't tell the Durocs about the pills."

"All right," the doctor said, turning from staring at the bay to look directly at Lafitte. "Not as a doctor but as the family friend, what happened out there?"

"Well," Lafitte said, pausing a bit to pick his words, "hopefully no one outside the premises will ever know about this, and in case they do, we chased 'em to the swamp, found 'em this morning and when we started in they shot at us, we shot back, and they ran."

The doctor raised a skeptical eyebrow, then nodded, not believing Lafitte for a moment. "I see. Well now, as the family doctor, I am forced to observe that the bandana around your head seems to have some dried blood on it."

"Huh!" Lafitte grinned. He'd forgotten about the bandana. He started to ease it off his head, but it was stuck on the left side.

"Here," the doctor said, taking the cloth in one hand and holding Lafitte's hair in the other. He separated the two without opening the cut and then leaned closer to examine it. "A good slice but it's closed. Be careful when you shower."

"Thank you," Lafitte said with an enigmatic smile.

"Now, sir," the doctor said firmly, flicking his ash to the wind. "Would you care to tell me what really happened?"

"No, sir!" Lafitte said quickly and emphatically. "That just might cause you a lot of trouble. . . . But, uh, I will go this far. I take it you do believe in the Hippocratic oath?"

"I would've been shot many times over by erring husbands had I not. Just tell me you got the bastards that caused my friend's death."

"Okay. They'll never be seen again. . . . By the way, the police haven't been called in on this, have they?"

"No. I did as you told me. There's been no one here but the ambulance with the oxygen, I didn't even have time to call for a nurse. He died while I was in attendance, so there'll be no necessity for an inquest, even. I've already filled out the death certificate. In fact, the funeral's tomorrow."

"So soon? My God. . . . Tell me this, Doctor. Did he regain consciousness?"

"No. After you left he never even batted an eye."

Lafitte shivered, flipped his cigarette into the bushes, and trudged wearily into the house.

Part Five

THE MOST IMPOSING STRUCTURE IN THE SMALL GRAVEYARD IN Bayard was the family mausoleum with the name LAFITTE carved in block letter on the weathered stone. With the exception of Dominique You, Dr. Glover and his wife, Attorney Davis and his wife, the undertaker and an apprentice (who had yet to learn to look properly solemn), the only people remaining at the gravesite were the members of the immediate family and Sedonia and Sam. The rest of the mourners, most hastily called members of the local business community, had retired after the preacher's brief service to leave the family to its grief. The women (the girls had been left at home in charge of Marcel and Blondy) were seated in the front row dressed in black, the men dutifully standing behind them. The minister had been whispering to the madam for some minutes now and she was still sobbing quietly. Lafitte presumed he would talk to her a bit more, then lead the group in a silent prayer and end with a psalm. To get his mind off the moment, Lafitte glanced again at the stone structure in front of him.

It was as he'd remembered from childhood. It was perhaps twelve feet square with a peaked, slate roof. The only break in the gray stones was in front; the heavy brass door, ornately carved and now weathered a dull green, was still open, as was the iron gate which was turned back against the wall.

A few minutes before, Lafitte had helped carry his grandfather's casket inside, where it had been put on the top shelf on the left. There were six spaces, three to a side, and all were currently filled, though Lafitte knew that a half dozen people had been buried there over the last seventy years, in addition to the current occupants.

Vaults in many places in the Delta had for over a century been constructed with a very wide outside footing in the soft, marshy land to enable the inside to be dug down to the few feet it took to reach water, then covered with a removable floor. As the years went by, the bottom casket would be dropped into the rich, disintegrating area below and then each coffin lowered a shelf. Thus the bodies were still legally buried and if the members of the family had the good timing to space their departures, the family burial place would last for centuries. No longer done in the cities, the practice, though seldom mentioned, was still followed in small, out-of-the-way graveyards. The only way it might be known was by the number of bronze nameplates on either side of the door inside the crypt.

When Lafitte had inquired the evening before if there was enough room in the vault, Jeremy had replied that the undertaker had, at his request, "disposed of" the remains of Uncle Granget Lafitte, a distant relative who had died over sixty years ago and who had been for many years the senior resident. Lafitte had nodded and shrugged; it was the way.

Lafitte shook his head clear of the reverie and turned slowly to stare at the mourners. Though they all probably missed the old man, the degree had a great variance, from the madam's overwhelming sense of loss down to Jeremy's ill-concealed eagerness to have the proceedings at an end and to be able to get on with his preparations. Lafitte smiled slightly for a moment, then covered the smile with his hand and stared at the back of his wife's neck and quickly ran through yesterday's events in his mind. . . .

After seeing that Sandy had taken her sedative and was asleep he went downstairs to find Dominique already asleep on the big leather couch in the den. He went behind the bar and got a bottle of Scotch and poured a tall one, added ice cubes from the little refrigerator, and took it up to his bedroom, sipping as he went. After a very long, very hot shower, a shave, and a change of clothes, he felt better, but a look at his sleeping wife and his anger rose; he couldn't relax, so he took his glass and went into the old man's room.

There was no one alive in the room and as he closed the door and went to stand by the foot of the bed to stare at what had once been his grandfather, he could hear the tick of the old clock on the wall behind him. The body was dressed in a dark red dressing gown and it almost looked as if he were asleep, except the hands were folded across the now still chest. Lafitte shook his head once, took a sip from his glass, and stared at the body for a long time, shaking his head occasionally in unresolved anger. After another sip he irreverently put his right foot on the bedstead, still mulling an idea which was not yet clear. He held the glass up in a toast and said in a low voice:

"You were right, you old son of a bitch. You said the map would make me a lot of money . . . I guess you just didn't realize what I'd have to go through to earn it."

Then it came to him and he grinned wickedly and took another drink. "And that's the answer . . . the map! Genesis and Revelation! Jeremy paid for it, I should give it to him, that's only proper. And it's also proper that I tell Tomas Mejia that his time was wasted. . . ."

Lafitte chuckled as he thought what the reaction would be. For a time on the way back across Barataria Bay he'd thought about getting Mejia alone. . . .

"Huh!" He said it aloud. "Mejia's just smart enough to outsmart himself. . . . Ha! By damn, it'll work!"

He raised his glass to the corpse again, put his foot down, and as his smile disappeared he said quietly, "So long, you old bastard. . . . And thank you."

He had a last drink to his grandfather and went downstairs.

Dominique was still asleep on the couch. Lafitte sprawled in a big leather chair and put his feet on the hassock as he continued to work out his plan. He grinned at the large picture of his grandfather, finished his drink in one long gulp, and yawned; he was finally getting sleepy.

He awoke to an almost dark room, the waning light outside told him it was late afternoon. He yawned, stretched, and looked at his friend who'd picked that moment to stop snoring. Lafitte smiled as the door opened and Jeremy entered, closed the door quietly behind him and went to the bar. He fixed himself a drink and looked up to see Lafitte staring at him.

"Oh, hi!" Jeremy said. "Have a nap?"

"Yeah, a good one. . . . How's Claudette?"

"Fine! Thanks to you. Jean, I'll always owe you a debt for saving her."

"Thank you. And I owe you a map."

"Yes," Jeremy said with a grin and a sad shake of his head. "But it'll do me no good tonight. I'll have to be here. The Davises are coming by, the preacher will be here, and the flowers are beginning to pile up. . . . Uh, where is it?"

"You're looking at it."

"Pardon?"

"It's behind the old man's picture, right there."

Jeremy put down his drink, looked at Dominique, and Lafitte shook his head; Jeremy went to the portrait and pulled it away from the wall and glanced behind it. He grinned, shook his head, and let the portrait slip back into place. He looked at Dominique again and whispered:

"My compliments, cousin. An ideal spot. In fact, I think I'll leave it there until I've tried the oak."

"All right, suit yourself."

"Good. Tomorrow night will be the time, everybody will be sitting around mourning, and they'll all go to bed early—"

He stopped talking as the doorbell rang, took a big sip of his drink, put it down and said:

"More flowers, probably."

As Jeremy left the room Dominique said, without opening his eyes, "I think I smell a small mouse."

Lafitte grinned. "Now what in the world makes you say a thing like that?"

"It has come to me, *mon ami*, that the map has always been the bait."

"Your perception is fantastic," Lafitte said in a monotone.

The funeral was finally over and the ladies were walked to the waiting limousines. As he helped his wife into the back seat Lafitte squeezed her arm and said:

"I've got some business with Mr. Davis. We're going to stop by the funeral home and check the bill to see that the madam doesn't get stung. We'll be a while."

He kissed her on the cheek and she nodded, though ob-

viously not too happy about it. He smiled quickly and closed
the door. When the two black cars were out of sight he
turned to the lawyer and shook his hand.

"Thank you," he said. "And thank you for not asking."

The lawyer nodded and said, "That's all right. I can check
the bill without an entourage. I'll see you at the house?"

"Maybe. We might be several hours."

The two men exchanged nods and Lafitte turned to get
into his waiting Chevy, driven by Dominique. When they
were out on the highway Lafitte reached under the seat and
pulled out a semi-automatic shotgun and put it next to the
door.

"Where did you get that weapon? It's a semi, no?"

"It's a semi, yes. I borrowed it from Dr. Glover last night."

"Does the doctor know?"

"No, not the details. But he suspects. He didn't quite buy
my official story about chasing the bad boys."

"That's a devastating weapon," Dominique observed. "And
it'll be pretty obvious."

"That may be, but I won't fuck around this time." Lafitte
reached into his inside coat pocket and brought out a list of
items on a piece of notepaper, "We'll need these things if I'm
successful. And if I am, I'll meet you back at the inn. I've
written my idea on the other side. When I return, tell me if
you agree with my big plan."

Dominique nodded and put the list in his pocket and
slowed as they entered town. He drove the few blocks to Mejia's office, stopped a half block short as big Abe stepped out
of a doorway and nodded. Dominique pulled to the curb and
Abe put his hands on the door and said:

"He's in there. Been in fer a coupla hours . . . and he ain't
alone."

"How many?" Lafitte asked.

"Three big bucks come in with him, one of 'em white, and
three high yaller girls."

"Uh huh," Dominique said, handing the keys to Lafitte.
"But we have no idea how many were already there."

"Ain't nobody come in since," Abe said. Then he grinned.
"One of 'em had a big sack, kinda lumpy, like bottles. So I
figger they come fer a party and I sneaked around the back
fer a look-see."

"Oh?" Dominique inquired. "And what did you see?"

"Well, sir," Abe said, obviously pleased with his bit of es-pionage, "this next building has a door to the roof and frum there it's an easy way 'cross several more and I sneaked down and looked in the skylight and I seen them three high yaller gals earnin' their pay!"

"And what do they do for a living?" Lafitte inquired with a grin, knowing the answer.

"Well, suh, you'll pardon the words, but I don't know how to say it in a fancy way, but them three gals was just a fuck-in' the hell outa them three men!"

Lafitte and You exchanged chuckles and Lafitte said, "No!"

"Yes, suh!" Abe said positively.

They got out of the car and met on the sidewalk, Lafitte holding the shotgun pointed at the ground. If the mixed pop-ulation in that section of town thought anything about a man carrying a shotgun they didn't show it. It wasn't particularly unusual for the men of the town to go hunting in the swamps.

"Abe," Lafitte said, "did you see Mejia in that room?"

"Yes, suh. He wuz in there for a while, just sorta watch-in'."

"It might be the best place to start," Dominique said.

"Yeah," Lafitte replied. Then to Abe, "Lead the way."

They went to the next dingy building, entered the dirty hallway, and Abe led them to the second floor and then to the back. There was a small door that opened up to a short flight of steps leading to the roof. From there they made their way across two flat roofs that almost touched and then to the peaked roof of Mejia's building. Abe pointed to the dirty sky-light and Lafitte nodded, handed him the shotgun, and said in a low voice:

"Cover us while we take a look-see."

Abe nodded and took the gun. Lafitte and You moved for-ward slowly, staying at the edge of the building they were on until they were close to the skylight. By putting their feet on the edge of the parapet they were able to lean forward to the edge of the glass. They inched their way into position and slowly raised their heads to look through the wired glass. La-fitte blinked in disbelief at the sight and turned to check Do-minique's reaction.

Though obviously a man of the world, You's expression

showed that he'd never seen such a sight. Mejia was propped
up on the bed, nude, with his back to the skylight. The three
women were also nude, dancing wildly to a portable record
player. But it was not the light from the skylight that made
the scene unreal. In a corner was a flashing red strobe light
that made the women seem like manikins, dancing in a jerky,
silent movie. From time to time they would come together,
fondle each other, and then two would throw the other one
to the floor and crawl all over her. Then Mejia would lash
one with a knotted rope and the one struck would leap up
and impale herself on top of him. He would allow her to stay
a few moments, then fling her to the floor where she was
engulfed by the other two. Then the rope would flash out
again. Dominique shook his head and backed below the window and nudged Lafitte who lowered himself out of sight.

"Malade!" Dominique whispered. "He's sick! Shoot the
son of a bitch now and rid the world of him!"

"No, no," Lafitte replied. "He has to talk to me first.
Come on."

When they were again on the street Lafitte said to Abe,
"Watch the car. If any more come in behind us, lean on that
horn."

Abe nodded and Lafitte took the shotgun, and he and Dominique started casually up the street.

"Mejia's men probably saw Abe a few minutes after he arrived," You said.

"Uh huh. And the moment we drove up we were probably
seen. And when we came out of that building a man probably ran up to warn him."

"Then why go into a trap, for God's sake?" Dominique
whispered.

"Two reasons," Lafitte said complacently, smiling at what
seemed to Dominique an incongruous time. "One, if you
know it's a trap, it isn't really. And two, unless that mutha
banger's got a machine gun, this shotgun's gonna be the big
equalizer. You got your .38?"

"Bien entendu!"

"Then what are you worrying about?"

Lafitte paused to stare through the dirty glass of the entry
door to see that the little hallway and the steps were empty.
He checked the shotgun again, nodded to Dominique, and

opened the door. But not quietly; the door squeaked loudly on its ancient hinges, announcing their arrival. As You loosened the gun in his belt, Lafitte started up a step at a time, being careful to keep his feet as close to the inside as he could, to avoid any further squeaks. He tested every step and they made their way slowly, but absolutely quietly, to the second floor.

The three doors were closed. Lafitte put his right foot in the middle of the hall and let his weight down gently on the bare wood. There was no sound and he took a long step to take up a position to the right of the middle door. He turned and nodded to Dominique who followed the example and stopped on the other side of the door. Lafitte nodded and the pistol appeared as Lafitte gently tried the knob. It turned quietly and Mejia called:

"Come in, Señor Lafitte, come in."

Lafitte shook his head, dropped his shotgun to his side, and indicated that You should back out of sight. Dominique flattened himself against the wall and Lafitte pushed the door all the way open so that it banged against the wall as he leaned against the jamb, the shotgun and his right hand hidden by his right leg. Mejia was seated at his desk, his hands in sight, the broom handle near his right hand. Lafitte blinked once, keeping his face composed as he saw the four men standing behind the desk, two Latins and two blacks.

"Come in," Mejia said again. "You might as well, you will never make it to your car. Luis, here, came to tell me of your arrival. In fact, we stopped a small party to greet you. We, uh, have some business about a map."

"No," Lafitte answered slowly, his racing mind telling that they might not know about Dominique, otherwise they would've had someone in the hall. But there was no sound from outside. "I'd rather not."

"We can convince you," Mejia said.

"I don't think so," Lafitte replied calmly. "I've got some help."

"Ha! You mean that big black out there? He is about as subtle as a firetruck! Luis reported his presence within minutes of his arrival. But your man didn't know it, did he?"

"No," Lafitte said, furrowing his brow as if it were a surprise.

"Yes," Mejia said with a grin. "And then Luis went to the bar across the street and he saw your car."

Lafitte shook his head and Mejia grinned again. But Lafitte was shaking his head at Mejia's lack of security. His man must have seen the empty car while they were on the roof, came in to report, and Mejia must have decided that Lafitte would leave Abe outside. Well, Lafitte thought, he was right about Abe. But Mejia was either more stupid than he'd thought or else his supreme arrogance told him Lafitte would come alone. Good, the arrogance could be helpful. Lafitte shrugged and hid a grin; they didn't know about Dominique.

"And," Mejia added, "I'm assuming that you're hiding a pistol by your side. I suggest that with five of us you'd be far smarter if you'd give it up. In fact, I'm somewhat amazed that you'd return. You must be angry enough to overcome your reason, especially after the funeral of your grandfather. And I suppose you blame that on me, also."

"As a matter of fact, I do," Lafitte replied calmly, only his eyes moving, fanning the four men. Their hands were all at their sides. When he spoke again his voice was calm, businesslike. "Now, which one of these shall I shoot? How about all four?"

Mejia's eyes narrowed and he frowned for a moment, but he quickly regained his composure, and his smile.

"No, Señor Lafitte. Not you. I do not think you are a killer. A good fighter, yes. I give you that, though from what I heard, the storm enabled you to get your wife back."

"Yeah?" Lafitte grinned coldly. "Then what happened to Lou? And George? And the others?"

Mejia frowned, then wiggled a hand, and the four men had suddenly shaken knives into their hands. Lafitte's eyes narrowed and quickly scanned them again, but there was no further movement. Each knife had a blade on either end with a small wrapped handle in the middle and each knife was held by a point; they couldn't all miss.

"Come on!" Lafitte said, trying to make his voice sound properly brave. "You guys watch too much TV. I can get three of you anyway. Mejia first, of course." Then the shotgun appeared, steadied on Mejia's chest, and the four men no longer looked so confident. Though no one moved, Lafitte knew that the next sign by Mejia and four knives would be coming toward him, shotgun or not.

"In case you're not sure, this is a semi-automatic shotgun. I've got one in the chamber and four in the magazine . . . and it's set like a scattergun, I'm bound to get most of you, so I suggest you drop the knives."

Lafitte waited but a second or two, then shrugged and took a deep breath. As he let it out he let the gun shift slightly; it pointed just past the man to the left and he squeezed the trigger. The explosion in the small room was deafening for a moment and there was a large hole in the wall. The man screamed, dropped his knife, and grabbed at his punctured arm. The shotgun moved to the right to cover the others and Lafitte heard Dominique come into the room behind him and say:

"Easy!"

The other three men held fast and Mejia took a deep breath and said, "Damn you, Luis!"

"Over here," Lafitte commanded.

The tall Latin, his face set and eyes narrowed in anger, got cautiously to his feet, moved clear of the desk, and advanced slowly. Dominique put his gun away and took a piece of nylon fishing cord from his pocket and grinned as he spun Mejia around and tied his hands behind his back.

"On the desk!" Lafitte commanded and the three knives dropped with a clatter. Lafitte turned and took Mejia's arm and pulled him away from the door. Then he nodded to Dominique. The Frenchmen smiled and pulled his gun and peered into the hall, then went through the door.

"Outside!" Lafitte said. "Any one of you wise bastards so much as blink I'll blow the back of his head off!"

The four men silently went out into the hall and Dominique backed down the steps as Lafitte forced Mejia through the door. Dominique opened the front door, looked both ways, then yelled:

"Hey, Abe!"

Then he turned back and nodded to Lafitte and waved his gun to the four, motioning them down the steps and into a corner. Lafitte nudged his prisoner in the back of the head with the shotgun and, keeping his left hand tightly gripping the shoulder of Mejia's expensive sweater, he slowly marched the man down the steps and outside. Lafitte backed against the wall and quickly scanned the street in both directions. Abe was approaching from the left and there was no one to the right. Across the street a couple of women were chatting and a fat black man was getting into a pickup truck.

"Bring 'em out, Dominique. Stand to the right of the door."

"Oui."

Dominique backed out of the doorway, holding the gun by his thigh, and motioned the four men to the sidewalk.

"Stand by the curb," Lafitte said to the now thoroughly frightened bullies. "If you move before we're out of sight I'll blast your asses with this shotgun. Now, if you don't want to be arrested for kidnapping my wife and that child I suggest you get the hell out of town. If you don't, the cops will pick you up within the hour! You dig?"

The four men nodded and Lafitte backed his prisoner to the waiting car. Abe got in the back seat, then Dominique, and Lafitte forced the sullen Mejia into the front seat and slammed the door. He handed the shotgun to Abe and walked around the back of the car, checking the street again. The two women glanced his way once, then turned and hurried up the other side of the street. The pickup was gone.

As Lafitte slowly turned the corner he glanced back once and saw the four men run in four directions. He smiled at Mejia and said conversationally, "Fuck you."

Dominique laughed and said, "Felicitations, *mon ami!* I didn't think we'd carry it off so easily. Uh, what about those women?"

"No trouble. Whores are not known to take their problems to the law."

"Umm, you're probably right."

Lafitte stopped behind the inn, at the employees' entrance. He got out and pulled the seat back forward, took the shotgun from Abe, and the big man climbed out, followed by Dominique.

"I'll see you later," Lafitte said to Dominique.

You frowned and said, "Are you sure you'll be all right?"

"With him?" Lafitte replied, nodding his head toward Mejia. "Certainly. Don't give it another thought. But I'd appreciate it if you'd check the corners of the building for a moment."

You frowned again and he and Abe went to opposite

corners, peered around, then turned back and nodded to Lafitte.

"Now, you'll try me, won't you?" Lafitte said amiably to
his prisoner.

Mejia's look of pure hate told him the answer.

"Uh huh," Lafitte said casually, "I thought so."

He brought the gun butt around in a tight arc, smashing
Mejia on the back of the head with a dull thunk. As his prisoner slumped into instant unconsciousness, Lafitte said in a
low voice:

"There, you son of a bitch, that's part payment!"

He turned to grin at his two friends for a moment, put the
shotgun on the back seat, and got into the car and headed
south.

When Mejia came to, he was hanging by his wrists and his
head was wet. Then he realized that someone had thrown
water at him. He shook his head for a moment and then
turned it from side to side. He was in the swamp somewhere,
suspended over the dark water by a heavy rope. He looked
up to see the rope attached to a block and tackle which was
tied to a stout limb some ten feet over the water. He kicked
his feet and spun around so that he was facing the edge of
the bayou and a grinning Lafitte. His captor was leaning
against the tree, holding a wet shovel in one hand, the other
holding onto the rope. Mejia took a couple of deep breaths
and stared down at the water for a few moments. Then, his
face blank, he looked at Lafitte and said:

"This is rather childish, don't you think?"

"Oh no," Lafitte replied in mock wild-eyed wonderment.
"You won't think so when the snakes come by."

Mejia whirled around and stared at the water again, but it
was smooth. Lafitte let up on the rope a bit, the pulley
squeaked, and Mejia dropped within a foot of the surface.
He tried to reach the rope, but his hands were tightly bound.
He glared again at Lafitte and the look was returned calmly.
Neither man spoke for almost half a minute and the silence
was almost complete, except for the buzzing of an occasional
insect. Lafitte stared at the late afternoon sky and then
looked at his watch.

"Who hired you?" he asked, as though just making conversation.

Mejia didn't reply and Lafitte shrugged and put down the
shovel to squat on the bank, still holding the rope in his left
hand. He smiled slightly and waited; for once, time was on
his side. A full minute went by before he saw a snake swim
toward his captive. He took the rope in both hands and eased
up on it until Mejia's shoes touched the water. Mejia quickly
doubled his knees and began to swing on the rope. Then he
threw his head back and got his ankles over the rope.

"Very good," Lafitte commented. "If you'd rather get bit
on the butt."

He let the rope down a bit more as the snake got closer
and repeated his question, still speaking calmly. "Who hired
you?"

There was still no answer and Lafitte shrugged and lowered the rope farther and Mejia's bottom was gently lowered four inches into the water. The big Latin was now
thoroughly frightened, but nonetheless he had the good sense
to remain still, though he couldn't hold back a shudder as the
snake approached. When the snake was but five feet away,
Mejia yelled:

"Jeremy Duroc!"

Lafitte nodded and hauled on the rope, not surprised at the
answer. The snake made a leisurely turn and disappeared.

"That's better," Lafitte said. "Now you know, and I know,
that a snake will normally run from a big disturbance in the
water, but on the other hand it just might bite at a small
quivering. It also follows that you will get tired enough some
time during the night so that you will just be able to move a
little, just enough to get bitten. . . ,"

"I told you Duroc hired me!"

"Yes, you did," Lafitte admitted, "but I just wanted to
point out the eventualities. Also the fact that you might not
die from the bite of a cottonmouth, but I don't think you'd
want to try it. By the way, it was you who had the snakes
dropped on my car, wasn't it?"

Mejia clamped his mouth shut.

Again Lafitte shrugged and eased up on the rope. He'd let
out but a foot when Mejia shouted:

"Yes! They were my men. But, so help me God, Lafitte, I
told them to use king snakes! It was that stupid Luis who
thought cottonmouths would be a big joke."

"Oh, yes," Lafitte replied dryly, "it was very funny. . . .
Now, why did Jeremy hire you?"

"To get the map, of course."

"And to kidnap his own child?"

Mejia took a deep breath and controlled his anger. "No!
They were to check your room and the old man's. The
woman and the child just happened to come in at the wrong
time and . . . and the boys panicked and they took them . . .
but you'll never prove it! I've got ten witnesses!"

"Sure you have!" Lafitte said caustically. "And I suppose it
never occurred to you that one of your creeps might rape my
wife . . . or kill her?"

Mejia clenched his jaw and remained silent. Lafitte let up
on the rope and Mejia was up to his waist in the water. He
kicked his feet and churned the water for a few seconds and
then his kicks grew fewer and he was panting with the effort.
He finally stopped and regained his breath and said:

"A deal, Lafitte. I'll make you a deal."

"Come on, now," Lafitte said. "You must admit you're
hardly in a position."

"Yeah? What about Duroc? You kill me and he'll send
someone else after you. I can help you!"

Lafitte grinned and pulled on the rope with both hands. It
was a harder pull with Mejia in the water. When his captive
was just clear of the water, Lafitte wound the rope around
the tree trunk and secured it with several knots. Then he
squatted by the bank and took out a cigarette and lit it.

"Lafitte?" Mejia said, an imploring note creeping into his
voice. "I'll call off my men and I promise on my mother's
grave that I'll get rid of Duroc for you!"

Lafitte tossed the match in the water and stared at Mejia a
moment, then snorted and got to his feet and studied the
block and tackle, turned and walked away. He'd gone but ten
feet when Mejia yelled:

"Damn you! Damn you!"

Lafitte stopped, grinned broadly for a moment, then the
grin disappeared; he turned around and came toward the
tree. It was time to deliver the message.

"Listen, you stupid bastard!" Lafitte said angrily. "You
think you're such a big man, pushing narcotics to children
and being the big frog in the little pond! Well, let me give
you a couple of things to think about tonight while the rope

slips. . . . Oh, yes. You tug a while and the first knot will give way, letting your lousy ass into the water. But the second one will hold forever! Now, you can take your chance the other way. Hold still and the knot won't slip. Then maybe you won't die of starvation until somebody comes along and finds you!"

Lafitte paused for the effect and took a long puff on his cigarette and flipped it into the water fifteen feet away, telling himself he was smoking too much. Mejia's eyes instinctively followed the cigarette and saw something hit it and quickly disappear. It could have been a fish, but Mejia shuddered in spite of himself.

"Oh, by the way," Lafitte added in a milder tone, "here's something else to think about tonight. As to your men; you ain't got any! The first bunch are all dead . . . and you'll never prove that! And you saw the other four. I imagine they've crossed the parish line by now. So, how many you got left? None!

"And, as to dear cousin Jeremy . . . he wasn't as dumb as you thought he was. In fact, you were the stupid one. How much did he offer you? A thousand? Five? Maybe even ten? No matter. See, you made a mistake, you underestimated him. Now Jeremy may be many things, but stupid? No. He wouldn't be so dumb as to hire you and then expect that you wouldn't either keep the map, or if Jeremy got it, that you wouldn't blackmail him once he dug up the gold. You were used, you dumb ass! You were the big patsy!

"No, Mejia. You suddenly decided to go into business for yourself. Only you sent idiots to do the job while you made sure you had an alibi, . . ."

Lafitte paused and checked the limb and the knots again and he was sure that by the time he got through talking Mejia would be so angry that he would try to get loose, and he'd make it. Once he got up a good arc he could wrap his legs around the branch and from there it would be but a matter of perhaps a half hour or so before he was loose. Then he'd have a half hour following Lafitte's car tracks back to the main road and from there it was only a few miles to town. Lafitte nodded to himself; he had a good two hours head start. He walked away a few feet, stopped and came back.

"Oh, by the way, I didn't tell you the real clincher. I sold

Jeremy the map. He's been real patient the last few days, but as soon as it's good and dark he'll be a rich man, richer than your stupid mind can possibly imagine. The gold of a whole armada's buried there! He's got the map, and a Geiger counter and, most important, the time. . . ."

"You lie!" Mejia shouted.

"Yeah?" Lafitte said, then added a lie. "I've got a hundred and fifty thousand dollars in a New Orleans bank. You see, dummy, there's something else you never considered, it's worth a fortune, but only to those of us who have access to it. You never thought of that, did you, you stupe!"

"You're lying!" Mejia screamed again.

He tried to twist his wrists and the rope slipped two inches, then held. Lafitte raised an eyebrow at the extra benefit; he thought he'd tied the rope securely. But Mejia was convinced; he held still.

"And tonight Mommy and I are on our way to Vegas for a little vacation," Lafitte said as he checked his watch again. "Incidentally, feel free to tell anyone you wish how much gold is there. Added to the rest of the hokey legends, nobody will believe you anyway."

Lafitte turned and walked away, grinning happily; the trap was properly baited.

Dominique was waiting at the rear entrance to the inn. Lafitte opened the right door and pulled the back of the seat forward. Dominique had two burlap bags which he put on the floor. As he got in and closed the door he said:

"I've got it all, but it seems awfully devious."

Lafitte grinned and stared at You's black denims and sweatshirt and said, "Maybe, but I gather you agree with the idea, otherwise you wouldn't have dressed the part."

"Yes," Dominique said slowly, "though I have some reservations."

"So?" Lafitte pulled onto the highway and headed toward the plantation. "Even if we flop, we won't be out anything."

"Maybe, but he's a dangerous bastard. Say, what'd you do with him?"

"I hung him over the swamp by his hands. I asked questions and when he wouldn't answer I'd let his ass down into the water for the snakes. He'd say something, he'd get pulled up again."

Dominique grinned. "Did he talk?"

"Yes, sort of. Half lies, but he thinks I believe him and that's what I was after. I fixed it so he'll get loose in a bit and I bragged about Jeremy digging up all that gold as soon as it's dark . . . he'll be there."

"Uh huh. And he'll damn sure kill you, if he gets the chance."

"Maybe," Lafitte said, "but I don't really think so. He's smart enough to know that I might've told someone else about him. . . . Oh, don't get me wrong, he might kill me in a fight, he's so mad now, but I don't think he'd go for out-and-out murder; too many people know he's involved."

"That's a thought," Dominique allowed. "But you're taking a pretty big chance with Jeremy, aren't you? I mean exposing him to Mejia like that?"

"I don't think so. Mejia wants that map and Jeremy wouldn't be so stupid as to carry it around with him."

You shrugged and leaned back to enjoy the ride and smoke his last cheroot for several hours. After a mile or so, Lafitte said:

"I should be there soon after Jeremy arrives, I might even be first but, just in case, you should know that Suzanne will probably show up at the oak."

The dark brows contracted and Dominique said, "That could be bad."

"No, I have every confidence in you. . . . By the way, have you eaten?"

"Yes, I'm ready to do my bit."

"Good. Dominique, I want you to know how much I appreciate this. I couldn't bring it off without you."

"Not at all. I owe you that. If I hadn't kept you so long at the Cove that night it wouldn't've happened."

"Nonsense! It happened. . . . Say, you sure you got everything on the list?"

"Yes, sir, yes, sir, two bags full," Dominique grinned for a moment, then became serious. "I know you laid it out in the note but perhaps I'm a bit thick. You're predicating all this on the fact that someone will get tossed into the swamp?"

"Not exactly," Lafitte said. "But I've set it up so there'll be a jim-dandy confrontation, and just in case you might not be able to stop it, I don't want that crazy Mejia pitching Suzanne or Jeremy to the snakes."

"Involved," Dominique commented.

"Preparation. But work it backwards. I want to get Jeremy and Mejia together and maybe I can solve this thing . . . but I don't want either one to think that I set it up. Now, it couldn't be in the house, could it?"

"No . . . you're right. Mejia would never go for that."

"Okay. And I want 'em to think they're alone. The logical spot? The oak tree. Unfortunately, I couldn't figure a way to fill in the pond on such short notice."

"All right," Dominique smiled and nodded, "you convinced me. . . . But what about Mrs. Duroc?"

"Oh, that?" Lafitte said, not being completely honest with his friend. "That's just an extra added attraction. . . . Now, you sure you've got everything?"

Dominique frowned a moment, knowing Lafitte was holding something back, but one didn't ask too many questions where a man's family was involved, so he let it pass. "Everything on the list. Rifle and extra bullets; two quart-bottles of oxygen, with valves; plenty of fish line; three gallons of chlorine; a small sack of sulfur, had to get that from the feed and fuel store; and the black pants and sweatshirt for you."

"Excellent," Lafitte said with a nod. "You think the chlorine will do it?"

"I think so. There's practically no tide in the backwater down there. It should stay all night. And it'll certainly drive the snakes out if there are any in there."

As Lafitte turned off the road onto the ancient bridge he throttled down so that they were barely moving. The bridge creaked and groaned, swayed slightly, but they couldn't be heard a hundred feet away. He eased the car along at a bare five miles an hour over the dirt road until they were within a hundred feet of the big oak, then pulled to the right and cut the engine. As they climbed out, he pointed to the brush and said:

"Snakes?"

"Probably not."

Lafitte nodded and picked up one of the sacks and they made their way carefully to the edge of the small cove. The giant tree was on the last bit of dry land next to the water. The pond was some forty feet across, closing to a small neck at the other end and where it joined the bayou, leading down to the bay. You pointed to a stand of brush some twenty feet from the oak. Lafitte nodded and they stooped down and made their way into the middle of the brush. Dominique peered through the leaves and then backed up to show Lafitte that he could see well from the spot.

"Good," Lafitte said. "I'll come in the same way."

Dominique nodded and took the three jugs of chlorine from a sack and gave one to Lafitte. Dominique took the other two and they circled the pond from opposite directions, staring into the water.

"See anything?" Dominique called softly.

"No, fortunately."

Lafitte worked his way back, pouring a bit of chlorine as he went. Dominique did the same from his side, saving most of the last bottle to pour close to the oak. Then Dominique picked up a long, dead limb and used it as a paddle to stir the water. Lafitte joined him and watched for any movement as Dominique probed the depth with his branch.

"It gets quite deep in a hurry," Dominique said.

"That's good."

"It's shallow around the tree, but the rest could be a swimming pool." Dominique turned from the water and pitched the limb into the grass. Then he pointed to the far end of the pond. "I'll put the line six feet or so from that end. I'll tie it to the bush, there . . . and there."

Lafitte nodded and took a last look around as Dominique began to strip to his trunks.

"Now, *mon ami*, there is something I must ask. . . ."

"Ask."

"The chlorine I understand, but the oxygen indicates that you plan on someone going for a swim. Am I right?"

"Not exactly," Lafitte replied with a smile. "Chlorine and all, I have no desire to swim in there at night, but let me ask you this; assume Mejia has a couple more friends and you and I have to bail out. What if my trap for him becomes a trap for us? Then what?"

"*Mon Dieu!*" Dominique said admiringly. "You did work it out! If he comes with a bunch, and he could have some, we would indeed have a problem running through this brush at night . . . and we wouldn't dare try the road. Excellent!"

"Yeah, I hope you're right. And I hope to hell we won't need it. . . . What about the sulfur?"

"I'll put it in after I get out. Being by it will be bad enough."

"You think it'll cover the smell of the chlorine?"

"Yes, when the water is calm the chlorine won't be much."

"Well, I guess that's it," Lafitte said, putting his hand out. "We pull it off and we take care of several things."

You's brows knitted for a moment, then he smiled briefly and gripped Lafitte's hand. Lafitte picked up the two sacks, one with the clothes for him, and headed for the car.

The house was quiet when he entered; the only sound came from the living room. He looked in the door to see them scattered about in small groups. Sandy, Suzanne, and Jeremy were on the couch, quietly sipping highballs. The children were in front of the cold fireplace playing Pick-Up-Sticks, and Marcel and Blondy were on the other couch with small brandy glasses.

"Hi!" Jeremy said and Sandy jumped to her feet to greet him.

"Hi!" he replied with a small wave and kissed his wife on the cheek. "Where're the rest?"

"Sedonia and Sam are fixing supper," Suzanne said. "The madam took one of her super sleeping pills, so she's through for the night."

"A drink?" Jeremy said, getting to his feet.

"Scotch and water, please," Lafitte said. Then, lowering his voice he said to his wife, "I have to talk to you."

"I'm glad you're finally here," Sandy said, picking up her cue and turning toward the couch. "I want to talk to you about the tickets."

"Okay." Lafitte grinned and crossed the room to take the glass from Jeremy.

"I'm ready," Jeremy whispered.

"All right," Lafitte replied in a low voice. "I'll have Marcel call from town that his car broke down, that'll spring you."

"Thank you!" Jeremy whispered.

Lafitte sipped his drink and turned to the two men on the couch. "All quiet?"

"Yes, sir," Marcel said. "And I guess we'd best leave now."

"No," Lafitte said, "wait and have supper, we'll eat soon. Have another brandy."

"Thank you," Blondy and Marcel chorused.

Lafitte nodded and took his wife by the arm and steered her upstairs to their room. As he closed the door she put her arms around him and kissed him fiercely for a moment, sighed, then kissed him again, her mouth working on his. He held her a moment, then decided that as much as he disliked the idea, the Tomas Mejia solution would have to come first. He pushed her away with one hand, balancing his glass in the other, and took a deep breath.

"Whew!" he grinned and added, "Enough! And you won't hear that very often. But there are foul things afoot tonight! I've still got to play pirate a while longer."

"Ha!" she said with a smile. Then the smile faded. "You're joking with the corn . . . but you're serious."

"Yes, honey, I am. For real. And I need your help. You've got to do a bit of play acting for me."

"Tell me," she said suspiciously.

"Now, now, don't worry," he replied gently, already having decided to lie to her several times, but nobly. "The bad guys are all disposed of, it's another sneaky little deal I've got with cousin Jeremy."

"Is he the louse I think he is?" she said, her feminine intuition coming out.

"He certainly is," Lafitte replied. "He was the son of a bitch who hired some men to drop those snakes on us."

"I thought that was phony!" she exclaimed, adding a satisfied nod to her deduction. "What are you going to do?"

"Well, you see, he thinks that map is for real and he wanted to get his grubby little hands on it so he would be free of Suzanne and her control of the family money. Now, the marks on the map are a fraud . . . the old man put 'em there, in hopes that I might sell it and make a few bucks. He was a smart old bastard. He had nothing to leave me, so he made up the pirate thing, put the X's on the map, and hoped I'd find a pigeon. . . ."

"And you found Jeremy!" she exclaimed excitedly, then lowered her voice though the door was closed. "And he already thought your grandfather would leave you the map! Go on, go on!"

"Well," he grinned. "When I figured that he was the one who was responsible for the snake thing I decided to get even. And, incidentally, your being kidnapped had nothing to do with this. They were just a bunch of local punks who thought that I'd give them the map in exchange for my wife. They were right, of course, but they didn't plan on Jean Lafitte having a friend named Dominique You. . . . Anyway, I followed the old man's advice and dropped a few hints to greedy Jeremy about the map. In the meantime I went out and bought some old coins and an old pot and buried some of them at an X. Then I leaked the news to Jeremy. . . . Honey, he was so greedy he was drooling."

"Yeah, you dog," she said with a big grin. "How much you sell it for?"

"Oh no!" he said, holding up his hand in mock protest. "You'd never believe it. Besides, it's better you don't know. But it was up in the thousands."

"Really! You mean I get a convertible?"

"Yeah," he allowed cautiously, "a used one. Anyway, here is the plan. He has the map and tonight he's going out and dig like a little kid looking for buried treasure. I'll follow him and then I want you to leak it to Suzanne, sort of. After we're gone and while she's wondering where each of us went . . . you tell her something like, uh, 'Didn't you know? Jean sold him the map and Jeremy's at the big oak, digging.' Then she'll get mad and when she cools off she'll ask you how much. You be reticent at first, then, when she keeps insisting, you proudly tell her twenty-five thousand dollars."

"Jean! She'll never believe that!"

"Sure she will." Lafitte couldn't help but grin at that one. "They've got a good thing in that business. And Jeremy, of course, has access to the bank account. Now, I suspect she'll get mad, and then decide to go after him. Remember, I'm not with him, or there at all. I'll fake a call that I've gone into town to see Dominique 'cause he's got a big trucker who may give me his account. Can you do it?"

"Yes," she said, considering the idea. "But I don't see why. You've already gotten even, you've sold him the map."

"Well," he said, lying again, "it's important, and I don't want to give it away, I'll tell you the whole thing later, all right?"

She thought of how frightened she was when that snake had dropped on her foot and then she grinned. "Yes. It's not very ladylike to enjoy revenge, but for Jeremy I'll make an exception."

"Good girl." He took a sip of his drink and added, "Now, there's just one thing more. We'll all come back to the house and they'll both be steaming mad. Jeremy may even decide to try me. Whatever, I don't want those nice children to hear all those nasty words, so after Suzanne has gone you make sure that the girls go to bed and, no matter what, unless I call you, you keep them upstairs, okay?"

"All right. . . . But what if she doesn't ask about you or Jeremy?"

"She will. And if she doesn't, I know you'll find a way to lead the conversation."

"You know something?" she said it like she would enjoy the bit of conspiracy. "You're right."

After that he managed the rest rather easily. When they came downstairs, Sedonia was just setting out a cold buffet on the sideboard. As they gathered for dinner, Lafitte managed to get Marcel to one side and told him to leave after dinner and get to the nearest phone and call Jeremy and say that his car had broken down, then wait five minutes and call back, try to sound like Dominique and ask for Lafitte. Then they were to get their rifles and come back and guard the house, one front and one rear; he was expecting Tomas Mejia to show up at the swamp, but he wanted to be sure Mejia didn't try the house. Marcel nodded that he understood, then grinned broadly and nodded as Suzanne invited him to get into the serving line.

They had a rather quiet dinner and then Marcel and Blondy excused themselves, bowing politely to the ladies. Lafitte saw them to the door, made sure the instructions were clear, then held them a moment and went back to the dining room door and caught Jeremy's eye. Jeremy was already on his feet and said to his wife:

"Excuse me. I have to thank them again."

Jeremy did as he said, shaking hands again with both men. As Lafitte closed the door behind them he turned to Jeremy and whispered:

"Marcel will call in a few minutes to say that his car won't run. That should spring you so that you can get right at it, rather than try to sneak out of the house after they've all gone to bed."

"Excellent!" Jeremy whispered, grinning broadly and barely able to contain his eagerness. "Everything's in my trunk."

"You don't have the map in there, do you?" Lafitte asked quickly.

"No, sir," Jeremy replied. "I never moved it. I wouldn't be so stupid as to take it out of the house. I'll just try the oak first."

Lafitte nodded in relief and mentally kicked himself; his big plan would've looked pretty bad if Jeremy had elected to try another spot. They exchanged quick grins and returned to the dining room. The women were just getting up from the table. Lafitte picked up his cup and went into the kitchen to get more coffee and found Sedonia at the sink and Sam clearing dishes with one hand. He grinned at both and poured himself a cup; he waited until Sam went into the dining room and then quickly went to the sink and whispered to the fat woman:

"Sedonia, it's not over yet. Tomas Mejia may show up here tonight."

She opened her mouth in surprise and he quickly put a finger to his lips.

"Quiet!" he whispered. "Now, you're the only one I can trust here, other than my wife, so you'll have to be the guard. I don't think he'll make it this far, but in case he does, I want you to protect Sandy and the girls. Can you use that pistol?"

"Shore!" she said. "On him? Easy!"

"No, I don't want you to, unless he comes in alone. If he shows up with me, or Mr. You, be sure to keep out of sight."

"Yes, suh. It's a big'n, but it still works."

"Good. Now, if you think anything's wrong, you be sure and get upstairs. I've told Sandy to stay with the girls, but she doesn't know what's up. And don't you tell her, you got it?"

"Gotcha man!" Sedonia grinned, proud that he would call on her.

Lafitte blinked at her hip reply and nodded and left the kitchen.

The first call was for Jeremy. He mumbled a couple of times, then said, and rather loudly, "Yes, yes, I'll be right there."

"Who was that?" Suzanne inquired as he reentered the living room.

"Marcel. His fuel pump went out. He's at the crossroads store. I'll have to take him into town."

"Why, for heaven's sake?" she demanded. "Can't he call a tow truck?"

"Suzanne!" he said it angrily, and loudly. "I'm going because I owe him! And you, too, if you'd think about it!"

He spun on his heel and marched out the door. Lafitte gave him an "A" for acting, hid his expression, and settled back to wait for the next phone call. It was right on time. Sedonia answered it and then called him. He went through his speech and returned to the women and said to Sandy:

"It's Dominique. That shipper he was telling me about is there. This just may pay for the whole trip."

"Good," Sandy said with a wide smile. She got to her feet and saw him to the living room door.

"Huh!" Suzanne said. "At least your call's business."

Lafitte kissed his wife on the cheek, winked at her, and left.

It was a clear, warm night with a half moon. It was fairly bright, enough to see by, yet Dominique would be safely hidden. He drove a good hundred yards down the road past the path to the oak before he stopped under a low tree. He opened the trunk, took out the dark clothes and changed quickly, slipped the knife into the back of his belt, and quietly closed the deck lid.

He started back up the road at a leisurely, quiet pace, listening to the few night sounds. He moved carefully from the road to the brush, testing every step until he was close to the bush. As he dropped to his hands and knees he saw Dominique's face above the rifle. The Frenchman grinned and moved a bit to his right. When Lafitte was in position next to him, Dominique leaned close and whispered:

"He's just started. When he got to the tree he just stood there for a good five minutes before he flashed on the light. He took a quick look around and since then he's been digging in the dark."

"What about the oxygen?" Lafitte said, turning his head toward Dominique and barely whispering.

"All in place."

Lafitte nodded and they watched the diligent Jeremy as he sweated and pitched damp sand into a pile. From time to time Lafitte would scan the surrounding area and then turn his eyes back to Duroc. Jeremy continued, grunting a bit more now, and pausing for longer rest periods. As Lafitte was deciding they'd watched about five minutes, they heard a stick snap and saw the flashlight. Jeremy jumped out of the hole and was about to hide behind the tree when Suzanne called:

"Jeremy?"

"Damn!" Jeremy muttered under his breath. Then he said, "Here!"

He flashed his light and in a moment she joined him. She flashed her light in the hole, then turned it on her husband's face and said in an icy voice:

"You damn idiot! Out here digging for pirate treasure like a schoolboy!"

"Yes, my love," he replied sarcastically. "You will think so, until I'm rich, then——"

"Then nothing!" she said in a loud voice. "And that's just what you are—and a damn fool! You thought you could get the money and then you'd be free of me, didn't you? Well, let me tell you something, Jeremy Duroc! I know how much you paid for that map and I know where the money came from. Now if you try to keep anything from me I'll have you in jail for defrauding the corporation!"

"But, Suzanne. . . ."

"But nothing! I've kept records on you for years and you just might go to jail for the rest of your creepy life!"

"Why, Suzanne," Jeremy said with mock solicitude, "I never planned to keep it from you. I only wanted to surprise you with our good fortune."

"Oh, you're such an inept liar!" She paused to get her breath, then looked down into the hole and said, "Find anything?"

"No, not yet. But I've barely started."

"And you're so stupid!" she said, starting in on him again. "Digging at night like this! Just think, you dum-dum, you live here. You can do it in the daytime! We can give the help the day off, I can slip the madam a pill and take the girls to a movie, and you can dig for hours!"

"I . . . I never thought of that."

"No, you wouldn't," she said, acid dripping from every word. "That phone call was a fake, wasn't it?"

"Yes."

"Uh huh. Well, what if Marcel just happens to call back from town? Then somebody gets suspicious. What about Jean? He left just after you for town."

"I don't know. I presumed he would stay with his wife."

"All right," she said, now speaking as though she were addressing one of her children, "come on. Let's get back to the house."

"All right," Jeremy said with a sigh as he began to shovel sand back into the hole.

"Hurry up!" she commanded, then added, "Where's the map?"

"Come on! I may be as stupid as you think, but I'm not that bad. It's at the house."

"Bully for you!" she said derisively. "I married a genius! Hurry up!"

She stooped and picked up his flashlight and held the two on him while he partially covered the hole, then said, "That's enough."

He nodded and she turned toward the house, using the two flashlights to light her way, leaving Jeremy to stumble along in the dark with his gear. Lafitte turned his head and saw You's white teeth flash as he shook his head. Lafitte nodded him close and whispered:

"Damn! The best-laid plans of Bobby Burns!"

Dominique nodded, showing some knowledge of Scottish poets; and then Lafitte had a sudden thought that made him clench his teeth.

"Son of a bitch! What if he's out there watching? You follow them, I'll give you fifty yards, then I'll come along."

Dominique nodded and backed out of the blind, stood erect for a moment, glanced from side to side, and then started up the faint path. Lafitte watched until he'd disappeared in the dark and then got to his feet and went quietly to the oak.

"Damn!" he said to himself. "And I was so smart! I made all those plans and, and . . . nothing!"

A swamp owl hooted and he stared down at Jeremy's partially filled hole. He shook his head and turned to follow Dominique. He got to the edge of the small clearing and suddenly he was caught by the neck and almost lifted off his feet. Before he could shout, a rope was closing on his vocal cords and he barely got his fingers under the half-inch line. He leaned back in desperation, then jerked forward, throwing the strength of his arms into the rope but only managed to ease the pressure for a moment; then he was able to drop to his knees, bringing the line with him. He rolled to one side and Mejia's knee grazed his side instead of fracturing his spine. Lafitte scrambled to his feet, but before he could do anything other than pull in a chest full of air Mejia was pulling on the rope, dragging Lafitte in a circle and forcing him to run to keep from being garroted.

Then he stumbled and fell heavily at the edge of the water, his fingers still on the noose. Mejia lost his footing for a moment in the damp sand and the line slipped from his hands. Lafitte spun to face him, still on one knee, and pulled the line free with one hand and reached behind him with the other, feeling for the knife. It was gone. His mind raced wildly, looking for a way out. He was no physical match for the big Latin and he couldn't outrun him. Then his thoughts came to an abrupt stop with the answer, like the last spin on a slot machine.

"No!" he croaked, putting out his hand toward the advancing Mejia, and hoped he was as good an actor as Jeremy. "I . . . I can't swim."

Mejia stopped, savoring his moment, and grinned broadly. "You wanted me to escape."

"No!"

"You wanted me to kill Duroc and then you were going to have your Frenchman shoot me while escaping!"

Lafitte was tempted to leap backward into the water, but Mejia was too close. The Latin's arm came up, the palm flat, and Lafitte paused a moment, gauging the distance. Then the arm descended and Lafitte moved forward at the last moment, hunching his shoulders as he tried to dart to his right. The crushing blow struck him on the left shoulder like a blunt sword and Lafitte was smashed into the sand, but still conscious.

Then a strong hand grabbed his left wrist and another one tugged at his belt and he felt himself being lifted easily and he was spun in a circle. Lafitte grinned and pulled in a deep breath as he was released at the completion of the circle and he was flying through the air. He managed one more deep breath and held it as he hit the water face first and began to sink. He let his body grow slack and ducked his head, mov-

ing his arms to swim deeper, resisting the urge to kick his
feet and make a splash.

When he was a good five or six feet down he began to
swim rapidly in what he hoped was the direction of the rope.
He let his breath out in small spurts, knowing his lungs
would last longer. His eyes were stinging from the chlorine,
but for that he was grateful. His breath was almost gone before he swam into the line and arbitrarily turned to his left.
He expelled the last of his air and was beginning to see red
when his groping hands found the oxygen. He fought off the
urge to rise to the surface; he put the nozzle in his mouth
and finally got the valve open and a stream of pure oxygen
poured into his empty lungs.

After a moment he closed the valve and exhaled slowly
through his nose, hoping the bubbles wouldn't be spotted. He
was uncomfortable, but after a couple of breaths he had the
hang of it and decided he could stay down as long as the cylinder held out. He pulled in another breath and tried to undo
the small tank, but Dominique had done too good a job.
Fearful that he might be spotted, he took another deep
breath, moved as far to his left as he could and still hold
onto the oxygen, then exhaled a bit at a time and allowed
himself to sink almost to the bottom. He could feel the sand
with his feet, but the line on the container wasn't long
enough to let him put his weight down. He waved his free
hand and began to take small breaths so that he wouldn't rise
to the surface and he started counting, kicking his feet slowly
so that he gently swayed back and forth at the end of the line.
When he'd counted to a hundred and eighty, taking a breath
at every five counts, he took in one final breath of oxygen,
closed the valve, and worked his way under the line until he
hit the shore.

He broke the surface quietly and found himself under an
overhanging bush. He waited a moment but heard nothing,
then turned in a complete circle. The surface of the pond was
smooth and he could see no movement on the bank. He waited a few moments, torn between the desire to hurry to the
house and warm Dominique, or wait some more until he felt
sure he was alone. His common sense decided on the latter,
as he thought that he'd been under the water a good three
minutes and Mejia had probably waited two, just to make

sure he didn't come up. This gave Mejia a good minute's start, possibly more.

Lafitte shrugged and started to swim across the pond, but after two strokes he changed his mind and suddenly realized why he was able to stay under the water with little effort— the sweatshirt and Levi's must weigh twenty-five pounds. He turned and made his way to the edge and climbed slowly out of the water and circled the pond to the small path. He stopped again to listen and turned in a full circle in the little clearing, but he could hear nothing. Then the owl hooted again, closer this time, and he decided he was alone. He went to the oak, leaned against it and pulled off one shoe, emptied it, replaced it, and repeated the process. Then he stripped off the sweatshirt and started wringing it like a large, black towel as he moved slowly up the path. It was still warm and though he was wet he was not uncomfortable. When he'd extracted most of the water, he replaced the sweatshirt and moved along at a good pace, still listening.

He was across the shell drive from the house, standing behind a large oleander and studying the front porch. The lights were on in the living room, the foyer, and upstairs, but he could see no one. He moved as quietly as he could across the white expanse of the drive and stopped at the foot of the steps and called softly:

"Marcel?"

There was a slight rustle in the bushes to the left of the porch and Blondy replied, "Here."

Lafitte went across the bottom step and joined the light-haired man in the shadows.

"Have you seen Dominique?"

"Just a minute ago. He brought in Mejia. The Durocs were with him."

"What'd he say?" Lafitte whispered.

"Not a word. I stood up after they passed and Dominique just shook his head."

"Okay," Lafitte replied with a frown. "Come on."

They climbed the steps and Lafitte was about to open the front door when they heard a voice from the open living room window. Lafitte held up a warning hand and they made their way silently along the porch to the square of light. From there they could make out the voice. It was Mejia.

". . . one minute to tell me. Then I start cutting."

"He's bluffing!" Suzanne said, though her voice sounded fearful.

"Damn!" Lafitte said to himself. Now he knew why Dominique had waved Blondy off; he was the captive, not the captor. He turned to take Blondy's rifle and Blondy held his trigger finger out and squeezed it several times and nodded. Lafitte nodded once and turned to peer cautiously in the room. Mejia was in the center, his back to the windows. He was holding Suzanne in front of him, a knife at her back. Dominique, his back against the door on the left wall, was looking at Mejia, and also toward Lafitte's window. Dominique's rifle, the bolt open, was against the far wall. Jeremy, a frightened look on his face, had his hands on the back of a chair near the fireplace, facing Dominique. Lafitte quickly moved in front of the windows so Dominique could see him. You smiled slightly and said in a firm voice:

"Before you start counting your minute, Mejia, there are a few things you should know about that map and this island."

"Like what?" Mejia said, pulling Suzanne in front of him as he backed to the fireplace.

Lafitte quickly pulled out of sight and grabbed Blondy and pulled him to the front door, returned the rifle and whispered:

"Get back to the window and watch, but be careful! Mejia is by the fireplace, so he can see the window from his left. Get prone on the porch with that rifle and if he gets far enough away from her, shoot him! But make sure the woman's clear. I'll take a try at the door."

"A pleasure." The blond man grinned and returned to the window.

Lafitte eased the big front door open and made his way across the tile floor on his damp, canvas shoes and stood at the living room door. Dominique was speaking rapidly.

". . . never get off! My boats are on the bay, there is a car at the bridge."

"Lies!" Mejia said confidently. "If you'd had your men here they would've been close enough to back you . . . and I saw none. Forty seconds!"

Lafitte quietly turned the knob and found some resistance. Then the knob turned back. Lafitte smiled. It wasn't much, but it was a help that his friend knew he was there.

"All right," Dominique said, a forced note of resignation in his voice, "it's in the den."

"How would you know?" Mejia said suspiciously.

"I saw him!" Dominique's voice had turned nasty.

Then it occurred to Lafitte that he needed a weapon, he still wasn't big enough, especially with Mejia holding a knife in his hand. He turned quickly and went into the den and to the gun cabinet. It was locked. He spun around looking for something to use as a club and stopped short as his eyes flashed to the wall and he grinned.

"Naturally," he said dryly.

He reached up on the wall and pulled down the two foils and ran back to the foyer.

"In the middle and stop," he heard Mejia say.

Lafitte flattened himself against the door and peered out to see Jeremy come out of the living room and stand by the large, circular entry table in the middle of the big foyer. As Lafitte worked his way along the wall, the foil in his right hand held high, Dominique came out of the door, paused and glanced down at the floor, then slightly to his right, grinned, and stepped forward to be out of the way. Lafitte was in position as Suzanne, with Mejia close behind her, came slowly to the doorway. Mejia's left hand was gripping the back of her neck. Mejia paused a moment, then pushed his captive forward another step and Lafitte could see the knife at her back.

Lafitte grinned coldly and brought the foil whistling down, aiming for the wrist, but Mejia caught a glimpse of the motion from the corner of his eye and turned instinctively and the foil caught the knife blade, knocking it to the tile floor with a clatter. Mejia grabbed Suzanne by the neck with both hands and spun her to face Lafitte. At the shock on Mejia's face, Lafitte grinned coldly and said:

"You didn't think you could kill the pirate so easily, did you?"

"But you're dead! You didn't come up!"

"You're the big voodoo man," Lafitte said, playing on the Puerto Rican's confusion, "you know better than that. Remember? The only way to kill a Lafitte is with a blade?"

Dominique You grinned as he backed to block the front door; he'd never heard that one before. Mejia glanced toward You, then shoved Suzanne at Lafitte, who barely had time to drop the blade to keep from impaling her. Mejia was right behind her, leaping to knock Lafitte to the floor. He succeeded better than he'd expected. As they landed on the floor in a jumbled pile of flailing arms and legs, the foil in Lafitte's left hand was knocked loose and skidded across the floor. Mejia leaped across Suzanne as Lafitte rolled the stunned woman off him and raised up on his left hand to see Mejia dive after the rolling blade. As Mejia caught it, his impetus carried him over on his right shoulder in a full roll. Lafitte scrambled to his feet and advanced quickly, but the nimble Mejia lunged at him from a three-point stance and the startled Lafitte barely parried the thrust and backed away.

Now Mejia was on his feet and Lafitte continued to back up, his eyes on the tip of the gently whirling blade in his enemy's hand. Lafitte backed into the big table and quickly put it between them. As the Latin took a moment to check the other two men Lafitte saw a movement from the top of the stairs. Sedonia was pointing the huge pistol waveringly with both hands. Sam and Sandy were standing behind her.

"No! For God's sake, don't shoot! You might hit anybody!" Lafitte shouted.

As he saw Sam step forward and grab the gun from his wife, Lafitte's eyes returned to Mejia who had spun around to lunge at the running Blondy who'd intended to butt Mejia with the rifle. The foil went into the fleshy part of the right forearm, came out quickly, and Mejia backhanded Blondy across the side of the head with the whipping edge of the foil. Blondy groaned, dropped the rifle, and staggered against the wall. Before Dominique could get from the door, or Lafitte could round the table, Mejia had stooped, picked up the rifle with his left hand, and was pointing it at Lafitte's middle.

"Hold it!" Mejia commanded and Lafitte froze, staring into the muzzle which suddenly looked six inches in diameter.

At the momentary impasse Lafitte had a chance to gather his thoughts. Though Mejia had a rifle, he wouldn't kill; there were too many witnesses and he couldn't get all of them. Then Lafitte wondered about Jeremy. Suzanne was sitting against the wall, Dominique was against the front door. Then it came to him. Jeremy had been leaning against the table when it had started, but since then he'd been out of the way. Instead of helping when Mejia was scrambling across the floor, Jeremy had panicked and had to be against the wall at Lafitte's back.

"Drop it!" Mejia ordered.

"No!" Sam's voice thundered from the stairs. "You drop it!"

Mejia froze for a moment, almost turning the muzzle away from Lafitte, then thought better of it. Keeping the rifle in place, he turned his head a quick second to locate Sam, then grinned and said:

"Old man, you know voodoo curse! You kill me and the curse goes on . . . pretty soon the other arm, then legs, then you turn into a dead man!"

"I know," the old man replied with quiet dignity. "But you'll not get any more of my family. Turn to shoot me and Mistah Jean's gonna cut you up!"

Lafitte shook his head once at the old man's courage and said, "Well, Mejia? You got as much guts as that old man?"

"If I do," Mejia said, "you're dead."

Lafitte smiled a little; Mejia had hesitated. But Lafitte knew Sam's chances of hitting Mejia with a shaky hand were slim. Lafitte made a quick decision and said:

"Tell you what I'm gonna do. Give you my word, you fence me and win, and you walk out of here. . . . You lose, it won't matter."

Mejia hesitated again, then shot a quick glance toward Dominique, ignoring Jeremy. Dominique, still with his back to the door, grinned slightly and shrugged.

"Your word as a Lafitte?" Mejia said.

"As a Lafitte." He hid a grin, knowing he had no intention of keeping it. Besides, Dominique had given no word.

"Him?" Mejia jerked his head toward Sam.

"Sam?" Lafitte said. "Put the gun on the steps."

As the old man stooped to put the gun down, Lafitte turned his head toward Dominique and winked quickly with his right eye and said, "See to it."

"I certainly will," Dominique replied in a dry voice, and in mutual understanding.

"Well?" Lafitte said, turning back to Mejia, the foil in front of him and slightly lowered.

Mejia glanced to his left, making sure that Blondy was no threat, then hesitated.

"You can't shoot," Lafitte said carefully. "They're too

many of us. Either walk out of here, or take my offer. I heard you were pretty good with that thing. After this afternoon I'd think you'd want to show me."

As Mejia's eyes narrowed, Dominique's flashed for a moment. Lafitte was deliberately baiting the Puerto Rican. So, Dominique thought, whoever he is, he's still the pirate. Mejia backed up a step and tossed the rifle into the living room, reaching back to close the door with his left hand, then turned to face Lafitte, who had moved to the right of the table.

Mejia put his right foot out, then danced forward quickly without a word, and lunged. Lafitte parried the blow easily, as his antagonist had anticipated, merely trying to see if Lafitte was any good. Instead of a riposte, Lafitte backed around the table again, putting it between them. He grinned and put his weapon on the table, though not letting go of it, and leaned forward, his left hand on the table. Mejia took the bait and advanced quickly with a flashing horizontal slice. Lafitte quickly raised up and backed out of the way as the blade whistled in front of him, cutting the top off a flower in the small vase. Lafitte countered with a rather clumsy downstroke, hoping to get Mejia's arm on the way by. He missed and whacked the table with a resounding thud. Mejia whirled in a full circle and advanced again.

"Sorta reminds you of an old Errol Flynn movie, doesn't it?" Lafitte grinned.

The look of hate on Mejia's face showed that he wasn't an old film fan and Lafitte's grin faded as he tipped the table toward his enemy. Mejia easily sidestepped it and advanced, smiling coldly now that they were in the open. Lafitte's stomach tightened and he backed up, his eyes flicking from the gently quivering tip to Mejia's upraised left hand. The fingers quivered slightly, and Lafitte had a split second's warning and was able to parry the thrust, though they came to a halt, blades up and guards locked. The heavier Mejia grinned and pushed Lafitte in the chest with his left arm, and Lafitte was sent sprawling to the tiles, landing heavily on his right shoulder, the damp shirt bringing him to a quick halt. He flailed his left arm and rolled to his left as Mejia lunged. Lafitte continued to roll and came up on his knees and scrambled around to face his opponent.

Mejia, too, had momentarily lost his balance as the tip of

his blade slid along the tiles at the spot where Lafitte had been and danced quickly to recover, but it gave Lafitte time to get to his feet, his foil up.

"Hey, you bastard!" Lafitte said as though it were only a game. "You're not supposed to do that!"

"Fuck you!" Mejia replied and advanced, the blade whirling in a two-foot circle this time.

Lafitte's right shoulder suddenly ached from the heavy fall, and he knew it would have to end quickly. Then Mejia telegraphed his lunge and again Lafitte parried the blow and they hooked guards once more. As Lafitte frowned at the Latin's clumsy delivery, Mejia grinned and then Lafitte knew—Mejia was toying with his less skilled opponent. But this time Lafitte didn't wait to be sent sprawling again or for his shoulder to give out. He shoved his thumb hard into Mejia's right eye, and as the big man screamed in pain Lafitte continued to raise his left hand and brought it down hard, fingers stiff, and smashed Mejia across the bridge of the nose. As the bones shattered, Lafitte dropped his left hand to his right and heaved, freeing his blade and forcing Mejia clear. The Latin stumbled backward a few steps and smashed against the wall by the steps.

Mejia grunted, fighting back the pain, and came in again with a quick lunge. Lafitte parried the thrust easily, but Mejia, showing that he wasn't yet finished, came back with a quick riposte and Lafitte was forced to grab the rounded shaft with his left hand because his right hand had lost its speed. He pulled on the foil and swung Mejia away from him and raised his weapon again, knowing he had but little strength left.

Mejia returned, but the thrust was a fake and Lafitte took a gouge in the skin of his neck as the price of a weak shoulder. He danced backward and put his hand to his neck and forced a grin and said:

"You son of a bitch, you're good! And it's a good thing you copped out that she'd hired you or I might not have figured it!"

"Yaa!" Mejia yelled, advancing wildly. "You're dead!"

"Come on," Lafitte invited, moving to his left. "I just wanted to make sure your employer saw you get it!"

Lafitte wanted to rub his shoulder but he dared not. He

gritted his teeth and kept the blade ready, though it was growing heavier by the moment.

"Dead!" Mejia yelled, getting within range.

His next thrust showed that his injured eye affected his depth perception. The lunge was not quick and clean; Lafitte saw it coming and instead of a parry he stepped forward and to his right and grabbed the blade in his left hand as he'd done a moment before. Forcing his left arm away from him, he swung Mejia in a half circle. True to his fencer's training, Mejia wouldn't let go of his foil and Lafitte knew he'd won. He let go of the blade and Mejia was propelled into the wall of the dining room with a breath-tearing impact.

Lafitte clenched his jaws in pain again and used his left hand on top of his right for the final thrust. The tip went in just above the belt and Mejia dropped his foil and stared at Lafitte with an amazed look.

"And you were the son of a bitch who almost had my wife killed!" Lafitte said the words in a low voice, and still using both hands on the foil he spun the hilt in a tight circle. Mejia's body dropped and Lafitte stepped back, freeing his blade.

He took a deep breath and turned to see a grinning Dominique leave the door and come toward him. He turned back to see Sam at the bottom of the stairs and Sandy hurrying down them two at a time. He held his hand up to her and shook his head and she stopped short, a frown on her pretty face. Looking at Sam, Lafitte took the foil in his left hand, guard up, and said:

"Hey, Sam! Catch!"

He tossed the foil and the old man's right arm instinctively shot out and caught the blade in mid-air. Then Sam blinked in amazement as he looked at his hand holding the weapon and he looked again at Lafitte and tears came to his eyes. He swallowed hard and choked out the words:

"Thank you."

"No, Sam," Lafitte replied quietly, "thank you."

Then his wife was in his arms and Dominique was pounding him on the back and he was suddenly very tired.

"Now it's all over, for real," he said to his wife as she kissed his cheek, the tears running down her face.

"*Magnifique!*" You said, whacking his friend on the

shoulder again. When he saw Lafitte wince he stopped, a pained look on his face.

"It's all right." Lafitte smiled. "But a man with bursitis shouldn't go around fighting duels."

They led him into the living room and put him on one of the couches and You helped Blondy to a place next to him. Lafitte grinned and Blondy grinned and said in a low voice:

"I am sorry. I should have just shot him."

"No," Lafitte replied. "It's awfully hard to shoot a man in the back."

Sandy leaned close to her husband and examined his neck and satisfied herself that it was a small cut, then sat quietly, squeezing his arm. Dominique returned from the bar and handed Lafitte and Blondy a glass of cognac; he looked at Sandy and she shook her head. Dominique smiled and turned to Blondy and was checking his wound when Lafitte turned toward the door, held up his hand to Suzanne, then pointed to the couch opposite him. She nodded, still numb with shock and fearful of what Lafitte might do. Jeremy, frowning because he didn't want to believe what he'd just heard, sat next to his wife, but at the other end of the couch.

"Suzanne," Lafitte said with a friendly smile, though his eyes were narrowed, "you're all through. When I worked Mejia over this afternoon he told me everything."

"Honest to God, Jean, I didn't intend for him to go that far!"

"Sure!" Lafitte's voice had turned nasty. "Just a little polite stealing, and maybe a polite mugging or two, nothing serious! And you didn't have sense enough to know that he'd go into business for himself. . . ."

"I swear it!" Suzanne said, beginning to sob.

"Shut up!" Lafitte commanded. Suzanne opened her mouth but closed it without speaking. "You had Mejia's men watch for our arrival, didn't you? And they put the first doll in the car, didn't they?"

Suzanne's eyes widened, but she did not speak.

"Answer me, damn it!" Lafitte shouted.

"Yes," she whispered.

"And you planted the dolls here in the house?"

She nodded.

"And after the old man gave me the map that night you

called Mejia and he would've had that broad call Jeremy, only Jeremy was obliging enough to call her first, right?"

Another shocked nod and Jeremy stared at his wife, a sick look on his face.

"And you did one more thing, didn't you, cousin? When you came home from the movie and found both me and Jeremy gone, you called Mejia again."

Suzanne stared around the room at the circle of shocked faces, her eyes finally coming to rest on Lafitte's cold face. She averted her eyes, then began to sob again.

"Oh, quit it!" Lafitte commanded. "Just sit there and shut up! I'll get back to you in a bit."

Jeremy, his face flushed with shame for his wife, got up to fix himself a drink. Sandy leaned close to her husband and whispered:

"Honey? Did she really hire that man?"

"Yes," he replied. "Dominique? Will that require the doctor?"

"No, I don't think so," You replied, looking up from examining Blondy's arm. He got to his feet and went to pour himself a cognac and added, "It looks clean. Not too deep. Not even much blood. The, uh . . . doctor might add to the problem. I'll tend it. If it's worse tomorrow I'll take him to have that gaff wound fixed. I certainly didn't intend to stab him when I struck at that gar in the bottom of the boat."

Lafitte grinned at Blondy and both men nodded.

"What about Mejia?" Lafitte asked.

"You mean the law?" You rubbed his jaw a moment, then shook his head with Gallic practicality. "No. I don't see where it would help. And you might have to explain about the others. Besides, there doesn't seem to be anyone here who would ever mention such a thing."

As You stared at the Durocs, Lafitte grinned and said:

"Certainly not them. And not Sam or Sedonia. But . . . uh, won't the disposal be a problem?"

"For Dominique You? And surrounded by swamp? Don't concern yourself, *mon ami*. . . . Come, Blondy."

With Sedonia leading the way, they went to play doctor. Lafitte sighed, sipped his brandy, and Sandy lit him a cigarette from the box on the table. Jeremy left the bar and came to stand in front of Lafitte, his eyes on the carpet.

"Lafitte, believe me, I would never have been part of such a thing."

"I know, Jeremy." Lafitte nodded. "I never cared much for you, but that's the one thing that set me to wondering; you would never have risked your child."

"Well, I thank you for that. As to the map . . ."

"Jeremy, that map is just as worthless as your greed made you think it was valuable. After the thing on the road with the snakes, when I thought it was you, I set out to hook you with it. I bought some old coins in New Orleans, soaked a couple of sacks in acid, and bought an old pot, just to salt a mine."

"Huh," Jeremy said. "Well . . . it's no more than we deserve."

"Yes," Lafitte said over the rim of his glass. "That's the way I see it. And I don't think either of you will care to debate the issue."

"No, no!" Jeremy said quickly. "Of course not. I would've paid that and more to get my child back."

"I agree," Lafitte said curtly. "Now, one thing more. Take her to her room and keep her to hell out of my sight. We're leaving early in the morning and I think it'd be better all around if you keep her out of the way. Go see to your children. . . . Hey, what about the girls? Did they waken?"

"No." Sandy chuckled. "Sedonia must've known something was going to happen. She had them all drink a big mug of hot chocolate, liberally laced with brandy. I could smell it."

Lafitte grinned and leaned back, took a final puff on his cigarette, and gave it to Sandy as Jeremy quickly pulled his wife from the couch and steered her from the room. Lafitte started to close his eyes and his wife took his glass and said:

"Oh no you don't. Upstairs and get those damp clothes off and into the shower before you get pneumonia."

"Huh!" Lafitte grinned and shook his head. "I goddam near get killed and you're worrying about me catching cold!"

He was refreshed, and much more relaxed, when he came down the stairs a half hour later in dry clothes, leaving Sandy to pack. The hot shower had soothed his stiffness and his shoulder no longer ached as much. Dominique, Blondy with his arm bandaged, and Marcel, all with brandy glasses in their hands, were standing near the living room door watching Sam as he finished covering the corpse with a rug and went about picking up the scattered flowers.

"Sam," Lafitte said with a grin. "You don't have to do that now."

"Yes, suh," the old man replied. "But I just wanna show off how good my arm works . . . and keep rememberin'."

As the men in the doorway grinned, Lafitte rubbed his shoulder and said ruefully, "I wish I could say the same."

"They have shots for bursitis," Dominique said.

"Not me. They hurt. Maybe if I give up fencing it'll get better."

"No doubt," Dominique agreed. "I was just telling these two what a magnificent feat it was to take a champion fencer, and with a bad shoulder . . . *mon ami!*"

"Naw," Lafitte replied, "it wasn't that much. I knew that if I got in trouble you'd jump him."

"*Oui!* I was about to, but you seemed to be having so much fun. But how were you sure I would do such a thing?"

"Well," Lafitte said, grinning at Marcel and Blondy, "I didn't hear you give your word. And I only gave mine as a Lafitte, and everybody knows he was a pirate."

As the men chuckled, Lafitte turned to Marcel and said, "Hey! Where the hell were you?"

"Monsieur!" Marcel protested. "I was guarding the back door as my leader instructed me. The enemy never got through that door while I was there! Besides, Dominique has promised me that the next time I can come in and get stuck in the arm."

"Ha!" Lafitte laughed. "Come on, we'd better drink some more of the old man's brandy on that one. Besides, I see little reason to leave it for cousin Jeremy. . . . Hey, uh, what about the late fencing champion?"

"Abe and Albert are on the way over with a boat . . . and lots of chain."

"Good."

They had another brandy while Sam sat on the front steps to make sure that no unwanted visitors might come to the house and somehow be disturbed by the lump under the rug. Twenty minutes later Sam brought in Abe and Albert who were quickly filled in by Blondy and Marcel. The new arrivals had a quick brandy and as Dominique's four men turned to their chore, Lafitte said:

"Wait, gentlemen. We're leaving early and I might not see you again. Because of you, my wife is safe, and the child, and I cannot adequately put it into words, but I would like to share some of my . . . uh, reward with you. . . ."

"No, sir!" they chorused and Dominique said:

"No, *mon ami.* We thank you, but we do not fight for pay . . . only for business and friends."

"Well," Lafitte shrugged. "I will never forget you."

He shook hands with each man, except Dominique, and they left the room. "You'll be back?" he said to Dominique.

"Yes. It's almost twelve. I'll be back before dawn."

"I'll wait."

"Get some rest."

"I'll rest while I wait."

Lafitte walked his friend into the foyer and held the door as the four men carried the heavy rug from the house. He exchanged nods with Dominique and closed the door and turned to Sam.

"Go to bed, Sam. It's late."

"Yes, suh. What about you?"

"I'll sit a while."

"Yes, suh. And, Mistah Jean, thank you agin."

"No, Sam. We're even. If you hadn't pulled that gun he would've killed me."

"Yes, suh, but you could've told me to shoot. I think you done it the way you did just to show me about the voodoo."

"Good night, Sam."

"Good night, suh."

Lafitte wandered into the living room and fixed himself another brandy, in a taller glass this time, and laced it with Triple Sec. He put the bottles away and left the bar to sit in a big chair while he stared at his grandfather's picture and sipped his drink.

He awoke at the sound of the front door.

"It's me," Dominique called softly.

Lafitte blinked and realized that it was morning. Then he realized that his feet were propped on a hassock and he was covered with an afghan.

"Hi," Dominique said as he crossed the room to pour himself a late brandy.

Lafitte sat up, stretched, rubbed his shoulder, and Domi-

nique pointed at the couch. Sandy was curled up, asleep. Lafitte nodded, got to his feet, and stretched again.

"I'm too old for this sorta thing," he grinned ruefully.

"It's done," Dominique reported, lifting his glass. "And
with three hundred pounds of chain."

Lafitte nodded and went to the drapes and pulled them and
the dawning sun poured onto the floor. Sandy groaned and
turned to face the back of the couch. Lafitte swallowed several times and went to the back of the bar.

"Brandy to celebrate the new day?" Dominique said.

"No," Lafitte swallowed again, "that doesn't sound too
good."

He searched under the bar until he found a small can of
tomato juice and fixed himself a Bloody Mary laced with Tabasco sauce. He added a couple of ice cubes and held the
glass up to his grandfather's portrait in a toast; he took a
healthy sip and blinked.

"Whew! That'll stop your teeth from itching."

"Mon ami," Dominique said, a frown on his dark face, "I
must apologize for letting Mejia take me that way. But I fool-
ishly thought he would be after the Durocs and not jump
me. I was so busy listening to them argue that I didn't hear
him come from behind. Then, even though he had a knife, I
decided to do as he said; I was sure you'd be right there."

"Don't feel bad," Lafitte grinned. "He outfoxed me, too.
He jumped me at the oak and tossed me into the pond.
Thank God for that oxygen bottle!"

"Say! Then your plan was a success!"

"Yeah . . . sort of. Though I certainly didn't plan on fencing the bastard. But I'll never tell Sam that!"

Dominique grinned and said, "Mejia didn't confess in the
swamp, did he?"

"No. But Suzanne thinks he did. Dominique, it couldn't
have been Jeremy. He was too weak and, no matter what he
was, he wouldn't have chanced any of his children being kidnapped. Besides, he wouldn't have set up that thing with the
wiring on the car as an excuse; too much chance that his
wife would've found that he was shacked up with that broad.
Then he might've lost his business and his children, too. And
it was too crude. Jeremy's a bastard, but he's a sophisticated
bastard."

Lafitte took another sip of his drink, a smaller one this time, then added:

"But . . . it had to be someone in the house. The chance of a stranger being able to get out all that alleged gold was too remote. Whoever he was, he had to have the acquiescence of someone here. Now, it couldn't have been the madam, she's too fragile, and certainly too old. Sedonia or Sam? No. They wouldn't know what to do with money if they had it. They live here. That's enough for them."

"But it could've been Duroc."

"Yes," Lafitte allowed, "it could've. But then he wouldn't have bought the map. Remember, he paid me a bundle for it. He wouldn't have done that if he'd hired someone to steal it for him."

"Uh huh," You nodded and sipped his drink. "And that left Suzanne."

"Yeah. And she thought she could control Mejia, pay him a few thousand bucks maybe, and he'd get her the map. That way she could throw Jeremy out and have all that money. . . . And she was taken in, too. The old bastard did a fine job of selling."

"Greed," You said. "It got to both of them. Or all three."

"And they were all so blinded that they didn't have sense enough to know that even if there had been all the gold of Jean Lafitte here, it wouldn't amount to enough to be worth the risk."

"I don't understand?" Dominique said with a frown.

"Dear friend, check your history. Jean Lafitte would've buried a few thousand, twenty-five at the top. Remember he once had a half million, and that was the most any historian gives him credit for, and that was taken from him by the federal raid at Barataria. Now, assume the pirate, by a wild stretch of the imagination, buried, say, a hundred thousand at various spots here, and that's damn remote; this is pretty far from Barataria. But assume he did. How much you think it would cost to get it out? Then, once you did, you'd have to cheat Uncle Sam and take it out of the country to realize any great profit. And then you'd be lucky. . . . No, *mon ami*, even if Lafitte's treasure had been here, the ravages of inflation would've made it only a nice amount, not a treasure."

Lafitte raised his glass to the portrait again and Dominique said:

"But your grandfather made it one."

"Yes," Lafitte nodded. "He certainly did." He tossed off his drink and went to his wife and shook her gently, "Come on, love."

She opened her eyes, turned on the couch, and smiled up at him.

"We've got to get on the road if we're going to make that morning plane," he said.

"I'm ready," she said as she threw her arms around his neck.

An hour later Lafitte and You were putting the bags in the trunk of the convertible which was parked in front of the door. Assembled on the porch in a line to see them off were the three kids, Sedonia and Sam, and the madam. Sandy shook hands with Sam, hugged Sedonia and the madam, and was engulfed by the girls. Lafitte slammed the deck lid and climbed the steps to smile at the girls and shake hands with Sam.

"Take care of my mammy, you hear," Lafitte said.

Sam nodded, his eyes wide, and Sedonia broke into sobs and hugged him. Lafitte pushed her away gently and said:

"Take care."

Sedonia wiped her eyes on her apron as Lafitte turned to the fragile old lady, took her hand gently, and said:

"Madame, it's been a pleasure."

"Monsieur," she replied in her soft voice, "you are his grandson. . . . Be sure to write us."

"We will."

As Lafitte turned away, Jeremy appeared with the map, rolled and tied.

"Here," he said. "The old man was right."

Lafitte stared at his cousin's husband a moment, then nodded and said, "Thank you. Raise your daughters. They're fine girls. And I can't help but add, she's your wife . . . and you deserve each other."

Jeremy started to extend his hand, then withdrew it in embarrassment, and merely nodded.

As Duroc backed out of the way, Dominique came forward to escort Sandy down the steps. As he put her in the car he was given a quick kiss on the cheek.

"Dominique You is Jean Lafitte's friend," she said, "and I will never forget it."

You grinned and went to the driver's side of the car and gripped Lafitte's hand. "Come back," he said.

Lafitte nodded. "The history books were right about Dominique You."

He got into the car, started the engine, and everybody waved again as Lafitte turned the car down the driveway.

Lafitte turned off the shells and onto the dirt road; he glanced at his wife and said, "Well, other than that, Mrs. Lafitte, how did you enjoy your vacation?"

She smiled and squeezed his arm, and put her head on his shoulder for a moment. They were halfway to the bridge when Lafitte hit the brakes and stared to the side of the road, not believing what he saw. At the edge of the brush was a large, shaggy, old swamp bear. Lafitte shook his head and took a deep breath because he shouldn't believe such things and then stepped on the gas.

At the bend a hundred feet away he slowed and looked back and the bear was still watching him. Lafitte chuckled and headed for the bridge.

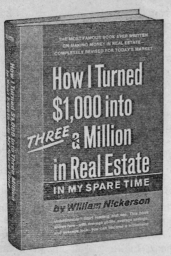